Change here accelerates with time. In a blink, new is old; fresh is stale; hip is passé. Each incoming wave of residents breaks over the last, overwhelming them with youth, style and attitude. But forever unchanging are the heat, the sun, the ceaseless roll of the ocean on the shore—and every generation's belief that the city belongs to them.

CHAPTER I

ZOE

Zoe turns on her rooftop light and settles behind the wheel of Zippity Cab. She loves her cab, loves the flamingo pink color she just refreshed with a new coat of paint, loves the fake zebra seat covers and the furry dice that dangle from the rear view mirror. For a sixty-year-old Caddy, it doesn't look its age. For an almost-fifty-year-old cabbie, neither does she. At least, she doesn't want to think so, despite the erosion time has carved into skin that once fit her compact little body like a shrink-wrapped tomato. Zoe glances at her reflection in the rear view mirror and adjusts her saucy pink cap, its visor embroidered with "Zippity Cab" in turquoise. Time to go to work.

A warm sea breeze swirls through her rolled-down window as she cruises Miami Beach, bringing with it a fragrant potpourri: burgers, burritos, sunscreen and incense, seaweed and smoke and sweat. She's on a morning run, although night time is her best time for fares, worth squeezing through the curb-to-curb South Beach traffic of club kids high on the drug *de jour*, rental-car tourists puzzling over maps of Miami, and suburbanites in bumper-stickered SUVs.

Last night, she worked Collins and Ocean Drive for a few hours but turned in early. For some reason, she had felt melancholy, and decided to head home to perk herself up with a dose of *South Park*. She just couldn't face the usual haul of late-night drunks who—as she knew from dismal past experience––were likely to barf in her cab. She kept Zippity in super shape, and the thought of cleaning, airing, and deodorizing her beloved taxi once more was too exhausting to contemplate. So she went home, climbed into her side of the bed she once shared with her late husband Albert, turned on the TV and promptly fell asleep.

The TV was still on when she awoke this morning to the flickering image of a wire-muscled woman pedaling furiously on some kind of machine. Zoe had watched for longer than she should, reluctant to get out of bed. She rolled over and stared at the flat sheet where Albert should have been but wasn't. It's been six years now since he died but there were still times in the middle of the night when she woke up and thought that his pillow was him. Then she'd slip back to sleep and dream happy/sad Albert dreams of a time when the present was still in the future.

She was still in bed at 8 a.m. Late for her. Something was off with her this morning. She couldn't figure it out. It happened now and then, when it seemed as if her Albert dream clung to her waking self, an invisible reminder of the big gap in her life. She shook it off, dragged herself out of bed, and pulled on her usual shorts and t-shirt—today a Hello Kitty tee to perk her up. She hadn't really been hungry, but selected a strawberry Pop Tart for breakfast from the assortment of portable food in her pantry––Pop Tarts, granola bars, Mallomars—and climbed into her cab. This was how her day had begun.

She takes several chugs of Diet Coke as she whips Zippity Cab in and out of Alton Road morning traffic. She's still feeling kind of funky, and needs a hit of caffeine to keep her on point. Pink cap at a jaunty tilt, elbow out the window, she scopes the curbside for likely fares with a practiced eye. Her crankiness is just beginning to lift when a slow-footed old woman pushing a shopping cart meanders across the street without looking. Zoe stomps on the brake with both feet; Zippity complies with a horrific screech.

"Cross at the light!" Zoe yells, leaning on the horn: *A-ooo-ga A-ooo-ga*. Her usual patience with the few old people still hanging on in South Beach––blocking traffic, crossing in the middle of the street, slowing her down—has deserted her today, replaced by a jagged edginess that has been surfacing lately at irritations she would normally ignore. "Move those bones," she adds, louder than she meant to.

"What?" The old woman parks herself in front of Zoe's bumper and leans over the hood to get a look at her. She's wearing a flower-printed floppy hat, plaid bermuda shorts that hang to her calves, and marshmallow-white Keds. "What you want?"

"Move! I want you to move!" Zoe leans on the horn again. *A-ooo-ga*. The old lady gives a little jump backward. The car behind Zoe sounds its horn.

"I'm moving!" The old lady looks grim. She doesn't move. "What you expect from a person with a hip replacement just last year and look, not even a walker?" She demonstrates, parading left, then right. "See? No limp."

A cacophony of horns erupts behind Zoe. She sticks her head out of her rolled-down window, sees the lineup of cars, hears a chorus of curses. Words she's never spoken aloud boil up and explode and she finds herself yelling to the honkers, "Fuck off!"

The old lady stops in mid-stride. "What's that you say? You say that word to me?" She hauls the grocery bag out of the cart and slams it down hard on the hood of the cab. "Nobody says that word to me. *Nobody*." She slams the bag down once again for emphasis. With a clang of cans and the crash of breaking glass, it splits and splatters the contents across the hood.

"My cab!" Zoe screams. Panicked, she throws it into reverse and rams the car behind her. Its driver emerges, a tall skinny Haitian who is bellowing something in what Zoe figures is Creole because it sounds more French than Spanish, not that it matters because she speaks neither.

The old lady is furious. She glares at the glass-strewn, bashed-in hood of Zippity Cab, now an abstract design of herring clots, borscht rivers, prune juice puddles, gefilte fish islands, and a slab of brisket already medium-rare from the heat. Unmoved by the sight, she reaches into her battered straw purse and pulls out a receipt.

"Forty-eight dollars and twenty-three cents," she announces. Spotting a tube of Preparation H that landed in the street, she picks it up, studies the price tag, tucks it into her purse and re-calculates on her fingers. "Minus three twenty-nine––it's okay, not squished too bad—so I'll be fair: Forty-four dollars and ninety-four cents."

"*What*?" Zoe can hardly hear her over the horns honking all around her and the bellowing Haitian whom she can't understand. He points to a fresh mark on his rusted bumper, a collage of dents from past mishaps, and shouts something incomprehensible but threatening. She staggers out of her cab to examine the damage. Her back bumper has crumpled, twisting the smiley-face bumper sticker into a snarly-face. Worse, the hood looks pulverized. Still recovering from the direct hit of a falling gumbo limbo tree during the last hurricane, its subsequent repair was recently undone after being trampolined by a drunken group of club-goers who used Zippity as a short-cut across Ocean Drive traffic. Now, this old lady's assault may have rendered the fatal blow—the hood's exhausted, age-thinned metal is dissolving beneath an acidic barrage of foodstuffs.

"You owe me forty-four dollars and ninety-four cents," the old lady calls out.

"WHAT?" Zoe feels something behind her eyes begin to pinwheel. Is she hallucinating? Is this all a dream, a horrible nightmare starring a hollering

Haitian, a nasty old woman and a car hood imbedded with kosher products? She steadies herself against the door of Zippity Cab and glares at the little old lady. She's short. She's slow. Zoe is sure she can take her.

Followed by the Haitian who is shouting indecipherable curses, Zoe advances on the woman. "I. Owe. You. NOTHING!" she says between gritted teeth.

The old woman waves the receipt in front of Zoe. "Look! Proof! A shopping trip's worth of groceries!" Zoe snatches the receipt out of her hand and tears it into little bits.

The woman glares at Zoe, at her shorts, her T-shirt, her Medusa-head of hair. "*Kurva*," she concludes gravely. Whore. "What kind of *schmatte* is that to wear in public, showing your boobies, letting your *tuchis* hang out? Feh! You should be ashamed." The old lady hugs her purse to her chest. "Forty-four dollars and ninety-four cents. Cash."

Zoe doesn't notice the siren. The Haitian does, and silently disappears. The cop breaks it up between her and the old lady. Zoe hears herself trying to explain in words that seem very far away. Forty-five dollars suddenly seems a small price to pay just to get away before she's arrested for elder abuse. The cop turns on Zoe.

"Whatya gotta jump all over an old lady for? Just let it go."

"Look at my car!" Zoe explodes. "Who's going to pay for that?"

The old lady shrugs. "Insurance," she says, then flips her hand in the air as if she's warding off flies.

"Insurance? Insurance doesn't cover food damage. Even if it did," Zoe adds, remembering her recent body shop repairs, "I've got a high deductible, and my rates will go up. Again."

The cop intervenes. "I'm charging you both unless you guys can settle it between you. What you wanna do?"

"I wanna sue!" Zoe says in a burst of legal vengeance.

"Look," the old lady says. "I'm in no mood. First, I can't deal with the crazy Publix parking, I had to pay to park down the street. Now I got to put money in the Park 'n Pay and go shop all over again." She holds out her hand. "Forty-four dollars. Ninety-four cents."

Inspired by the cop's narrow-eyed glare, Zoe pays up, counting out several hours' worth of fares and tips into the old lady's upraised palm. "Okay. I paid my share. Now it's your turn. I've gotta get this fixed. It's how I make my living."

"Settle this, ladies," the cop says, "or I will. I'm trying to cut you a break here, but you're making it hard."

"Okay, okay," the old lady concedes. She reaches into her purse, pulls out a yellow pencil stub, scribbles something on a scrap of grocery bag she's torn free. "Here," she says, waving it at Zoe. "How much can a little scratch be? Get an estimate and send it to me. Then we'll see."

"Don't think I won't," Zoe calls after her.

The cop eyes her warily. "Maybe you oughta sign up for some anger management class or something."

Anger management? What's his problem? She was fine, just fine, until that old bat came along and gave her a really really good reason to be angry. She's normally pretty mellow--sad sometimes, maybe, but a mellow sad. But, she has to admit that lately, out of the blue, she'll explode for no reason at all. Those days, she'll start out great. Then, to her great surprise, she'll inexplicably plummet.

Something has changed.

It's not just the fiery flashes that recently, without warning, drench her from the inside out. Or those sudden crying jags that overcome her when she's watching *Golden Girls* re-runs. It's not even that she looks any different, aside from the effects of gravity on certain portions of her anatomy and the epidermal price paid for too many summers spent frying in the sun. It's only close-up when it's noticeable that her skin keeps smiling when her face has stopped. From a distance she looks, well, not so bad for a half-century's worth of living.

But the crack that opened beneath her feet when Albert died has widened into a chasm, and she's asking herself a question she never asked when she was married: Is she happy? And what does "happy" mean, anyway?

Something's missing, and it's not just Albert. She's never craved fame or fortune, or wanted much in the way of material things. All she had ever coveted was the Caddy: 1959 Cadillac Sedan Deville. Roomy, cushy, plenty of space for six, with glorious sweeping fins that any rocket would envy, the four-door Caddy was forty years old when she bought it despite Albert's protests ("It's a boat!"). But it was also a deal, garaged for most of its life and kept in primo condition by its owner, her fellow employee in the auto parts department of Home Depot. He was selling it to buy a Mustang. When Albert died, the Caddy was almost all she had, aside from the little blue stucco-and-concrete-block house they owned in the Surfside area. This she discovered when his attorney told her Albert had stopped paying on his life insurance, had no pension plan, and p.s. he owed a bunch of money to the IRS. But no problem, she could keep the car. It was all hers, bought with the money she had saved from her job.

The Caddy was a solace but not much of a companion. For months after Albert's death, she lived a solitary life of mindless TV, takeout food and––after being laid off from her job––sleeping till noon. Her only real friend had been Albert, who had been all she ever needed. Sometimes she thought they shared a brain, that's how together they were. She had never allowed herself to think that someday he might not be here.

But then he wasn't. And she had needed a job. She discovered that her age wasn't a plus when she started looking for work, but when she heard Click and Clack on NPR's *Car Talk* extolling the virtues of maintaining old cars, she realized her Caddy could be more than just transportation. It could provide her with much-needed income.

Inspired by the memory of the car Albert drove when they first started dating––a used '57 Chevy he had revived by painting it pink, adding zebra seat covers and furry dice—she borrowed its décor to transform her beloved Caddy into Zippity Cab and found her way back from oblivion. Zippity Cab became a familiar but much-feared streak of Pepto-Bismol pink plowing through the constipated streets of Miami, and Zoe became part of the world again.

And so the years had passed, measured in miles and gallons of gas, with hope always on the horizon that someone would come along to share that life with her. Although time had eventually worn away that hope, leaving a patina of resignation, Zoe was determined to find happiness again.

But today is not a happy day. It did not begin well, nor would it end any better, judging from the looks of her food-battered cab. Zoe stares as the groceries ooze slowly into Zippity's innards. She scrapes off the loose pieces, gets in and starts the engine. It sounds funny. It wheezes and stutters down the street, sounding not just sick, but terminal. Zippity has been badly injured. This is a job for Boyd.

* * *

Boyd's Body Shop has kept Zippity Cab in pretty good shape since Zoe has owned it—periodic paint jobs, upholstery re-do's, various ding/crunch/smash repairs needed after run-ins with assorted solid objects—but this time, Boyd is less than enthusiastic about the possibility of returning Zippity Cab to its former state. He walks around it, scratching at chest hair which peeks through the vent holes of his grease-stained Dolphins t-shirt. "I don't know what you hit this time," he says, poking at the congealed remains of food hammered through the hood, "but whatever it was, I betcha a nickel it's dead."

"So what does it need—a little patch, some repainting?"

"Repainting? You gotta be kidding. Look." He pokes an oil-blackened finger at a spot on the hood. It crumbles into particles of rusty metal and bits of food. "I toldja them puncture wounds would rust through in this salt air."

"You also told me it would cost twice as much to fix if you did it right."

"Yeah. Well." He opens the hood and peers inside. "Alla them other repairs? From alla them other accidents? Well, looka here. The metal got so fragile that whatever landed on it ate right through to the motor. It's like, glued. This baby's headed for the
Cadillac Ranch."

"Ranch? There's a ranch for cars?"

"Well, it's in Texas, but it's not really a ranch. This millionaire guy buried ten old Cadillacs nose-down and called it art. They're covered in graffiti. It's like a fancy graveyard for old Caddies."

"A graveyard?" Her eyes fill and spill over. "Zippity Cab is *dead*?" She throws her arms over the roof of the car and sobs. "Sixty years! She was perfectly healthy for sixty years, and now she's gone, just like that."

"Well, hey," Boyd says, uncomfortable at this outpouring of automotive emotion, "she's not dead. She still runs. Sort of." He scratches his chest thoughtfully, studies the clumps of food solidifying in the engine, comes to a diagnosis. "It's more cosmetic than anything. If I can clean up the motor, we might be able to keep her going a little while longer." He scratches some more. "You know, maybe it's time to think about selling her."

"Sell?" It's not something Zoe has ever considered, but––it pains her to acknowledge it––maybe Zippity's time has finally come. It's getting way too expensive to keep the old girl alive, not to mention the pukey mileage she gets what with the price of gas these days. "How much you think I can get?"

"Jeez. I dunno. Considering she's never been restored, maybe five hunnerd. Tops. Maybe a little more on a trade-in. And that's after we fix her up some. Scrape off the food and all."

"Five hundred? Dollars?"

"Maybe some antique car collector would be willing to give you a little more, but my guess is not much. She could be a nifty number, but it'll cost a bundle to fix her up. Her innards'll hafta be replaced, and even before this food attack, she wadn't in such great shape to begin with, what with all those dings and scrapes and dents and stuff all over."

"I'm a good driver, don't talk to me about dings and dents," Zoe huffs. "There's some real crazies out there I've got to dodge every day."

"Yeah, well. She's also got about a jillion miles on her, and she's making noises like a meat grinder."

"What do you expect? She was practically pummeled to death. Plus she's sixty years old."

"My point exactly."

"Is she worth fixing up?"

"Not probly, to be honest with you," Boyd says.

Zoe slumps down on Zippity's bumper. "What am I going to do? This is how I make a living. Now I can't even sell the clunker." Frustrated, she slaps its fender like a cheek.

"Hey," Boyd says, clumsily patting her back. "Tellya what. I'll fix her up cheap so she don't look too terrible."

"How cheap?"

"I'll get my mechanic to take a look at that engine, but I'd guess fifteen hun-nert if you want her to run halfway decent."

"Fifteen *hundred*?"

"And that's a deal. We can probly get her running pretty okay for a while. And she'll look almost like nothing happened. Think positive," Boyd says with a cheer-up smile. "Could be she'll last ya another sixty years!"

Does she have a choice? She can't afford a new car, and without at least minimal repair, Zippity is doomed to the Cadillac Ranch. "Make it a thousand," she says. "Give it a cheap paint job. Just make it run."

"Twelve fifty, if I can fix the hood without too much trouble," he says, ballpoint poised over an estimate sheet. "That's my bottom line. Take it or leave it here for the junker."

"Okay," she concedes with a sigh. "Twelve-fifty. I guess I can sell my body." Zoe is swamped with sorrow, self-pity and a hot flash. She reaches into her shorts pocket for a Kleenex and finds the crumpled paper bag remnant the old lady had scribbled with her name—Mrs. Wolfe—and address. No phone number.

Collins Avenue, in the fifties. Huh. The old lady can afford it. Let *her* cover the damage.

Zoe decides to pay her a little visit.

CHAPTER II

HAL

The doorbell still doesn't work. Hal repeatedly bangs the knocker on his parents' apartment door. Teeth bared in a cute canine face, the brass wolf's-head knocker resembles a pissed-off Disney character. Hal can hear the TV on the other side. Giving up, he lets himself in with his key. Max, his father, is folded into his La-Z-Boy, staring at the TV screen positioned squarely between his propped-up slippered feet. The top of his head, smooth, pale, iridescent as a pearl, is visible above the back of the chair.

"Hey, Pop," Hal says, his voice slightly slurry from the joint he smoked in the parking lot before he went upstairs. Weed is the only way he can get through these Friday night dinners with his parents, especially after another surreal day with his fellow Miami Beach city commissioners. In these instances, he considers it not recreational but pharmaceutical. Without it, he would rather shoot himself than be here.

Max turns around and peers at him through coke-bottle glasses. His magnified eyes hover above his nose like the bug eyes of an alien being. "What?" says Max, turning back to the TV.

Hal sits on the couch, feeling rather mellow by now. His father has a bowl of peanuts on his lap. Hal reaches over and takes a handful. "What're you watching?"

"News," says Max. "All bad."

"Where's Mom?"

Max jerks a thumb in the direction of the kitchen. "Burning dinner."

Tootsie is stirring something frantically on the stove as Hal comes through the door. Something *is* burning. Tootsie is a limited cook, specializing in recipes featuring gobs of chicken fat, wedges of onions, overdone cuts of stringy meat, vegetables boiled to exhaustion, and desserts with too many raisins. Burning is not an unheard-of occasion. Yes, at the moment, something is burning—smells like kasha——and Tootsie is muttering as she stirs and scrapes the frazzled grains.

Hal bends down to give her a kiss on her cheek. It's damp and hot from her efforts, which don't stop as she reciprocates with an air kiss and the complaint, "See what he makes me do? Burn the kasha. I can't concentrate. He makes me crazy."

Hal shrugs. "So what else is new? You make each other crazy. It's mental aerobics, keeps you healthy."

"It's gotten worse. He yells at me, he yells at the TV, he even yelled at Dr. Weinberg's nurse because the blood pressure cuff was too tight." She gives the pot a vicious stir. "Maybe it was a mistake to take away his driver's license. He's been mad at the world ever since."

"Better he should be mad than let him kill somebody," Hal says. He opens the refrigerator. "What's for dinner?"

"Every Friday you ask that, every Friday I tell you the same: brisket." She stops stirring and waves the kasha-caked spoon at him. "Do you know what happened when I went food shopping this morning? First, I refuse to park in that crazy Publix garage with the ramps where I scraped the car last time, I should sue, so I had to park down the street, so I'm coming back with my groceries and what happens? This *meshugganah* lady almost runs me over and then says that word to me."

"What word?" Hal finds a jar of pickles, opens it and sniffs. "These sour or dill?"

"*That* word. You know what word."

His face puckers as he bites the pickle. "Sour," he pronounces. "You mean the S word?"

"No. The other one."

"The Z word? The P word? The..."

"Stop it. You know what I'm talking about. F. The F word."

"Frog? She said Frog to you? Fuzzy? Fat? Flanken?"

"You're making fun."

"Fun. That's it! She said Fun. Arrest that woman!"

"Ha! See?" Triumphant, Tootsie resumes stirring with a vengeance. "You think I'm making it up. She *was* arrested."

"Come on."

"Well, she was almost arrested." Tootsie shakes her head. "What a day. I can't begin to tell you. I'm exhausted, *exhausted*. First the grocery store. Then pick him up and take him to the doctor's. Every day he's got to go someplace, the periodontist's, the barber shop, Macy's to get socks. For sixty-five years he never let me drive with him in the car, never, and now it's me with the bad hip who has to do all the schlepping in the crazy traffic with all the *meshugganah* drivers out there. And then what? I have to come home and listen to this," she nods in the direction of the living room, "crazy person."

"Ca-razy world," Hal agrees. Max is yelling something from the depths of his chair. "What?" Hal answers.

"Get the door!" Max repeats.

"I didn't hear it," Hal says. "You should get your doorbell fixed."

"I've been telling him to fix the doorbell," Tootsie says.

"Nag nag," says Max.

Hal opens the door. A middle-aged woman with unkempt hair and too-short shorts is bristling on the other side. "Is Mrs. Wolfe here?" she asks, waving a sheet of paper in his face. "She wrecked my car."

"Who are you? How did you get up here?" Some security, Hal thinks, if this nutcase can get past the doorman.

"Where's Mrs. Wolfe? She's an old lady about," she holds her hand up to her chin, "yay high."

"Whozzat?" Max calls. "Shut the door. There's a draft."

"Look," Hal says to her. "I don't know who you are or what you want," although he's getting an inkling of the situation, judging from his mother's expression as she comes out of the kitchen, wiping her hands on a dishtowel.

"It's her! The *kurva*!" she says.

Zoe deftly steps through the portal before Hal can shut the door. "I just want what's fair. You said to send you the estimate. Here it is. This is what you cost me today," she says, waving the paper in the air. "My cab is ruined. I had to take a *bus* here." Her lip trembles at the word.

"So take a bus home," Tootsie says. "I didn't tell you to show up in person. I don't know what you want from me. I got enough problems without *tsuris* from you. Go home! Comb your hair! Put on some clothes!"

"I'm not leaving without a check. Twelve hundred and fifty dollars. That's what you owe me. Here." She thrusts the estimate at Tootsie. "This is what you did to my cab. It won't even run any more, and I *need* it to run. It's how I make my living."

"You drive a cab?" Hal says.

"I *did*, until this lunatic smashed it with her groceries."

"Twelve hundred and fifty dollars? For a little paint?" Tootsie says. "Who are you kidding?"

"You smushed the hood and damaged the engine! What did I do to deserve that?"

"You said the F word to me," Tootsie says. "The *F* word. Nobody says the F word to me. And," she adds, "you tried to kill me."

"I *what*?"

"I'm walking nice across the street, like a person, and you tried to run me down like a dog."

"She's crazy," Zoe says to Hal. "This woman is a crazy person."

"She's my mother," Hal says.

"Is she incompetent? Maybe I should be talking to you."

"Don't talk to me. Talk to her. I'm staying out of this." He heads for the kitchen. Zoe follows him. "I mean it," he says, reaching into the pickle jar for another. "You settle it between you two. I've had a hard week. I'm just here for dinner."

"What's burning?" Zoe asks. Black smoke is rising from the kasha pan.

"What's going on?" Max yells from his chair. "What's the big commotion?" He points the remote at the TV and turns up the volume. The jingle for a toilet-paper commercial fills the room with happy sounds.

Tootsie rushes into the kitchen, grabs a grease-stained oven mitt in the shape of a chicken, and tears the smoking pan off the stove. "See? See? See what you made me do?" she cries. "Dinner is ruined! You ruined my day, and now you ruined my dinner."

"What is it?" Zoe asks. "Popcorn?"

"There's popcorn?" Max asks. "Bring me some."

"Look," Zoe says to Hal. "Can I just get a check and go?"

"Don't give her any money," Tootsie warns. "I'm not paying her a cent. It wasn't my fault."

Hal examines the bill. "This *is* pretty steep. What happened?"

"She said the F..." Tootsie begins.

"Not to you! To those guys honking at me!" Zoe turns to Hal. "Is that any reason to bash in my hood with her *groceries?*"

"Which I had to shop for all over again," Tootsie reminds her.

"I paid you back. And now I've got to pay for *this*," Zoe says, waving the bill wildly over her head.

"Insurance...?" Hal begins.

"Won't cover it," Zoe finishes. She suddenly shields her eyes with her hands, then looks up tearfully. "I don't want to rip off anybody. I just don't know what to do. My cab's sixty years old, and really ready for the ranch."

"Ranch?"

"The Cadillac Ranch. Where dead Cadillacs go. That's what the body shop guy said. My cab is pretty much doomed, thanks to her," she says, nodding in Tootsie's direction, "but if I can keep it alive a little longer and scrape up a down payment, maybe I can trade it in on a new car."

Damsel in distress. A little *old* for a damsel, but still, in distress. The politician/public servant in Hal rises to the occasion, especially since he just can't deal with yet another nutty constituent, not after today's commission meeting which was loaded with them. Besides, it's not worth the *mishegoss* of Tootsie's insurance. Her last mishap resulted not only in a higher rate, but an escalation of his own stress level just dealing with Tootsie.

He examines the bill. "Look," he says. "We'll compromise. I'll give you half."

"Just half?" Her eyes well up. "I need *two* halfs."

Jeez. More tears. He's in no mood for drama. He extracts a check from his wallet. "I'll make it out for $625. When your cab is fixed, I'll send you the rest. Just promise to go away and not come back for more. How should I make it out?"

Zoe pulls a pink card from her back shorts pocket and hands it to him.

"Zippity Cab," he reads.

"Yep. If you ever need a cab, you know who to call."

"Sure thing. I'll do that."

"I mean it. What with Uber and Lyft, all that competition, I'd really like to make some steady money. You need someone to chauffeur your folks around, I can do that, too. Drive old people around. When they can't drive themselves any more. Or shouldn't."

"I drive just fine," Tootsie says, insulted. "I don't need a cab." She bangs a pot on the stove, dumps in a fresh batch of kasha. "Forget it."

"I drive, too," Max pipes up despite his fixation on Wolf Blitzer and what appears to be more bad news. "Only they won't let me. But," he adds darkly, "we'll just see about that."

Hal regards the card with renewed interest. "You know," he says to Zoe, "you've got a point. Maybe I'll give you a call."

* * *

Hal's black boot whacks the kickstand up; his leather-gloved hand grabs the clutch. The engine's puttputtputt erupts in a black cloud roar; a kick into gear and he's off. He takes the turn on Brickell *easy now, easy*, doesn't want to skid like last week when he almost lost it in a heartstopping slide, tattooed the asphalt with one blocky heel braking the Harley as if it were a scooter, fighting gravity until somehow he swung upright again, head ringing with relief and the whine of the wind. Rigid with the memory, Hal grips the handlebars with palms sweating beneath the gloves, orders himself to relax. He lifts mirror-goggled eyes to the sky and gives thanks there's no longer a helmet law. Free at last, free at last, his unfortunately receding hairline is free at last. His grey-threaded ponytail whaps him fiercely between the shoulder blades like a rabid ferret on a leash. He thinks his earring is coming loose.

The Harley stutters as he climbs the ramp onto I-95 and his nostrils widen in fear with the sudden image of his brains sunny-side-up on the pavement. Last time this image came to him he almost merged with a truck, but then he was wearing a helmet, very uncool. Now he just wears a red bandana tied around his forehead, much groovier than that plastic prison. But what if...?

All right all right relax relax, and then he's okay again, doing a smooth 65 side-by-side with a little white Porsche driven by a blondie who pretends he's not there. He releases his grip to give her a cool-guy wave, slams his hand back on the handlebar when the bike jitterbugs over the white line. Control. Got to keep control.

Stress, that's his problem, it's always something, first he had to rush downtown, now he's heading back to the Beach again, meetings, meetings, meetings, Jeez, it's enough to make him nuts. What's he doing, anyway, bored out of his skull with those political geeks? He's been asking himself that question more and more these days: What is he doing? He finds himself wishing he wasn't who he is, doing what he does. Miami Beach commissioner, *Harold Wolfe* in stick-on block letters on his imitation-wood nameplate. Sitting in that swivel chair rocking back and forth, the damn chair making that eeerk sound that drives him bonkers, doodling geometric women with cubic tits on the yellow legal pad, glaring at his fellow commissioners and thinking: Losers.

So what does that make him? Not what he thought he'd be at this time of his life, that's the sad sad fact of it, he hates to admit it but there it is. He's 55 and stuck in city politics with nowhere else to go.

But politics does have its perks, perks that have kept him going, kept him sitting in that swivel seat down at City Hall. Perks like fame, little flashes of fame, the odd satisfaction of seeing his face on TV now and then, of being rec-ognized when he's tearing into a steak at Smith and Wollensky or waving from a float in the Mango Strut parade.

Perks like women. A pool of women from which to choose, needy women, adoring women who believe in white knights, who scribble their phone num-bers on bits of paper and matchbook covers he stuffs in his wallet alongside business cards from Chanel-clad executettes whose eyes meet his across ma-hogany desks. Women he chose over his wife, a wife now long gone except from his checkbook.

Perks like random hits of cash that just happen to come his way for the occa-sional favor he bestows, pocketed without guilt because with the pathetic salary he's paid as a public servant, hey, he deserves a bonus now and then, especially when the bonus is big enough to wind up in his bank account in the Caymans.

Perks like the adulation of constituents who vote for him––pony tail, ear-ring, Harley and all––because his constituents are Miami Beach constituents and to them, weird is okay as long as you're charming and glib and smart.

Especially if you're Ivy League smart, which is what Hal Wolfe is, Yale smart, poli-sci-major smart, the kind of smart that comes with expectations: CEO, Supreme Court, Nobel expectations. Once, he had expected that much of himself as he rose through the political ranks, his name bandied about as a candidate for state representative, state senator, and once––during a particu-larly chaotic time when Miami Beach politics went even more berserk than usual—for mayor. But it never came to pass. He blamed it on the Cubans. They had taken over. There was no room for an Anglo like him, a charming, glib, smart, ponytailed, earringed Anglo. Hal dismissed the fact that the present mayor was not just Anglo, but hugely popular across the board. Hal tried, he really tried, but he could never impress the Cubans. The best he could hope for was a seat on the city council, which he won handily and resented daily. This was not why he went to Yale.

He had believed in himself. Believed what others had believed, that he was smarter, sharper, and better-looking than they, until the day came when smart, sharp, good-looking Hal discovered he had been running on a hamster wheel while everyone else was running track. If he didn't catch up now, it was never going to happen.

When he hit fifty, he had ignored the number and convinced himself that he was on a roll, that things were percolating, that all that preceded this big birthday were mere precursors to the main event (whatever that might be). Didn't he have all the signs of success? The slick oceanfront condo with the girlfriend-impressing Williams Sonoma-equipped kitchen—Miele espresso machine, Breville juice press, a complete set of All-Clad cookware—a kitchen he used mainly to microwave takeout from Boston Chicken. The giant flat-screen TVs in every room that he still can't figure out how to turn on without screwing up and having to call the cable company to tell him (again) how to use the controls. The four-foot neon penis sculpture he bought at Art Basel when he was smashed on champagne and later regretted when its blinking orange presence took over a corner of his living room, but which he kept because it announced to visitors, "I have ten thousand dollars to spend on a blinking orange penis sculpture."

Then he was 51, then 52, and now he was 55 and the main event had failed to occur. He felt he was fading, a captured firefly in a glass-jar condo whose value, thanks to the proliferation of even-newer condos around him, had decreased along with the years he had ahead of him. Now it was the minutae of life that littered his condo and marked his days: the baggie of grass that needed straining; eight years of dog-eared Sports Illustrated swimsuit editions; a bathroom cabinet stocked with Xanax, Viagra, Rogaine, Just for Men haircolor, tooth whitener strips, self-tanning lotion, and an ex-girlfriend's razor that he keeps for sentimental reasons. Something had to happen soon, or this could be his life forever.

Hal angles the Harley onto the MacArthur Causeway, threads his way through a steady line of cars heading towards the sunset-painted horizon of South Beach, moving at a pretty good clip now for rush-hour traffic, easy traffic compared to the caterpillar of cars that will climb the causeway in just a few hours, the late-night weekend bumper-to-bumper stereo-blasting Ecstasy-fueled nightmare traffic he dreads. But he had agreed to meet his developer pal Milo on Ocean Drive for a drink and a little chat about the historic designation and height restrictions on Milo's projected condo whose plans have been delayed due to same.

When they last spoke, Hal had told Milo he was crazy to start this project in a city that was exploding in too-much too-soon construction after the recession nightmare, a city that was first on every climate change environmentalist's list, slowly drowning as sea water gurgled upward, turning the streets of Miami Beach into white-capped rivers. Downtown Miami, once packed wall-to-wall with mid-construction condos––some dead in the water, some deserted by walkaway buyers whose expectations of flipping them for huge profits had sunk even deeper than the pilings they were built on––had come to Frankenstein life again in the latest incarnation of Miami's boom-and-bust history. After the spectre of abandoned condos, their unglassed windows hollow-eyed reminders of a crash-and-burn market that was hopefully in the past, developers savvy to the lure of South Florida knew that deep-pocketed foreigners were looking to drop big bucks into Miami real estate once the economy took an upturn. Those who saw this were quick and connected. Unfinished buildings were finished; new buildings sprang out of the ground overnight like glass mushrooms. Thanks to them, Brickell Avenue became an even higher-rise city, with traffic bumper-to-bumper at every point of the compass from there.

Milo had insisted that Fantabulissimo, with its three sixty-story towers stretching high above its lowly South Beach neighbors, would be different from all the other crystal palaces across the bay. Not only would it be away from the compressed city Miami had become, but its height alone would make it a magnet for buyers eager to invest their euros/pesos/rubles/yuan in a landmark building, open to the traffic-free ocean. While glitzy multi-million dollar condos were proliferating along the beaches farther north, they were away from the action of Miami Beach, second, third or fifth-home excuses for international investors to launder their dollars––condos unoccupied for much of the year. Fantabulissimo would be the crown of Miami Beach—close in, luxurious, and really, really tall. When Hal reminded him that Beach zoning forbid such grandiose heights, Milo said, "I dream the impossible dream." Hal couldn't argue with that.

He had promised himself that the last deal with Milo—lucrative as it almost was––would be the last one, period. He had done legalistic cartwheels to try to get a variance passed on the height limits for Milo's previous project, which ultimately failed and wound up falling several stories short of the Beach's tallest buildings, the 44-floor, 559-foot-tall twin Blue and Green Diamonds. The Miami Beach commission would be on high alert if he attempted this new one.

The challenge put Milo into overdrive. "Sixty stories? What's the big deal?" Milo had countered at Hal's objection. "That's Ted's Shed-sized next to what's gone up in the Brickell area. Panorama Tower––85 floors! One Bayfront Plaza––92 floors! And don't even talk to me about SkyRise Miami. It's going to be humungous––1000 feet! They're worried planes might fly into it, it'll be so tall."

"Well, that's city of Miami," Hal reminds him. "Sixty stories is still too tall for the Beach."

"Miami Beach isn't City of Miami. Different zoning, different everything. So maybe it's a little tall for Beach zoning, so what. You can handle that."

Hal didn't want to attempt the tall thing again––looking for loopholes, lobbying people, making enemies along the way. He needs friends, not enemies. Never again, he had told himself then, despite Milo's promise of an impressive bonus should he succeed. Which he didn't, so no bonus. And now he wants Hal to do a repeat performance? Not going to happen.

"I can't do that again," Hal had said. "That was it. I'm done, I can't handle the stress. Fini."

"Hey," Milo said. "I just wanted to give you the opportunity. Fantabulissimo will be outrageous, the most talked-about condo complex on the Beach. I promise you, say 'No' to this, and you'll forever regret not being a part of it."

Hal was intrigued, but unmoved. Still, he was curious. "Where is it? Somewhere on Collins, right?"

"You know the Louis Quinze?"

"The Louis Quinze?" Hal wasn't sure he heard right.

"Yeah, yeah. Everybody knows the Louis Quinze."

Hal felt disoriented. "My father built the Louis Quinze."

"You're kidding. He was the developer?"

Hal nodded, trying to sort out his feelings. Max had built the hotel so long ago that Hal thought of it as a distant memory, a playground of sorts when he was a kid, but, sold years ago to a hotel chain, no longer a part of his life. "The Louis Quinze," he repeated, trying to fix it in a now-altered reality. "*That's* the site of your new condo?"

"I just closed the deal to buy the property. I got the plans, I got the location. It's all still pretty hush hush."

"Why there? Aren't there other properties on the market you can build on?"

"I figure with the condo market the way it is, you gotta have a gimmick. The gimmick here is, this won't just be a condo, or just the tallest condo complex on the Beach. It'll be a landmark, a condo with a history."

Hal knew its history—decades of fame and infamy had guaranteed the Louis Quinze a solid chapter in Miami Beach's history—but history was being rewritten, times had changed, and the Louis Quinze had become an anachronism, a temple from another time considered ancient by the young and the hip who now peopled the Beach. Maybe it was time to rethink its image. "What are you doing with it?" he asked. "Renovating? Adding on?"

"Knocking down."

"Knocking down?" It hadn't registered. "You mean...bulldozing?"

"Imploding, actually." Milo's hands flew either side of his gerbillian face, and his cheeks puffed out with a kaboom sound. "From the inside out. It's really cool to watch."

"You can't do that," Hal said, suddenly protective. "It was built in the fifties. You can't just go around knocking down historical buildings. There's a law, all kinds of regulations."

Milo rolled his red-rimmed eyes. "Give me a break. Sure, the Deco nutcases won on South Beach, making a historic district out of those crappy buildings from the thirties and forties, like they were built by Frank Lloyd Wright or something. Now the preservationists have slapped a fancy name on the stuff from the fifties and sixties: MiMo. Miami Modern. How original."

"The Louis Quinze is MiMo," Hal said. "It's in a historic district. It's protected."

"That's taken care of," Milo said. "It's just a *local* historic designation, meaning the Preservation Board makes the decision for any kind of changes to those buildings in the district. So the first order of business was to get around the historic designation thing. Our attorneys figured out the legal angle—no offense to your qualifications, but they're experts at circumventing all that preservation stuff––and, thanks to someone on the board who was, shall we say, convinced, it's a done deal. It's easy, if you know what you're doing, to ..." He completed the sentence with a chopping motion of his hand, then added, "It's all in who you know."

Hal had sat for an uncomfortable moment with the implication that *he* is the Who Milo Knows, the Who with the pull to escalate Milo's condo from forty stories to a sixty-story mondo condo. That would make him an accomplice in reducing his father's building to a pile of rubble, even if it is just fifties MiMo rubble. "Do you *have* to knock it down?" Hal hedged. "It's not falling apart. It's even written up in books." He wasn't sure about where but pursued it. "Architecture books. History books."

"That's right. It's history. Out with the old, in with the new," Milo said. "Implosion's the way to go: Now you see it, now you don't. It's like the building never existed."

But...it did exist. And then Hal had remembered a moment with Max, so, so long ago when he was just a kid, standing on the roof of the hotel holding Max's hand and looking out over the beach below. How small his hand felt in Max's as they leaned over the balcony and gazed down at the alabaster curve of the Louis Quinze that stretched beneath their feet. How proud Max had been when he turned to Hal and said, "I am a builder. This is what I do." And how in awe Hal had been, believing his Pop had built this thing, all by himself.

Back then, the Louis Quinze uncoiled like an albino snake along the ocean-front, the biggest hotel ever built on Miami Beach. It had a lobby with windows three stories high, chandeliers with enough wattage to light up Cincinnati and a Busby Berkeley stairway to nowhere. There were three pools: one kidney-shaped salt-water, one square-shaped fresh-water, and one round kiddie pool the color of pee. There was a coffee shop with orange plastic booths and purple plastic orchids in pink plastic pots. There was a nightclub with stars like Judy Garland and Frank Sinatra who would walk around the hotel when they weren't performing, just like real people.

But that hotel exists only in memory, unlike the Louis Quinze of today. Today it preens like an aging movie star, Norma Desmond ready for the close-up that never comes, while newer, brighter, shinier faces hog the paparazzi's cameras. Its time has come and gone, along with the famous and the fabulous who once composed its clientele. Perhaps a mercy killing wouldn't be such a bad thing for the old girl in order to make way for the future.

Still. It was too much. He was going straight, no more deals, no more stress, just do his job, that's it, just do his job until his term ran out and then do something else, he didn't know what, but he did know this much: He wasn't going to be an accomplice to the murder of the Louis Quinze.

"Well?" Milo said. "You in?"

"Forget it," Hal said. "I can't get involved. It's my father's hotel."

"*Was* your father's hotel," Milo had corrected him. "It's not any more. Why would he even care?"

True, Hal had admitted. His father didn't seem to hold nostalgia for anything, much less a building he sold to a hotel chain when Hal was still a kid. After that, Max continued to build, but nothing compared to the Louis Quinze. At times, Hal felt Max's subsequent decline may have begun on the day of Hal's graduation from Yale, when Hal announced that he wanted to go into politics, as befitted a political science major who who had spent the previous summer in Tallahassee as an intern with the state representative from Miami.

The representative had paved the way to a scholarship at the University of Florida's law school, and that's where he was headed after graduation. So there went Max's dream of inserting "...and Son" into the company name, "Wolfe Development." The grand argument that ensued cancelled the small celebration Tootsie had planned at the Holiday Inn, ruining the day and whatever was left of Max's hopes for Hal's future, which was supposed to be linked to his own.

Hal's legal education led to a drudge job as a law clerk in a monster firm in Miami, which he knew from the start was a means, not an end. Law, he acknowledged, was almost a prerequisite to becoming a politician; joining the firm would be his apprenticeship. He had climbed in the ranks but never sought to distinguish himself amidst the more ambitious young attorneys more willing than he to conform to the rigid rules, conduct the tedious research, calculate the billable hours, and endure the mind-numbing boredom. There was no excitement, no applause, no recognition of the talents he knew he possessed. But he made a decent salary, and as an attorney (lowly as he was), he acquired validation and legitimacy to pursue what he knew for certain was his true calling: politics. This he had known from the age of 17, the moment he stood on the podium before the student body of Miami Beach High to make his acceptance speech as the new student council president—his first flush of political fame. As the applause washed over him and he glimpsed his defeated opponent slumped down in his seat, the taste of triumph gave him a hunger for more, and he had sought it ever since.

Yale gave him his first inkling that perhaps he wasn't so special after all. True, he had been president of the Beach High student council, but Yale was packed wall-to-wall with past student council presidents, valedictorians, science fair winners, and perfect SAT scores. What Hal did have was looks, charm and charisma, so he amped up those attributes and regained his mojo as a star debater in the Yale Political Union, then handily won several campus offices. His first real campaign after law school was an easy success (school board), and thus began his career.

But he had yet to achieve what he had visualized in those early, heady days when it seemed he was headed for greater heights; when the natural order would be city, then state, then national office; when it seemed as though his choice of career would be vindicated in Max's eyes, and he would make him proud. Max has made it clear Hal had yet to achieve that, implying that if Hal had only listened to him way back then, they all would have been the better for it.

Years of unacknowledged guilt had embedded itself in Hal's psyche like a kidney stone that never passed, buffered by ego and pride until —like now—it would occasionally surface, a painful reminder that maybe life could have been different. He wasn't about to add to his guilt by participating in this adventure of Milo's. Plus, he had plenty of other reasons for not getting involved with Milo, and they all added up to No.

But Milo had not been so easily deterred. "We need to talk. Just hear me out. I'll make it worth your while—I mean *really* worth your while, and I'm not just talking major bucks, although that's part of it. But it's bigger than that. Let me lay it all out for you, and if you're still not interested, we can say Adios."

Really worth his while? What did that mean? Could this be the event Hal had waited for all this time, something that would bestow the blessing of recognition, the "I told you so" he had never been able to say to Max?

Well, it couldn't hurt to listen, Hal had figured. Just hear him out. What's the harm in that?

So now he's on his way to meet Milo. Not to make a deal, no no. No deal. Just...to listen.

Hal death-grips the Harley's handlebars, squints into a constellation of oncoming lights from cars aimed right at him, yes, he's going to die, this is it, the moment he's always feared but then *whew* he's on the ramp and off the causeway. Giddy with the realization that he made it without being creamed by some kid with a fake driver's license and no insurance, his cockiness returns. He resumes his Easy Rider slouch over the handlebars, roars down Ocean Drive with a motor-revving head-turning I'm Here and I'm Cool grand entrance, only to find himself circling several blocks in search of a spot. Disgusted, he parks illegally in a loading zone. Hey, he's a public servant, they owe him, no problem, he gets a ticket, he'll get it fixed.

He flings his Harley jacket over one shoulder and weaves through the maze of sidewalk tables into the cool dark of Hot Tamale, striding with the cowboy bowleg gait he feigns after dismounting the bike. He straddles a seat at the bar to wait for Milo, signals the bartender for a beer. Where's Milo? He checks his Rolex: 6:45. Milo told him 6:30. He busted his ass getting here on time and here he sits, twiddling his thumbs at a bar with a bunch of TGIF slackers staring up at the ...what is that? A *golf* tournament? They're watching *golf*? He swings around on the stool, swigs his Samuel Adams, wipes his mouth with a furry forearm. Golf, he mutters. Give me a break.

He scans the tables, looking for Milo, but Milo's pinched gerbil features are nowhere to be seen among the multitude of upturned faces staring at Tiger Woods, a half dozen Tiger Woods cloned on the TVs overhead. Tiger's still around. A good sign. Hal punches Milo's number into his cell phone, realizes it's as dead as a cell phone he forgot to charge can be. He makes circles on the bar top with his beer mug. Tears his napkin into little bits. Wonders once again: why is he in this business anyway, bored, underpaid, dealing with creeps like Milo.

He's doing it. He's sinking into one of his funks. They've been coming on him lately, usually when he's home alone at his granite-topped counter in his shiny condo kitchen eating warmed-over Boston Chicken or a sad frozen Hungry Man Turkey Dinner he picked up at Publix. Tonight will be no different. After he scrapes the last bit of turkey from the tray, he'll drop his fork into the dishwasher, turn off the kitchen TV, light up a joint, then flop face-up on his sofa, staring from its buttery Natuzzi depths at the ten-foot ceiling of his ocean-view condo bought years ago at the peak of rising condo prices, when it seemed they would continue to rise forever.

Then the condo's value tanked with the sinking market, not helped by the fact that the street where he lived was periodically underwater during the King Tides, a foreboding of Miami Beach's future as Waterworld. Politicians ignored that dire forecast, and life went on to the throb of pumping stations, one of which hummed away within earshot of Hal's condo. Nevertheless, his condo has regained its original value and then some, no consolation to Hal, who lately has felt that his own value has diminished with the times, that he's on the downslide with no up in sight. Fifty-five. He's fifty-five. By fifty he should have been mayor.

He feels a tap on his back, startling him back to Now. He turns around to face deep cleavage at eye level framed by a palm-tree printed shirt unbuttoned low, tied high, and adorned by a plastic badge that reads "Staci." His gaze moves up to a wide mouth painted a juicy shade of tangerine.

"Hal Wolfe?" the mouth asks. He is fascinated by its moist orangeness, fights a sudden urge to perform a litmus test by sticking his tongue into its depths. It would not do to act on such urges in public as he learned from experience when, under the influence of some primo pot just arrived from Mexico, and oh, all right, just one nostril's-worth of coke offered by Milo in the mens' room during a fundraising event, he indulged in a discreet caress of the mayor's wife's satin-clad butt which was met with a loud objection. Said scene made the lead in the Talk of Our Town column in the Miami Herald. The incident, hardly an astute political move, wasn't fatal since his constituents, for the most part, understood. The mayor, however, didn't, and despite Hal's subsequent eloquent and very sincere apology, has been his political antagonist ever since.

"Yeah, I'm Hal," he says, pleased at the recognition by such a young and juicy morsel as this Staci. "How did you know?"

"You got a call from a guy who couldn't reach you on your cell," she says. "He said I should look for a middle-aged guy dressed like a biker. You can take it up front."

Middle-aged? He sucks in his gut, then bowlegs it to the front desk to pick up the phone where Milo informs him that he's not meeting him, the deal's off, at least for now. Seems that the *Herald's* doing an investigative piece on developers and politicians and, um, they got wind of this latest venture and asked him about that last, uh, deal, and well...

"Shit!" he yells. "What did you tell them?" He immediately regrets the volume of his reaction when heads swivel and—great, terrific—he's recognized. He forces a smile and gives the celebrity wave of acknowledgment, the index-finger-point in their direction. He folds himself around the phone and growls softly into the receiver, "You say anything to the *Herald*, you'll never build in this town again."

He slams the phone down before Milo can reply, and stalks back to the bar. His rage rises in increments of scarlet from his neck to his ears, and by the time he's straddling the bar stool again, his face is as furrowed and red as a chili pepper. This is all he needs. If he were paid a decent salary, he wouldn't need to do favors for scumbags like Milo. Sure, he gets a steady income from his practice with the firm, plus his investments which he was at least astute enough to put into the hands of a financial advisor. With the escalating market of the past few years, they bring in good money, but not enough, especially not now. He needs more. He's got to live. He has expenses. The condo. The Alaskan cruise. The Mercedes. The diamond Rolex for the last girlfriend. The alimony. The alimony. The goddamned alimony.

A tsunami of self-pity overtakes him. He slumps forward until his forehead rests in a beer puddle on the bar top. He doesn't care. He can't move. Life sucks. He hates his job. His bald spot is growing. He has toenail fungus, eroded gums, and side effects from Viagra. His parents make him nuts, his ex-wife *is* a nut, and their grown son Wally sells time shares in Tucson. This is not the way it was supposed to be.

"You okay?"

He looks up, bleary-eyed. He recognizes the cleavage, the palm-tree shirt, the tangerine mouth. The badge that says "Staci." "Fine," he says, turning away. "I'm just peachy." He busies himself with his beer bottle, circles it on the bar-top.

"You don't look so fine," she says. "You look kind of sick."

"Look, Staci with an *i*," he says, still smarting from the middle-aged biker reference, "why don't you just mind your own business?"

"Sorry," she says. "I thought maybe you were having some kind of heart thing." She turns to leave, and he gets a whiff of her scent, a citrus-y honey that seems to pulse from between those palm-framed breasts. His depression lifts substantially, as it often does in the presence of nubile young women wearing minimal clothing.

"Wait," he says, grabbing her arm, which she disengages with a shake. He re-arranges his features into a semblance of contrite apology. "I just got some bad news and I took it out on you." He gives her his trademark killer smile, lopsided and a little shy. "I appreciate your concern, though."

"No problem," she says, and she's gone. Her incandescence—the white of her shorts, the blonde of her hair—fades into the gloom, then reappears, elusive as a firefly among the tables. He should have caught her when she was within reach. He's losing his touch. She should have been the latest entry in his mental list of conquests, a list that began early in his now-defunct marriage and was added to with regularity. But the entries have sunk lately in both quantity and quality.

He had always been an equal-opportunity schtupper, offering his services to a broad range of bimbos—Marilyn the meter maid, Sally the judge, Lauren the hippie, Diane the realtor, Delia the Publix cashier—until he sank to a new depth with Ruth the prison guard and her butt-sniffing dog Chico. *ChicoChicoChico* she had yipped during sex, which had immediately deflated him. When he realized that being replaced by a dog in a prison guard's fantasy was about as low as he could go, he lost his libido until now, when it's revived at the sight of Staci. Who thinks he's middle-aged.

He mournfully turns his gaze to the screen above him which no longer focuses on infinite golf course green but on the Channel Seven news anchor, the dark-haired one, not bad, a little chunky but nice tits. She's smiling into the shar-pei grin of Mayor Martinez, who wouldn't be mayor if things had gone Hal's way because if things had gone Hal's way, it would be *his* face grinning on the TV overhead. Hal's head is drifting south toward the bar top again when a hand lights on his shoulder. He snaps to attention at the frontal view of Staci, whose tangerine lips are asking, "You *sure* you're okay?"

He shakes his head to rid it of Mayor Martinez's grin, a movement Staci takes as a negative. "Is it your heart?" she asks. "Should I call 911?"

"What? No!" He uncoils from his slump and assumes Biker Pose, crossing one big boot over his knee, leaning back with both elbows on the bartop. "I'm great. Never been better." He attempts a cocky grin, but can only produce a sickly smile. "Just conducting a little career review," he confesses, surprising himself in his misery.

"Me, too," she says with a sigh. "I do it every day."

"Yeah?" Ah. Damsel in distress. Never fails to perk him up. "Why's that?"

"This," she says, indicating the beer-stale gloom of Hot Tamale with a nod of her head, "was not in the plan."

"What plan?"

She shrugs, her lips a tangerine slice of embarrassed smile. "The plan was to be a model."

"And...?"

"The agency said I was too...buxom."

"Buxom? Buxom is bad?" He takes this opportunity to do a complete body scan from top to toe. "You've got a great figure," he assures her. "Just *great.*"

"Yeah, well, thanks." she says with a sad little shrug. "But they told me I'm just not cut out for fashion." She takes his empty bottle and swipes the bar top's puddle dispiritedly with a cloth. "I feel like I've hit a dead end."

"How so?" he asks, his voice cracking with suppressed but all-too-real understanding.

"Oh, I don't know. Sometimes I think I should have done what my friend did. She used to work here, too."

"Used to?"

"Yeah. *Maxim* was doing a South Beach feature. Some guy asked us both to take scouting shots. She did. I didn't."

"Why not?"

"My father would have totally freaked." She pauses. "So she wound up being a *Maxim* Girl. She got paid more in a month than I make in a year of waitressing."

Hal feels the cogs turning, flipping his brain cells through his favors-owed file. "So you'd do it, if you had the opportunity again?"

Staci shrugs. "I don't know. It's *something*, I guess. I just don't want to do this," she indicates with a hand wave at her surroundings, "forever."

"Well," he begins, "this guy I know owes me a favor." He pauses for effect. "He's from *Maxim*."

"Yeah?" She tips her head and eyes him with skeptical amusement.

"Yeah. I got him permission to shoot naked in places that don't permit naked." He makes his move. "If you want, I could give him a call about you."

"Sure thing," she says with a laugh that curls her lips into a citrus twist. "You just do that, Harley Guy." And then she's gone. He watches her incandescence fade once more into the darkness.

Once, there was a time when she wouldn't have left, he thinks. She would have known who he was, would have met him after work. That was the time of power and prestige, the daily tingle of anticipation as dawn leaked through his Levelors, the promise of conquest at nightfall. Now day brings with it the fear of defeat, and night makes its certainty seem imminent.

He descends the barstool, boots landing with a hollow thunk before they carry him outside, bowleg walk reduced to a shuffle, heels scuffing the ground until he reaches his parking place––now empty but for a grease spot where his Harley should be.

The Harley reposes in the ignominious custody of Beach Towing. Hal pays the $250 fee while expressing his outrage about illiterate immigrant crooks who hold vehicles hostage despite his threat to shut the place down because he knows the mayor. He exits Beach Towing in a roar of fury, narrowly missing a turn which would have dumped him into the bay. It is then, overcome by the image of himself weighed down by the hulk of his Harley and sinking beneath the dark waters, that he has a vision.

That vision is Staci.

She appears to him like an angel, one of those Victoria's Secret angels wearing little but a push-up bra, a diaphanous veil and a pair of fluffy wings. And in this vision, he sees her on the cover of *Maxim*, thanks to him of course, which would result in Staci's undying gratitude, leading to generous favors of the sexual kind delivered by Staci herself. And so, with the germination of a plan to make at least *this* dream come true comes the revelation that after all the pain he has suffered, all the hopes that lay shattered, that life could just possibly be good.

CHAPTER III

STACI

Staci glides on silver skates. Her body, fluid as molten gold, sways to the music only she can hear. She dances over truck-pocked heat-buckled asphalt, weaves through the sunset crush of rush-hour traffic, a butterfly among beetles. Darkness descends as she turns onto Ocean Drive where neon heralds the coming night with jeweled brilliance. She quickly unlaces her skates by the light of the flashing red Hot Tamale sign, ties on her Nikes and hustles inside. She's already wearing her waitress uniform, green palm-patterned shirt knotted high above tight white shorts, but her shift has begun and here comes Roberto, the restaurant manager, to chew her out.

"Late again," he says. "Third time this week."

She shrugs. "Traffic," she says. She pulls the Scrunchie off her wind-tangled ponytail, rakes fingers through sun-striped hair and leaves it loose around her shoulders, the way she once wore it when she had an occasional modeling assignment. When she believed this waitress gig was just a way to make some money until she got a solid contract with Elite or Wilhemina or Michele Pommier. When she believed it was just a matter of time and dropping oh, fifteen pounds the agencies said, even twenty wouldn't be a bad idea. And then when she realized that diet, exercise and all the Rollerblading in the world wouldn't shrink her to model size, she shifted her career fantasies to *Maxim*. The one part of her that refused to deflate just might be her key to fame: 32-D genuine real-thing breasts that Roberto is now staring at in silent appreciation before he growls, "Okay, okay, okay. Get to work."

Get to work. Get to work. Work means sweating in a sports bar, hostage of a Cyclops army of TV sets tuned to ESPN. Work means taking orders, toting trays, enduring complaints about cold food and slow service from guys fixated on the circle of overhead screens alive with muscular bodies manipulating balls:

big balls, little balls, white balls, brown balls, red balls, yellow balls, every hue but blue balls, an affliction apparently shared by guys who can't keep their hands away from Staci's shorts-encased butt, guys who brush against her generous breasts, guys who whisper nasty wishes into her ear with Bud Lite-saturated breath.

This is Staci's work, her job, her future until something better comes along, a something which better come along sooner than later. She's 22, too old to be living at home with Mami and Papi and a couple of teenage brothers whom she caught charging their friends five dollars to catch a glimpse of her in her underwear. If her parents had their way, she'd still be chaperoned on dates, like Mami had been in Havana, like her older sisters had been in Miami until they married just to get out from under the rules. She's tired of the ongoing fiction she's forced to enact, that she's spending the night at a girlfriend's whenever she has a hot date. As soon as she can, she's getting her own place, even if Papi insists that in Cuba girls stayed home until they married. She's not in Cuba. She's her own person. She didn't change her name from Stefanie to Staci for nothing.

She deftly dodges the guy in the University of Miami sweatshirt who expresses his desire for the check by plucking at the hem of her shorts. Be back *momentito*, she promises sweet as can be because she doesn't want to lose that tip, not after putting up with him for the last hour, him and his sloppy drunk friends, jamming cigarettes into their salsa, knocking over bottles of beer, sticking straws up their noses and into their ears. College boys. The pits.

Almost as bad as the boomers who hang out here, beer bellies ballooning over khaki Dockers, painfully-placed strands of hair plastered over shiny skulls. What is it with those guys? Do they seriously think she's turned on by disco dialogue and jokes featuring tongue tricks and tiny dicks? It's a good thing she doesn't want to get married or she'd be depressed by the selection.

Not that she's still a virgin by any means. No, that disappeared long ago, the night of her *Quinceañera*––the elaborate fifteenth birthday party her parents scrimped and saved for. When the dancing was done, when the last bit of *dulce de leche* and cake had been downed, when Mami and Papi, sated with pride and pleasure at the success of the party, agreed to having Tía Ana drive her home, Staci managed to talk Tía—a hipper version of Mami—into letting Juan, her boyfriend, drive her home instead. And, parked in Juan's car, in a flurry of satin and lace, Staci lost not just her *Quince* crown, but the one thing Papi assumed she had kept: her purity, her innocence.

She never missed it. After Juan, there was Luis, then Orlando, then Richie, then Pepe, then—oh, she's lost track. Now there's no one, but it's just a hiatus. She has her eye on Angel, a copper-skinned raven-haired hottie who works at the Lincoln Road Gap and goes to school at night. She knows that after Angel, there will be another, and yet another, for she is blessed with passion. She also knows that passion dies, but marriage is forever.

Staci hears her name called as she passes the bar. It's that old biker from the other night, the one who got so purple and agitated she thought he was having a heart attack. Today he looks a little healthier. Poor old guy, he tried so hard to impress her she feels sorry for him, so she smiles and says hello.

"I'm back," he says.

"Yes, you are," she agrees. He's wearing a T-shirt that reads "Harley Hog" above a tattooed pig straddling a motorcycle. The pig is wearing an earring and a red bandana and resembles Billy Bob Thornton. It's sad but sweet that this is what the old guy thinks is cool.

He goes into his pose, one clunky-booted foot crossed over the opposite knee, elbows against the bar. "I was thinking about your wish," he says.

"My wish?"

"You know, about being in *Maxim*."

"Oh, that." She's embarrassed. Why did she ever confess her hope to this complete stranger? "I wasn't..."

He reaches into the back pocket of his jeans and pulls out a card: Harold Wolfe, Councilman, City of Miami Beach. She supposes she should be impressed. "Oh," she says.

"Yeah. I know people, people know me. Now, like I said, someone at *Maxim* owes me a favor."

"I sorta remember." Now she really remembers. Something to do with naked, taking naked pictures. "The permission thing?"

"I made it possible for him to shoot nudity in fairly public places. You do know *Maxim* shoots a lot of nudity, don't you?" he asks. "Is this something you'd be willing to do?"

Nude. Naked. Staci hadn't really allowed herself to think seriously about *herself* being naked. Would she dare? Papi would disown her. Mami would spend the rest of her life in church. Her brothers would up their viewing fee to ten dollars. "Are *Maxim* Girls always naked?"

"Sort of."

"Oh." She hadn't been sure. She's never looked inside an issue of *Maxim*, but the covers displayed on magazine racks didn't show the girls all-the-way naked. "I didn't think they were *really* naked," she says. "Just nearly."

"Well...it's more than nearly. Although," Hal adds at her look of dismay, "I think it's up to the individual girl. If you don't *want* to be completely nude, I bet you wouldn't have to be."

"Really?" she says, brightening. "You think?"

"Besides, we're just talking about scouting shots, you know, test photos. There's no guarantee it'll go any further than that. I don't want you to get your hopes up. It's not an easy thing, being chosen for *Maxim*, and I'm not just talking the cover girl. I mean just for one little photo in a feature."

"Even that would be such an honor."

"Well, if this is what you want, then I'll make the arrangements. Give me your number and I'll have the scout call you. And maybe it wouldn't be a bad idea if you got a few things together for the scouting shots."

"A few things? Like what?"

"Um--lingerie? Something...brief?"

Time for a visit to Victoria's Secret, she thinks. She does have nice lingerie, but this calls for something new and special. It could make all the difference for the future she envisions. She beams a sunshine smile at Hal. "I can't believe this is really happening," she says as she happily scribbles her phone number on a napkin. "I don't know how to thank you."

"My pleasure," Hal says. "It's my job to be of service."

* * *

The rich aroma of roast pork is in the air. Mami is busy in the kitchen, her broad back to Staci, who takes the opportunity to sneak by quickly with her pink-striped bag from Victoria's Secret, filled with freshly purchased bits and wisps of fluff—sheer, lacy, barely-there fluff that although provocative, nevertheless covers her in all the appropriate places should the *Maxim* promise from her new friend, Hal, come to pass.

Staci rounds the corner of the hallway to her bedroom when she hears Mami's querulous voice call out in Spanish, "Stefanie? Are you home?"

"*Sí*, Mami," she answers, throwing the package under the bed, her childhood bed, buried beneath a stuffed animal menagerie that multiplies with each new boyfriend. "It's my night off." She pauses. "I have a date, so I won't be home for dinner."

Silence from the kitchen. Staci can picture her mother's face, frowning, elongating her Modigliani features even more as she turns from her pork-tending at the oven and draws to her full height of five-nine. Staci gets her height from her mother, Maria, as statuesque, full-bodied and strong after six children and thirty-five years of marriage as she was on her wedding day. Pepe, Maria's husband, first spotted her working in a bodega on Calle Ocho after his tumultuous arrival in Miami on one of the rafts that escaped Cuba and landed on Hallandale Beach. She was much younger and taller than he, but he wooed her with tales of terror and bravado and she, still a virgin and ripe for the picking, fell for his macho style. After several chaste dates chaperoned by her cousin, she agreed to marry the brash man with the bristly mustache who came up to her eyebrows. And, as she often says to her willful daughter as a windup to one of her interminable lectures, *that* is what courtship should be.

But Staci thinks otherwise. Courtship, first of all, is a ridiculous, outdated, Victorian word. In America, you date. You date lots of men. You sleep with whomever. You fall in love, never. Love is a treacherous thing, a painful thing, a thing to avoid at all costs. When men are as plentiful and attentive as her lovers have been, what's the point of love? It just gets in the way.

She refuses to tie her future to one man. Once upon a time, she wanted a career. She wanted to go to the community college to see what she could be. But when she blurted out at dinner one night that it was right that Elián went back to his father in Cuba, her enraged father withdrew his promise to send her. "Let Janet Reno pay for your school," he had shouted. And since Janet Reno was no longer around and she couldn't send herself, she never went.

Still, she feels she is bound for greatness. It's something she has known since she was very young, when the sight of her walking down the street turned men into bobble-heads. It was a power she took for granted, and felt obligated to use for good—her own. It was too generous a gift to waste on one man; it should be shared with many. Preferably thousands, who would applaud not just her beauty, but her talent. She just had to figure out exactly what that talent would be.

CHAPTER IV

TOOTSIE

A grey curtain of rain obliterates the ocean view from the sliding door of the balcony. "I don't know about this," Tootsie says. She wipes the foggy glass with a vein-bubbled hand and peers out. "Maybe we should cancel."

"I'm not canceling," Max says. "It took me three weeks to get this appointment with Dr. Whatsisname, three weeks I have to wait for him to take a look at this thing on my nose and now it's twice as big. I'm not canceling."

"It's not twice as big. It's a pimple. It can wait."

"So now you're a doctor?" He leans close to the mirror over the hall table and pokes at the pinkish bump on his nose. "I'm not waiting. I wait, it grows, next thing I know he's cutting the whole nose off." He moves into position at the front door. "Let's go."

Tootsie wipes the glass again. "Look at that. It's like a hurricane. I'm not driving in that."

"You make such a big deal. So you get a little wet." Max thrusts his hand out. "Give me the keys. I'll drive."

"What? So you can kill us both?" Tootsie flaps her hands against her hips like a fidgety hen, then throws them up into the air. "I give up. Such *tsuris* over a pimple." She yanks open the hall table drawer, pulls out a clear plastic rain bonnet and ties it under her chin, exposing only a row of tarnished silver curls coiled so tightly they seem buttoned to her forehead. With a huge sigh that puffs out her little pigeon breast, she churns out the door ahead of him. They wait in steamy silence for the elevator, which doesn't arrive any sooner for all of Max's impatient poking of the down button.

"I can drive," Max says, but since Tootsie has taken charge of the keys, he can't. He sulks in the passenger seat as Tootsie backs out of the garage parking space, her galosh-clad foot pouncing on the brake in head-jerking spurts until the big black Lincoln clears its Audi neighbor by a hair. She exits the garage, peering through a windshield suddenly opaque with rain. The wipers are ineffectual in their stuttering passes across its surface, leaving wide, smeary paths as she inches the Lincoln through storm-stalled traffic.

She never was much of a driver, just here and there, the store, the beauty parlor, her weekly mah-jongg game until, one by one—this one got sick, that one died, it was always something—the girls dropped out and the game ended. Before Max's license was yanked from him, he had insisted on driving whenever they went anywhere together. She never thought to protest, even when it became clear that he had no business sitting in the driver's seat. She rarely questioned anything he did because it just wasn't worth the aggravation, but she was relieved when Hal, after one particularly harrowing trip with Max behind the wheel, realized that not only had his father's driving ability declined, but that Max, as Hal put it, couldn't see worth shit. Hal ratted on his own father, much to Tootsie's relief, and when the license bureau made him re-take a driver's test, he flunked.

Tootsie glances over at Max, tucked into the seat belt despite his complaint that the strap is rubbing his neck. He mutters angrily to himself, oblivious to the spastic start-and-stop of the car. She picks up speed as the traffic accelerates, ignoring Max's escalating demands to slow down slow down slow *down* until, at the explosive shock of hitting a deep puddle, she swerves wildly out of control. A sheet of khaki-color water envelops the car. Helpless, she skids, misses an oncoming car, fishtails to a stop at the entrance of what looks like a parking lot. Exhaling in relief, she inches up a ramp into the lot to wait out the storm.

A sharp jolt bounces her off the seat. She's hit something big, rolled right over it, a parking bumper probably. "Huh," says Max, momentarily stunned. Dislodged from his position beneath the seat belt, he leans at an angle to his left. "What the hell?" he asks, but his question goes unanswered. The jolt seems to have knocked the needle off his non-stop muttering, replacing it with a grim silence Tootsie has come to recognize as the prelude to a proclamation.

"I have to pee," Max announces. "I didn't go before we left."

Rain beats a tom-tom rhythm on the roof. Tootsie puts the car into reverse. The engine revs, the wheels spin. The car doesn't move. This is some big bumper, she thinks. She puts the car into drive, presses the accelerator. Nothing.

She jams her foot hard on the gas pedal. The engine revs to a whine. Nothing moves. She stares at the windshield wipers, hypnotic in their metronomic rhythm, back, forth, back, forth. They make her want to go to sleep.

"I have to pee," Max repeats, pulling on the door handle. "Where are we? I'm getting out."

"There's nowhere to go here," she says. "We got a little problem."

The rain isn't letting up. She's got to do something. What did she hit? She tries to see out the windshield. There's nothing beyond it but gray. She opens her door a crack to peer out and is instantly drenched. *Gottenyu,* she says, but climbs out and looks.

She didn't hit a bumper. She's hanging over a wall. It's about eight feet to the ground below. The chassis of the car is resting on the barrier of the wall and the front wheels are resting on nothing. She's not going anywhere.

She gets back in the car and tries to think. She's soaked to the skin. Max faces her; his big pale eyes swim behind the thick lenses like sick guppies. "It was all that iced tea," he says. "How many times do I have to tell you, don't make iced tea before I take a trip."

Tootsie wipes the fog from the windshield, and makes out the blue and red lights of a gas station across the street. "I'll be right back," she says, taking the keys with her. "Don't move."

She splashes across a river that once was the street and reaches the security-glassed cashier's booth of the gas station. She pounds on the glass. The attendant, groggy with boredom, looks up, alarmed.

"Help!" she says. "My car is stuck. Can you help me?"

"¿Qué?"

Oy vey. He doesn't speak English. She points frantically in the direction of the car, a big black blur overhanging the ledge across the street. "Help!" she repeats. "Car off cliff!"

He shakes his head. Shrugs.

She's delirious with frustration. "Car!" she pantomimes, right hand moving horizontally towards the vertical left. "Cliff!" she shouts as she drives right hand over left. The attendant frowns with concern. He peers out of the booth, looks where she's pointing, nods his head. "No problem," he says, and follows her through the rain.

"Ay ay ay," he says upon closer inspection. "*Tienes un problema grande.*"

"Tow truck," she says. "I need a tow truck."

That he understands. He holds up a finger, runs back to his booth. She can see him calling from his phone. He flashes ten fingers at her twice. Twenty minutes? The tow truck will be here in twenty minutes.

Forty-five minutes later, the tow truck arrives. Windows closed, air conditioning off, the car has become a sauna on wheels. Tootsie's blood pressure has risen along with the temperature while, soporific from the heat, Max has dozed off. Either his need to pee wasn't that urgent, or the Depends he wears when he goes out has absorbed the problem. In any case, help has arrived. The rain has let up. The crisis is clear. She has driven the front of the car off an elevated parking lot. Her rescuer, a burly, fortunately bilingual guy, is studying the situation from the base of the ledge. He looks up at the overhanging car. "How'd you do this, lady?" he asks.

"What, it's your business?" Her dress is sticking to her skin, her shoes are soggy sponges inside her galoshes, and this nudnik is asking stupid questions. "Just tell me you can fix it."

He hooks the tow truck cable to the bumper of her car, winches it up, and tugs. Tootsie grips the wheel and releases the brake, as he has instructed, then puts the car into reverse. Max is awake. "What? What?" he wants to know. The car rocks crazily with each yank as the tow truck attempts to dislodge it from its perch. Max's head jerks with each tug of the truck.

"Where are we?" he asks.

"Almost there," she says.

The yanking becomes more desperate. The wheels spin in empty air. The bumper is making scary creaking sounds, as if it's going to disconnect from the car. The tow truck driver gives up.

"You need the big tow truck," he says. "It's got a elevator bed that goes up and down. Maybe it can lift your car from the front. Only," he adds, studying the height of the wall, "I dunno if it'll go that high."

A half hour later, she finds out. It doesn't go that high. It rises to six inches below the front of the car, and that's as far as it goes. The new tow truck driver sees this as a challenge. He considers borrowing a nearby cement block that is imbedded with a "no parking" sign to increase the range of the bed. Tootsie is numb by now. She doesn't care what he does. She walks across the street and uses the bathroom in the gas station. Max, judging from the odor that has arisen within the confines of the car over the past hour and a half, is no longer concerned about his urination situation. He has, however, regained his energy enough to share his thoughts with her upon her return:

"I knew it. I knew it," he says. "Look what happens when I let you drive. If I miss my appointment, I'll have to wait *another* three weeks to get him to take a look at this thing." He pets the malformation with a knobby forefinger. "What does *she* care? It's just a nose to her, but to me, it's *my* nose." He slumps into a cross-armed knot behind the seat belt. "I shoulda driven. I'm a good driver. I passed that test. I can prove it."

Tootsie sees the bed of the tow truck slowly elevate beneath the front of the car. The cement block is on top of it. It rises until it hits the chassis with a crunch. "I think we got it," the tow truck driver yells.

"The test guy said I didn't stop at the stop sign," Max says. "I didn't *need* to stop, I told him. I was going very slowly."

The car shudders, creaks and moans as its front end lifts away from the ledge, tipping Tootsie and Max back in their seats. "Reverse, reverse," the truck driver yells, and Tootsie throws the car into gear.

"I've been driving for 75 years. How many people can say that?" Max asks.

"Gun it!" yells the truck driver.

The car jerks, tossing them like crash test dummies. The front drops with a thud onto its wheels and the car rolls back several yards. Heart leaping, Tootsie stomps on the brake. The tow truck driver jumps down from his cab and gives her a thumbs-up.

"What happened?" Max asks, searching the windshield for a clue. "Where are we?"

"We had a little problem. It's fixed."

"Are we at the doctor's?"

"No," Tootsie says, focusing on getting out of the parking lot without another mishap. She listens for sounds of damage to the car. "We're going home."

"I've got a *doctor's* app..." Max begins, but stops short when the car skreeks dangerously on the slick asphalt as Tootsie stomps on the brake. She turns to him with a menacing glare, speaking in a voice he hasn't heard since she told him forty years ago if he so much as *looked* at that tramp Wanda Feinstein again, she would serve him his *putz* on a platter.

"We are going home," she says. "And I am *never*—understand me?–– *never* driving you anywhere again.*"

* * *

The pimple was just a pimple. That was the doctor's diagnosis when Max was driven there by Zoe, hired after Tootsie called Hal at work to tell him he was now in charge of transportation for his father. "I'm in the middle of a meeting," Hal had said, and hung up before Tootsie finished relating the events of the day that led up to her demand. She didn't hear from him again for several hours, and when she did, the news was not good.

"I've hired Zippity Cab to drive Pop," he had said. "Your troubles are over."

"Who? What?" Tootsie said.

"Zippity Cab. Remember Zoe? The woman whose car you bashed?"

Tootsie's brain stalled momentarily, then it all came rushing back. "The *kurva*. Not the *kurva*!"

"Relax, Mom," he said in the slightly slurry voice she's noticed he has lately when he's dealing with her and Max. "She's going to help. Her cab's fixed. She's back in business. And she's available to drive Pop whenever he needs to go somewhere."

"I'd rather schlep him myself than pay that *meshugganah* woman to do it."

"She's pretty reasonable, Mom. Cheaper than a regular cab. She's giving us a deal because it means a steady job for her."

"I don't like her," she had said, twisting the telephone cord sullenly. "And," she added, "she's a terrible driver."

"So you're Mario Andretti?"

"Who?"

"Never mind. Listen, it's a done deal," he had said with finality. "Zoe's going to take him to his next appointment."

And that—given Tootsie's determination never to repeat an expedition as horrific as that rainy day with Max—was that.

She refuses to go to the door when Zoe shows up to collect Max, who walks right by her as she feigns busyness in the kitchen, rifling through the junk drawer—bag clips, twist-ties, pencil stubs, old Publix receipts, coupons, orphan bits of hardware, an old rusty toilet chain preserved in an envelope—as if she were looking for something crucial. A pang of guilt knifes through her when she hears the door slam, followed by a feeling of abandonment. She paces the kitchen, gradually substituting righteous anger for the guilt she's feeling as she ticks off all the things Max said he'd fix but never did: burned-out refrigerator light, broken burner on the stove, grease-clogged exhaust that makes a funny noise.

Even Viola, the maid who has worked for them since they moved to this apartment––what is it, 30 years? 40?—complains about those things. Viola's down to a half day every week, declining over the years from three full days a week, still too much time for Max who says *What do we need her for? I pay her too much, what does she do, a little cleaning, a little laundry, what's the big deal?*

but Tootsie was never one for cleaning, she can only do so much, what does *he* do, he can't even change the bulb in the refrigerator and besides, they've only given Viola a couple of raises the last ten years, and who's going to hire her at this age? *I don't like strangers here poking around in my business* Max said but Viola's not a stranger and she doesn't poke although maybe she's stealing from them because one of Tootsie's bras is missing and so are those cans of Star-Kist tuna she just got on sale.

Tootsie takes her grievances into their bathroom when she hears Max open the front door. They're back. She doesn't want to see Zoe, but she's not that happy to see herself in the bathroom mirror, either, the furrows in her face etched even deeper in the glare of the overhead row of lights, one of which is flickering. Max was supposed to replace it, and do something about the rust around the faucet, and fix the towel rod that collapsed when he grabbed it getting out of the shower. Maybe she should redecorate. The bathroom hasn't changed since they moved in: brown-spattered beige tiles, orange-mono-grammed brown towels, metallic wallpaper in a geometric pattern. She did get a new shower curtain with fish on it.

Zoe must be gone because Max is rapping on the bathroom door. "You in there?" he asks, like who else would be in there? "I gotta pee."

"How did it go?" she asks when he comes out.

"I still got my nose."

"Her car got fixed okay?"

"We made it back home."

And for that, Tootsie is truly grateful.

When did she begin to worry that Max might never come home again? There was hardly a time when she could remember not being with him, they had married so young. It just seemed a natural thing to do at that age: get married. She didn't think all that much about it, but fell into life as you did in those days: the husband goes off to work (what did he do all day, she sometimes wondered, to make buildings rise up out of nothing?), the wife stays home and has babies (baby, in her case), cleans, shops, cooks, whatever it takes to be the *balabusta* her mother was, who brought all her old-country ways with her to the Bronx and died at the age of 84 sweeping dust bunnies out from under the bed. They said it was her heart, but Tootsie suspected it was from inhaling all that schmutz.

Once Max was making money, she didn't have to clean, thank God, but she took pride in her cooking. That she could do: cook, and if she couldn't earn her *balabusta* points by dusting and scrubbing, she'd make up for it with her authentic Jewish recipes, handed down in painfully scrawled and creatively misspelled recipes from her mother: brisket, kreplach, borscht, chicken soup, schav, even gefilte fish made from scratch, which she did when she was younger and didn't mind hauling whole fish home from the market and grinding it herself. And then she discovered Manischewitz. Maybe fish in a jar isn't as good, but it was a hell of a lot easier.

Besides, Max never noticed. Not since they were young marrieds, when neither could do no wrong and her first attempts at cooking were uniformly charred past recognition yet praised as manna by Max, that's how much in love they were. Then (she couldn't say when) that kind of love—where they couldn't keep away from each other, where she laughed at his jokes and he complimented her cooking, where they assumed that this feeling would never end— ended. It wasn't marked on any calendar, there was no particular time that it happened any more than old age happens, just a steady day-by-day devolution that wore away at love as surely as water carves a canyon.

And so, without realizing it, they slipped into the strange comfort of togetherness, the slow waltz of daily life interrupted by brief jitterbugs of illness, annoyance, and momentary crisis of one kind or another. But beneath it all remained a caring, the remnants of love, and an underlying fear that someday, one of them would go missing.

Max is slumped into his La-Z-Boy. A big white bandage covers most of his nose. As he flicks channels with the remote, his thumb freezes when he hits the history channel. He leans forward, squinting at the screen. "Is that Reagan?" he yells at Tootsie, who is sitting across from him on the brown plaid sofa, absorbed in catalog shopping. "What's with him? You never hear nothing about him these days."

"Not since the funeral."

"Oh," Max says. "Yeah."

"He had the brain thing," she says. She won't say the A word, like she won't say the C word. Say the word, and next thing you know, either you or somebody you know gets it. *Kine-ahora,* so far, so good, unless you count Mrs. Adelman down the hall who Tootsie heard has got the C word, but nobody Tootsie could call a friend has had that for maybe a year. "And don't yell at me. I'm in the room, you don't have to yell when I'm in the room." She flips the page of the Lillian Vernon catalog. "I'm not deaf, you know."

Max's attention returns to the screen, where a replay of Reagan taking the oath of office is flickering. "But he did important things before he got the brain thing," he says. "He was President, for instance."

Tootsie nods in agreement. "*And* he was a movie star. Don't forget that." She had a crush on him when he was a young ruddy-faced actor. Those blue eyes. Or were they brown?

"Two careers. The guy had two careers. How many people can say that?" Max wants to know. "And famous for both of them." He leans back and gingerly pats his bandage. "I think I'm gonna have a hole in my nose where that quack popped this thing."

"I told you it was a pimple," Tootsie says with a satisfied sigh. "It would have gone away by itself." She turns another page and wonders who buys all those clocks in the shape of cats. "If you'd left it alone, you wouldn't have needed to pay that crazy woman to drive you to the doctor."

"It was more than a pimple. It was a *serious* pimple. Infected. You can die from an infection on your nose, the doc said so himself."

"You can die in a car driven by a crazy person too."

"At least she drives better than you."

Tootsie turns the page with an annoyed snap. "If you're trying to get me to drive you again, it won't work."

Max doesn't answer. He's staring at the TV. "He made a difference," he says.

"Who?"

"Reagan." Max is engrossed in the next segment, Reagan smiling and waving to a crowd. "There was no bad news when he was president."

"There's always bad news," she says, dog-earing a catalog page displaying a sunflower-shaped potholder mitt. The potholder chicken she's got has been looking pretty shabby since the kasha-burning incident. "Doesn't matter who's president."

"Not like now. Now there's nothing *but* bad news. Nobody makes a difference now. The world is going to hell."

"What do you think of this?" she asks, holding up a catalog page featuring a flowered over-the-door shoe bag. "Would you bother putting your shoes in it if I go to the trouble of ordering it?"

Max stares glumly at the TV screen. "I've never made a difference," he says. "Eighty-nine years old and I haven't done one damn thing that's ever made a difference."

Chapter V

ZOE

Zoe can see the pale dome of the top of Max's head in the rear view mirror. She stretches higher until his magnified eyes come into view, expressionless behind his glasses. "How you doing back there, Mr. Wolfe?" she asks. "You got your seat belt on?"

"I don't need any seat belt," he says. He sinks down lower so she can't see his eyes.

"It's the law," she says. "You got to wear a seat belt."

"Whose law?"

"My law. Zoe's law." She looks in the rear view mirror, but now she's lost him altogether. She turns around. He's moved to the far right corner of the seat and is glaring out the window with a sour-lemon look on his face. A small round flesh-colored bandage sits on the tip of his ruddy nose like a beret on a beet. "Put the seat belt on, Mr. Wolfe. We don't want to mash that pretty nose now that it's almost better, do we?"

"Who's We?" he says.

"Me. Zoe. *I* don't want your nose mashed, okay?"

"What kinda name is Zowie? Who names their kid Zowie? I never hearda such a thing."

"It's ZO-ee," she says. "I don't know. It's what my name is. I don't think about it." She stops to think about it. "There's a famous book with somebody in it named Zoe. So I'm not the only one."

Max falls silent at that. This is how he rode to and from the doctor's the other day—silent as a stone, despite her attempts at conversation. But if his showing signs of life means an argument each trip, Zoe hopes for his return to muteness. It's going to be a long day if he keeps this up. They're done with the check-up at the doctor's, but now she's got to brave the mall with him. Haircut. "And socks," Tootsie had called after her as they waited at the elevator. "Macy's. Black. No stripes."

Zoe turns up the radio, taps her fingers on the steering wheel to the music. Abba. She loves Abba. "Gimme gimme gimme...." she sings along, "a man after midnight...."

Max lunges over the seat and punches buttons on the radio with a finger the shape of a lamb shank. "Hey!" Zoe yells. "Sit down!" The cab swerves as she tries to push him back. His shoulder feels bony as a chicken wing.

"Put it on NPR," Max demands. "I don't want to listen to that crap."

"Sit *down*," Zoe says, jerking the wheel and flinging Max back into his corner. She steers the car laterally across traffic and comes to a screeching halt in the emergency lane. Zippity Cab shudders with post-convalescent hangover—a warning that, despite Boyd's expert ministrations, its innards are still fragile from the encounter with Tootsie's groceries. Pressing her lips together, Zoe gathers what's left of her patience before she turns around. "Now. Listen up. I will not drive another inch until you put on your seat belt," she says, but her patience ends there. "And you will never," she yells, "*never* jump over the seat like that again. Understood?"

Max doesn't answer. He looks out the window, suddenly interested in the baffle wall that stretches along the side of the expressway. "When did they put that up?" he asks.

"I'm not kidding. Put your seat belt on. I'm not moving until you do."

Max studies the wall a moment longer, then, as if it were his own idea, pulls the belt around his thin waist and fumbles until it snaps. "What are you waiting for?" he asks. "We don't got all day."

"No jumping over the seat," Zoe repeats. "All you have to do is ask me to change the station. And," she adds, "it wouldn't kill you to say 'please.'"

"Hmf," Max says.

She pulls out of the lane into the path of an oncoming car which expresses its surprise with a prolonged goose honk. "What's *his* problem?" she muses as she punches the radio back to the music station. Abba's song is over, but Stevie Nicks is wailing one of Zoe's favorites, which inspires Zoe to accompany her: "wo wo wo, gypsy woman...."

"Couldja put it on NPR now," Max interrupts. He waits a beat. "Please?"

Zoe holds the barber shop door open for Max. He turns and shoots a farewell glare at the hairdresser, who ignores him. Max shuffles glumly as they trek through the mall parking lot. "He cut it too short," Max complains, open-ing the cab door and climbing in. He combs his fingers through what's left of the white fringe around his ears. "Every time, I tell him, 'leave it a little longer in the back' but it's like I'm not there, I'm just some head without a brain in it."

"It looks fine," Zoe reassures him. "You look like Bruce Willis. Look. I brought you a surprise." She holds out a tiny sample box of chocolates. "They were giving them out in the mall. I got two. One when I went in to Macy's to get your socks, and the other when I came out. One for you and one for me." She opens a box and extracts a brown blob with a curl on top. "Ew. Squishy. I guess they kinda melted while I was waiting for you." She pops it into her mouth. "Here," she says around the ooze, "take your box."

"Keep it." After a moment, he asks, "Who's Bruce Willis?"

"A movie star." She sees his dour face pick up a little at that, so adds, "A very handsome movie star. He's in a lot of action films."

"So he's a man of action."

"You might say that." Zoe licks her fingers and turns the key to start the en-gine. The cab bolts from its spot, startling a woman loaded down with packages into dropping a few.

"A man of action," Max repeats with sudden fervor, and she feels her seat being pulled backward as he grips it with both hands.

"Sit back and put your seat belt on," she orders, "or I'm pulling over right now."

She hears a satisfying click, accompanied by indecipherable muttering. "Thank you," she says, and to show her appreciation, punches up NPR on the radio. Max listens intently for several minutes as a debate concerning the Mid-dle East escalates until the two opposing politicians are arguing above the voice of the host.

"Like they're going to solve it," Zoe comments idly to Max at the break. "Like it's something they can fix."

"Politicians. Some career, politics," Max says. "Their real career is getting re-elected, so look at what we got. A buncha idiots. Not like it used to be when the idiots were smarter."

"They aren't *all* idiots," Zoe corrects him. "Just most."

"There's no Truman any more," Max laments. "No Roosevelt. No Churchill. There's nobody around worth two cents any more who can fix things like they could."

"How about Kennedy?"

"He's not around any more. And what about the Bay of Pigs? Not such a smart move."

"But he was a good man." What was it Albert had called him? "The last hero. That's what he was."

"He was a man of action," Max says. The NPR moderator is attempting to sum up the previous discussion over interruptions from both sides, but Max's attention has drifted. "*I* am a man of action," he declares.

"How's that?" Zoe wonders if now would be a good time to change the station, maybe he won't notice.

"I built hotels. I made Miami Beach into Miami Beach." He pauses for effect. "You built hotels? Which hotels?" She slides her finger to the Y-100 station on the radio and gives it a push. Max is oblivious as the voice of Bruno Mars replaces NPR.

"Mostly little ones. But one big one, over sixty years ago. The Louis Quinze."

"You built the Louis Quinze?" Zoe is impressed. "Holy moley. The Louis Quinze. That's a famous hotel."

"I know," he says, a touch modestly. "I sold it a long time ago."

"How come they're tearing it down?" she asks.

"What?"

"Tearing it down. To build a big condo."

"What?"

"It was on TV this morning. Some developer bought it. He was going to renovate it but he said it's old and has too many problems, and it's cheaper to tear it down. He wants to build three sixty-story condos there."

"*What?*"

Zoe turns, alarmed at the strangled timbre of Max's voice. His face now matches the color of his nose. "You didn't know?" she asks. He shakes his head. "You okay?" He shakes his head again. He doesn't look well at all. She'd better get him home ASAP.

"Hang on," she says, and Zippity takes the challenge, sliding in and out of the sludgy traffic as if it were pudding. The change of pace revives Max.

"LOOK OUT!" he yells, stiff-arming the seat in front and pumping both feet on a phantom brake on the floor. "*Slow down!* Are you crazy?"

"Crazies!" Zoe agrees. "They're all maniacs!" They exit the causeway neck and neck with a car full of kids, only to stop next to them at a traffic light. She sticks her head out of the window to glare up at the driver of the offending car, a Dodge Ram truck that vibrates with rap music punctuated by words resembling English.

"You oughtta be arrested," she yells.

The kid grins happily back at her, his backward-facing-baseball-capped head nodding in rhythm.

"You call that music?" Zoe yells. "Listen to the Beatles!"

The light changes and the truck takes off, leaving Zippity in the dust, still panting from its recent exertion. Zoe reflexively guns it, but then heeds Max's panicked warning, *speed limit, there's a speed limit*, accompanied by his fist pounding on the back of her seat. She drives back to the condo with determined moderation.

"I'm taking you up, Mr. Wolfe," Zoe insists when they pull into the driveway.

"I know how to take an elevator," he grouses, but allows her to take his elbow and steer him into the lobby. He seems more fragile now. The bad news about his hotel has compressed his features into a knot in the middle of his face. They ride up in silence until they reach the apartment door. Before Zoe can knock, he turns to her with a more hopeful look. "Maybe it's some other hotel," he says. "You can't believe everything you hear on TV."

"Maybe." She bangs the wolf's-head knocker several times. "You never know." She's sure Tootsie is on tiptoe on the other side, spying on them through the peephole. She bangs the knocker again until Tootsie opens the door.

Tootsie's gaze bypasses Zoe completely and lands on Max's head. She purses her lips critically and studies the silver tundra that patchworks the base of his skull. "Why'd you let him cut it so short?" she asks.

"I think Mr. Wolfe isn't feeling so hot," Zoe tells her. "He got some bad news." She pauses. "It may not be *true* bad news, but still..."

"What? What bad news?" Tootsie gives her what could be interpreted as the evil eye: one eye squinched, the other steel grey and accusatory.

"The Louis Quinze," Max says. "Did you know?"

"Know what?"

"They're tearing it down. To build a..." he gathers his strength to utter the next word, "*condo.*"

"Really?" Tootsie's sparse eyebrows shoot up. She mulls the news over for a moment, then shrugs. "I never much liked it anyway. It was too fancy-schmancy for my taste."

"It was *swanky*," Max protests. "That's what they called it, swanky. Miami Beach was schlocksville before I made it the most famous resort ever, and if you wanna call it fancy-schmancy, okay for you, but for me, it was the pinochle of my career. It *means* something to me. I put my *heart*," he thumps his chest, "and my *smarts*," he thumps his head, "into the Louis Quinze, the most swanky hotel ever on Miami Beach and that's what everybody said, not just me."

"Okay," concedes Tootsie. "But what's the big deal now? We haven't even been inside since you sold it."

Max turns to Zoe, thrusting a trembling hand in Tootsie's direction. "See what I have to live with? She doesn't care. She never cared about the business, nothing, never mind it paid the rent..."

"Rent, schment. We never paid rent. We always owned," Tootsie corrects him.

"You know what I mean. Bills. Cars. Trips to visit your crazy sister in New Jersey. And you wanna talk about fancy-schmancy, how about college––*Yale* yet, Harold hadda go to Yale? To do what? I still don't know what he does. Politics?" he asks, his voice cracking. "That's a job?"

"Um," Zoe interjects. "If you don't need me any more today, I guess I'll get going."

"What do you know from a job?" Tootsie challenges Max with a pugnacious thrust of her chin. "You haven't worked for twenty years."

"I'm retired. So now she says I'm not entitled to retire?" Max's offense is writ large on his cheeks in blotchy patches of pink. "I worked hard. I built half of Miami Beach. I built..." his face crumples, "...a *monument* when I built the Louis Quinze."

"The Taj Mahal, it ain't," Tootsie says.

"Well. Bye," Zoe says, making her way to the door. "See you Thursday, right? Periodontist." She shuts the door behind her, but can hear, as she hurries down the hall, Max's hoarse announcement: "I am a man of action!"

It's been six years since she buried her husband Albert, but Zoe still wonders about him. Like why did he have to go and die on her? They were happy. Maybe they didn't have the perfect marriage, but compared to couples like the Wolfes, she and Albert were a regular Ozzie and Harriet. They had fun together, laughed a lot, and the sex was good––too good, apparently, since after a particularly strenuous but rewarding bout, he keeled over and died.

"Well," her friend Keisha had sympathized after the funeral, "he was kinda older than you are, so, you know, that can happen." Although their paths had crossed occasionally at Home Depot––Keisha had worked in Appliances, Zoe in Auto Parts––their friendship began with Albert's death, when Keisha heard sobbing coming from one of the stalls in the ladies' room. It was Zoe, overwhelmed with grief. Keisha had consoled her, then taken her home to dinner with her family––strangers who soon became the family Zoe had always wanted.

And Keisha became the friend Zoe had always needed. But as welcoming and consoling as Keisha is, Zoe feels she can't understand loneliness. Keisha's life is an enviable one, as far as Zoe is concerned. Whenever a fare takes Zoe somewhere near Keisha's house, if Keisha is off work Zoe will drop by to be submerged, if only for a time, in the delicious stew that is Keisha's home, full of kids from toddlers to teenagers, noisy, busy, curious and funny. They blend together, shifting and changing in bright designs like a kid kaleidoscope. The house is littered with juice boxes, Pop Tart remnants, homework papers, board games, and sneakers of all sizes; a TV tuned to BET is a raucous soundtrack punctuated with shrieks of laughter and wails from one kid being pummeled by another. The air is always infused with the scent from whatever is baking in the oven––usually chocolate chip cookies or Keisha's sinful Triple Berry pie. Sticky little hands hold Zoe's in theirs; chubby brown arms encircle her neck. Keisha's kids are Zoe's for the moment, the children she'll never have.

Later, when Zoe goes home to her cozy little house in North Beach, it seems as empty and cold as a cave. In this transitional neighborhood, houses like hers are succumbing to the high-rise wonders of Canyon Ranch and the latest Trump triumph. Their shadows creep down the strip of shabby shops on this part of Collins––Argentinian bakeries, dust-caked pharmacies, second-hand stores going out of business––their future forecast by the ringing gong of ever-new construction.

Zoe intends to stay put. Most times, she likes her house and the memories it holds. She and Albert bought it when they were first married, a little blue-stuccoed three-bedroom with a tile roof and wrought iron railings in need of replacement after all these years. She occasionally touches up the pink flamingo on the screen door, and that, with the blue dolphin welcome mat, enhances her tropical decor. She's amazed that her blond deco bedroom furniture, the rattan sofa with the palm-patterned cushions, and her old Fiestaware are trendy now, expensive even, in antique stores she wanders into now and then. The house is paid for, thanks to Albert, although escalating property taxes and insurance rates have taken such scary bites out of Zoe's income that she has nightmares where she sees herself living under the I-95 overpass.

So when she comes home from Keisha's to her empty house, she consoles herself with a big bowl of Edy's Mint Chocolate Chip with a side of Mallomars, and watches Dancing with the Stars or maybe an old movie, especially one with Judy Holliday. But still. She's alone. And neither ice cream nor Mallomars will fill that vacant space, the space she had reserved at one time for a husband who loved her (she did have that, she reminds herself) and lots of kids, like Keisha has.

That would make her happy. A full house. A home. A family.

One way of coping after Albert died was to have a boyfriend. At first that was no problem. Men were drawn to Zoe, more for her exuberance than her looks, which, Keisha had advised, could be improved with a good makeover—a decent haircut, pluck the brows a little, a free makeup session at the Clinique counter at Macy's, and for God's sake, girl, ditch the shorts and t-shirts, you're not sixteen any more. Well, Zoe sure didn't want to be sixteen again, but she did want to be comfortable, and when you're driving a cab where the AC is ancient and unreliable and you keep the windows open unless a passenger complains, then shorts and t-shirts are the uniform of the day. Her cap camouflaged her hair on bad hair days, which were almost every day, given the heat and humidity of Miami and her reluctance to make a trip to Supercuts until her hair had taken on a life of its own.

So despite her less than *Vogue*-ish appearance, she had had her share of boyfriends. She never loved any of them the way she had loved Albert, but as long as they were decent and kind and bathed fairly regularly, she welcomed them into her life. The last time she heard the words "I love you" was from Albert, just before he plopped over and died. She never expected to hear those words again, but deep down, she still had hope. She liked having someone just to hang out with, and she did love to make love, so as soon as one boyfriend dropped out of sight, he would quickly be replaced by another.

Until recently. Recently, she noticed, she had become invisible. Sure, construction workers still whistled and yelled their version of compliments as she passed by, but she took into consideration that they were several stories up in a building, which could possibly hamper their judgment. She figured that distance alone, not to mention a certain lack of discernment when it came to females, probably colored their perception of her age, and while it momentarily buoyed her spirits to be catcalled by younger men, she rarely would wave back.

No, it was the up-close and personal encounters that had changed. Where, before, she hardly ever dined alone when she ate out, now her Big Macs and fries are eaten in solitude as she watches, through the grimy plate glass window haze, the rough-and-tumble of kids in the play yard outside and wonders why she and Albert had put off having kids. And where before, some guy would invariably ask, even if there were empty booths all over the place, if she minded if he shared the booth with her and then they'd share the ketchup packets and he'd buy an apple pie for her and they'd eventually wind up, a couple or three McDates later, in bed––well, nowadays it never happened. These days, a guy will look at her, she'll smile what is becoming an ever-more crinkly smile, and he'll move right along to one of the empty booths. These days, she's invisible. She's getting used to it.

But that doesn't mean she likes it. When she was in her forties she didn't think much about her age, but now that she's borderline 50 and having all these weird things going on with her body, she wonders if this means she'll never have sex again. Never wake up next to someone she cares about again. Never sit in front of the TV with another pair of usually bigger feet next to hers on the coffee table, never have more than one toothbrush in the bathroom, never find nose hairs in the sink again. She wonders if this means she'll always be alone.

And then she gets really pissed off at couples like the Wolfes. What's the matter with those people? Here they've managed to make it together all these years, and then they go and waste what little time that's left, just picking at each other. There must have been something each liked about the other or they wouldn't have gotten married in the first place. Is that Something gone now, or is it still there and they just don't want to see it?

She wonders if she'd still have felt all the good stuff she felt for Albert if they had both lived that long. Sure, maybe his little pot belly would have turned into a serious gut; maybe his habit of clipping his toenails in bed would have gotten to her; maybe even sex wouldn't have kept on being so good, or maybe it would have stopped altogether. That happens, you know. But she thinks the love wouldn't have stopped. That they would have just kept on loving and caring about each other until they got very very old and then both died in their sleep on the same day, which––one night as they lay entwined in bed, wondering about the future––is what they agreed would be the way to go.

But that's not how he went, at least the being-old part, although he did die in bed. Zoe felt a little guilty about the circumstances, having played a role in his demise, but as Keisha had reminded her, he died happy, and that's not something everybody can say.

Still, she misses sex. Maybe she'll never again have what she had with Albert, but sex, she wants to believe, isn't really over for her forever. So one day, it happens. Not out of gratitude or uncontrollable passion or even loneliness, although that plays a role because she *is* lonely, that middle-of-the-night-single-person-in-a-double-bed loneliness that doesn't strike in the middle of the day unless the day is Sunday and raining and nothing's on TV worth watching.

But it happens on a Saturday morning at Boyd's. Zoe has brought Zippity in for a check-up, for, despite Boyd's recent repair work, Zippity still isn't up to speed.

"The old girl's doing fine, considering," Boyd says after fiddling around under Zippity's hood. "She should be good for a while. Just keep her away from old ladies with heavy objects."

Boyd's radio, tuned to reruns of NPR's "Car Talk," teeters on a shelf above what passes for a couch in his back office: a sunken mattress covered in a worn plaid blanket, frosted with cat hairs from his ancient tabby, Edsel. A "Car Talk" caller is imitating a noise her car is making: *tucka THUCK tucka THUCK-tucka THUCK*.

"Engine knock," pronounces Click—or is it Clack?—who then tells a knock-knock joke which dissolves into static.

"Damn radio." Boyd reaches up and gives it a thwack. It settles back into a crackling reception. The brothers Click and Clack laugh raucously over another caller's story involving valves. Zoe lowers herself onto the couch and listens attentively until the end of the program.

"I love them," Zoe says. Boyd clicks the radio off. "It's my favorite show."

"Me, too." He reaches up and pats the radio. "I've got all their CDs."

"Omigod. Me, too!" The air is pungent with the odors of paint and gasoline. She takes a deep breath and feels a little giddy. She knows she spends more time at the gas pump than she should whenever she fills up, but she has so few vices that she allows herself a Citgo high now and then.

"Wanna see the "Car Talk" website?" Boyd lumbers to the computer and clicks the mouse with a fuzz-knuckled hand streaked with bright green paint. Zoe never noticed his hands before: strong hands, working hands, hands that grip large tools. His back is to her, and she fights an urge to pet the furry path that leads down his neck to his shoulders, disappearing beneath the tank top emblazoned with an open-mouthed shark.

"Hey, this is the best feature of the website." He moves the mouse and clicks again. "You know how they figured out that girl's problem on the radio, just from the sound her car made? They do that, here, too––imitate the noise an engine makes when there's trouble, then tell you what the problem is. Listen to this. You'll love it."

Bad differential, Click's voice announces: *vooooOOOOOOOOOOooooo.* Boyd clicks on the next sound.

Dieseling: blubBLUBblubBLUB. Zoe notices that Boyd's shirt has ridden up to expose the crevice peeking from the top of his low-cut jeans. It's not the first time his body has been exposed in such a way, but it is the first time she's had the urge to run her hands over those particular parts. She tucks her hands beneath her armpits and scans the garage to distract herself. A raggedy 1950s girlie calendar flipped to August is tacked on the wall next to the computer. Its big-breasted nude licking an ice cream cone seems to wink at Zoe over one shoulder.

Bad Axle: gulla, gulla, glugluglugluglug. Zoe runs her tongue slowly over her lips, contemplates Boyd's bare shoulders, round and tan as Parker House rolls as he hunches over the keyboard.

Sticky Lifters: dicka, dicka, dicka, dicka. "Funny, huh?" Boyd laughs and turns to Zoe. She isn't looking at the computer. She's looking at Boyd with sleepy eyes and a moist mouth. "Hey," says Boyd, turning away from the computer when she runs her hand lightly over his shoulder.

"Hey yourself," she says.

Vacuum Leak: vwishhhhhhhhhhhhhhhh. Boyd slides his hand beneath her Hello Kitty T-shirt. She can't help herself. It's been way way way too long since she's been touched. So she lets him. And when he nibbles her neck softly with his chipmunk teeth, she lets him lead her to the blanketed couch in his back office.

Water Pump: grrgula, grrgul, grrgula,vum wum wum wum wum. She had forgotten how well lubricated parts could work together, how quickly things can accelerate, how... oh, yes! Piston! Caliper! Talk dirty to me! Spark plug! Exhaust valve! Yes! Vacuum diaphragm! More! Connecting rod! Crank shaft! Yes! Injector! Oil pan gasket! Combustion! Combustion! Combustion!

Loose Belt: YEEeeEEeeEEeeEEeeEEee!

And when at last they rest atop the tangled plaid blanket—naked, sated, and prickly with cat hairs—it's clear that neither *Misfire: puhVROOpuh-HOOpuhVROO* nor *Weak Battery: wurrrrRRRRrrrrwuRRRrrr* applies.

* * *

Max sinks into the back of the cab and clicks on his seat belt without being asked. "Tootsie wanted to come with me," he says in greeting to Zoe. "Fat chance. I'm not going anywhere with a person who thinks killing the Louis Quinze is no big deal." He looks grim.

"Maybe she thought you'd need her after the periodontist." Zoe attempts once again to crank up Zippity, who is still balking of late. The cab finally coughs and rumbles into action, rattling a bit but picking up the pace as they meld into morning traffic. "Last time, you had a little problem, remember?"

"What? So my gums bled a little."

"A little? This time I brought a towel." She immediately regrets that confession as she sees Max's eyes widen in the rear view mirror. "You'll be fine, Mr. Wolfe," she reassures him. "She's just feeling protective."

"Nah. She's jealous."

"What? You've got to be kidding."

"She thinks I'm a ladies' man."

"Are you?"

"Not so much any more."

Zoe decides to leave it at that since her attention is distracted by the escalation of a funny sound Zippity started making this morning, a kind of scraping noise coming from the engine, only now the scraping increases alarmingly to a screeeek. Zippity shudders like an old shivery dog and then with one last wheeze, gives it up in the center lane.

"What?" Max asks.

Traffic veers around them. Frozen in the middle of Biscayne Boulevard, Zippity sits like a big pink target. Zoe ratchets the ignition key back and forth while she flamencos the gas pedal, but nothing happens. Zippity is stone cold dead. Zoe leans forward in despair, thumps her forehead on the steering wheel. "Shit," she says under her breath.

"What?"

"Twelve hundred fifty bucks down the tube," she says, and gives her head another thump.

"Are we at the periodontist's?"

Zoe sighs and pulls out her cell phone. "Listen, Mr. Wolfe. I'm calling AAA for a tow, but first I'm going to call your wife and tell her she's got to come and get you. My cab has broken down."

"It's broken? How did it break?"

"It's old." She checks her address book for the Wolfe's number. "I hope she's home," she mutters as she dials.

"Who?"

"Mrs. Wolfe."

"Why?"

"She's got to take you to the periodontist."

Now it registers. "*No.* I'm not driving with that woman again." He reaches over and tries to grab the phone. "Gimme that."

"Hey, cut it out!"

He slumps back into the seat. "Call Hal, then. Call a cab. Call anybody. But I'm not going anywhere with Her."

Zoe contemplates the alternatives. True, Tootsie Wolfe wasn't anyone she'd care to share a vehicle with, driving or not. And Hal? He made it pretty clear that he wasn't in the transport business, at least not when it came to his parents. And Zoe refuses to humiliate herself by calling a rival cab. Or Uber. Or Lyft. She does have her pride. She has no choice. She punches the Wolfe's number into the phone.

Tootsie's belated arrival, just before the AAA tow truck pulls up, is far from a happy reunion. Speaking neither to Zoe nor to Max, Tootsie glowers behind the steering wheel, staring straight ahead as Zoe folds Max into the seat. Then, with traffic soaring around them to the tune of multiple horns, Tootsie edges out into the boulevard.

Zoe watches the Lincoln rumble down the road, two little heads barely visible over the top of the front seat. If she hadn't been so crazed over her own dilemma, she might have worried about their safety, but right now, the Wolfes' transportation problem takes a back seat to her own vehicular sorrow.

When the tow truck arrives, she can't even look as Zippity is winched up onto its hind tires. She climbs into the truck's cab, mutters Boyd's address to the driver, and slumps wordlessly beside him for the mournful drive back. She hears the creak and whine of the winch, the thumpety-thump of rear tires on pavement as Zippity is dragged behind the tow truck for what could be its funeral procession unless Boyd can perform one last resuscitative miracle. If not, Dead car = Dead career. *Then* what will she do?

* * *

Zoe doesn't know what took her on this serendipitous path but now she believes in love at first sight. Why is this day different from all other days? Why did she, on this particular morning, oversleep till noon, thereby skipping her Captain Crunch-and-Diet Coke breakfast and instead, run into McDonald's for a takeout Big Mac, an indulgence she ordinarily would reserve for dinner? Was it the restless, guilt-ridden night she spent after having left the moribund Zippity in Boyd's greasy hands yesterday, knowing that Boyd's may be its final resting place? Was it Boyd's solicitous manner that implied that they now had a relationship she wasn't sure she wanted? Was it the emptiness she felt when she saw the happy family in the McDonald's commercial on TV this morning that lured her towards the comfort of the golden arches? And why this McDonald's on this particular day, a day she was forced to walk, not drive, right past the BMW dealership she had whizzed by in the past without so much as a glance into its gleaming showroom window, the window she now presses her nose against to better see what is posing as provocatively as a Victoria's Secret model: a sleek, sparkling, sassy little 230i convertible.

Her craving for the Big Mac in the bag she's carrying morphs into a consuming desire for this car. She must see it, touch it, feel it. She must have it.

She ignores the raised eyebrow of the salesman who ambles over and asks if he can help her, ignores his pursed lips as he takes in her frazzled hair, her Rolling Stones t-shirt, her shorts with the torn back pocket, her grease-spotted McDonald's bag. "Can I take a look at that one?" She points to the car that seems to wink at her in the tinted-glass-filtered sunlight of the showroom window.

The salesman hesitates, then shrugs, a shrug that says *It's a slow morning. Why not?* When he opens the door, she feels as if she were entering Cinderella's coach, and when she glides into the driver's seat, she knows her love is real. She slides her hands across the buttery leather seat, fondles the pert little buttons on its flashy dashboard, inhales its new-car perfume. She's never felt this way before.

A hot flash of guilt envelops her, then subsides. It's not that she doesn't love Zippity Cab, she reasons. She's just not *in* love any more. Look. She's been faithful all these years. Well, almost. She did have a fling with a Harley but that was when she was lonely, impressionable and dating a biker after Albert died. She only rode on the back; it wasn't a serious thing.

But let's face it. Zippity is old, even though Zoe has done all she could to keep it in good shape: weekly trips to the carwash; fill-ups with premium gas; a new paint job so it looks almost, if not quite, brand new. Out on the town, Zippity still turned heads. Zoe was proud to be known as its owner.

Still, a '59 Caddy is a sixty-year-old Caddy that has seen far better days. Zoe had been willing to overlook the creaks and sags, the slowing down and the stalling out, until the fateful day of its mauling and its subsequent deterioration. She tells herself it was an act of God when Tootsie Wolfe bashed Zippity's hood with her groceries. Until then, Zoe never thought she'd betray Zippity for another, but now she knows the relationship is over. She is looking at her new cab.

"How does the top go up?" she asks, mindful of her future passengers' comfort. The salesman shows her: a button, and presto. Top up, windows shut. "How much?" she asks, and when the salesman points to the sticker price on the window, she sucks in her breath with dismay. The salesman's thin lips pucker into an anal smile and he nods sympathetically as she woefully gets out of the car. He spots a blue-suited businessman who is inspecting a sedan, and spins to attend to him. "Wait!" Zoe calls after him, and grabs his arm. Alarmed, he jerks away, but Zoe persists. "Will you take a trade-in?"

"Certainly," he says, brushing at his sleeve where she touched it. "We're always happy to consider that." He straightens his tie and heads for the more promising customer.

Zoe quietly opens the BMW's door and slides back inside. She might as well have entered a time machine: the years fall away and she's twenty again, a girl on the threshold of life, dewy fresh, wrinkle-free, as daring as Wonder Woman, her girlhood heroine. In this car, she can be that girl again. It's not too late to dream big dreams, to renew herself in a spiffy new cab that revives her hopes for the future. She adjusts the mirror, grips the steering wheel, fantasizes herself zipping through traffic in this nifty little car. She's got to have it, got to figure out how to work the financing. *Zippity Two*, she'll call it, she thinks as she dreamily unwraps her Big Mac. Her first bite is a drippy one that squirts ketchup and mustard down the front of her t-shirt. *Damn.* She hastily dabs it with a napkin and stuffs the resulting greasy wad into the ashtray, safely away from the upholstery. She takes another bite.

BAMBAMBAM. Zoe yelps in terror. The salesman is banging on the car window with a fist.

"What are you doing? Are you *eating*?" The salesman's nose, white with fury, is pressed like a mushroom to the glass. He yanks the door handle and she tumbles out. He pokes his head into the car and sniffs, his nostrils rattling wetly. "*Onions,*" he announces. "The new car smell is gone."

Zoe responds with a hacking cough from the bite she just inhaled.

"The ashtray!" he cries, poking gingerly at the greasy napkin within. "What have you done?" He removes the ashtray, bangs it against his shoe until the dislodged napkin pops out onto the floor. He spits on a well-used handkerchief from his coat pocket, wipes out the defiled ashtray, then buries his nose inside. He inhales deeply and moans. "This car will never smell the same. You've taken its innocence."

"I'm going to buy it," Zoe protests as the salesman leads her out of the showroom by her elbow. "I'll be back."

"I don't want to see you around here unless you've come to lay down some cash."

"I'll get it," Zoe says. "Swear to me you won't sell that car."

Smirking, the salesman deposits her outside the showroom door. "Don't even *show* it to anyone," Zoe warns as he retreats inside. "When I come back with the money, I better not see footprints on the paper carpet cover."

Back on the sidewalk, all appetite gone, Zoe presses her nose once again to the showroom window. The salesman has lowered the top once more and is fanning the air in what Zoe assumes is an attempt to dispel the Big Mac aroma. The headlights of the BMW—*her* BMW—gaze back at her with heavy-lidded bedroom eyes. Cold reality smacks her in the forehead like ice cream eaten too fast. He's going to sell the BMW. This little jewel, so fresh and sassy with her top down, will be gone in a flash. The first guy who waves a wad of cash at her grille will be the one who steals her away. If Zoe can't raise the money fast, she'll lose her ticket to happiness.

CHAPTER VI

HAL

This time Milo is waiting for him. Hal spots him in a shadowy booth, already scarfing down a *media noche* between sharp little gerbil teeth that nibble away at the sandwich in double time. Milo chose the location: La Casa de Puerco. Tiny, obscure, tucked into the corner of a bland shopping plaza way out in Sweetwater, the café is away from anyone who might recognize either of them—–or for that matter, understand English, a plus when conversation just might lean a teeny bit towards the unethical, as others might see it.

Not that either Milo or Hal is doing anything *illegal*. No no. Hal is there reluctantly, but he did agree to listen, and besides, he's curious as to what exactly Milo has to offer. Just curious. And Milo is there to lobby, to suggest, to convince Hal that three sixty-story condos would be a plus for the city, and incidentally, for Hal as well.

Hal's eyes dart around the restaurant. "What happened to the *Herald* story?" he mutters. "I thought they were doing a story on...you know."

"They did. Didn't you see it? Big story, old news, about that jerk on the Miami city commission who disappeared with the payoff and the hooker he was keeping and who then surfaced in Thailand or Taiwan or some T country over there. They can't get him, in any case, and now the company's in deep shit."

"*That* was the story?"

"Looks that way. That reporter, whatsisface, Gomez, never called me again."

Hal takes a noisy slurp of his *cafecito*, dumps in another spoonful of sugar. The jolt of concentrated sugar-laced caffeine magnifies his relief at hearing this, and he feels oh so much better. Of the many shards that compose the mosaic of his dismal life, at least that particular chip has fallen away. The possibility of an investigative reporter ferreting about his business had been a contributing factor to his gathering gloom; this news is a welcome ray of sunshine.

"So," Milo assures him, "looks like I freaked out over a false alarm. There's no story here."

"And I don't want to be the next story. I'm just here to listen. Don't get your hopes up."

"All I'm asking is just a little wheel-greasing."

Hal examines the muddy dregs left in his cup before signaling the counter guy for another. "First of all, I'm still freaked out that it's my father's hotel you're tearing down."

"I get that."

"Second of all, I'm done with doing favors. It's too stressful."

Milo nods. "I understand. The stress. The Dad thing. I get all that. But I thought you might be interested, given the high reward and low risk involved."

High reward? Low risk? "What are we talking about here?"

Milo tells him, and the figures are impressive. The reward could be *very* high, high enough to be an incentive to finally quit this rat race and have a real life.

Could this be the key to the main event, the offer he had waited for all these many years, the opportunity to take the big chance and get the big payoff? Could this mean he could quit politics and all its sleaze, have enough stashed away to never think about money again, then do whatever he wanted to do with whatever time he has left? He has to face the painful truth: he had become part of the political machine at the expense of his integrity. He wants to believe that's not who he really is, even though that is who he really was and might have to be this one last time. Could he say "No" to this big "Yes" moment, if it meant he'd never have to say Yes again?

But then he'd be taking a chance. A big chance, even though Milo insists the risk is low, how could he know that? People get found out, they get stories written about them, is anything worth that?

And then there's the all-consuming question of Max. Even though the Louis Quinze is no longer in Max's thoughts (Hal wants to think), he would feel betrayed if he found out that Hal had a hand in its demise. But then, maybe not. Hal doesn't know. He doesn't know what Max is thinking, or, better put, he doesn't want to know. Whenever Max expresses what's on his mind these days, it's rarely favorable.

He remembers a time when he was young and he and Max saw eye-to-eye, both literally and figuratively, right at the time of his bar-mitzvah. They were momentarily the same height as they faced each other on the *bimah*; the ray of pride that shone from Max's blue eyes into his own was a light Hal had rarely seen since. As Rabbi Fendelman yodeled his Hebraic blessing and the congregation murmured in response, the realization dawned in the thirteen-year-old brain of Harold Arnold Wolfe that all those years of tedious study were finally culminating, not only in the big party with the space-travel theme that awaited them in the Starlite Room of the Louis Quinze, but in the look of love he saw in his father's eyes. Their level gaze was probably their last as Hal shot up and within weeks surpassed Max's height. The taller he grew, the less they saw eye-to-eye, and the day came when he knew that the light he had seen at that moment on the *bimah* was as ephemeral as lightning. Now and then it appeared as a promising glow, but disappeared forever when Max realized that the future he had seen for Hal was not what Hal had planned. He no longer could dictate what Hal would do with his life, for Hal would not be his partner.

Now Hal is at another turning point as momentous as that at the *bimah,* only this time it's Milo bestowing the blessing of choice: would it be the big party that could be his future, or oblivion cushioned by integrity?

"I need some time," Hal says, wavering. "It's not just that it's a building. It's history. It's my father's history. That's what makes it...difficult."

Milo leans back and belches softly. "Well, think it over. But you've got to let me know pretty soon because there's someone else with pull who's interested." He signals the counter guy who is studiously composing an elaborate sandwich. "Hey, amigo," he calls. "Check-ay, okay?" He turns to Hal. "Listen, it's just a building. It's been owned by a hotel chain, for God's sake. What kind of history is that? Make your own fucking history."

Milo has a point. What kind of history *has* he made? City commissioner? Unsung attorney? Overeducated underachiever? Some history. This could be his last chance to make something of himself, to leave something of himself behind when he's gone: the footprints in the sand, the glistening trail of a snail, the breadcrumbs in the woods that say "I was here."

Actually, he'd prefer to leave something behind more permanent than that.

So maybe Milo's right. But Hal has an important caveat: "I wouldn't want my father to know."

"What's to know? *I'm* not telling." Milo waves both hands over his head to attract the counter guy's attention. "Hey!" he calls. "Check here!"

"Well, I guess it's no different from the other times," Hal says, more to himself than to Milo. "Circumstances are different maybe. But basically the same." Something else occurs to him. "That reporter—Gomez? You sure he's gone?"

"Gone." Milo pushes his chair away, slaps some money on the table. "This should cover it, amigo," he calls. "No tip," he says to Hal. "Lousy service."

"I'll leave something. I want to finish my coffee." He studies his coffee-cup dregs as if they were fortune-telling tea leaves. "I need to think about it."

Hal thinks about it as he angles the Harley out of the shopping center lot. Thinks about it as he wedges himself into a lane of cars waiting at the light. Stops thinking about it when the light changes and the bike stalls and a car blares its horn, triggering a domino effect of other cars' horns which escalates the curses he hears in the language he speaks only well enough to exchange basic pleasantries with his Latino constituents and to order from the deli at Publix. Neither Berlitz nor Rosetta Stone really worked for him but he does know enough to yell back at the honkers with a few choice words *en español*.

His increasingly frantic key cranks finally work: the bike comes to life, jerking away from the cacophony, swerving and jittering into the approaching vehicle stampede. Hal barely escapes, hands welded to the handlebars, eyes glued to the road ahead, mind racing between intermittent flashes of his imagined demise––steel crushing bone, asphalt ripping flesh, flowers by the roadside at the site of his accident—and Milo's offer.

Life is short, he tells himself. If he can't make history, he can at least make a pile of money and then get out. It's just a building, a building whose time is up, and his own time isn't up. Not yet.

* * *

He can see them from his balcony, tethered to brightly colored kites that arc against the sky like candy wrappers caught by the wind, lithe surfers balancing on boards that skip the waves at high speed, knees bobbling over frothing waves like skiers over bumps. Graceful as Baryshnikov, flexible as Gumby, focused as a kid thumbing a video game, the kiteboarders leap, spin, and cartwheel beneath the billowing U of their kites. Hal's body flexes in phantom harmony with theirs, pantomiming the careless freedom he once had when all that mattered was the next move.

Once upon a time he was lithe and muscular, too, before his broad shoulders sank, before his carved legs became stringy, before he lost his nerve. When did that happen? When did the years settle over him like a fog, obscuring all those things he thought he was and would be, leaving him high up here on his balcony watching kiteboarders skim the whitecapped waves as lightly as a cat laps cream?

He doesn't even know what he wants any more. Once he wanted power, women, acknowledgment. It's not that he still doesn't crave those things, but what once seemed possible has become less and less probable. What he took in himself for granted—looks, brains, charisma—he had squandered in his youth, reducing his life to the trivial pursuit of acclaim which he once seemed to find everywhere, even in the trends of the time such as Werner Erhard's est Training.

His pontificatory powers found their moment in est. When he rose to speak, he was a star, a standout in the audience of seekers of self-knowledge who were charmed by his wry but astute commentaries on life and its problems —other people's problems, not his own, since he was loathe to admit that he had any. Women loved him. It was the biggest pond he'd ever trolled, and he caught a lot of flesh.

As the years went by and his appeal to women lessened, he turned to a later trend: Internet dating. He was a J-Date junkie, a Match.com maven, which lasted until one of his dates confessed she only contacted him out of curiousity. She had noticed he'd been on Match for years, same old face, same old profile. Same old, same old. Hearing that discouraged him from the online chase, leaving a vacuum until he met Staci.

What has he done? Where is he going? Is he just a has-been womanizer and fuck-up extraordinaire? What is he doing, mixing it up with Milo? Has it really come to this?

Apparently so.

The kiteboarders are depressing him with their youth and exuberance. He goes inside and starts flipping channels on the TV, stopping at the visage of Dr. Phil. Maybe Dr. Phil can give him some insight, a path to the future that will satisfy his needs. Hal is desperate for guidance. But Dr. Phil is dispensing, not wisdom, but accusations to the hapless guy he's grilling onscreen, a guy who cringes at each of Dr. Phil's questions: "Do you feel disgusted? Do you feel dirty? Do you feel cheap?"

You talkin' to me? Hal wonders.

The phone's ring shatters his melancholy. It's Tootsie on the caller ID. He does not need this, not now. He considers not picking up, but he does, compelled, as usual, by the fear that *this* time it could be a true emergency. And, as usual, it's not. He holds the phone away from his ear, reducing his mother's voice from a bark to a squeak. "What a day," she says, "first the crazy woman calls to tell me her cab broke down, come and get him, so I have to run out and pick him up in the middle of godknowswhere and then I have to schlep him to the periodontist and after that he's so busy yelling at me about how to drive home he goes and spits blood all over the inside of the car, the seat, the door handle, everything, so I have to scrub and scrub with Fantastic but does it come out, No! so next time he can take the bus for all I care."

"Slow down," Hal says, massaging his neck muscle that goes into contraction at the sound of her voice. "What happened to Zoe's cab?"

"It broke! Who knows? What am I, a mechanic? All I know is it stops in the middle of the street, the *meshugganah* woman calls me to come get him, I get him and they take it away, I guess, who knows, all I can tell you is he makes me crazy what with the directions and the complaints and the spitting blood all over, you have no idea, but here's what: He's got more gum surgery coming up and if she can't take him any more, somebody *else* is gonna take him there because I'll tell you this: *me*, it's not gonna be."

So who's it going to be? It's not going to be Hal, for sure. Another driver? Not likely, given Max's distrust of strangers. Max won't even call a cab because Max doesn't like calling a cab, waiting for a cab, riding in a strange cab with a strange person because, as Max had said at Hal's earlier suggestion that cabs could be an acceptable mode of transportation, "How do you know who the guy is? He could be a serial killer. Serial killers drive cabs. What was that movie where the killer was a cab driver?"

" 'Taxi Driver,' " Hal had said, regretting it immediately.

"See?" Max had said, and that was the end of the conversation.

Hal sighs, a great heaving sigh. "Okay, Mom. Okay. I'll take care of it."

Delaying the inevitable Friday night stint, Hal sucks on a tightly-rolled joint in the parking lot before he heads upstairs to his parents' condo. He checks to make sure his cell phone is on. Milo should have returned his call by now. Now that Hal has made up his mind, he's antsy to tell Milo that okay, he'll do it, he'll go along just this one last time, don't even ask again. The Louis Quinze is just a building, he tells himself. An old building. It's not like he's doing anything *wrong*. He bets there's not one person on the commission who hasn't done the same at one time or another, in one way or another. That's what politics is all about: Influence. Power. Prestige. Why else would anyone take such a shit job at such low pay if they didn't see some advantage in it? Sure, you can talk all you want about community service and crap like that, but, really.

He's going to insist on even more money than Milo offered. He'll tell Milo it's hazard pay, plus it's the Louis Quinze they're talking about, not just any ho-tel but a hotel that was once family, and even though it's now a distant relation, he feels––well, guilty. But hey. He's not doing anything wrong, just guarantee-ing a little insurance for his future, a cushion so he can retire from politics and do the things he's always wanted to do, which he hasn't figured out yet but there's got to be something. Maybe he'll write a book. Maybe a thriller. Thrillers sell big. Or he could write an expose. Boy could he write an expose. Political exposes, they sell big time. Or maybe he could announce Heat games.

He takes another drag off the joint, puts it out on the sole of his boot and carefully folds what's left into the Hot Tamale matchbook he keeps in his pocket. He may slip out on the balcony between dinner and dessert for another lungful. He thinks he'll need it. His jumpiness about his decision, combined with what awaits within the walls of Casa Wolfe, will no doubt call for another hit or two to get him through the night.

"It's a little chewy," Tootsie apologizes as she saws away at her brisket. "It was on sale."

"Chewy?" Max says. "Where'd you get this? Tire Kingdom?" He studies the masticated chunk of gristle he's just spit out, then sticks it on his plate. He pokes a finger into his mouth. "I think I loosened my bridge," he says around his wiggling finger. "Something doesn't feel right."

Hal gazes at the grey wad stuck on Max's plate like old gum under a school desk. He relates to the gummy wad: chewed up, spit out, and stuck in place. The only really bright spot in his life is the possibility of Staci, but whenever he stops by Hot Tamale to say hello, all she wants to talk about is her upcoming test shoot with that sleazeball scout from *Maxim*, Winston Gurney. The only time he sees her are those treasured moments stolen when she's between tables in the restaurant. He lives on dreams of her future gratitude. Lost in his fantasy, he picks at the kasha on his plate. The tones of his cell phone startle him from his reverie.

"What's that?" Max says, looking around for the source.

Hal grabs his phone and jumps up from the table. Maybe it's Milo. He feels a flush of incertitude. Maybe he should tell him he needs more time, he needs to think about it some...

"Hal?" says the voice. It's not Milo. "It's Zoe," she says.

Zoe? "What do you want?"

"I've got a big problem."

He doesn't want to hear about her problem. He's got enough problems of his own.

"My cab. It died on me. I guess you heard."

"Yeah," he says. "Is it fixed?"

"I don't know if it's fixable. It's still in the shop." She pauses. "Boyd says he might be able to get it running long enough to trade it in."

"Good idea. Trade it in. Get a good used car."

She pauses. "I won't get much on the trade-in. It's pretty old. And, well, after your mother bashed it in..."

"Hey, I covered that, didn't I?" Now he's really annoyed.

"...it's never been the same," she continues, her voice rising. "It was just fine until then and now it's *terminal*." She pauses. "So I need to ask you something."

"Yeah?"

"I need to ask a big favor."

Oh no. Everybody wants a favor. "What?"

She pauses so long he thinks she hung up, then: "I saw this car. It's perfect. Only the agency won't give me decent financing. I could handle the monthly payments if you'd lend me enough for a really good down payment. I'll work it off driving your father around, no charge. It might take a while but I'll take him wherever he wants to go whenever and I'll even drive your mother if she'll let me. I really really have to have a new cab, wouldn't you rather have your father driving in a brand new, really safe, totally cool-looking car anyway?"

"What kind of car?"

"Um. A BMW."

"A BMW? Are you crazy? What do you need with a BMW?"

"It's a *little* BMW."

"Are you crazy? You're telling me you want me to buy you a BMW for a cab, a *little* BMW yet?"

"No! No, not *buy*. Lend. I want you to *lend* me the money, just for the down payment."

"No."

"No?"

"No. What do I look like, a bank? Go to a bank. Borrow the money."

"They won't lend me the money. I tried."

"Too bad," he says. He's so tired of people asking favors. Favors favors favors. He's sick of it. "Maybe you should consider another line of work."

"I'm almost *fifty*. I can't change careers now!" she says. "You don't understand. I really *love* this car."

"Well, we can't always get what we want."

"Who are you talking to?" Tootsie calls from the dining room, then scurries into the living room where he's on the couch, hunched over the phone. "Who's that?"

"Is that your mother?" Zoe asks.

"Dinner's not over," Tootsie says. "Who's calling you during dinner?"

"Where are you?" Zoe asks.

"I've gotta go." He mashes the off button with his thumb and looks up at Tootsie, who stands over him with a hurt look on her face.

"What's so important you got to leave the table to talk on the phone?"

"I was expecting a call." He wearily pushes his hands onto his knees and stands up.

"You didn't eat your brisket," she complains as she follows him back into the dining room. "And you hardly touched the kasha. Are you sick?"

"I've got a lot on my mind." The sight of congealed brisket on his plate does not cheer him and he gives it a little push away. "I'm not really hungry."

"Eat," she insists, pushing the plate back at him. "Just a little bite."

He stares at it a moment, then gets up. "I'm going out on the balcony for a minute. Get some air."

"I have bread pudding for dessert," she calls after him.

He knows there's an ocean out there because he can hear its muffled roar. The moonless sky gives itself away with a chalky smear of clouds and a feeble twinkle from a fading star. But mostly what he's staring at is Black. He feels around in his pocket for what's left of the joint he smoked in the parking lot and lights up, taking deep breaths of the humid salt air along with his tokes. He turns away from the endless dark and watches his parents through the sliding glass door. They sit opposite each other beneath the glare of the fake-Tiffany lamp that hangs over the table. His mother is animated, waving her fork like a baton as she leans over her plate and says something clearly being disregarded by his father who methodically chews, removes and lines up little chunks of grey on his plate.

At least Hal's not staring at his own future, he thinks. At least when he and Arlene divorced ten years ago he escaped the dismal prospect of someday re-enacting the scene before him. Although it costs him alimony to this day, he's not sorry he did it, even if Wally didn't invite him to his college graduation, the thankless little shit, all that child support and then tuition for college, Jeez, that took a serious chunk out of his income, even though UF is only a state school and not Yale because (Hal had argued and won) why should he pay Yale tuition for the kid when Gainesville is a perfectly good school—didn't Hal go to law school there, on a *scholarship* yet?––and what did fancypants secret-club Whiff-enpoof-warbling Yale ever do for Hal anyway, he's fifty-five years old and all his Ivy degree got him was a seat on the Miami Beach commission.

He turns back to the blackscape of night sea and sky and peers over the edge of the balcony. Fifteen floors below, the illuminated condo pool glows like an aquamarine on velvet. The image of a well-aimed dive into its six-foot depth passes through his mind, more for the glory of the success of such a feat than for its more likely consequences.

Something's got to happen. Something's got to change. Sure, he's got the Staci thing going which does occupy a goodly portion of his mind these days, but that's entertainment. He needs something solid, something that will turn things around for him and make all that has preceded this fuzzy time in his life mere prologue to his glorious future.

This deal with Milo doesn't count. It's a means to an end, a last financial blast to carry him over the hump and into a new beginning. And once it's done, that's it, the end, *fini* to that kind of income forever; this time he's going straight, he really means it.

He's inhaling one last toke when he sees Tootsie push her chair back. In-stead of heading into the kitchen, she aims herself towards Hal's retreat on the balcony. He hastily flicks the still-burning roach over the balcony, immediately regretting that action because there were at least a couple of tokes left that he had intended to save for a post-parent decompression session once he got home.

"You spending the night out here?" Tootsie asks. Her nose wrinkles and she purses her lips. "What's that smell? Is it you?" She buries her nose in his shirt and takes a deep breath. "If it's cologne, I don't like it. I never did like perfume on men."

"I'll try to remember that," he says.

"Come in. Eat dessert. Your favorite. Bread pudding."

"Since when is bread pudding my favorite dessert?"

"It's not?"

He sighs. This has become an Abbot and Costello routine. He hates bread pudding. He hates warm raisins. They remind him of flies. He's told her that since he was five. "I'm not hungry," he says instead of repeating the usual routine. "I'll pass."

Tootsie looks around shiftily, although Max is nowhere near. Hal can see him sitting at the table, gloomily observing a pale pile of yellow that Hal assumes is bread pudding. "I'm worried about him," she says *sotto voce*. "Something's not right. He hasn't been himself lately."

"Who has he been?" he says lazily, letting the rising tide of mellowness wash over his brain.

"Don't smart-mouth me. You know what I mean."

"Is he depressed?"

"Maybe that's it," she says. "He's been a real *farbissener*, such a grouch like you can't believe."

"Worse than usual?"

"Worse."

"For how long?"

Tootsie shrugs. "I think ever since he found out about the Louis Quinze."

"The Louis Quinze?" The name pulls the chain on his mellow mood and he's flooded with a sudden flush of guilt. "What about the Louis Quinze?"

"They're tearing it down and putting up a condo. Why he's so upset I don't know. We sold it, what? Forty years ago? And even though we lost a lot on it, it was still enough so we live very nicely thank you very much, so what's his problem?"

So what's *his* problem? Hal asks of himself. Why does he feel responsible somehow, as if he were the cause of the hotel's destruction? It's not as if he were Milo, doing the actual deed. It's happening anyway, no matter what; he can't stop it, it's a done deal whether he's in on it or not.

"I never really missed it when we sold it," Tootsie is saying. "It was too fancy-schmancy for me. Besides, that big fight with whatsisname, the architect, all over the papers taking credit for the whole thing when if it wasn't for your Pop it wouldn't have gotten built, I still have bad feelings from that. And I hated the decorating. All that fake French stuff in the lobby, curliques and columns and chairs with animal feet for legs. I didn't like those feet. They had toenails."

"I don't remember the feet," Hal says.

"*Ongepotcht*," she exclaims. "Everywhere you looked—half-naked statues, big satin bows, chair feet with toenails––that fancy decorator didn't miss a trick. She called it high-class; I call it *ongepotcht*." She points to Max, who is slouched over the bread pudding mound and poking it with his fork. "Now he's depressed about a hotel he hasn't set one foot in since we sold it? Go figure."

"So what do you want me to do?"

"Talk to him."

"About what?" Hal asks, guilt rising in his gullet at the prospect of mentioning the Louis Quinze to Max.

"*I* don't know. Get his mind off it. Cheer him up. I try. God knows I try."

Hal shudders at what he knows to be Tootsie's efforts at cheer: Food and *nudging*. Food, of course, the cure-all, as if kishkes, creamed herring, and gribbenes could be the prescription for happiness. *Nudging* is another, because Tootsie believed that if she repeats over and over again what you should do to improve your life, eventually you'll give in and do it and be forever grateful to her that you did. And then there's Hal's particular favorite: warnings of her own demise due to some defect in one's personality, as in "your (choose one: *a.* grouchiness *b.* stinginess *c.* lack of appetite) is killing me."

"Maybe he doesn't need cheering up," Hal says, avoiding the responsibility of even having to try. "Maybe he just needs to get out more."

"Not with me," Tootsie says. "You take him."

"Oh no," Hal protests. "Not me."

Now Tootsie is saying something Hal never thought he'd hear from her: "Well, it looks like we got no choice. We got to use the *meshugganah* driver. She's the only one crazy enough to put up with him."

The reality that Zoe could be his father's only mode of transportation seeps into Hal's weed-fuzzed consciousness like razor-cut blood through a toilet paper patch. He has no choice. Max needs Zoe. Zoe needs a car. But what Zoe *doesn't* need is a brand-new BMW. Amazing how out of touch with reality she is, fixating on a fantasy of something totally out of her realm.

Whatever. He guesses it won't kill him to give Zoe a loan—a small loan. It won't get her a BMW, but maybe a pre-owned Chevrolet. If she's so dead set on a BMW, that's her problem. As long as he gets wheels for Max, he doesn't care what they're attached to.

"Come eat dessert," Tootsie is saying. She leads the way back to the table where Max has finished most of his bread pudding, leaving the raisins in a little pile on the side of the plate. Resigned, Hal sits, jumping up again at the sound of his cell phone.

"There's that music again," Max says.

Hal grabs the phone. It's Milo.

"Again with leaving the table?" Tootsie calls after him as he heads for the living room. "Tell your friends it's dinnertime!"

"What's up?" Milo is saying. "You called."

"Uh, yeah." Why *had* he called? He's fuzzy with grass and the grate of Tootsie's voice and the sadness of Max picking raisins from his pudding. Now he remembers; he called because he was going to say Yes, he's in on the deal, but seeing Max's gloomy reaction to the news has given him second thoughts. If only it had been some other hotel, any hotel but the Louis Quinze.

"Hey, man," Milo says. "You still there?"

"I think maybe it's not such a good idea. For me to get involved. In the deal."

"What are you talking about?" Milo asks. "From your message, I thought you were in on it."

"Changed my mind."

"Listen," Milo says after a thoughtful pause. "Let me tell you what I've been thinking."

"Wouldn't matter. I'm out."

"You ever think of running for mayor?"

"Not lately."

"But it's something you've thought of before, I know. Because you ran before."

"I lost."

"You lost because you weren't ready. This time, you can be ready."

"How's that?"

"You didn't have the right backing last time. This time, you could have a real campaign fund. A serious campaign fund. I've been talking to some people about you. There are many, many persons of substance—*substantial* persons of substance, myself included––who would be happy to support—*generously* support––a development-friendly candidate." Milo pauses. "You could be mayor."

Mayor. Hal feels as if he's just gotten a kick start, a reawakening of the moribund ambition that drove him to politics in the first place, the possibility that he still may have some worth in the world. Or is he falling for one of Milo's snake-oil promises that usually end up nowhere? "I don't know," he says warily. "I lost pretty badly last time." He doesn't mention that the winner--the present mayor--was overwhelmingly chosen because he was well-liked. And honest.

"You didn't have the right *backing* then," Milo persists. "Times have changed. The Beach has changed. You'll have big-bucks people behind you. With numbers like that, you can't lose."

Oh yes he can. It takes more than numbers to win; it takes what Hal knows he no longer has, and maybe never did have: single-minded obsession. He lacks that certain hunger innate to powerful men––not just ambition, but the driving force that lifts them above lesser beings and transforms them into legends. There are those with ambition who lack smarts, and those with smarts who lack ambition. He has come to the realization that he is in the latter category. Politics, to him, wasn't so much an avenue to making the world a better place; it was the road to making it a better place for *him*.

Along the way, he did do admirable things, good deeds that won him effusive thanks from innumerable charities, organizations and individuals, allowing him to acquire enough engraved brass-and-wood plaques to fill up the storage bin in his condo. The public once seemed to love him, but the public is a fickle audience who now applauds the young, the flashy, the bi-lingual. Once he had existed in a bubble of adoration, borne aloft by his charm and charisma. The bubble hasn't popped yet, but it's rapidly deflating, and beneath him is nothing but air.

Milo apparently thinks differently. Milo believes in him. "With my people behind you, you can do it," he says. And then comes the clincher: "The Beach needs a leader like you."

A leader? Like me?

"You've still got a following," Milo continues. "Your name is known. Run now, before it's forgotten. Mayor: It's a logical next step for you."

Mayor! But it didn't have to stop there. Maybe politics *is* his calling. Not piddly city commission politics, but the big time. Mayor could lead to the House, the Senate––presumably where the present mayor might go when his term is up. Mayor: the first step to glory.

How quickly one's outlook can change! How briskly one's fortunes may rise! Milo has opened the prospect of a glorious future where just moments before, Hal thought he had none at all. He hangs up and returns to his plate of bread pudding and his pissed-off parents. He returns their sullen stares with a grin. He is suddenly, happily, dizzily energized, a feeling he hasn't felt in a long, long time.

Things have taken a brand new spin. Maybe life can be good after all.

CHAPTER VII

STACI

Is she crazy? Accepting a ride home from work on the back of Hal's Harley seemed like a good idea at first. She wanted to get there before the family arrived for Sunday dinner, fearing that her curious nieces, who love to play with the stuffed animals in her bedroom, might discover the Victoria's Secret bag she had hidden beneath her bed. Her skepticism about Hal's Harley facility rises as he straddles the seat to explain the finer points of her riding in the sissy seat. The bike begins to tip slowly to the left and he loses his balance. His long, keening wail (*yiiiiiii*), escalates as he and the bike crash in a metallic clatter to the pavement.

"I think I changed my mind," Staci says. Hal crawls out from beneath the machine and gingerly checks his knee and elbow for damage.

"Not a chance," he says, grunting and sweating while wrestling the bike up-right again. "You're in for a treat." He dusts the grit from his jacket and jeans, climbs aboard once more. The engine roars to life. "Ready?" he yells over the racket.

She shakes her head. "I'll take a bus." But buses running on Sunday were even more unreliable than usual. She can't take a chance she'll be late.

"Come on." He pats the sissy seat with a black-gloved hand. "I'll get you home on time."

"What about helmets? Aren't you supposed to wear a helmet?"

"Hell, no! No helmets! Too hot! Too much stuff on your head!" He pats the seat again. "Hop on."

Well, she should probably give him that much. He's trying to make the *Maxim* thing happen, even though it hasn't happened yet. The least she can do is take a stupid ride on his stupid motorcycle because after all, she owes him.

"Hang on," he says as they bolt away, and she does, clutching him tightly around his waist. "Fingernails!" he yells. "You're stabbing me!" They pick up speed and annoyed glances from outdoor diners as the Harley zooms crazily up Ocean Drive, takes a knife-sharp corner and almost runs down a couple of platinum-headed nipple-ringed guys in Speedos who scream something in German that sounds profane.

"Slow down!" she yells, but he speeds up and bee-lines it to the challenge of stop-and-go Alton Road. He barrels through without stopping, even for the red light that she sees before he does. "*Stop!*" she screams, but he doesn't and a florist's truck misses them so narrowly that Staci can almost smell the roses.

"Fingernails!" Hal yells again, but she can't, she won't, she refuses to release her nail-bending grip on the fleshy roll stretching the sweat-wet Grateful Dead t-shirt under his jacket. A massive appliquéd eagle glares meanly at her from the jacket's back. Hal's grizzled grey ponytail, whipped by the wind, repeatedly slaps her in the face. She knows that she is doomed.

"Take me back!" she screams, but the wind erases her words and they head east on Arthur Godfrey Road, up the ramp and out on Collins. To their left is a blazing sun; to their right, a Roquefort blur of white hotels veined with glimpses of blue ocean. Traffic has eased, the road is smooth, and the ride has become a glide.

"Great, huh?" he calls back to her. "You love it?"

"NO," she yells.

But does she really, now? Men's heads have been bobbing as she zooms by, and she knows the signs when she sees them: goofy grin, popping eyes, a sudden improvement in posture. And then she sees herself as others see her: blonde hair flying in the wind; breasts bouncing beneath a low-cut shirt; long legs spread wide over chrome. She suddenly feels like queen of the world, just like... well, almost...a *Maxim* Girl.

* * *

"Let me off here," Staci yells before they get to her house. But Hal doesn't hear her until it's too late, and they arrive in a roaring Harley blast that ends in a screeching stop.

Something is terribly wrong. Papi's Honda is still parked in front. He should be at Domino Park, competing with his old *campadres*, a place he spends his Sundays before dinner since the Elián González Museum closed. He had loved volunteering at the Elián Museum––the Little Havana house where the Elián saga occurred, a place revered, enshrined, and sacred to believers in the legend of the beloved abductee. Papi, dressed in his best *guayabera*, would hand out souvenir calendars and lead tours through the house-turned-museum crammed with mementos of the sainted boy: teddy bears, toys, religious icons, Cuban and American flags, paintings, plastic flowers, and collages chronicling the media moments of Elián's all-too-short time in Miami.

And Mami should be in the kitchen, preparing for the big family dinner, rolling dough for *pastitos*, boiling beef for *ropa vieja*, telling Staci's older sister Elisa for the fifth or sixth time to set the table and use the good china, and would she tell her kids to keep the TV down and get the other sisters to stop gossiping and help out in the kitchen?

By now, her younger brothers should be off somewhere, she never knew where, somewhere where they could watch girls and smoke weed and play video games and do all the things that Mami and Papi insisted their sons would never do.

But no one is where they are supposed to be. Instead, Mami and Papi sit grim-faced on the porch in white plastic chairs, while (she can see their faces in the window) her brothers and sisters and sisters-and-brothers-in-law and nieces and nephews are all in the living room, anticipating something, she knows not what.

And then she knows. Because clutched tightly in one of Papi's veined and hairless hands is the Victoria's Secret bag. The other hand holds its forbidden contents—lacey, black, see-through, push-up, flimsy naughty nighties—visible for everyone to see.

The window of the living room is fogged with many breaths: nieces and nephews on the lower tier, sisters and sisters-in-law on the next, brothers and brothers-in-law jostling for space at the top. The last time Staci had an audience like this was at her *quinceñiera*.

Why is everyone here now? And then she remembers: there's a Dolphins game on TV this afternoon. When that happens, they gather to watch it before they eat.

Finally Papi speaks. His usual fast-tumbling Spanish syllables are slowed to an ominous growl. "You set an example for your nieces with this trash?" Staci sees her niece Juanita giggle behind her hand. Traitor. "What is the meaning of this?" He waves the lingerie in the air like a black flag.

She hesitates. "It's a career move."

"What kind of career?" he says, his face turning to ice.

Her mind skitters over possible answers and lands on "Modeling. I'm auditioning to be a model."

"What kind of model wears this kind of trash?"

"Um. Victoria's Secret?" She knows better than to try to explain the *Maxim* girl thing, but Victoria's Secret doesn't appear to be a wise second choice.

"Naked ladies!" Papi yells. "You want to be a naked lady? Where do you get these ideas? That bar where you work?" He glares at his wife. "You said it would be good for Stefanie to earn her own money, and now, see what you did?" He stuffs the lingerie back into its bag. "This goes into the garbage."

Hal is discreetly attempting to start up the Harley, presumably to make his escape. Its roar and sputter, as well as his failure to get it going, swings Papi's attention away from Staci to Hal. "Who is that?" he demands. "Why were you riding on that...thing?"

"His name is Hal," she says. "Harold Wolfe." She needs to make him respectable. "He's in politics."

Papi's face goes from ice to fire. "Politics? What kind of politics?"

"He's...um." What does he do? "He's going to run for mayor."

"Mayor?"

"Of Miami Beach."

Papi propels himself off the porch, waving the Victoria's Secret bag with its naughty booty in Hal's direction. "This is your idea, Mr. Mayor of Miami Beach?" he yells in Spanish. A wayward thong slips from its prison and lands at Hal's feet. He picks it up and, not knowing what to do with it, stuffs it in his jacket pocket.

Unable to escape, unable to fully translate what Papi is saying, Hal attempts conciliation. "*Staci quiere una carrera,*" he begins in what he hopes is Spanish. "*Staci es una hermosa mujer....*"

"Don't tell me what she is," Papi booms back *en español*. "I will tell you what she's *not*. She's not going to be a model. And," he adds, "you're not going to be mayor."

From the pained look on his face, it was clear that Hal understood. "I'll be in touch," he calls out to Staci before attempting, at last successfully, to stomp the Harley into action and is gone.

Tears of righteous anger fill Staci's eyes, fueling her defiance. She has never challenged Papi before, but if she submits now, her possible career is over. She plants her feet and stares him down. "I'm not a little girl any more," she says.

"I'm," she takes a deep breath, "a woman." The three-tiered fog on the living room window thickens to near-obscurity.

Staci slams the door to her bedroom and throws herself across her stuffed-animal-crowded bed. She doesn't sob pitifully––the soundtrack of her usual boyfriend-induced tantrums. This time she's dry-eyed, stunned by the recognition that for the first time in her life, she has openly defied her father.

She rolls over on her back and looks around her room, unchanged since Mami allowed her to decorate it herself as her *quince* gift when she turned fifteen. Ruffled in pink chintz and white eyelet, it remains a virgin's room, frozen in a long-ago innocence belied by her surrogate zoo of stand-ins for her sexual conquests, each furry creature a reminder of certain acts of pleasure she can conjure up as she strokes its pastel fuzz. She'll bequeath them to her cherubic nieces (except the one who ratted on her) who will remain unaware of their prurient origins. It's time to leave them behind, along with her past, and enter the world of her future.

Her future. A hot thrill of anticipation warms her, melting the anxiety that froze her just a moment ago. If it takes leaving home to make her dream come true, then this day will be her turning point. Her world is changing, but once she's a *Maxim* Girl, her world will have no boundaries. She'll have money to spend, autographs to sign, TV shows to star in. Everyone will know her name: It's Staci, not Stefanie, she'll tell them.

That'll show Papi.

CHAPTER VIII

ZOE

Happiness is the cradle of a contoured seat, the perfume of new leather, the spring of untrod carpet. Happiness is the plump grip of the BMW's steering wheel, the hard shaft of its gear shift, the one-fingered tip of its rear view mirror. This is the day Zoe will possess the car of her dreams, and then she'll be happy forever.

Zoe had polished and vacuumed and spiffied up Zippity in a wave of guilt before leaving for the dealership. She tossed her collection of empty Diet Coke cans and McDonald's bags, and packed up what would be transferred to her new car: tissue box, water bottle, nail clippers, Rain-X, Swiss Army knife, tire pressure gauge, a weather radio that needed batteries, and back issues of *Car and Driver* she kept handy to read during slow times. She even shampooed the fuzzy dice and hung one of those Christmas-tree deodorizers from the rear view mirror, banishing the faint but lingering aroma of years of Big Macs and fries. Zippity Cab never looked so good.

Boyd did a great job of resuscitation, although it was mostly cosmetic. Zippity's new lease on life, Boyd had warned Zoe, was merely temporary; her innards worked on borrowed time. But he assured her that the cab would make it past the trade-in, and then it wouldn't be her problem any more. *On the road again*, she sings as they tool down Collins in a circuitous route to the dealership. She doesn't want Zippity to know that, rather than being back in business, they are traveling the last mile.

She tunes the radio to a salsa station, tries to liven up the mood. But Zippity is dragging ass, chugging a little as if aware that something is up. Zoe's guilt is washing over her in waves now, alternating with the excitement of claiming, at long last, the BMW, which in her mind is already Zippity Two. She makes a quick stop at the bank to deposit the check from Hal, the money he grudgingly advanced as future payment for chauffeuring Max. The amount isn't enough, but Zoe is determined to talk the salesman into letting her put less down in exchange for higher monthly payments. She'll worry about those later.

Zoe can barely contain herself as she drives into the BMW lot. She slams Zippity's door without a goodbye. She had intended to make a brief but meaningful speech about the years they had spent together, explain the difference between love and being in love, offer reassurance that someone new will come along who would appreciate Zippity's good qualities. In short, goodbye and good luck, she would have said had she not been overcome with joy. Her beloved new car awaits. She rushes into the showroom, eager to claim her car at last.

But her BMW is gone. Vanished. Nowhere in sight. In its place in the showroom window is a funereal, shiny black 540i sedan. "Did you sell her?" she wails as the salesman approaches. "Is she gone?"

The salesman adjusts his goulash-patterned tie and shifts into sorrowful mode. "I'm afraid so," he says. "Just moments ago, as a matter of fact. The young lady and her father are signing the papers right now."

"Young lady?"

"She just got her driver's license this week. The car is her sixteenth-birthday present." He lowers his voice confidentially. "Her father owns a chain of souvenir shops. Big bucks," he says, making a movement between his fingertips and thumb. "Airport deal."

Zoe feels as if her heart has been splintered, vacuumed and emptied into her toes. "Where is she?" she manages to ask.

"You can see her through the glass in the office over there." He nods discreetly in that direction.

That's not what Zoe meant—she meant where is her BMW, her love, her Zippity Two? But she looks anyway. She can see the tops of their heads, the girl's blonde hair artfully banana-clipped into a trendy spray, her father's dark hair sleek and pomaded, nodding at something their salesman is saying. Zoe trembles, resisting the impulse to rush into the room, throw herself onto the desk and cry, "*No no no!*"

Now she's angry. "You *knew* I wanted that car," she hisses to the salesman. "Now it's going to some private-school twit who's going to cram it with her stoner friends and play Beyoncé on its radio."

The salesman backs off, eyes flitting nervously from side to side. "I can't save cars for people like seats in the movies. We've got lots of others. There's a nice little pre-owned sedan I can get you a deal..."

"I don't want it!" she cries, clapping her hands over her ears. "Don't talk to me about other cars." She glares in the direction of the father and daughter, who are now shaking hands with their salesman, preparing to leave. "I told you the other day that I would have the down payment, but you just couldn't wait, could you?"

She scurries away, trailing the father and daughter to the lot where the BMW preens, freshly bathed, top down, gleaming in the sunlight. Crazed with jealousy, Zoe watches the daughter slide into the driver's seat and caress the steering wheel with multiple-ring-fingered hands as the salesman explains the logistics of the dashboard.

Zoe can't stand it, can't watch as her dream car is fondled by this stranger. She slogs across the lot to Zippity, fires up its slumbering engine, and aims its shuddering body homeward. Blinded by tears, she's unaware that –– steered hesitantly by the girl backing it out from its parking spot –– the BMW, her would-be Zippity Two, is directly in her path.

"Look out!" the salesman yells. Too late. Zoe plows into the BMW's shiny new fender with a sickening crunch. The howling duet of "Shit!" from both father and daughter awakens Zoe from her lugubrious trance. She jumps out to see if she's damaged her lost love.

"You never look!" the father is screaming at the daughter, who is bowed over the steering wheel, sobbing. He is, Zoe notes as he emerges from the car, a very large man. He towers over her, jowls quivering on a face the color and texture of a tangerine. "You stupid slut!" he is yelling, and with a start, Zoe realizes he is addressing her.

"She didn't look!" Zoe whimpers, although she knows she is equally at fault. In exquisite slow-motion, she replays through the fog of memory the moment before impact: the backing-up of the convertible, the turning of the blonde-tasseled head to the side, the twin expressions of horror registering on father and daughter's faces at the crunching sound of metal on metal. Zoe crumples in fresh tears as she sees what her spaciness has wrought: the BMW's fender resembles a disco ball.

She retreats to the safety of Zippity Cab, notices that its bumper is now partly detached and bent into the shape of a licorice twist. She glumly observes the chaos around her: the father arguing with the salesman, the daughter blubbering she doesn't want the car any more, the manager running on pigeon-toed feet to stop the father and salesman from coming to blows.

Zoe stifles a sob as the BMW is driven away, tire scraping noisily against the bashed-in fender. They gradually disperse—father and daughter driving off in the car they came in, their salesman skulking back, muttering epithets about big shots who cancel contracts. In the sudden silence, Zoe has a flash: her sorrowful blunder may have paid off.

The BMW is now a used car.

Newly energized, she runs back into the showroom and flags down the salesman who, upon seeing her, attempts to hide behind a plastic potted palm. "What's going to happen to the convertible?" she asks.

"I guess the body shop'll fix her up," he says, his eyes twitching. "Then she'll be up for sale again." He pauses. "Damaged goods. Could be a real deal."

Zoe grabs him by his tie. "Okay. Listen up and listen good. She's mine, you hear? *You are not selling her to anyone.* Understand?"

He nods, eyes wide.

"It's a deal," she says, and grabs his hand in a hearty shake. "Call me when she's ready." She hands him her card, then marches out to Zippity, parked, bumper askew, in the middle of the lot.

Zippity starts up with a shudder. Zoe guides the cab onto the highway, ignoring the screech the bumper makes as it drags along asphalt. "Jeez," she complains, "now I've got to make another trip to Boyd's to fix this clunker. It's like giving CPR to a corpse."

* * *

Boyd shakes his head as he studies Zippity's sagging bumper, gingerly lifting it, testing to see if it's broken or just seriously mangled. "I don't know," he says, frowning. "We might have to amputate."

"Do it. Do it quick, and do it cheap. I don't care what it looks like. I just need it to run until the new car is fixed."

"The *new* car needs fixing? What..."

"Don't ask."

"I understand," Boyd says, eyes shiny with compassion and leftover lust. "No charge this time. I do pro bono work for special customers."

Uh oh. Zoe sees what's happening here. Pro bono? More like pro boner. If there's going to be a repeat performance of their roll in the plaid blanket—a good possibility, since it was more fun than she'd had in a long time—she wants no strings attached. "No thanks. I pay my way," she insists. "But if Zippity's beyond help, give me the bad news right now."

Boyd bows his Mr. Potato-Head head. "This car has suffered," he says after a moment of contemplation. "I'll do what I can to save it."

"No heroics," Zoe says. "I can't afford heroics. Just keep it going, that's all I ask. If I don't get back to work soon, I'll lose my best customer."

The next day, her best customer is slouched in the back seat of the freshly patched-up but bumper-free Zippity cab, poking at the roll of blood-blotched gauze pack stuffed between his lip and gum.

"Don't mess with it," Zoe admonishes Max, watching him in the rear-view mirror. "The periodontist said to leave it alone." She gamely steps on the gas to pass the slowpoke weaving in front of her, but Zippity's only response is a wheeze. Zoe drops behind the slowpoke again, an SUV driven by a woman with a cell phone glued to her head. Zoe honks, *A-ooo-ga*, but the woman is zoned out, so Zoe floors it, shocking Zippity into action of sorts. As they chug past the SUV, Zoe mimes holding a phone, shaking her head vehemently at the woman to indicate her disapproval. The woman, oblivious to Zoe's tactics, chats on. Undeterred by Zippity's violent shuddering, Zoe cuts in front of her and slows down for spite.

Max, Zoe notes as she checks her rear view mirror to see the woman's reaction, has removed the gauze from his mouth and is studying its bright-red blotchiness. "Put that back," she says. "Don't take it out till it clots."

But Max stretches over the seat to catch a glimpse of his gum in the mirror, pulling his lip aside for a better view.

"Sit down," Zoe yells. "Where's your seat belt?"

"Ith thtill bleeding," Max says. "Wook. Fulla blood." As proof, a big drop plops on the seat next to Zoe.

"Stop bleeding all over my cab! I've got to trade it in!"

Max drops back into the seat. "Twade in?" he asks. "Why?"

Blaaaaaat! A horn blast from the SUV aborts Zoe's answer. The woman is apparently now off the phone and unhappily aware of Zippity's chugging presence ahead of her.

Blaaaaaat! Blaaaaaat!

It's music to Zoe's ears. She tappity taps on Zippity's brake to slow her pace even more. Zippity decelerates in a series of shudders as Zoe's mood climbs. Ah, sweet revenge. She tries to catch a glimpse of her honking nemesis in the rear view mirror, but the swollen face of Max blocks her view as he leans forward once again.

"Why aw you twading it in?" he asks.

The SUV swerves wildly across the double line, honking madly as it passes Zippity. Zoe shoots it a bird through her open window. "Asshole!" she yells at its rear bumper, ablaze with a sticker proclaiming "My child made the honor roll at Palmetto Elementary."

"Why?" Max persists.

Zoe glumly watches the SUV vanish into traffic. "Because," she says, "I want a new car."

"Whath wong wif dis one?"

"It's old. It's time." She hands him a wad of tissues from her Kleenex box.

"But thereth nothin *wong* wif it." He jams the tissues to his mouth and stares out the window.

"There's nothing right with it, you mean," she says, then perks up. "Wait till you see my new car. You'll flip out."

"I wike dis car."

"I like this car too," she agrees. "But I *love* my new car." Her mood elevates as she visualizes the hopefully near future, shimmying through traffic she's crawling through now, her hands gripping, not the time-worn ridges of Zippity's steering wheel as she is presently doing, but the baby-butt smoothness of the BMW's leather-wrapped wheel. "It's a convertible. We can ride with the top down, get ourselves some sun."

"Thun? Tho I can gwow another thing on my nothe?" Max stretches toward the mirror and points to the still-pink scar from their previous medical outing. "The doc thays *no more thun.*"

Unfazed, Zoe agrees. "You don't want sun? Push a button, the top goes down. Push it again and it's up. It's got all kinds of gadgets. Jeez, I'm way way way overdue for something new. This old clunker has outlived its usefulness."

Max sinks back into the seat. Zoe stops at a red light, takes a swig from her water bottle, hums along with an old Herman's Hermits song—tinny on Zippity's ancient radio—thinking happy thoughts of musical times to come, times filled, not with the mono-music leaking from these useless speakers, but heart-thumping Surroundsounds from the BMW's audio system: sounds to caress a steering wheel by, sounds to inhale new-car perfume by, sounds to reawaken her senses and make her feel young again.

Lost in her erotic auto fantasy, she fails to notice that Max has disappeared until the light turns green and the door, open from his escape, bangs shut when she accelerates. She swings her head around and her heart stops: the back seat is empty. She jams on the brake; Zippity Cab jolts to a dead stop, a boulder in the swirling river of cars pouring around her. Where did he go? Cars swerve crazily around the door she has flung open, their drivers mouthing curses as they lean on their horns, but Zoe doesn't see them, so focused is she on what she's desperately seeking among the whizzing hunks of steel on wheels: a bright yellow golf shirt and little pink head.

"Mr. Wolfe," she screams. "Mr. Wolfe! *Max!*" Is that him, that flash of yellow dodging cars up the street? The sudden outbreak of horns from the vicinity heightens her hope. Still gripping the water bottle, she runs after him, waving her arms over her head in a futile attempt to stop traffic, an action which serves only to escalate, rather than calm, the rage seething within every car that passes. A glimpse of gold skitters in and out of her vision, teasing her with its unpredictability, now here, now there, now nowhere at all. Where is he?

Aha! She spies a yellow splash along the center line and races toward it. "Mr. Wolfe! Mr. Wolfe! Come back!" she cries until she realizes it's not a golf shirt she's screaming at, but a fluorescent vest on a guy brandishing a spray bottle who, despite the head-shaking protest of the driver of the car he has targeted at the light, is grinning happily as he swipes a dirty rag across its windshield. He looks up, startled, as Zoe realizes her mistake and skids to a stop.

"Hey," he yells at her, spotting her water bottle. "Beat it. Git your own corner, bitch." Sensing an opportunity for escape, the driver of the car runs the red light, barely missing a mini-bus festooned with bosomy ads for Club Madonna. The rest of the cars at the intersection rev their engines, anxious to avoid the ministrations of the windshield washer, whose primary prey has vanished. He turns his fury on Zoe.

"Look whatcha did!" He snaps the dung-grey rag at her and advances menacingly. "You made me lose my customer."

"Here, take it." She throws the water bottle at him, hoping to appease him, an attempt which fails when it hits him in the face.

"*Fuckin' bitch!*" He clutches his battered nose. To her horror, he lunges at her, and the chase is on, a zig-zag race through a dumbstruck audience of drivers stuck in traffic. She reaches the light where her cab should be, but it's gone. It was here, right here, just a minute ago, wasn't it? Right here? Where she's standing? Cars whiz by, horns blasting at her and the advancing windshield washer who, after dodging a turning bus, shakes his fist with a final curse. Satisfied that she's not returning to his territory, he reverses course back to his station. Zoe, however, remains rooted to the spot in bewilderment. Where is her cab?

The siren she hears in the distance provides a clue. She runs in its direction, feet slapping asphalt, heart clanging in her chest. Traffic ahead is at a standstill, heads poking through rolled-down car windows. And then she sees the focus of all this attention: piloted by Max, Zippity has had a grave mishap, its grill forked by a No Left Turn sign in the median strip. Impatient drivers are swinging around the scene, but a hard knot of Samaritans have formed a protective shield around the cab. Zoe's yell of "Mr. Wolfe, Mr. Wolfe" parts the crowd, and she sees Max staring dazedly at her through the driver's side window, his face smeared with blood.

The cop nudges her aside and opens the door. "Are you all right?" he asks Max, who is still gripping the steering wheel. "You're bleeding. Don't move. I'm calling an ambulance."

"No! No ambuwance!" Max cries, suddenly alert.

The cop, unheeding, is speaking into his radio, which is ripped out of his hand by a surprisingly agile Max. "No ambuwance," Max repeats. "I'm okay, awright?"

"You're bleeding," the cop protests, grabbing his radio back.

"Not me. My *gumth*." Max waves the bloody gauze pack he has fished from his mouth. The cop jerks backward at the sight.

Zoe elbows her way between them. "He had gum surgery. That's why he's *bleeding all over my car*," she yells, turning to Max. "Where did you go? What did you *do*? You ran away! You stole my car! You *crashed* it! Are you crazy?"

Max sinks low in the seat. He stuffs the gauze pack back in his mouth and stares ahead at the blood-smeared steering wheel.

"Can I see your driver's license?" the cop asks Max.

"He doesn't *have* one," Zoe says. "He's not supposed to drive. That's why I was driving him."

"You were driving?" the cop asks.

Zoe rolls her eyes and throws up her hands. "Does it look like I was driving? NO! I *was* driving, until he jumped out of my cab and I had to stop and he disappeared and this guy washing windshields started chasing me and I get to my car and it's *gone* and guess who took it, Mr. Toad here, and then he goes and smushes it and bleeds the hell all over it and who's gonna wanna buy it *now*?" she wails.

The cop is unmoved. "I gotta give you a ticket."

"Why me? Why not him?"

The cop shrugs and keeps on writing. "License and registration," he says, and holds out his hand. Zoe complies, glaring at Max, who ignores her as he slides across the seat, opens the door and gets in the back seat. He casually regards the faces outside his window as if they were just passing scenery.

"Can you start 'er up?" the cop asks Zoe as she contemplates the ruined grillwork with resignation. Sighing, she gets behind the wheel, wipes the blood off with a tissue and gingerly turns the key. With an exhausted shudder, Zippity starts up. The cop is done. The crowd is gone. Zoe edges away from the mangled No Left Turn sign and eases out into traffic.

"Don't move," she orders Max. "You make one move and you and your bloody gums can hitchhike home."

"Hmf," says Max.

They ride in steamy silence for several blocks before Zoe erupts. "What is *wrong* with you? What makes you do something so *crazy*? Jumping out of my cab, stealing it, crashing it into a pole. You coulda been killed!"

Max doesn't reply. He examines the clump of bloody gauze with great intensity, turning it over and over in his palm before he sticks it back into his mouth.

"Well, I'll tell you this," Zoe continues. "I don't want you riding in my new cab if you're gonna act like that. No running into traffic, no cabjacking, no bleeding all over my leather seats. You want to act like a nutcase, you better get yourself another driver."

"I'b not a nuccase."

"Then give me one good reason what made you eject yourself from your seat," she says in a grim attempt at control.

Max removes the gauze, rolls down the window and tosses it out into the wind. "Outlived its usefulness," he says.

"What?"

"That's what you said. 'Outlived its usefulness.'"

"What are you talking about?"

"What do you need a new car for?" he mutters, staring out the window. "Nothing wrong with this car."

"Nothing wrong? You mean before, or after, you creamed it today?"

"This is a good car. I like this car. I don't know why everybody always wants something *new* alla the time."

"It's sixty years old. It's falling apart. It's got three wheels in the grave. *That's* why I'm getting a new car."

Max leans back and pats the seat with both hands. "They don't make 'em like they used to."

"Yeah. They make them *better*," Zoe says. "The BMW's got power steering. Power brakes. Air bags. Better mileage, too. This thing eats gas like a Sherman tank."

"Hmf."

"It's got leather seats!" Zoe cries, getting pumped. "Plush carpet! Audio system! And," she says in a final burst of conviction, "it's a convertible!" She looks for Max's reaction in the rear view mirror, hoping he's sharing her enthusiasm, but he's disappeared. Alarmed, she swings around, fearing a repeat performance, but there he is, scrunched down in the seat, arms folded, bottom lip covering the top in a pout.

"*Now* what's wrong?" she asks, but his answer is swallowed by the wail of a fire rescue truck behind them. Zoe jerks the cab into the right lane which fortunately has no occupant. The truck overtakes them, then fades into the distance as Zoe picks up speed once again. "Sirens always remind me of Anne Frank," she says.

Max doesn't respond.

"You know, Anne Frank," she says, attempting to steer the conversation in a cheerier direction. "The Nazis? The kid with the diary? It was a movie. Remember when they hid from the Nazis in the attic, and you knew that the Nazis were coming because you heard the sirens, *wa*WA*wa*WA, like that?"

"They don't sound like that here," Max says. "They don't go *wa*WA.*"

"Well, *waaaAAAAaaa*, then, if you want to get technical about it."

"Sirens," Max says after a moment of contemplation. "When I hear one, I think, Watch out who that bell tolls for because you never know, it could be for you."

"Wasn't that a book or something?"

"Yeah. I forget who wrote it."

"Hemingway?"

"No—no, not Hemingway. Singer maybe."

"Singer? What singer?"

"*Singer!* Isaac Singer! The writer!" Max says, his voice cracking in disbelief.

"You never heard of Isaac Singer? He was famous. They even named a street for him."

"A street? Where?"

"Here! In Miami Beach. He usta live here."

"Where does he live now?"

"Nowhere," Max says. "He's dead." He is silent for the rest of the ride home.

* * *

The salesman sees Zoe coming and heads her off at the door. "The car's still not ready," he says, attempting to block her way. "I told you this morning, like I told you yesterday and the day before and the day before *that*: These things take time." He wipes the back of his neck with his handkerchief, stuffs it back into his pocket and sighs. "I'll let you know when it's ready. Yours isn't the only car in our body shop."

"I've got a check." Zoe waves it at him. "I'm ready to buy. What's with you people?"

The salesman closes in on her with a pointing finger. "I am giving you such a deal, even taking that clunker of yours in trade, that you should get down on those knobby knees of yours and thank me," he says, jabbing the air. "But what do I get? A car stalker!" He waves away the check she is snapping at him. "I don't care! Go home! You're bad for business."

"I'm taking damaged goods off your hands," she says.

"And who *did* the damage?" he snarls. "For all I know, you planned it, running into it with that heap of yours."

"Are you crazy?"

"Crazy, yes! Crazy to do you a favor, crazy to sell that car so cheap..."

"*Cheap?* It's costing me money I haven't even earned yet! It's peanut butter sandwiches for lunch from now on. No more Big Macs for me," she says, forgetting the significance of that particular menu item until she sees his face blanche.

He smooths his tie with a manicured paw. "Do not return," he says icily, "until I tell you it's ready. If you do, I will not sell it to you. If you do, I will sell it to anybody but you. If you do, I will donate it to charity, I will give it to a homeless person, I will shove it off a bridge. Do not come back until you are invited or you will never see that car again. *Understand?*"

Back in the parking lot, Zoe climbs dispiritedly into Zippity Cab. The engine turns over gamely, but Zoe is too dejected to notice that Zippity is giving its best. She has lost compassion for the car in her zeal to claim its successor, and hasn't bothered to wash it, much less spiffy it up as she had before. Now that the cab's grillwork has been mangled and the bumper has gone the way of the dump, Zoe doesn't attempt to keep up appearances.

She has presumed that each day will be Zippity's last, but the days have stretched out to a week. It becomes hard to pretend everything is the same as they drive around picking up fares. She wishes her passengers would just shut up, but they fill the silence between clicks of the meter with irritating observations she tries to stifle with a scowl. Her thoughts are occupied by fantasies of the new car languishing in the dealer's body shop––unrepaired, unclaimed, waiting to be loved as only she can love it.

Oops. Almost missed them, the bunch of blue-hairs frantically waving her down, hands flying above their heads like competitive kids in a classroom. Zoe yanks the wheel; Zippity Cab takes a 90 degree, clanks its way across traffic so pitifully that the four ladies at the curb look shocked at its intact survival.

"Lawdamercy," says the squattest of the four, adjusting her perky straw hat with "Nassau" embroidered across its brim. "I thought for sure you weren't going to make it."

"I always make it," Zoe says as they scurry into the cab. Nassau-hat lady plunks herself into the front seat next to Zoe while the other three settle into the back seat with the flurry of setting hens.

"Where to, ladies?"

"Jai-alai," says Nassau-hat. She pronounces it "Jayalay."

"I won last night," pipes a voice from the back seat. "I won $50!"

"Me, too!" says a second voice with equal pride.

"I bet the quiniela, that's the way to go," says the third with a cackle. "Won myself 75 smackeroos."

Nassau-hat stares glumly ahead as the cab zig-zags across the causeway. "So," Zoe asks her, "how much did *you* win?"

The woman clutches the armrest with a tiny sunburned hand and gives her a grim look, then turns her attention back to the road. "I'll win it all back tonight."

"Good luck!" says Zoe, summoning up false gusto. She is wearing her smiley-face "Have a Nice Day" T-shirt tonight, one of her favorites. Its sunny grin and licorice eyes usually make her feel like a roving goodwill ambassador, but today it merely mocks her.

"I *will* win it back," declares the woman with sudden fervor.

"That's what you said before the slots ate your twenty bucks on the cruise ship," says one voice from the rear.

"Yeah," says the second. "Just kept poppin those quarters in, poppin 'em in, poppin 'em in, and what did I tell you? I said, 'Emma Sue, you're gonna feed your whole retirement into that one machine, it's a jinx.' But did you listen?"

"It was fixed," Emma Sue snarls between clenched teeth. "I ought to report them." She sinks lower into the seat until Zoe can only see the top of her hat. "Crooked bastards," she mutters.

"Well," chirps the third voice, "I've got a good feeling about tonight. I'm betting on that same cute little guy I bet on last night, whatsisname."

"How you gonna bet on somebody you don't know his name?" asks the second back-seat voice.

"It's a kind of Spanish name."

"They're *all* kind of Spanish names."

"Albuerga. Albita. Al-something."

"Maybe Al was his first name."

"The dark-haired guy with the big neck."

"Which dark-haired guy? They've all got big necks."

"Shut up!" Emma Sue's Nassau hat flips back as she spins around in her seat, exposing her face: hard, tan and wrinkled as a walnut. "Just shut up. I've had it with the three of you." She turns back around, whaps the hat back in place with the flat of her hand, and sinks even lower in the seat.

The pavement whirs beneath the cab, white divider lines whizzing like arrows. The meter breaks the silence at regular intervals. Tsk, it goes. Then tsk again.

The brightly lit jai-alai fronton looms ahead. Zoe swings the cab over with a curb-scraping screech. Emma Sue throws open the door and, hat and all, disappears into the crowd. The remaining three count out the fare, painfully pooling nickels, dimes and quarters. They say not a word about the vanishing Emma Sue, spare not a second to glance in her direction, but pour a cascade of silver into Zoe's waiting palms.

Zoe stares at the handful of change. Something about Emma Sue's "Shut up!" has scratched the surface of Zoe's ragged mood like a needle across a Sinatra record, bolstering her impulse to say out loud what she ordinarily would have stifled: "What the fuck?"

Two of the ladies recoil, then scurry off. The third stares hard at Zoe, pokes her right in the smiley face of her t-shirt with a stubby little finger, and says, "Well, have a nice day" before trotting away.

"Yeah, *you* have a nice day," Zoe calls after her. Right now, she doesn't give a shit about the kind of day anybody is having.

The call that the BMW is ready comes the morning Zoe is scheduled to take Max to the podiatrist. Giddy with excitement at the long-awaited news, she forgets Max's appointment, loads some music onto her phone to christen the BMW's sound system—Abba, her favorite––and fires up Zippity for a last, unsentimental dash to the dealership. She is undeterred speed-wise by morning traffic which she deftly maneuvers until her cell phone rings enroute. It's Tootsie, barking "Where are you? He's gonna be late to his appointment with the foot doctor, his bunions are *killing* him," and Zoe is suddenly flung back to reality.

"Just this once you've got to drive him," Zoe says.

"Are you crazy?" asks Tootsie.

"*Please.* I'm on my way to pick up my new car."

"So? It's not going anywhere. Get it later."

"I'm almost there," Zoe pleads. In the distance, she sees the showroom window reflecting the morning sunlight. She pictures the little car awaiting her, resting comfortably after its traumatic restoration work. She needs to be there to assure it that they'll be together from now on, and she'll never, ever hurt it again.

"You shouldn't be almost there," Tootsie says. "You should be almost here."

"How about Hal?" Zoe says in desperation. "Can't he drive him?"

"Hal? *Hal?*" Tootsie says. "Are you kidding?"

Resigned to the inevitable, Zoe yanks Zippity's wheel, makes a sharp U-turn and heads back to Max's condo. He's waiting on a bench out front with a sour look on his face, one shoe on, one shoe off. He limps to the car carrying the shoe in a plastic Publix bag, which he shakes at her once he's settled into the back seat.

"I can't even get my shoe on," he complains, "and now I'm gonna be late." He peers into the bag, then pulls out the shoe, a squishy orthopedic number that, like its mate, has a peninsula-shaped bulge worn into it that conforms to the shape of his bunion. "I hope he can fix my foot so I can wear this home."

Zoe is too aggravated to be diplomatic. "Bunions don't get fixed like that. Why don't you just cut a hole in your shoe and save yourself the trip." When she sees his stricken look in the rear-view mirror, she backpedals. "Look, I'm sorry. It's just one of those days."

"Yeah," he says.

"Hot flash," she offers by way of an excuse.

"I don't know from that."

"He'll fix your foot. He's a good doctor."

The good doctor keeps them waiting a good two hours, and then pronounces that surgery is called for. "He's not cutting me," Max says as they leave the office. "I'll just make a hole in my shoe."

"Good idea," says Zoe, who is thinking about cars, not feet, and how she's got to get back to the dealership before the salesman leaves for the day. She'll never make it, she realizes as rush-hour traffic proceeds in increments of inches, not if she has to drive Max all the way back to the Beach, and then turn around and go back to the dealership, just a few blocks from where she is now.

"Are you in a rush to get home?" she asks Max.

"I'm not in a rush to get anywhere," Max says. "Especially not home."

"You want to go with me to get my new car?"

"No."

"Come on," she chides. "You'll love it."

"I won't love it." He folds his arms around the bag holding his shoe and slumps low in the seat. "I want to go home."

The dealership is just ahead. Caught in the vortex of desire, she can't turn back now, not now, not this close to consummation, so she grips the steering wheel which has taken on a life of its own beneath her sweaty palms. She dodges the papaya-selling guy in the middle of the street yelling "*frutas!*" then swings right at the dealership parking lot and into an open space.

"Where are we?" Max wants to know. "What's going on?"

"It won't take long," she promises. "We're just going to pick up my new car."

"I'm staying here," he says through the half-open window.

"You can't. I'm trading it in." She goes around to open his door. He mashes the door lock button down. "Open up," she says. He refuses. She opens the door with her key. "Come on, it's cooler inside." He shakes his head.

"Okay," she concedes. "Stay here until I finish with the paperwork. Then we'll go home. In my new car!" His lack of enthusiasm fails to dampen her own. "Just wait–– you'll change your mind when you see it. It's awesome!"

Max's woeful face doesn't deter her from heading to the showroom, and when she returns later—much later than she had anticipated, what with haggling with the salesman, signing all the papers, and hyperventilating from both the excitement and the hassle of it all—Max is gone. At least he appears to be, since his face is no longer visible through the window. Panicked, she opens the door and finds him lying on the seat.

"Oh my God, he's dead!" the salesman cries, but no, Max is not dead. Max is conducting his own form of protest. He refuses to get up.

"I'm calling the cops," says the salesman.

"No! No cops!" Zoe has seen more than her share of law enforcement officers in the recent past.

"Well, he can't stay here," the salesman says. "It's our car now. He doesn't come with the deal."

Zoe crouches next to Max. "Listen, Mr. Wolfe. This isn't my car any more. It's theirs. I traded it in. I have a new car now. Come and get in my new car. We'll put the top down. We'll take a ride. Won't you ride in my nice new car?"

Max raises his head and sits up. "Why are you talking to me like some kind of moron?"

"I'm not," she says. "I just want you to..."

"I still got my brain with me. It's not going anywhere."

"I just want..."

"Tell him to get his shoes off the seat," says the salesman.

"*One* shoe," Max corrects him. "The other one's in the bag."

Zoe sees her new BMW glide to a stop nearby. "All set," calls the service guy, and leaves the door open for her. Like an impatient lover, the car beckons her into its warm, dimly-lit interior. She sees the shimmer of its dashboard, hears the soft bongbongbong warning that the door is open. She can't wait a moment longer.

"Get out!" she yells at Max. "Get out, or I'll call Tootsie to come get you."

Max bolts upright, gathers up the bag with his shoe, and sullenly obeys. The salesman leads the way to the BMW. Zoe follows, eyes shining with joy, and opens the door for Max. "Look," she says, sweeping her hand in a car-show-model flourish. "Isn't it fantastic?"

"Where's the back door?" Max asks. "How am I supposed to get in?"

"There's no back door." Zoe slides the passenger seat forward. "See? It's easy to get in the back."

Max peers into the car. "No back door? You call this a cab?"

"It will be when I get it painted and all."

"Painted?" the salesman asks. "It was just painted."

"Wrong color," says Zoe. "It needs to be pink."

"*Pink?* You're covering Glacier Silver Metallic with *pink?*"

"Soon as I can afford a paint job." She indicates the former Zippity now abandoned in the parking lot. "That's the official color of Zippity Cab."

"*That* pink?" The salesman clutches his tie for support. "You're painting it that atrocious...that tacky...that *pink?*"

Zoe is indignant. "It's my trademark. Pink, with *Zippity Cab* in turquoise letters. I may be upgrading, but I'm not changing my style." She leans into the BMW and caresses the leather seat. "I'm still not sure about zebra seat covers, though. I really hate to cover the leather."

"Zebra?" The salesman staggers back and leans against a neighboring car. "What are you thinking?"

"I'm thinking it's my car now and it's none of your business." Zoe's had it with this guy. "Come on, Mr. Wolfe." She attempts to guide Max into the back seat. "Let's go home."

Max doesn't move. "I can't climb back there."

"Sure you can," she assures him. "See how far the seat moves forward? It's easy."

"I'm sitting in front."

"Fine, fine," she says. "Sit in front, sit in back, I don't care, just get in."

"Some cab," Max mutters, and plunks himself into the passenger seat.

"Let's put the top down," Zoe says. "Live a little."

"Keep it up. I don't need the top down to live."

Disappointed, Zoe settles in behind the steering wheel. Grasping the wheel cheers her up; it's hers now, all hers—her soft seats, her plush carpet, her cute little cup holder. She takes a deep breath that instills within her a zen-like calm, then tears out of the parking lot, reducing the seething salesman to a dot in her rear-view mirror. *Her* rear-view mirror. She accelerates, her foot light as a fairy's on the gas pedal as they roar onto the expressway.

"Feel that power," she exults as they overtake a rumbling truck hauling a precariously-stacked load of lumber.

"Slow down," he yells, pressing his hands against the dashboard. A tattered orange flag stuck on the end of the lumber load flaps just inches in front of them.

"Gotta pass this guy." Zoe swings into the left lane. The speedometer hits 75. The driver of the car she has just cut off indicates his displeasure with a honk that endures until she moves back into the center lane, far ahead of the offending lumber truck, and drops her speed to 65. Max opens his eyes.

"Smooth, huh?" Zoe says. "Handles like a dream."

"More like a nightmare." Max turns his face away and stares out the side window. "The old one was better."

A sudden image of Zippity, left without a goodbye in the dealership parking lot, flashes before Zoe's eyes. Her mood plummets with the speedometer. Max is trashing her high, spoiling the thrill of new ownership, infusing her joy with guilt. "Be happy for me," she pleads.

"Why should I be happy for *you?*" he asks. "I can't even be happy for my-self."

She's not going to let this mean little man ruin her day. She's waited too long for this, spent too much time fantasizing how it would be. And now her dream is real. She's really gripping the leather wheel, really inhaling the new-car odor, really hearing Abba through the sound system. She's really happy.

She *is.*

CHAPTER IX

HAL

Hal stares at the Disney Wolf doorknocker before he bangs it twice. Another emergency call from Tootsie. Why does he keep doing this to himself?

"Four hours at the podiatrist's!" Tootsie greets him. "To look at a bunion! How long does that take? It's there, you see it, you fix it, goodbye. So he gets home, what time? six thirty, and does he sit down to dinner like I ask, NO, he doesn't say a word and goes to bed, covers over the head, no dinner, no nothing. And now he won't come out."

Hal enters the darkened bedroom. Max is cocooned deep beneath the rumpled bedspread. "Pop?" Hal peers under its scalloped edge, which snaps shut, tight as a clam. "Come on out."

Max's answer is muffled but clearly negative. Hal watches the lump that is his father shift beneath the bedspread. He thinks of anacondas and small furry animals. He wishes he had a couple of tokes beneath his belt to give him some perspective on the situation.

"See?" Tootsie asks, startling Hal and causing the Max lump to contract into a ball. "What did I tell you? Straight to bed! Not a word, nothing. I asked him 'So, what did the doctor say?' but does he give me an answer? Never mind it's 6:30 already, dinner's on the table getting cold but who cares that I made stuffed cabbage, all day it takes me, but it's the inconsider*ation*: four hours since he left here. Four hours! No explanation, no nothing, then zip, under the covers."

"Where was he for four hours? Did Zoe's cab break down again?"

"Ha! *Now* we get to the gritty nitty, don't we, because what I want to know is what's with this cab, it breaks down all the time, that's what she *says* but who knows what's really going on between them for four hours yet..."

Hal feels his guts—picturing them pink, warm, porous as a sponge—compressing into a hard little bubblegum ball. He has to get out of here. He backs toward the door. "I have to go," he says.

"Go?" Tootsie blocks the doorway with her arms flung wide. "You can't go. He's still in bed."

"He's got to pee sometime." Hal edges by her. "He'll come out then. Or when Anderson Cooper's on TV." He makes a break for the front door. If he doesn't get out of here right now, he's going to...what? Hit the wall? Pass out? Throw up?

And then he's out. He thinks he said goodbye to Tootsie. He doesn't remember. He doesn't care. He takes a deep breath of frigid hallway air conditioning, redolent with the smell of onions, cabbage, some kind of mammal meat from dinners being prepared in the various apartments on the floor. He punches the elevator button. He rides down with a wide woman in a muu-muu who is clutching a dead plant in a pot. He doesn't respond to her cheery hello.

He peels out of the condo driveway, revving the Harley to the max as he cuts through Collins Avenue traffic. He can't take this insanity much longer, acceding to every wacko thing his parents expect him to share. Maybe he just won't answer his phone any more, that's it, just act like they're a robo call that he won't pick up, hope they'll get the message and never never bother him again. Unless it's an emergency. Like this one was but wasn't.

Holy shit they're driving me crazy, he screams into the wind. The bike swerves suddenly, evoking an angry honk from the car he almost hits. To his right, the offended driver of the near-missed car rolls down his window and addresses him: "Asshole!" Hal responds in kind: "Asshole!" This exchange continues briefly until Hal ends it by cutting the guy off, signalling his intention with a middle-finger-thrust before swinging into his lane. The resulting blast of the car's horn rattles Hal into an instinctive stomp on the brake. And then he's flying.

High, high he flies; up, over, and under he tumbles through rushing air studded with rhinestones, the sparkle of many lights. And now the direction is down. Down down down. He does not want to go down. He climbs the air like a ladder but he just can't get a grip, so it's all downhill until there is no more down. Something hard and unforgiving smashes into his side. The lights spin and go dark, and when they go on again, he is being jolted on a stretcher beneath a starry sky. His right arm and leg feel as if they were composed of hot metal shavings, and he thinks his ear has been barbecued.

He can hear the siren. *wa*WA*wa*WA*wa*WA.

Hal's right leg and arm are broken. His hip, shoulder and ear are badly abraded. With time, the doctors say, Hal will be fine. He was lucky he didn't land on his unhelmeted head. Since his libido has been momentarily flat-lined by his injury, he doesn't even fantasize about Staci, much less contact her. Besides, he still has no news about the promise he made her since the *Maxim* scout hasn't returned his calls (bastard, after all the trouble Hal went to so *Maxim* could shoot naked volleyball photos on the beach). Sex is on hold for now; he's got enough problems. For starters, he's had to move in with Tootsie and Max until he can manage by himself. Who else would have him? Not his ex, not his son, not one of his many former girlfriends, several of whom had expressed the wish when he dumped them that he'd meet with some terrible fate. Which he has, thank you very much, ladies. And worse: the doc has told him he can't drive, at least for quite a while.

Of course he's going to drive. Not the Harley, which was totaled in the accident anyway. But drive a car? You bet your ass he will.

"I can't bend my knee." Hal stares at the new cast the doctor is putting on. "You told me I'd have a walking cast and I'd be able to bend my knee."

"I never told you that." Dr. Merkin finishes smoothing out the plaster of Hal's new cast and regards his sculpture with professional satisfaction. "You did some major damage. Your leg's got to be immobilized for a few more weeks."

Hal slumps on the examining table. His leg is frozen, his arm is in a cast, his ear is covered with a lumpy Van Gogh bandage, and now he's told that he's not allowed to drive yet. It's been a month already, and he thought that this new cast would be more forgiving. But the new cast looks the same as the old: a plaster tree stump with roots of pale, hairy toes. With his arm still in a cast, he can't use crutches, so he'll be one-handing it on a rolling walker for a while, not to mention one-handing the rolling of his joints, a difficult but totally necessary task. One day bleeds into the next like tie-dye in shades of grey, a dismal calendar that seems to have no end. The miserable life he lamented before this all happened looks idyllic in retrospect. He wants his miserable life back.

The only positive to this whole experience is that his accident roused Max from his cocoon. Disaster gave Max a focus and while it didn't lift his depression, it did get him out of bed and, reluctantly, into Zoe's new cab for a checkup at the periodontist's. He has returned to the La-Z-Boy and resumed his caustic commentary on the state of the world as he watches TV. Hal, imprisoned on the sofa with his leg up, gazes impassively at the running loop of disasters, talking heads and bad-news bulletins that feed Max's chicken-little outlook on life.

He had thought he'd be out of their place by now but no, he's still here, stuck in a condo that's stuck in the '70s, its shag carpet a flattened mat of avocado green, its harvest gold and orange plaid couch sunk like a hammock in the middle. The windows, terminally smudged from salt air, are never opened, trapping decades of air musty with the odors of Tootsie's cooking and Max's cigars—given up years ago, doctor's orders—that tinged the white walls a tea-stain tan. When the ambience of the living room gets to Hal, he retreats to his room.

But Hal can only spend so much time on the narrow twin bed in the guest bedroom staring at the pimply-textured popcorn ceiling dimly lit by a rotund light, its 40-watt bulb silhouetting long-deceased bugs that expired in its belly. He thinks too much when he does that. Wonders why the people who he thought were his friends don't call. Why the *Maxim* scout hasn't returned his calls. Why none of the women he slept with haven't offered to take him in. Why Milo has seemed to put his mayoral future on hold. Milo hasn't even called since he sent the big purple orchid that died within a week.

He's got to get out of here. His social life, with the exception of the rare foray out to dinner with a sympathetic acquaintance or two, has disappeared. None of the girlfriends have called. What's wrong with them? Hadn't he told them he loved them? The word "Love": Easy to say, and it always worked. A couple of times when he said it, he almost believed it himself.

He wasn't even sure what "Love" meant. He guesses he was "in love" when he married Arlene, but what did he know? He was only 25—time to get married, according to the timetable of those times. He was dating Arlene at that moment, so by the laws of chance, the spinning wheel of fortune, she was the one. Despite the catch about having to be faithful (which he abandoned before their first anniversary), for a few years it was fun, playing grownup, being a couple with couples friends, having fancy wedding-china dinner parties featuring something Arlene had learned in her French cooking class but never quite mastered. Things were pretty okay.

And then Wally came along. Life came to be All About Wally. Sleepless nights, sexless weeks, babysitters, PTA, Khoury League, acne, girls, drugs, grades, college applications, one dreary thing after another until he got careless and Arlene found out about his lunchtime-diversion-of-the-moment, and then about all the rest. By then he didn't care what Arlene thought because he had stopped caring about Arlene, so when she told him she wanted a divorce, it was easy for him to say Yes.

Divorce was fine with him. He was free! (Aside from the goddamned alimony.) He went a little crazy then with the women, admittedly, but that settled down to a routine of serial relationships that inevitably crashed, not his fault. Arlene moved to Arizona, a relief because now he didn't have to dodge her if he saw her at a party or at Publix. And with Arlene went Wally.

As Hal lies on the narrow bed in his parents' guest bedroom, staring up at the bug-congested light, his wandering thoughts turn to Wally. For some reason, thoughts of Wally have been recurring lately, triggered by something as benign as a TV commercial with some kid eating Captain Crunch. Yesterday, as he sat in the lobby in a brief respite from Max and Tootsie, he watched a young father waiting for the elevator, his baby's sleepy head nestled on his shoulder. Hal felt suddenly transported in time, felt the heft and weight of holding Wally just like that, the baby powder smell, the little toes pressed against his stomach, the fear of dropping him, the startle at seeing the same pale blue of Max's eyes in Wally's. And then he'd wonder: Did Wally ever think about him?

What happened? Why doesn't Wally call now and then to see how he's doing? Hal's his *father*, for God's sake. It's not like he abandoned Wally. He sent him birthday money every year, paid for his college, encouraged him to find something better than that time-share job he has in Tucson, what kind of job is that anyway? Did Wally forget what a good father Hal had been when he was growing up? Didn't Wally remember that when Hal had time, he'd go to his Khoury league games, even took him to Dolphin games when he got an extra ticket? Now it's like Hal doesn't exist for him. Like he doesn't have a father.

The bugs in the light blur as Hal succumbs to sorrow. Here he is at 55. An old man. He could have grandchildren and not know it. (Did he hear that Wally got married? Or did he dream it?) Where did it all go? Where did it all go?

He allows himself a short wallow in regret, then wills himself to occupy his time with better things. Eventually the tedium of flipping through magazines and trying to nap overcomes Hal's better judgment; he hauls himself onto the walker and joins Max once again in front of the TV. This, of course, puts him within range of Tootsie, who alternates over-solicitude *(What's wrong, you don't want another knish?)*, complaints about life *(I asked them to slice the corned beef thin but look at this! Like a brick!)*, and irrelevant admonishments *(I don't understand why you never asked out Sophie Goodman's niece.)*

He's here, he tells himself stoically. Deal with it.

Now every night is Friday night. Dinner conversation revolves around Tootsie's replay of the same "I told you so" tune about the Harley and Max's predictions of imminent doom. Hal has had it.

Tootsie is making it clear tonight that she, too, has had it. "I'm not cooking," she announces as Hal settles his leg onto the couch. Max acknowledges this news positively: "Good."

"We're going out," she says. "There's still time to make the Early Bird at Humperdink's if we hurry. You can still get brisket––not bad, mine's better–– but not bad. The chopped liver's not terrible either."

This is not Hal's idea of escape. He's as thrilled about going to Humperdink's now as he was when he was in high school and his parents dragged him there for dinner, where he might run into some of his friends: the ultimate humiliation.

"Order a pizza," Max says, aiming the remote at the TV. "I don't want to go out."

"Good idea," says Hal. "Pizza."

"It's Friday night!" Tootsie says. "Who eats pizza on Friday night?"

"Sophia Loren," says Max.

"Benito Mussolini," Hal says.

"Frank Sinatra."

"Tony Soprano."

"Gina Lollo..."

"Stop it!" Tootsie yells. "You're not funny."

Hal thinks they are. He was liking their game. He and Max exchange looks, joined at last on common ground: the satisfaction of tormenting Tootsie.

"...brigida," finishes Max.

Tootsie gets her way. They are halfway to Humperdink's, Tootsie at the wheel of the Lincoln, Hal stretched out in the pushed-back front seat, Max scowling in the back. Tootsie inches into the left lane and slows down. "So just once I don't cook on Friday night, is that such a crime? I can't do it. *I can't do it.* Spend all day shopping and cooking, *then* put dinner on the table, *then* do the dishes, and *then* go and do it all over again the next day."

"You don't have to go to special pains for me, Mom."

"What pains? It's a pleasure! You're my son!" She glares in the rear view mirror at the driver behind her, who is honking furiously at her snail's pace. "Everybody's in such a hurry," she says. "Where's the fire, what's the rush, they have to be in such a hurry?"

Hal slumps down in the seat, attempting invisibility. "Going too slow causes accidents, too," he mutters.

"Not like motorcycles!" Tootsie declares. "Motorcycles! Why don't you just say to the world, 'Okay, here I am, come kill me.'"

"I won't be riding it any more," Hal says. "It's totaled."

"I know. It should only be totaled totally."

Hal's not sure how he feels about the demise of the Harley. On one hand (the undamaged one), he's bereft. The Harley was his swagger, his strut, his "fuck you" to a world he was forced to deal with thanks to his unfortunate choice of profession. It was a tether to youth, a shield against age, and a babe magnet when he needed it most.

On the other hand (the one in the cast), the Harley had scared him shitless.

Well, it's gone, so the matter is moot. He sees the big neon Humperdink's sign blazing against the nighttime sky. It's late. They may have missed the Early Bird. He hopes so since he deliberately forgot his wallet in a silent challenge to Max's cheapness. He won't order the early bird special, and Max will have to pay.

Tootsie is having a problem wrestling the Lincoln into a parking spot that's big enough for two. She lurches backward and forward several times before she's satisfied. When they exit the car, Hal notices that it's straddling the line. Not wishing to evoke unnecessary conflict, he is careful not to point this out.

He doesn't order the brisket despite Tootsie's urging, and gets the smoked fish platter (*Since when does lox cost as much as steak?*) instead because it's not on the Early Bird menu. He orders a beer (*So what's with the drinking?*), another beer, and a giant slab of chocolate cake for dessert (*What, you don't want bread pudding?*) Max is busily mopping brisket gravy from his plate with a piece of rye bread when the check comes. He doesn't look up when the waitress places it on the table. Tootsie ignores it as well. "Your brisket was fatty," she says to Max. "I never make fatty brisket."

Max continues to scour his plate. "Don't you want dessert?" Tootsie asks, clearly annoyed that Max's brisket dinner has vanished so thoroughly. "You must be hungry, to eat all that fat."

Max's gaze skims the pale blue check on the table and lands on the metallic pot of pickles. He reaches in with his fork, stabs a chartreuse tomato, and slices it up on his spanking-clean plate. "My mother used to make these," he says around the morsel in his mouth. "These remind me of my mother."

Tootsie responds with a sigh. "Your mother couldn't cook. Everything was stewed. Stewed tomatoes, stewed meat, stewed prunes. Stewed stewed stewed. It all tasted alike."

The check has a drop of pickle juice on it now. It spreads unevenly, blurring the writing. Hal gives it a little push towards Max, who looks away. Hal pushes it again. Hal always winds up paying when they go out. He's not backing down. He's meeting the challenge. This time, Max will pay.

"Pop," Hal says. "The check."

Tootsie's leftovers from her Early Bird special–chicken fricassee––have been scraped into the Styrofoam takeout box. Now she's stuffing rolls from the bread basket into her purse while Max regards Humperdink's décor with unusual interest. The check lies untouched on the table.

"Pop. I don't have my wallet," Hal finally says. "I hope you brought some money."

"Oh," Max says with feigned surprise. "Did she bring the check?"

"It's the blue thing in front of you," Hal says. "The thing with writing on it."

Max picks up the check, squints through the magnification of his glasses. "What's this say?" He points to where the pickle drop has dissipated the ink to a blur.

Tootsie takes the check. "Let me see that." She examines it. "Sixteen ninety-five for a couple slices of lox? Seventeen ninety-five for brisket? I can buy a whole brisket for that. What happened to the Early Bird special?" She looks around. "Where's the waitress? Something's not right here."

Hal gives an exasperated sigh. He should have known this would happen. Should have brought his wallet. Should have just slapped down the old Visa and gotten out of here. Now it's going to turn into a Tootsie/Max/waitress confrontation down to the penny. He lifts the check out of Tootsie's grasp. "Let me see," he says, and quickly scans the bill. "Okay, Pop, it's $59.75..."

"Fifty-nine?" Max asks. "I never heard of a Early Bird that costs fifty-nine bucks."

"...plus tax and tip, so just leave eighty bucks and let's get out of here."

"Waitress!" Tootsie calls. She spots her, stands up and waves. "Yoo-hoo! Waitress!" The waitress regards them sleepily from beneath blue-frosted eyelids and turns back to the order she's taking from the couple in the corner booth.

Hal can't take another minute. He grips the walker and hauls himself upright. "You two battle it out. I'm going to the car."

Several long minutes later, his parents join him. Tootsie looks grim, Max even grimmer. Tootsie grips the steering wheel, her foot skimming the brake the entire trip home. They travel in silence. Hal doesn't know what happened. He really doesn't want to know. But this he does know: if he spends one more day with Tootsie and Max, they'll all wind up as a gory story on the 6:00 news.

Max has found The Scrapbook. Years ago, Tootsie had wedged it into a closet that bulged with stuff that should have been sent to Goodwill long be-fore the millenium: moth-ball-scented wardrobe bags of outdated fashions; wilted feather pillows flat as a road-killed duck; elderly plaid suitcases mottled with mold; boxes of time-stiffened gloves and veiled '40s hats. In a search for something he forgot he was looking for as he pawed through the detritus, Max spied the worn leather binding of The Scrapbook peeking out from beneath a box labeled "Fancy Shoes."

He pried it out and took it to the dining room table. He didn't open it at first, but slowly ran one finger over the lettering embossed on its cover: Louis XV. The pages stuck together as he turned them; he separated each one care-fully so as not to disturb the newspaper and magazine clippings that had been pasted in decades before.

Hal watches from the living room couch as Max, magnifying glass in hand, studies the scrapbook pages, commenting, more to himself than Hal, on each one. "Come here," Max says, indicating the chair next to him. "I want you should see this." Hal obeys, trundling over in his walker and seating himself at the table. Max starts again from the beginning.

The first page is a yellowing clip from the *Miami News*, 1955: an article about the groundbreaking of the Louis Quinze, and a photo of a young Max, his mentor, Reuben, and the architect, Bernie Diamond, whose face Reuben had scribbled out with a ballpoint pen after their big fight. Reuben had taken credit for the innovative curve that architecturally separated the Louis Quinze from all those other boxy hotels on the Beach, so Bernie sued for defamation. It was a legal dead end, but history has given Bernie the acknowledgment that Reuben had not, and Max has never forgiven him for that. "Bastard," Max comments.

He pauses at the page with Reuben's yellowed obituary taped on it, head-lined *Pioneer Developer Reuben Solomon*. "He died before it was finished. I took over, sooner than he had planned." Hal had heard the story often: how when Max arrived in Miami, newly married, ambitious and eager to learn, Reuben had hired him as his assistant. His protégé proved to be brilliant at what he did, and moved quickly into the position of Reuben's second in charge. And then Reuben died, prematurely bequeathing the completion of the Louis Quinze to Max, which he accomplished not only competently, but to great acclaim. "They called me a *wunderkind*," Max says.

This photo makes him happier: a mustachio'ed Max stretches his arms wide in victory before the now-completed Louis Quinze, while the then-mayor beams in the background. "He was a big help," Max says. "The re-zoning stuff. Big help." He turns the page. Hal nods without comment. He can—unfortunately–– relate.

Several pages later, Max breaks out in a smile. "Marilyn Monroe," he says as if Hal wouldn't recognize the buxom platinum blonde sitting on Max's lap. An unlit cigar is plugged into the corner of Max's big grin; he doesn't seem to know what to do with his hands which hang uncomfortably in the air next to her. "The ladies," he says. "They loved me."

Hal guesses they might have. The Max of Hal's childhood memory was gregarious and fun, someone who, when they walked down Lincoln Road to get an ice cream or see a movie at the Carib, acknowledged his celebrity with a handshake and a word or two before strolling along, straw hat tilted at a rakish angle, a little bounce in his step. He reveled in being Max Wolfe, the hotel king, the man who made Miami Beach, *Miami Beach*.

Hal would give anything to be whisked back to that time, a more innocent time when he took Max's love for granted and assumed it would always be there. He wants to be that little boy, not this big boy riddled with problems that seem to have no end. He wants Max to be the Pop he remembers, to be happy—as happy as he was the day of Hal's bar-mitzvah.

With the turning of each page, Max becomes more absorbed in the past, the once-upon-a-time that would never be again. What's going on behind Max's eyes is overriding what's in front. "Gone," he says more than once, and Hal begins to wish that he, too, were gone—away from here, away from wishing things were the way they were, and not how they really are.

He needs a break from guilt. So when Zoe offers to take him out for an airing the next day, Hal does the unthinkable. He says Yes.

"Good God," he says when Zoe arrives and emerges from a blazing pink BMW with "Zippity Cab" in swirling turquoise letters across its doors and trunk. "This is your cab?"

"Pretty cool, huh?" She points to the Z on the matching pink-and-turquoise t-shirt she's wearing. "I had a bunch of these made to go with it." She spins to show him the back which reads "Zippity Cab (305)555-1212. Let's Ride!"

"Maybe you should change it to 'Ride It and Weep.'" He peers inside. "You've got to be kidding. Where do you put people?"

"In the back. Or the front. Depends."

"On what? Their degree of insanity?"

"Get in." Zoe opens the door for him. "I don't have the zebra seat covers yet. I have to special order them, would you believe."

"Unbelievable."

"See? I knew you'd love it. What's not to love? It's a convertible! How many cabs are convertibles?"

"Yours must hold the singular honor," Hal says.

"You bet."

"I'm not riding in that. There's no room for my leg in this cast."

She reaches in and pushes a lever. The seat glides backwards until it almost touches the back seat. "See? Lots of room." And there is. She helps him into the front seat and maneuvers his cast into place. He has to admit, as the wind ruffles his hair and the sun bathes his convalescent-pale face, that maybe a BMW convertible isn't such a crazy idea for a cab after all.

"How about a walk on the boardwalk?" Zoe suggests, and that's fine with Hal, just fine, anything would be fine that takes him away from the stuffy gloom of Tootsie and Max's condo and out into the sunshine. He hasn't been to the boardwalk in years; what exercise he's done has been in his condo's workout room, puffing on the treadmill, straining at machines that seem to have less and less effect the older he gets. He tried working out with a trainer, but cute as she was, that was too much work. Now, with the physical therapy he's been forced to endure since his accident, he's noticed that his body is beginning to regain some semblance of its youth, and that exercise might account for it. A walk would be a good thing.

They park at a meter; Hal's pace on the walker quickens as they approach the beach boardwalk that stretches for miles between the ocean and the hotels that face Collins Avenue. To their right, the ocean is alive with silhouettes of swimmers bobbing in its sunlit glitter. To their left, sunbathers cluster around hotel pools like rotisserie chickens, their tans as varied as a display of Home Depot paint chips.

It's Saturday, a cool and sunny day, crisp as a new box of matzah. Hal feels alive for the first time in weeks, every sense tingling with the novelty of being in a place he had always taken for granted. Joggers, power walkers, and leisurely strollers pass him in sound bites: not just English in all its accented forms, but a tangle of languages–– Spanish, French, Hebrew, Japanese, German, Yiddish, Swedish, something Eastern European with that guttural *ch* sound he finally mastered after years of Hebrew school. Their voices are woven into a sound track of crashing surf, boom box music, the snuffle of wind through dune grass. A wave of guilt washes over Hal when he hears the screech of building cranes and the bang of falling concrete as another old hotel is gutted to make way for the new, but his guilt subsides in the clean fresh air.

"What's that?" Zoe points at a thin, barely visible line strung high on slender poles that bend gracefully above them. "I always wondered." A pale scratch against the blue sky, too fragile to support birds or conduct electricity or hang clothes from, the string snags the curiosity of boardwalkers who wonder, like Zoe, *What is that?*

Hal knows what it is, but how can he explain the *eruv* to a shiksa? How can he explain the import of a simple string that permits those black-clad Chasids they've passed to walk a Sabbath walk, a post-shul walk, a walk made kosher by the mere presence of the string? How can he explain that the *eruv* allows those bearded men in yarmulkes and big brimmed hats to carry keys and money? That the *eruv* allows those long-skirted women, hair covered by scarves, hats, and wigs, to push strollers as they gossip amidst a sea of kids? That the *eruv* allows the boys, their little yarmulkes colorful with embroidery or cartoon appliqués, to skateboard? How can a thin white string make all those forbidden things okay to do on the Sabbath? He can't explain its logic, so he doesn't even try.

"It's a Jewish thing," he says. "Hard to explain. Kind of like making the sign of the cross before you try a free-throw."

A couple of bling'ed rapper types, their shorts hanging dangerously low, jogs by, followed by a strolling clot of conventioneers—men in suits, women in spike heels, all wearing plastic name badges. A sweating, ruddy-faced heart-attack candidate slogs past, head low, arms flopping, panting painfully. And here comes the inevitable guy with a bloated jelly belly that almost obscures his miniscule Speedo. "What's he thinking?" Hal asks. "Okay, wear a Speedo if you're a competitive swimmer who shaves all his hair and needs to wear a banana-hammock that doesn't cut his speed. But not if you're some fatso who thinks swimming means wading up to his knees in the surf."

"Speedos," Zoe agrees. "Too much information."

Hal feels as if he's been released from prison into a cartoon world sculpted from flesh. When's the last time he saw so much flesh? Tattoo'ed, pierced, wrinkled, waxed, furry, burned, pasty, veined, scarred, pimply, taut, stretch-marked, navel-ringed, lipo'ed flesh. Some good flesh––an iPhone-plugged-in babe in a bikini––jogs past, catching not only Hal's eye but that of a young Chasid whose averted eyes scoot surreptitiously sideways as his head-to-toe-covered wife chats obliviously on. How could any man not look at those bobbing boobs barely covered by tiny triangles of fabric, that firm butt divided by a strip of thong? Hal can read the Chasid's thoughts, thoughts like his—and why would they be different? They're both men, they're both male, they can't help it. It comes with the package.

The cats are gone, he notices. The last time he was here, the boardwalk was overrun by them, fed by the Cat Lady who put out tin pans of cat food. When strollers complained about the often overwhelming whiffs of cat poop, the Cat Lady was forbidden to continue her soup kitchen, and the cats disappeared along with their food source. Apparently some managed to survive without free hand-outs; a scruffy grey tabby scoots across their path as they walk, then dives into the sheltering shade of sea grass. Hal has a flashback of the kitten he once had as a kid —his last pet, unless you counted the painted turtle that melted when he forgot to put water in its window sill habitat. Or the gerbil that escaped and was found, mummified, by Tootsie behind the refrigerator. The kitten lasted until it became a cat and shredded the couch. Tootsie found it a good home. She said.

His stamina is dwindling. Trundling the walker encumbered by casts is hard work, but he doesn't want to seem like a pussy so he slogs on until Zoe notices he's dragging. "Let's take a break," she says, and heads for the nearest bench, occupied on one end by two of the turban ladies that he's noticed gathering in groups along the boardwalk, their clusters of brightly-colored turbans looking like mobile bowls of M&Ms. They eye him suspiciously, and move further down the bench as he and Zoe sit.

"What's going on there?" Zoe points at what looks like a construction site across from where they're sitting. "Another hotel going down?"

Hal doesn't recognize the Louis Quinze at first. Its great arcing sweep, partially obscured by a chain-link fence covered in plastic fabric, rises like a ghost of itself, windows blinded by plywood, carefully-tended landscaping now a dirt meadow of ruts and upended roots. He pulls himself back onto the walker and peers through the fence. The lagoon pool is empty, its fake-rock waterfall now obvious in its falseness without the concealing veil of rushing water. Chunks of concrete are missing in the once-pristine façade of the hotel, leaving mud-colored wounds that reveal glints of its steel-boned infrastructure.

"It's the Louis Quinze." His mouth feels as dry as the sun-baked dirt that once was a carefully-tended garden supposedly patterned after the gardens of Versailles. "I didn't know it looked like...this. Now."

"Yeah, that's right. It's closed now. They're going to tear it down." Zoe shades her eyes with her hand and tiptoes to see through the opening. "Your father's really upset about it. I feel kinda guilty because he didn't know till I told him. But when he mentioned to me that he had built the thing, I just blurted out that I heard they were tearing it down to build a condo. I didn't know he'd react so badly or I wouldn't have broken the news like I did."

Guilty? Hal thinks. She has no idea. Until this moment, the demise of the Louis Quinze was an abstract idea that hovered on the periphery of his consciousness. Now, seeing the hotel in shambles like this, its glory reduced to chipped concrete, broken windows, bare earth and barren pools, makes the abstract painfully real. A feeling of guilt gushes through his innards, and he's not sure if he wants to throw up or lie down.

"What's wrong?" Zoe asks. "Do you need to sit down?"

"No. I'm okay." He's not okay. He's transfixed by the awful sight but can't tear himself away, seeing, not just what's before his eyes, but what once was, as if the past were overlaid onto the present, reconstructing in some crazy rewind the pool alive with splashing swimmers and screaming kids, the curved expanse of alabaster, the crystal clear windows, the garden bursting with flowers. He never imagined it would come to this.

"I guess it's upsetting to see your Dad's hotel this way," Zoe says. "It's probably not a good idea to tell him what it's like. I already told him too much already, and boy, am I sorry about that."

"Don't sweat it," Hal says, trying to lighten her guilt. He feels a sudden need to confess what his role in this sad tale is, and what it will be. At least the burden can be shared, because, after all, if Zoe hadn't told Max, maybe he wouldn't have found out at all.

"Of course, he would have found out anyway," Zoe says, shattering that illusion. "He spends half his life watching the news, so it couldn't have been kept a secret for long."

Can Hal keep *his* secret? It's growing a rock in his chest. It's making his heart hurt. He needs help.

It comes inadvertently from Zoe, who says, "Oh well. He'll get over it. Old people, they just can't adapt right away to new stuff. Like my new car. Max hates it, but I know he'll come around because, well, it's *new.*" She peers through the opening in the fence and shakes her head. "Look. The place is falling apart. It's overdue for a fixing up. Or," she adds, "a flat-out replacement. Sometimes that's what you have to do. Replace." A shadow dims her features for a second, and then is gone. "It's progress."

That's right, Hal tells himself. It's progress. Without it, the world would stagnate. And by helping Milo to move things along, he'll keep himself from stagnating, too.

* * *

Max is spending more time with the scrapbook than in front of the TV. "At least I can listen to some of my programs without him switching the channel on me," Tootsie says. "He's looked at that thing so much I think the pages are coming loose."

It's true. Max is hunched a good part of the day over the scrapbook, barely speaking to anyone other than the scrapbook itself, which is the recipient of broken commentary ("Bogie's girl," "shoulda kept the mustache") and gutteral sighs. Communication with Hal, which had seemed on the verge of becoming close to normal at one point, has resumed its previous brevity.

Hal feels the walls are closing in on him. He needs the space of his condo. He announces his imminent departure at breakfast, and to his wonder, there is no objection. Tootsie actually offered to drive him, but he declined, thinking he'd rather hobble there barefoot on nails than drive with her again. He said he'd take a cab, but, surprisingly, Tootsie suggests that Zoe drive him instead after she returns from taking Max to the periodontist.

Although he doesn't expect Zoe to return with Max for another fifteen minutes, Hal's already in the lobby, reluctantly clutching Tootsie's three-day-old Humperdink's takeout box at her insistence, which he intends to deposit in the nearest trashcan at the earliest opportunity. Tootsie fidgets next to him on the lobby couch where he sits with his leg propped up on the coffee table.

"Where are they?" Tootsie asks him for the third time. "It's getting dark already. How long can it take to look at gums? It's just a checkup. You open your mouth, the dentist pokes around, nothing's wrong, goodbye."

"How do you know nothing's wrong?" Hal asks.

"I can tell by the way he chews. Like a garbage disposal. You saw him at dinner the other night. Even that fatty brisket didn't stop him."

Hal feels his jaw muscles tighten up. He checks his watch, considers getting an Uber if Zoe doesn't come within—okay, he'll give her five minutes. Five more minutes with his mother and then he's outta here.

He spots her cab half a block away, a bright pink spot in the gathering darkness. Max climbs out of the cab almost before it stops in front, ignoring both Zoe as she offers her arm for him to lean on, and Tootsie when she comes to lead him back upstairs.

"Next!" Zoe calls cheerfully.

Hal rises from the couch, leaving the takeout box behind, and wheels the walker to the curb.

"I can drive you if you want," Tootsie calls out from the doorway. Where did she come from? He thought she had taken Max upstairs, but no, Max is parked by the elevator, watching the numbers overhead change as they indicate the elevator's excruciatingly slow descent floor by floor. He's as mesmerized as if he were watching breaking news on CNN.

Hal hastily deposits himself in the cab. Zoe screeches away from the curb. The night sky opens wide above them. Stars pop out like neon chickenpox. And when he feels the wind whip his pony tail against the nape of his neck, hears the engine roar with power, and smells close up the aroma of the street—hot asphalt, diesel fumes, the pungent odor of gas—he's overcome by a sudden surge of longing for his lost Harley. Beaten and battered beyond salvation, thanks to the series of bounces it took in the accident before being flattened by a bus, the Harley was his last fling. That short happy burst of wild abandon is over. He knows now that nothing could ever match the freedom he felt during those few times he actually had the machine under control. He could weep for the loss, and almost does, stifling the urge with a stuttering sigh.

"You okay?" Zoe looks over at him. "Am I going too fast?" She downshifts and the car *uuurr*s into a slower speed. "Your Dad gets a little nervous when I drive fast," she admits. "Sometimes I get carried away."

"No, no." He hastily rubs away the suppressed tears prickling his nose. "Speed's not a problem."

Zoe responds by shifting into high gear and zipping around a sluggish Town Car that Hal for one arrhythmic moment thinks is his parents', but the face glaring at them through the window as they pass is not his mother's. His sense of relief is almost palpable. He leans back and drinks in the sky.

"Cool, huh?" Zoe gives the wheel a sassy wiggle.

It *is* pretty cool. Now he feels good about his contribution to this car, his generosity in conceding to her wishes. They are partners in a funny way, and he is almost moved to reveal his role in the upcoming demise of the Louis Quinze. He needs someone to confide in, and for one insane moment, it seems to be Zoe.

He regards her out of the corner of his eye, notes the wildness of her hair as the wind threshes it like wheat, the determined set of her lips as she runs a yellow light. She's blithely oblivious of his appraisal, so consumed is she by the challenge of traffic. He grudgingly admires her style: the way she presses the heel of her hand on the gear shift; the casual resting of her elbow on the window frame; the light control of the steering wheel with just the tips of her fingers, just inches away from the rounded profile of her breast. She pounds the brake with a caramel-tan leg, lean and muscular from the top of her Nikes to the bottom of her shorts.

Shorts! He mentally slaps himself on the forehead for his momentary slippage into admiration. What was he thinking? *Shorts*, for God's sake. The woman has no concept of what's appropriate. She must be...what had she told him? Almost fifty?

At 55, he doesn't even look at women in their fifties. *Forties* is pushing it. Fifty. Good grief. He was actually skirting danger there, idly wondering what those breasts beneath that Rolling Stones t-shirt might feel like. He's not well. Staying with Tootsie and Max has fried his brain.

"The Pinnacle, right?" Zoe swings the cab onto the stone sheen of his condo driveway. The last time he left here was in a manly roar of Harley might; now he's returning on a walker. He hopes no one will see him.

Zoe insists on escorting him to the elevator, but he refuses to let her advance further into the chicness of the spare and gleaming lobby. Already they are attracting stares from the young Euro-hip residents whose detached gazes glide over his plaster-bound leg and arm with neither pity nor amusement. He could well be invisible, as he fervently wishes he were right now. He hurriedly shuffles into the elevator as Zoe waves farewell with her last words, "Call me when you need me," mercifully cut off by the closing of the doors.

When he finally and gratefully collapses into his own bed, he can't fall asleep. Behind his closed lids plays a movie starring Zoe: the voluptuous profile of her breast, the lean tan leg pounding the brake, the teasing way she fondles the gear shift. *Stop it!* he orders himself, but not only does his self not listen, a particular part of that self insists on rising to the occasion. He turns over and tries to think of other things, but Zoe's last refrain loops incessantly through his brain: "Call me when you need me."

He may have to do just that.

CHAPTER X

ZOE

Where is Max? Zoe can't wait here much longer, engine idling in the no-parking zone in front of Dilly Deli, windshield wipers whining in concert with the drumroll of rain on the convertible top. She was on time, so why isn't Max waiting out front? The cop's already given her a warning, and here he comes again.

"I'm waiting for my fare," she tries to explain as rain gusts through the partially rolled-down window, drenching both her and her new zebra seat covers. She frantically attempts to blot up the damage with a handful of Kleenex. "He's an old guy. He can't walk far." The cop, unmoved, waves her on.

She circles the block, peering through the fog-glazed windshield for a parking spot until, in desperation, she parks in a loading zone behind the store. She could kill Max. He *would* pull something like this when she gave in to his insistence that he didn't need a nursemaid.

"Don't park!" he had demanded as they approached Dilly Deli earlier. "Don't come in. Pick me up later. I don't need another kvetch telling me do this, don't do that, like I'm brain dead or something. Whaddaya think, I don't know how to shop by myself?" So Zoe had dropped him off, said she'd be back in 30 minutes, and used that time to pick up an extra fare.

She makes a run to the store through the downpour. A sudden gust blows the umbrella inside-out and she dashes inside, dripping. He'd better be here, she mutters as she traverses the aisles, spattering raindrops from the tangled umbrella over neat rows of imported gourmet crackers and bow-tied jars of jam. She sees the manager, arms folded over his crisp white jacket, eyeing her curiously. He would have noticed Max.

"Did you see an old guy, bald, plaid shirt, about yay high?" she indicates with her hand. "I dropped him off about 30 minutes ago. He was supposed to meet me out front, but he's not there."

The manager rolls his eyes, nods his head. "Oh, you mean Mr. Wolfe," he says with a sigh. "He left."

"Left? What do you mean, left?"

"Left," the manager repeats, "in a huff. After a series of unfortunate events." Beginning, he explains, with Max's uncalled-for insult of the Cheese Lady, who was merely conducting her weekly cheese-sampling duties which included the offering of a low-salt cracker to serve with the cheese. This, for some reason, triggered an inexplicable rage in Max, resulting in an altercation between himself and the Cheese Lady which was escalated by his nasty references to her hat, leading to the manager's suggestion that he should leave the store and do his shopping at 7-11. That insult, combined with Max's taking very vocal offense at the price of the olives he wanted and the fact that they were out of pickled herring, was enough to send him out into what was beginning to resemble the Storm of the Century.

"I don't believe this!" Zoe says, but, knowing Max, she does. Waving the now-inoperable umbrella overhead, she rushes back to the cab and throws the ticket she's gotten into a puddle. She's got to find Max.

She plows through traffic clogged by white-capped rivers of rain, wiping the hazy windshield to peer at every passing pedestrian in her desperate search for Max's round peanut head and orange plaid shirt. Would he hail a cab? Take a bus? Or would he––stubborn, pig-headed fool that he is—walk all the way home just to spite her?

Just as her anxiety is evolving into panic, her cellphone rings.

"Where *are* you?" says a voice that, despite its being an octave higher and a few decibels louder than usual, she recognizes. It's Tootsie.

Zoe freezes. She grips the steering wheel and tries to soften the news. "I'm looking for Max. He left Dilly Deli before I was supposed to pick him up."

"You left him? Alone? In Dilly Deli?"

"He told me to pick him up later," she explains. "But I came back early and he was gone..."

"Gone? By *himself?*"

"I'll find him," Zoe says, reassuring herself more than Tootsie.

"It's *pouring down rain!*"

Zoe doesn't need a weather report. The rain is so torrential that she can barely make out the road ahead, a smeary grey blur broken only by the flare of brake lights ahead of her.

"I told him not to go to the store," Tootsie raves on, "but did he listen? No! And what does he do? Calls you to take him! So now he's in the pouring down rain, and where are *you*?"

"I'm driving, looking. In case he's walking."

"He's *walking*?"

"Maybe he took a cab. Or a bus." She hopes.

"He'll walk. I know him. He'll walk," Tootsie says. "He had to go to Dilly Deli! And what was the big deal he had to go to Dilly Deli? Salt! And does he need all that salt? No!" She takes a breath. "Who told you to take him to Dilly Deli?"

"Well, he called..."

"I just *did* a big shop at Publix. Everything: toothpaste, toilet paper, you name it. So I get home and what does he ask? Where's my pickles? Where's my salami? Where's my herring? All *salt!* So I said, The doctor said *no more salt!* You want your heart to go into those, whatchacallit, pippitations like you had after you ate all that lox at the Goldblatt shiva? You wanna eat salt, go eat salt, but I'm not buying it for you, I said. So what does he do? He calls you! You took him! And then you *left* him."

Zoe clutches the cell phone in a tight, sweaty vise. "It hasn't been that long. I'll find him..."

"You'll find him? You'll find him? He's walking in a downpour. Pneumonia! That's what he'll get. And all because of *salt!*"

Zoe hangs up. She can't deal with this lunatic. She needs to concentrate on looking for Max. Traffic picks up speed as she turns onto Collins. She turns up the radio on the oldies station to calm herself. *Shake it up baby*, her hands nervously beat out the rhythm on the steering wheel, *twist and shout,* alternating in counterpoint with the whackety whack of the windshield wipers. Sheets of rain blur the lights of rush hour traffic. *Shake it shake it sha...*

The music cuts. The lights go out. The power steering freezes. Without a blip of warning, Zippity Two has died.

The BMW glides to a silent stop. No last gasp from the AC. No twinkle from the panel that a split second ago was lit up like a carnival. No glimmer from the digital clock that just read 5:27 before it went black. Zippity Two—Zoe's sassy, brand new trophy cab––is dark, silent and dead as a rock.

Cars streak by like meteors. Horns blowing. Lights flashing. She reads a guy's lips as, passing her side window, he yells at her: "Moron!" His lips move around the word again. "Moron!"

She grips the wheel, frozen. She's imprisoned, hermetically sealed in a trophy tomb in the dark, in the rain, visible as licorice on asphalt. She's gotta get out of here. She tries to open the door but the lever won't move. Pushes the window control switch till her finger is numb. The electric locks are frozen. She presses her face to the glass and pounds with both hands.

Help! she mouths at the whizzing cars. A guy in a red Camaro flips her a bird. She furiously presses an answering birdie against her rain-soaked windshield but he's already a faint red streak being carried up the road by the streaming flow of traffic.

"Moron!" she yells at him anyway and the word fills the silence of the car.

She's doomed. She's incompetent. Max. Pneumonia. All her fault. Help. She needs help. She punches 911 *beep beep beep* in the cell phone with a shaking finger. HELP she yells at the maddenly calm voice asking *What's the problem*? I am a black hole on the highway, Zoe sobs. I am a moron.

Call highway patrol, says the voice. Zoe shrieks as a Range Rover misses her by an inch, she can tell it's an inch, her car is shuddering with the palsy of a near-miss. *Where are you*? asks the voice and Zoe answers I don't know I don't know, somewhere on Collins, you can't miss me I'm a pink BMW cab. *BMW*? the voice repeats. *Cab*?

YES she yells into the phone as it crackles with static and dies.

Then he's there, tapping on her window. A cop. She presses her face to the glass and mouths Help, no power, get me out. He makes a pressing motion with his thumb. *What*? He repeats the pressing motion until what he's doing seeps through her frenzy: he's miming pressing the lever for the door lock. I know that, she yells. What do you think, I'm stupid? She suddenly remembers the gadget she bought to break a window in case she ever drove into a canal, grabs it from the storage compartment and smashes the driver's side window.

The cop helps her out. He doesn't say anything as they push the car to the side of the road. She knows what he's thinking: *Moron*.

It's not just the battery, Zoe discovers when AAA finally arrives. The guy can't resuscitate it. It's the entire electrical system. Kablooey. Drenched through from the downpour, she hunches glumly, T-shirt and shorts dripping big drops in the cab of the tow truck as Zippity Two is mortifyingly hoisted, rear end up, for the trip to the dealership. The tow truck driver's attempts at conversation only serve to depress her further.

"Howya like your car?" he asks.

Silence.

"Pink. I never saw a pink BMW. It a taxi or somethin'?"

Silence from Zoe, accompanied by a vicious sideways glance.

"Yeah. Well okay." He drives on through the rain, humming to himself.

"Would you just shut the fuck up?" she snaps.

He jumps, startled. "Well, Jeez."

Yeah, thinks Zoe. Jeez.

"Tomorrow? It can't be fixed till tomorrow? I need it *now*." Zoe pounds on the dealership's service counter for emphasis.

"We're closing now," says the receptionist without missing a chomp of her gum as she fills out the service request. "Open tomorrow at eight."

"Eight? I can't wait till eight!"

"I didn't say it'd be ready at eight. I said we *open* at eight. You can call then and ask when it'll be ready."

"I've got to find someone *now*, not tomorrow." Zoe clenches and un-clenches her hands in an escalating rhythm. "What am I supposed to do?"

"Get a Uber," she suggests. Zoe shudders at the word. She would die before she rode with the enemy.

The receptionist pushes the phone over to her. "You wanna call a cab?"

Call a cab? Zoe doesn't call cabs. She *drives* a cab. Or used to. She stares at the cab company's number stuck on the phone. No. She can't do it. She can't call a cab. It's too demeaning.

Zippity Two has reduced her to this.

Zippity Two is a lemon.

She stalks out of the service area and heads to the showroom. The salesman sees her coming, tries to duck into the men's room but she follows him, oblivi-ous to the startled customer at the urinal.

"It's a lemon," she accuses, cornering the salesman at the hand-drying ma-chine. It turns on with a *whomp* as he backs into its button. "You sold me a lemon!" she yells over the blast of hot air.

"BMW doesn't make lemons," he says defensively. "It made the ten best list in *Car and Driver*." His eyes plead for help from the customer who zips up hurriedly and dashes for the door.

"All right then. Damaged! You sold me a damaged car!"

"You're the one who damaged it, remember?" he counters bravely, and then recoils when she grabs his tie, today the color of cheese grits.

"I'm not here to argue. I have to find a missing person. Now," she says, yanking his tie for emphasis. "It's life and death."

"Call a ..."

"Don't say it!"

"...cab."

Zoe's eyes narrow into slits of warning. "Where's the courtesy car? Get me a courtesy car."

"Service is closing," he pleads. "Maybe tomorrow."

"*Now*. Get the papers for me to sign. Then get me the keys."

Keys in hand, led by his tie to the parking lot, the terrified salesman is pointedly ignored by his fellow employees. Zoe snatches the keys, slams the door to the courtesy car and peels out of the lot, leaving the salesman awash in a fan of water.

It's dark. The rain has let up. She still hasn't found Max, and Tootsie hangs up on her when Zoe tries to call. She's fidgeting in the courtesy car in front of Max and Tootsie's condo, gathering the courage to go up and see if Max ever made it back, when the familiar tune of her cell rings. It's Hal. She lets the musical refrain replay, bracing herself for the worst, and answers in a small voice, "Hello?"

"You're fired," Hal says.

"What happened? Is Max okay?"

"No thanks to you, yes."

Zoe sighs a long, grateful sigh, releasing her anxiety and launching her anger. "He didn't wait for me! I told him to wait, and he left! Fire me, go ahead, I'm *begging* to be fired. You're a buncha *lunatics*." She pauses. "Who found him?"

"The police picked him up."

"The police? You called the police?"

"What else could I do? You weren't answering your cell..."

"I didn't hear it. I was having my own problems."

"...and I'm still not supposed to drive. My mother was freaking out. I had no choice."

"Where did they find him?"

"In Peesa Pizza on Alton Road. Eating a piece of pizza."

"With anchovies," she hears Tootsie add in the background. "*Anchovies*, for God's sake."

"Where are you?" Zoe asks.

"At my parents' place. I took a cab."

"A *real* cab," she hears Tootsie add.

"Well, I'm sitting in front of their building," Zoe looks up at the grey edifice looming overhead as if she could spot him in a window somehow. "If I weren't fired, I could take you home."

"Why are you here?" he asks, interrupted by Tootsie: "She's here? *Now* she's here?"

"I was worried!" Zoe protests. "I wanted to know if he made it back. Don't you understand what it's been like for me? I *lost* him. I've been crazed all day, riding around in this rain, looking for your nutcase father. And then my new car dies on me," she says with a sob. "It's a *lemon.*"

"Just God's way of telling you pink convertibles make lousy cabs."

"God's got other things to think about," she snaps. "Like whether your parents oughtta share a room in the mental ward."

"Look," Hal says. "I want to go home. What are you doing about a car?"

"I'm using a courtesy car till my lemon is fixed," she says, glumly surveying her temporary mode of transportation, a nondescript beige sedan.

"Well, can you take me home?"

"I'm fired, remember?"

"I'll be down in a minute."

She should leave. Who does he think he is? She knows his type. Pushy. Arrogant. That ponytail! That earring! He's as mental as his parents. She swings the car up the condo drive and parks beneath the overhang. Maybe she'll wait until he comes out and then drive off, just to aggravate him.

She waits, brain idling along with the engine. People come and go through the glass doors of the lobby: A couple lugging a kid and kidstuff: stroller, diaper bag, platter covered in foil—brownies, she bets. Dinner with Grandma. Or, she corrects herself when she hears snatches of their conversation, dinner with Abuela.

Older woman, younger man. Woman: around 60, sanded, bleached and pummeled into shape. Man: 50s. Sinewy, possible runner, definite toupee. Dinner at Joe's, she guesses, maybe a foreign film. And then back. Her place? His place? Their place? Good for her.

Totally buff gay couple. Ripped muscles. Still-damp teddy bear hair. Tight tees and lowdown jeans, coming from the gym, judging from their matching gym bags. One carries an Dilly Deli bag, triggering a painful deja vu of today's events in that location. They're bringing dinner in, she imagines: Cornish hens with orange sauce, wild rice, salad. A good red wine. Blackout cake for dessert. Candles. Flowers. Romance.

They all seem happy, Zoe thinks, sinking into the green pit of envy. Why can't I be happy, too? I'm tired of living in the land of lost love.

She tries to make it okay that her life isn't okay by remembering when it was, when Albert was there to share a pizza, to see a movie, to drive with on A1A, radio blasting the Stones, crescent moon hanging over the ocean like a gypsy earring.

Those moments could be triggered by a scent or a few notes of music; she'd light on them like a bee on a flower, suck out what honey she could get, then move on to another moment, then another, a connect-the-dots tour of her happier past. She wanted that again: someone to sense under the covers, feel his warmth, hear his breath. Someone to care for who cared about her.

She doesn't allow herself to slip very often, to be sucked into the vacuum of self-pity and loneliness that loomed large after Albert died. For years, Zippity cab had filled that space; she had wanted to believe she was happy. But Zippity's recent decline had mirrored her own, and she needed something to make her feel young again. Boyd does that in a physical sense, reminding her that her parts still work in wonderful ways. Still, she could never get serious about Boyd; he's too much of a Nascar guy whose idea of entertainment is a six-pack of beer, ribs at Hooters, and the latest Iron Man movie. She can't do that on a full-time basis--but now and then, not bad. She'll stop by his place for a lustful refill, giving the name *Boyd's Body Shop* new meaning. But sex with Boyd, mindblowing as it may be, is just a momentary thrill, like Space Mountain: wild, screaming, breathless excitement that, when it's done, it's done.

When the BMW—shiny bright, perky and beguiling--came into her life, it veneered her sense of loss and buoyed her spirits. The pleasures she had once shared with Zippity One--the taste of an well-constructed Big Mac from the drive-thru; the satisfaction of beating the warning gates before a bridge opens; the elation of asking an on-air question on *Car Talk*—were forgotten in the excitement of her new relationship with the cab she called Zippity Two.

But Zippity Two is a lemon.

She had sensed it, even before its recent demise. She never felt that connection she had felt with Zippity One, with its cozy, well-worn interior, its comfy seat that conformed to the shape of her butt over the years. She had an uneasy feeling that she wasn't well-dressed enough for the BMW, that maybe she shouldn't wear shorts or drive barefoot, which she sometimes did on sultry days. She was in denial, unwilling to acknowledge that the thrill of the new had peaked and faded. The reality of her solitude had risen in its place. Despite all of Zippity One's faults––its sluggish performance, its fits and starts––she missed her old companion.

She wanted her old Zippity back.

Through gathering tears, she sees Hal limping through the lobby on his new walking cast. She wipes her eyes and honks as he pushes the glass doors open. He looks around blankly, spots her in the unfamiliar courtesy car and thumps over.

"Sporty." He slides into the front seat with a grunt, adjusts his leg.

"It's temporary. Till the lemon gets fixed."

"So now it's a lemon. How soon the sweet turns sour."

Zoe jerks the wheel and squeals out of the driveway onto Collins, throwing Hal against the door before his seatbelt clicks.

"Hey! Slow down! Don't take it out on me. *I* didn't tell you to buy it."

Zoe doesn't answer. She takes a deep, snotty breath which becomes a sob; her face crumples. "*Nothing* is going right for me," she wails. "I'm a *disaster.*"

"Slow down!" he pleads as she accelerates to pass a bus.

"I try and try to do the right thing," she says through burbly tears, "but I can't do *anything* right. I lose your father, I pick a lemon, I lose the best friend I'll ever h-h-ave," she sobs.

"You lost your best friend?"

"Zippity," she cries. "I sold her down the river!"

"What are you talking about?"

"My cab! The old one. The Caddy. Oh, Zippity," she wails, leaning her forehead on the steering wheel in sorrow. The car momentarily swerves over the line, eliciting a "Watch it!" yelp from Hal.

She swings back into her lane, and tearfully resumes: "What was I thinking? So she was getting old. So what? She was loyal, faithful, never looked for trouble. Even her mileage wasn't terrible. Considering. And then I *dumped* her," she concludes, her voice collapsing.

"Turn here," Hal says.

She takes a sharp 90 degree, throwing Hal once again into the door and banging his leg against the side. "You think I could get her back?" she asks over his howl of complaint.

"Holy shit! Would you calm down?"

She turns and gives him a lugubrious stare. "You don't even care, do you?"

"Left at the next corner."

"Have you ever lost anything that meant something to you?" she asks as they approach the curving driveway of his condo.

"Here! We're here!" he yells. "Stop!" But Zoe doesn't. They sail right past the valet whose arm is still outstretched in door-opening position. She exits the driveway and heads north.

"Maybe you'd understand if you had real feelings," Zoe says. "Maybe you wouldn't be so mean."

"Mean? I'm not mean!" Hal grips the dashboard as she abruptly changes lanes. "I just want to go home."

"What do I have to go home to?" she asks. "Nothing! Nobody!"

Hal hunches down and stares out the window.

"Know what I do when I get home?" she continues. "First I pee. Then I look for something to eat. Chicken leg, Pop Tart. I turn on the TV. I sit at the counter. I eat the leg. I eat the Tart. I watch more TV. I shower. I brush my teeth. Maybe I floss. I watch Trevor Noah. I go to sleep. That's it. That's my life."

They ride in silence for several blocks. "Can I go home now?" Hal asks.

Zoe sighs and, energy dispelled, makes a sudden U-turn. "Hot date tonight?" she asks.

"No. No hot date." He pauses. "Okay. Here's what I'm doing when I get home tonight. First I'll pee. Then I'll look in the fridge for something to eat. No chicken leg, no Pop Tart. Maybe a piece of leftover brisket my mother sent me home with last week. I'll check my email. I'll shower, brush my teeth, maybe floss. I'll watch Stephen Colbert till I fall asleep." He looks at her. "That's it. That's my life."

Zoe huffs a derisive laugh. "Yeah, sure."

"Okay, so I lied about the flossing part." After a few minutes' silence, he says, "Look, I'm sorry about today. My father and all. It wasn't your fault." He rubs his eyes with the heels of his hands. "They just make me crazy. They're nuts, I'm nuts, we're all nuts." He looks up and laughs ruefully, and it's then that Zoe notices he's got a nice smile, a little lopsided, and that his eyes crinkle up kind of like Albert's did before he started wearing glasses.

"We all get a little nutty sometimes," she agrees.

"Unfortunately, my folks are nuttier than most."

"No, they're not. They're just..." She searches for a diplomatic way of putting it. "...old."

"They were like this when they were young. Now they're just distilled versions of who they were. Boiled down to their essence." He takes a deep breath. "I know it's hard to put up with their crap. I just want you to know I appreciate it. And I'm sorry about your car and all."

The magic word. *Sorry.* Something inside of Zoe melts like a Popsicle in a microwave. She sees Hal's condo up ahead and slows to a crawl. "Sometimes I just wish I could rewind and start over," she says. "Like today with your Dad. Or what I did to Zippity, just dumping her like that. I feel like I lost something really important and it's all my fault." With unusual caution, Zoe steers the car up the entrance ramp to Hal's condo. "Okey dokey," she announces with attempted cheer. "Home again. Go pee." When he doesn't move, she asks, "You need some help getting out?"

"No. No, I'm okay." He hesitates. "Want to come up? I've got some brisket in the fridge."

"Uh." She's taken off-balance. "Well, yeah, well, I don't know. It's kinda been a long day, so..."

"Sure." Hal opens the door and extricates himself awkwardly. "Listen, for what it's worth, here's what I think. You want your old cab back? Go and get it."

"How can I do that? It's gone," she says, her voice both mournful and hopeful.

"Nothing's ever really gone. Not if you want it badly enough."

She watches through the glass doors as Hal clumps through the lobby on his walking cast and waits for the elevator. She feels a surge of affection for him in his vulnerability. Maybe she should have gone up. But then what? He's good looking, a real charmer, a bad boy—she always fell for the bad boys. Trouble. She doesn't need more trouble. He turns and gives her a wave before he gets on the elevator. And then he's gone.

But Zippity may not be. Maybe what Hal said is true. Maybe nothing's ever really gone. Not if you want it badly enough.

* * *

Zoe creeps through the aisles of the dealership's used car lot in a Groucho Marx crouch, knees bent, shoulders hunched as she looks for Zippity One. Dull cousins of the shiny new cars inside the dealership, the "pre-owned" cars crowd together in their segregated lot like Tootsie Pops that have been licked and thrown away. With colors a little off and dents poorly disguised, they seem to struggle to maintain their dignity. Blindfolded by signs plastered across their windshields proclaiming their bargain status, they are the prisoners of rejection.

Zoe can't find Zippity anywhere in the lot. She must have been sold. Gone forever, that sweet pink confection, that faithful companion, that dear and comfy cab. Zoe puts her head on her knees and weeps. She hopes Zippity has a good home. That she's swept clean daily and fed high-test gas and taken to an honest car wash, not those high school fund-raising things with scummy water and harsh detergents. Oh, Zippity, where are you now?

A tangerine sun nests low on the horizon in a pile of pink and purple clouds. As darkness descends in an indigo stain, an arc of overhead lights pops on in the lot. Their paparazzi suddenness startles Zoe and she drops into frog position between a 2010 Ford and a 2013 Subaru.

She hears footsteps, looks under the Ford and sees the Teva sandals of a couple scouting out cars the next aisle over, followed by a pair of brown wing-tips. Is that her salesman? She's got to escape. She scuttles between aisles until she's out, then takes off on a run, short-cutting through another lot: the employees' parking lot, bristling with late-model BMWs.

With one exception: a spiffy, candy-apple-red, polished-chrome, perfectly restored 1959 Cadillac Sedan Deville.

Zoe screeches to a halt. Backtracks to the Caddy. Walks around it, studies it inside and out. Tentatively, she touches its shiny red hood, unblemished and pristine. But Zoe's fingertips sense something else, something deeper and darker beneath the surface––a ghostly indentation, damage beyond the repair of the most costly restoration, a scar that never healed completely.

"Zippity," she whispers. "Is it you?"

Zippity glitters coldly beneath the arcing lights, a beautiful but silent rebuke to Zoe's folly. Zoe flings herself in repentance across the shiny hood. Her tears bead on the glossy finish.

"What in the hell are you doing?" booms a voice that's frighteningly familiar. "Holy cow, it's you," the salesman says. He grabs her leg and yanks her to the ground. "Get off my car!"

"What have you done to my Zippity?" she wails. "You've ruined her."

The salesman takes his sleeve and polishes the smeared area where Zoe had blubbered. "It's my car now. Get out of here before I call the cops." He rubs the spot with increasing frenzy but little success. "Look what you made me do. It's losing its gleam."

"I want Zippity back!" Zoe flings herself once more onto the hood. "She's *mine.*"

The salesman lunges for Zoe, but this time she's taking him with her. She grabs his oatmeal-raisin-textured tie and they tumble across the hood where Zoe pins him with her knees. "I'll trade you my new BMW, even steven, no questions asked," she offers.

"Are you out of your mind?" With a mighty heave, he throws her off. She bounces hard onto the car on her butt. She can feel the hood, fragile from its history of injuries and repairs, bend beneath her. Aghast that her beloved Zippity has once again been pummeled, fearful that this time it could be fatal, she allows the salesman to escape. He runs to the Caddy's door, fumbles with his key and shuts himself inside.

Click goes the door lock. *Clack* goes the ignition.

Clack clack.

He cranks it again. *Clack.* And again, *clack.*

Zippity refuses to start.

The salesman punctuates his curses by repeatedly pounding his head on the steering wheel. He takes a break and gives Zoe a long, evil stare through the windshield. She is too distraught to notice; her attention is focused on the crater she has hammered into Zippity's shiny hood. Her dismay turns to anger at the salesman.

"Look what you did," she accuses, pointing to the hood's newly concave shape. "It's all your fault."

"My fault?" He throws open the door. A fellow salesman leaving work looks away, scurries to his own BMW and climbs in quickly, surveying the scene through his rear view mirror as he safely exits the lot.

Zoe senses an advantage. The salesman has no allies. This disaster might be opportunity in disguise.

"Okay, here's the deal," she begins, backing him against the door. "Zippity won't run for you, so you know where her loyalty lies."

Silence from the salesman.

"That bit of hood damage will cost you lots to fix now, right?"

He shrugs.

"And that lemon you sold me cost me a lot of money, which made *you* a lot of money, right?" She closes in on his sullen face with her own. "So listen up. I'm making you a one-time offer, today only: One slightly pre-owned lemon in exchange for one battered but loyal old Caddy. Deal?"

"The lemon is *pink*!" he protests.

"So paint it. Paint it red, like you painted my Zippity. Paint it purple, paint it puce, I don't give a shit what color you paint it. Just take it and give me back my car."

"Why would I...?"

"Because if you do, you'll never see me again."

Zoe and the salesman lock eyes. She stares into the dead space of his widening pupils. "Never?" he asks tremulously.

"Yes."

"Swear on the life of this car."

"I swear to Zippity. You'll never see me again."

"Okay," says the salesman. "In that case, it's a deal."

* * *

Boyd is dazzled. "That's a classic," he says when Zoe shows up with Zippity for a little hood repair work. "Where'd you get her?"

"It's Zippity––don't you recognize her?" Zoe says. "She's had a facelift, but underneath it all, she's the same old Zippity Cab."

"Get outta here." Boyd circles the car slowly, taking in the candy-apple paint job, the meticulous upholstery work, the bright silver grin of the grille. "I wouldn'ta recognized her. She's pretty slick." He examines the bashed-in hood with Vienna sausage fingers. "What happened here? Another crazy old lady attack your car?"

Zoe doesn't feel like explaining her role in Zippity's most recent demolition. "Something like that."

"I dunno if I can match that paint." He scratches his belly through a convenient hole in his Nascar T-shirt. "Looks like a custom job, specially mixed. I can come pretty close, though."

"I don't want you to match it. I want it painted pink, the same color you painted the BMW, with "Zippity Cab" in turquoise letters. Like it used to be."

"You wanna cover this beauty up?" Boyd says, his voice rising in disbelief. "With *pink*? Why would you wanna do that?"

"Because pink is who she really is."

Boyd's pumpkin face softens with lust as he strokes the curve of a crimson fender. "But this is who she *was*, when she was new."

"Well, she's not new any more. She's better. She's got character."

"Character," Boyd repeats. He shakes his head in resignation. "Okay, you're the boss."

"You bet." She turns to go but stops and places her hand on his shoulder. "Oh, one more thing. I need something else from you."

He looks at her hopefully, and jerks his thumb toward his back office. "Are we thinking the same thing?"

"Order me some zebra-skin seat covers."

CHAPTER XI

HAL

"I love a loophole," Milo announces. His eyes are glassy from the eucalyptus oxygen he just inhaled through a tube connected to one of many flavored-air scents offered in glass vials. He lifts a chocolate martini from a tray offered by a bird-boned waiter dressed in neck-to-toe black, and gazes happily at the party-goers who swirl around them, agog over the free goodies abounding at the pro-motional festivities showcasing the model and plans for Fantabulissimo, Milo's condo project.

"Let's not discuss that here," Hal says, uneasy at Milo's loose-lipped expan-siveness, triggered not by his inhalation of oxygen but by a more potent sub-stance which Hal had watched disappear up Milo's nostrils in the men's room.

"If not for loopholes, we wouldn't be here," Milo says, ignoring Hal's plea. "It's like old times again, those happy days when we pulled off these classy pre-sentations all the time." He raises the martini glass high in a toast. "To loop-holes," he cries before gulping the martini down, leaving himself a little chocolate mustache. Hal lunges for a passing tray of hors d'oeuvres in an at-tempt to disengage from Milo's manic good cheer, but the tray is quickly emp-tied by hands much quicker than his, hands bedecked with rings of diamonds and emeralds, hands smooth and veinless and spot-free, the hands of youth and money.

These are the new breed of high-end real estate-crazed crowds that Milo has lured with food, drink and flavored air to ooh and ahh over elaborate mock-ups of high-tech kitchens and sleek granite baths. Their numbers once dwindled along with the economy, but there were those whom the plunge hadn't touched––the fortunate few who could continue to feed their cravings for the biggest, the newest, and the best. Now, with the surge in Miami's building boom, the competition is fierce among developers to attract the 1% in this new market, augmented by the new crop of buyers from Russia, China, Saudi Arabia and Brazil. Milo has staked his future on Fantabulissimo's being, with Hal's help, the best of the biggest and the newest.

Along the walls of the room are framed computer-generated illustrations promising what life will be like in this fantasy: endless views of sapphire sea and sky; cocktails served on a balcony populated by stone-faced models; a dip in an infinity pool that gleams with the peachy reflection of sunset. And in the center of the party room, spotlighted in its glass-walled cage, is a scale model of the condo-to-be itself: Fantabulissimo.

Hal weaves through the glittery throng to examine the model, a perfect miniaturized replication of the condo's three proposed towers: teeny trees, tiny balconies, teeny tiny people, itsy bitsy umbrellas around three beensy bintsy pools. Soon these mini glass-walled towers will become maxi reality, perched in grandiose splendor upon the acres of land on which the Louis Quinze now stands. A nauseating wave of regret unrelated to his recent ingestion of a pastry filled with some kind of green meat sweeps over Hal.

Hal stares at the model and sees, instead, the Louis Quinze. He shrinks himself to six years old, imagines himself by the pool. He's wearing the puffy orange lifejacket Tootsie makes him wear because he can't swim yet. He dangles his feet in the water, willing the hour she makes him wait after eating his hot dog to pass quickly so he can jump into the pool again. Every day he does this. Every day he swims in the pool, eats a hot dog in the coffee shop, rides up and down, up and down the elevator. This is where he lives, in the penthouse apartment of his daddy's hotel, high on the top floor where he can see all the way down the beach from their balcony.

Hal sees his little sunburned self playing on the beach. He packs wet sand into his bucket, carefully turns it upside down until he has a row of flat-topped cones of sand. These are his army men. Each attempt is better than the last, until the last one reaches perfection: brown as toast, smooth as concrete, not a nick or a crack to be found. This will be the army men's castle. He gingerly presses tiny shells into its side for windows, then tops it with a seaweed flag.

But then the surf arrives with the incoming tide. It churns with white-frothed anger, attacks the row of army men, nibbles at their squat solidity until they finally surrender, crumbling and sinking into the maw of the sea. The castle is next, collapsing into a sliding mush. Sated, the surf creeps back into itself. The place where the castle with its proud army men once stood is as flat and shiny as glass.

"Pretty slick, huh?" Milo's voice jars Hal back to the present, back to the dazzling miniature towers of Fantabulissimo. "That's some knockout presentation the architects put together, right? Impresses the Russians—thank God for the Russians! We've already got a bunch of signups that look like sure sales." Milo points to the model. "They said it wouldn't be a problem to alter the model once you get the height allowance changed. Just stack on another twenty floors. No problemo."

Loophole, loophole, loophole. Hal doesn't need reminding that he needs to come up with a loophole to resolve the height thing with the city planning board. He doesn't want to think about that now. He doesn't even want to think about the reason he's doing this in the first place. Does he really want to be mayor that badly?

He wants to go lie down somewhere. Just smoke a joint, lie down and pull a blanket over his head. He wants to think happy thoughts. He doesn't want to think about what he's done or what he's got to do or what Max will do with his anger when he finds out Hal had a hand in this, because he *will* find out. And when he does, Max will crawl under his quilt like he did before, only this time he may never come out. Hal will be under his blanket, Max will be under his quilt, and people will say this compulsion to burrow when stressed must be genetic.

"Hey." Milo waves his hand in front of Hal's face. "Anybody home?"

Hal blinks. Milo comes into focus.

"I want you to meet someone," Milo says. A large form in Hal's peripheral vision moves closer, a boulder in a bow tie. "This is Carlos."

Hal's hand is grabbed and sandwiched between two immense, damp paws. "Carlos Cruz," booms their owner with a hearty shake, "contractor to the stars."

"Carlos is my general contractor," Milo explains. "I want you to meet him since he's helping you in the campaign."

"Helping me?" Hal says, flexing his battered hand. "How's that?"

"*Helping* you," Milo emphasizes. His right eye twitches in an attempt at a wink. "You know."

"Mister Mayor," Carlos says. "Your Honor."

Caramba. Now it begins. "Listen," Hal says to Milo. "We need to talk."

"Nothing to talk about," Milo says. He reaches up to clap a friendly hand on Carlos's beefy shoulder. "It's a done deal."

"It's my pleasure," Carlos says, his grin exposing small teeth set into a vast expanse of gums. "The pleasure is all mine."

"I appreciate that, but something has come up. Your help may not be needed." Hal fixes Milo with a stare. "I need to talk to you."

"You heard the man," Milo says. "It's his pleasure."

"Pleasure or not, I need to talk to you. Now." Fearing another knuckle-crusher, Hal nods to Carlos but keeps his hands in his pockets. "Nice meeting you. I appreciate the offer. It's good of you. But I don't think it's going to be necessary." He tips his head in the direction of the door. "Meet me downstairs in the lobby," he says to Milo. "We can't talk here."

Milo doesn't appear for fifteen minutes, and when he does he's wiping his nose with a crumpled linen handkerchief that he stuffs irritably into his pants pocket. "Okay okay, what's the problem, you got a problem, I don't see any problem," he says, his voice more highly pitched than usual. "That was pretty rude, what you said to Carlos."

"What's Carlos got to do with me?" Hal asks, even though he knew from the start that at some point the abstract idea of payoff would become hard cold reality. And here it was, in the flesh: Carlos.

"Do I hafta spell it out for you? I told you people want to help you out. You know, you scratch my back and all that crap. He just wants to scratch my back."

"And you'll scratch his? And I'll scratch yours?" Hal is so tired, so tired. He needs a nap. "Listen. I'm thinking I don't want to get any more involved in this than I already am. I don't like being associated with the historic designation being changed. Bad enough that I've made enough enemies, doing stuff for you, but we're talking about my dad's hotel here. I *lived* there, for God's sake."

"We all gotta live somewhere." Milo says. "So what?"

"It's not worth it. I can't sleep. I..."

"Too late. Too late. You're in it up to your eyeballs." Milo pinches his nostrils together and sighs. "Look. This is going to work. You saw the model, you saw the crowd, this is too good to fuck up now. And am I asking so much? You know what you're doing, you've done it before. And that was terrific, great work. I commend you. I really commend you."

Hal doesn't want to be commended. No commending. He wants to rewind his agreement, forget about his promise, eliminate his role in the whole thing. Whatever happens to the Louis Quinze is going to happen one way or the other. He just doesn't want to help it happen.

But Milo sinks his sharp little gerbil teeth into Hal's reasoning. "I'm telling you it's a done deal, and so it is. I went to a lot of trouble to make the arrangements. You think it didn't take balls for me to get Carlos in on this deal? What, you think he jumped in right away, happy as a pig in shit to take me up on my offer?"

Pig in shit? An appropriate phrase, Hal thinks.

"But no," Milo continues. "*I'm* willing to take chances just so I can help you out. So I call up Carlos, remind him I'm paying him $80 million to build this project for me. I tell him Hal Wolfe is a terrific guy, he'll be a terrific mayor, and wouldn't it be great if you, your company and your company's employees each contributed $500 to his campaign for mayor? Just a suggestion."

Oh, what a clever guy Milo is, Hal concedes. Since it's illegal for one person to contribute more than $500 to a candidate, the sneaky little rodent works it out this way: blackmailing his compatriots. Who concede. With great pleasure.

Milo's not finished yet. "What's he gonna do? Tell me No? And neither did my comptroller. So I call him up, ask him how many limited partnerships and entities do we have. He says fifty or so. So I suggest that he might want to cut a check from each of them to give to that really terrific candidate for mayor, Hal Wolfe."

"Done deal," Hal says. He leans against the marble wall of the lobby. It's cold and hard against his back, sending a bolt of frozen lightening to the base of his skull.

"Done," agrees Milo. "Except for that last little bit of business you have to take care of." He grins. "Just another loophole."

The height requirement change. He's done it before, so this should be a piece of cake. And then. And then.

He could get what he wants.

But does he really *want* to be mayor?

* * *

Max has seemed to be in better spirits lately. Hal attributes that to Max's re-lief at the resuscitation of Zoe's old cab, the sight of which eased Max's first slide into the newly zebra-covered back seat. Hal is equally relieved, because now that he's driving once again, he was afraid that he'd become Max's desig-nated driver if Max refused to ride with Zoe. Max now goes without complaint to his appointments––actually seems to look forward to them, dressed and waiting impatiently long before the buzzer announces that Zoe is downstairs to pick him up. And when he comes home, he's in a reasonably good mood until he turns on the news and goes ballistic.

Hal toys with the idea of breaking his own news to Max before he hears it somewhere else, putting a spin on the upcoming demolition so it sounds like *good* news.

Hey, Pop, he'll say. You'll appreciate this. They're going to build the biggest, tallest, most magnificent condo on the best piece of property on the Beach. The *best*. You always said so yourself, and you know what? You were *right*.

Where's that? Max will say.

And Hal will say...what can he say?

New scenario: Hey, Pop. I know how you feel about the Louis Quinze. Listen, I feel the same way, I really do. I have great memories. But it's falling apart, it really is, and it's had its day, it really has, and...guess what? I'm running for mayor!

No. Better to tell him after the fact: Hey, Pop. Guess what? I *am* the mayor.

Right now, that's the only good reason he can think of for running: to balance the destruction of what Max considers his monument with the possibility of making Max proud of him for the first time in his life.

Well, he can't bail out now; he's already scheduled a meeting with the city planning board regarding the height thing. The mechanism has been set in motion, and he's the only one dragging ass. He's committed, the ball is rolling, it's picking up momentum and has a life of its own. He's running for mayor, like it or not, and he'd better get pumped for the first campaign event next week: a serious wooing of the Hispanic community at its very core: the Versailles restaurant in Little Havana. A media event coordinated by his newly-appointed campaign manager, Jorge Delgado, one of Milo's connections, it's going to be a blow-out: TV, Spanish radio, the appearance of a couple of *telenovela* stars he's never heard of. There is even talk of roasting a pig.

After his accident, Hal had dropped the ball on Staci and her *Maxim* Girl interview. Well, not dropped the ball. He had never really picked it up. All his calls to his *Maxim* contact were never returned, sinking him even deeper into the depressive acknowledgment that he was a nobody to anybody, even someone he did a real favor for, that bastard. And then the accident...well, he had other things on his mind. Out of guilt, he gathered his nerve and called her at Hot Tamale to see how she survived being left in the clutches of her Papi, to explain his not getting in touch because of his accident, and to break the news that the *Maxim* thing was, um, not to be.

Staci seemed more surprised that he had called than at the dismal news about *Maxim*. "I figured," she said, sounding despondent. "I'm just trying to decide what to do for the rest of my life." Her voice dropped to a whisper. "I moved out. I'm living with my sister Alicia till I get a better job and can afford my own place."

"Moved out? That was gutsy. Good for you."

"Yeah, I guess it was time. Papi's pretty unforgiving." She paused. "You know he trained with Alpha 66 decades ago."

Hoo boy, Hal thought. Alpha 66. A bunch of old guys in a faded counter-revolutionary militia of exiles-in-arms who dreamed of invading what was once their homeland to take it back.

"Yeah. It's a good thing you left my house when you did. Papi might have turned all those years of frustrated revenge into a shotgun blast at you."

"Me? Why?"

"Oh, lots of reasons. The lingerie. The Harley. And he hates politicians."

"Well, I'm still planning on running for mayor," he said. "Let him chew on that."

"At least you've got plans," Staci said. "More than I have. I may be stuck here forever, the oldest living barmaid in Hot Tamale's history."

Hal had no response to that, since he had no solution. Until one possibility popped up, one he had never considered until this moment, one that might assuage his guilt for not making *Maxim* happen for her. "You know, one of my first campaign efforts is going to be an event next month in Little Havana." He paused. "Would you like to come along?"

"Why would I want to do that?"

"You can tell how bad my Spanish is. I need someone to interpret for me. I'd rather have an attractive girl like you than some guy. To make sure the crowd pays attention and all."

"I don't know. I'm not a professional interpreter."

"Doesn't matter. You'd be an informal one. But we'd pay you."

"Pay? Like money?"

"It would be fun for you! You'd get to meet some important people. Who knows where that could lead?"

The clatter and chatter of bar noises filled Staci's momentary silence. And then Staci's voice: "*¡Sí! ¿Quién sabe?* I'll do it."

* * *

Replicating its mirrored namesake in humble but sincere homage, Versailles restaurant, its brave little rooftop finials reaching for the sky, rises from its surroundings: the storefront clutter of pawn shops, botanicas, cafeterias and gas stations that shoulder each other for sidewalk space along traffic-clogged Calle Ocho. Despite the proliferation of rival establishments of equally stupendous decor, Versailles remains above it all.

Inside, the crowd seems bigger than it really is, multiplied in Versailles' maze of mirrored walls into an infinity of faceted faces, glittering in the harsh light reflected and reflected and reflected again until there is no distinction between the real people and their mirrored clones. As the crowd grows, the conversational buzz heightens into raucous exchanges punctuated by laughter. Spanish is the spoken tongue here, the mother tongue in this mother of all Cuban restaurants, an established, time-honored culinary magnet for politician and peon alike.

Tonight, the parking lot is packed, filled with late-model German and Japanese sedans, their owners headed for the private reception inside. It's an open bar night, a free-food-and-booze night, a night for Hal to gather his deep-pocketed Hispanic compatriots to his bosom—a bosom which, not incidentally, is fashionably attired Cuban-style in a custom-tailored, multiple-pocketed, finely pleated linen *guayabera*. Hal feels foolish—an imposter, a fraud––wearing the shirt, but Jorge, his campaign manager, convinced him that he needed to ditch the coat-and-tie bit if he wanted this group to contribute *mucho dinero* to his mayoral cause. Hal, however, feels no shame in bridging the cultural divide by having Staci, with her fluent Spanish and impressive hooters, by his side. *Au contraire*, in the language of the original Versailles, Hal beams with pleasure as she interprets his words in a rapid, musical cadence that flows from her tangerine lips, then reverses course to interpret the response into English.

Staci looks respectably sexy in the tailored but low-cut suit Jorge's wife picked out for her, overriding her own flounced and flowered choice, a dress designed for salsa dancing in a South Beach club. Something has changed in Staci that goes beyond her now-serious appearance. Today her confidence has crystallized: Hal realizes she's doing more than just interpreting; she's evolving from girl to woman with each hand-shaking, cheek-kissing circle they make of the room.

Jorge steers them with Gucci-suited arms toward the media lineup of local TV cameras and Spanish-radio mikes. The first words of introduction by a state senator who owes Jorge a big-time favor are drowned out by the parrot shriek of a malfunctioning microphone; the startled senator overcompensates with a tedious, painfully complimentary introduction that threatens to go on until the open bar runs out. This only accelerates Hal's antsiness to just get it over with.

He has prepared his speech, with Staci's help, in Spanish as well as English, and leaps into the English version with the false gusto of someone who has discovered that the diving board is a lot higher from here than it looked from the ground. He wraps up the English portion, segueing in the next breath into the Spanish version. He begins hesitantly, unsure of his pronunciation despite the two years of Spanish he took in college and sporadic politically motivated Berlitz-class attempts to master a language that has so far eluded him beyond the basics. Up to now, the basics have served him well enough to get by in political settings that don't involve fluency in Spanish. Here, where it matters, he needs Staci, who is performing beyond his expectations, as well as looking hot.

Hal recognizes several faces in the Milo/Jorge-accrued crowd, faces of cronies, hangers-on, and a few members of the group he most needs for support: the Latin Builders Association. Carlos Cruz, Milo's contractor, hulks in a corner, munching on a cheek-puffing something from the nearby buffet. Aside from the split-face-grins of ardent supporters, many of the faces are folded into expressions of skepticism and––he doesn't want to think it—suspicion. He amps up the charm, hoping body language will make up for his language deficiency; he waves his arms in great Latino swoops, flashes his killer smile, then, receiving no reassuring response, turns to Staci and gestures in what he hopes is a winningly helpless shrug.

To his great relief, Staci saves his Anglo ass. "What Señor Wolfe would like to express to you all," she says in Spanish, "is how happy he is to be here with such a distinguished group of people who represent the Hispanic way of life he so admires." She tosses her blonde hair, flashes her tangerine smile, and adds, "He hopes you enjoy the food and drink, and that with each delicious bite, you'll think of him...then write a check."

Hal isn't quite sure what she's saying until she interprets her own words, but he is deeply gratified by the response, a solid round of applause which, he suspects, is more for Staci than for him. Impulsive in his gratitude, he thanks her profusely, introduces her to the crowd, then plants a big kiss on her cheek, a gesture that momentarily stiffens Staci's posture and freezes her smile. But then she's back in sync, very media-aware at this point and playing right to it. She whispers into his ear Spanish words: thanks for their support and the hope that he'll make them proud if elected, which he then parrots into the bouquet of Spanish radio microphones blooming before them.

More applause, and the crowd heads back to the bar and buffet like a moveable beast intent on devouring freebies. Several people break off from the group to cluster around Hal, shake his hand and ogle Staci, who is beaming as if she hatched him. That's fine with Hal. She has become his biggest asset, and he's only too happy to acknowledge that and collect the checks that are inspired by her presence.

The salsa ringtone from her cell, barely audible above the crowd noise, catches Staci's attention. She detaches herself from Hal and, hand over one ear, heads outside to talk. She returns moments later, her upbeat cheerfulness replaced by wide-eyed panic. She gestures wildly at Hal, who waves happily back, misinterpreting her mania for glee. But it is not glee that animates Staci's features; it is terror, and her words confirm it: "My father's on his way here."

Hal momentarily blanks out at that news. *Great,* the dull part of his brain says, *he's coming to support me.* Then, *uh oh,* says the reality-check part, *he's coming to kill me.* This thought is shared by Staci, who verifies it with the statement, "He says he wants to kill you," a direct quote passed on by her sister Alicia, who had just called with that information. Apparently their father had been listening to WQBA's news coverage of the Versailles event, and, upon hearing the name and voice of his estranged daughter, called Alicia and demanded to know Staci's whereabouts. Which is where he's headed, right about now.

"Keep him away from me," Hal says to Staci.

"Keep him away from you? It was hard enough keeping him away from Castro."

"Castro wasn't in the same room as your father. I will be. Keep him out."

"You don't know my father," she says, grabbing the sleeve of his *guayabera* in an attempt to steer him toward the exit.

Too late. Hal knows that the Red Sea-parting of the crowd is for her father, a churning tornado of a man, small in stature, broad of shoulder, wide of neck, red-faced, bald-headed and dressed for battle in a Radio Mambi T-shirt. "*¿Donde esta?*" he is shouting, and the crowd divides to give him a straight shot at Hal, whose Donald J. Pliner loafers feel velcroed to the tile floor. Staci is equally immobile, her features melting as her father, shaking his fist, storms headfirst through the last remaining admirers until he is almost standing on Hal's loafers, his furious face level with the pockets of Hal's *guayabera.* His snow-white mustache resembles those in the "Got Milk?" ads. Hal focuses on it as it twitches above a mouth that is spewing words he cannot understand.

"What's he saying?" Hal asks, eyes darting toward Staci. He gathers that whatever it is, it's not good, since the words are accompanied by fine sprays of saliva that Hal is reluctant to wipe off his shirt for fear of instigating the man even further.

"He's saying, 'Stay away from my daughter, you bastard son-of-a-bitch, or I will keep you away permanently!'" Staci dutifully interprets.

"Permanently? Is that a threat?" Hal asks him. "Are you threatening me?"

Staci's father looks quizzically at Staci. "*¿Que?*" he asks her.

"*El dice '¿Tú me estás amenazando?'*" she interprets.

"*¡Si!*" her father shouts. Tiny beads of sweat are surfacing on his nose. "*Permanente. Muerte.*" He draws his hand across his throat. The tip of one finger is missing. Hal wonders why.

"Papi!" Staci pleads, her hand on his arm. "*No hagas eso, por favor. No hagas una escena dramática, no me amenazes. Vete a casa. Nosotros podríamos hablar después.*"

"*No hay nada más que hablar,*" he says, nudging her aside. "*¿Y tú estás trabajando por él? Tú eres un desgraciad. El te está embarazoso mi y a toda tu familia.*" He crouches into attack position, bracing himself on sinewy legs that emerge from wide knee-length shorts. "*¡Pelea como un hombre!*"

"What? What's he saying?" Hal asks, backing off.

"He says to fight like a man," Staci interprets.

"I *am* a man. I don't *want* to fight." Hal's attention flickers to the onlookers who have given them wide berth. He sees Milo and Jorge pushing through the crowd, but before they reach him, her father punches Hal in the gut.

Hal gasps, clutching the front of his *guayabera,* and then is punched again, this time on the chin. Her father assumes a boxer's stance in preparation for the next blow, but is grabbed from behind by Jorge, whose surprise when elbowed in the stomach in response is expressed by a very loud "Oooof!"

"Get him!" Milo shouts, leaping wildly about, but Jorge does not since he is temporarily without enough breath left to get anyone. Milo continues his frantic dance around the participants, but does not join in.

"Papi, Papi, stop, stop!" Staci cries, but her Papi does not stop, he just keeps pummeling whomever is within range, including a hapless waiter carrying a tray of glasses who inadvertently has joined in the fray in a failed attempt to detour the scene. The tray goes flying and red wine rains down upon the scuffling threesome. The upwardly propelled glasses twinkle and glimmer, sparkle and shine, their mirrored reflections a dazzling infinity of toasts until they reach their apex, then aim for the tile floor, exploding in a splintering crash. A crystalline spray of shards sends the onlookers scattering, leaving an abstract design of red and purple splattered across the floor.

"Blood!" Hal moans, staring at the magenta-stained front of his *guayabera*. "I'm bleeding!" He feels faint. A flashback to the accident plays across his vision. Blood. Pain. Trauma. His knees begin to buckle. He's caught by Jorge, who attempts to drag him away from the melee with the reassurance, "It's just wine. Come on, let's get out of here." But Jorge, decked from behind by an unseen assailant, suddenly disappears into a dazed heap on the floor, and Hal feels short but sturdy arms grappling him from behind. He turns as a fist belonging to Staci's father plants itself on his nose. Hal reels back in shock, puts a hand to his face. Now he's really bleeding.

Staci pulls her father away from Hal. Help has arrived: Fire Rescue. Police. TV cameras.

Fire Rescue, realizing it's just another false alarm triggered by an avalanche of 911 calls by cellphone-gripping bystanders, leaves first. The police leave next, encouraged to do so by several of the more influential patrons of this gathering who easily convince the jaded officers that there are more pressing problems out there.

The TV camera stays.

It focuses on Staci's sputtering father as he is steered away from the melee by his daughter Alicia's husband, who has come to the rescue. It focuses on Staci who, responding to Papi's accusations with new-found pride, announces that she has a career now and she's *never* coming home. Then it focuses on Hal who glares into its lens above the blood-soaked napkin he is holding to his nose. The camera pulls back to take in Milo's efforts to escape unobtrusively but unsuccessfully, having been blocked by his contractor, Carlos, who apparently needs a frantic word with his boss. Jorge has evidently resigned his post as campaign manager, according to the hasty statement he is making to Renaldo Cohen, the channel 7 newsman who, mike in hand, has appeared on the scene. When Hal spots Gomez, the investigative reporter from the *Herald* who Milo had assured him months ago had dropped off his trail, he knows that his political aspirations, as well as life as he knew it, is doomed.

It's Friday night, and he's not invited to dinner. The invitation, instead, is a command from Tootsie: "Get your *tuchis* over here. I can't do anything with him. He's going *meshugge* watching the news all day long like it's going to explain what's going on with you. Now *you* have to explain. What's going on with you?"

What's going on with him? You mean aside from the broken nose, the ensuing black eyes, the pain in his gut and the fact that his life has been put through a shredder?

"I don't want to talk about it."

"So don't talk about it. The TV is doing the talking. It's saying goodbye Louis Quinze! Since when did you have to stick your nose in that business? And mayor? You have to run for mayor? What is that? What's with the fighting? What's with the girl? What's with..."

Hal hears a crash. "Wait," Tootsie says, and she's gone. He hears a series of thunks as the phone bounces from its curly cord, then Max yelling, "That crook, that Milo guy, what's Hal doing mixed up with him?" Hal can hear their TV faintly in the background echoing the news from his own TV. Bad news, news that isn't good, news that's been bad all day. Like a voyeur passing the scene of an accident, Hal can't stop himself from looking even though the same scene has been broadcast on the morning, noon, 5:00 and now 6:00 news. He's even on YouTube, thanks to the multiple cellphone cameras whipped out to record the fight as it happened, right down to the punch to his nose. This morning's *Herald* carried a brief recounting of the event, but the investigative story—the first in a series, apparently––for which he gave a reluctant and evasive interview today, is coming out tomorrow.

He looks over at his TV screen. There he is again, napkin to nose, staring viciously at the camera. Cut to Milo and Carlos, seeming to wrestle. Cut to Staci and her father, shouting. Last shot: an aerial view of the Louis Quinze. He's memorized the voiceover by now: *A campaign kickoff for Miami Beach mayoral candidate Hal Wolfe ended in chaos last night at Versailles restaurant. Pepe Mateo, the father of Wolfe's interpreter Staci Mateo, stormed the gathering to protest Wolfe's candidacy and relationship with his daughter. Caught up in the bloody melee were developer Milo Minkoff and his contractor, Carlos Cruz. Cruz's financial backing of Wolfe has raised questions about his connection with their latest condo project, Fantabulissimo, to be constructed on the site of the historic but soon-to-be demolished Louis Quinze hotel in Miami Beach. In light of the escalation of controversy over Wolfe's influence concerning the override of historic designation for the hotel, as well as his prospective role in regard to the height*

*limits of the planned condo, Wolfe's campaign manager, Jorge Delgado, has an-
nounced that Wolfe will withdraw from the race.*

Tootsie is back on the line. "He threw his bowl of peanuts at the TV," she
reports. "Peanuts. All over the rug. Right after I ran the carpet sweeper. Next
thing you know he'll throw the TV! You have to get over here. Talk to him. Tell
him it's not what it looks like." She pauses. "Is it?"

What does it look like? He's not sure he cares right now. The pain in his
nose is taking priority, having increased as the Percocet wore off. What was just
an ominous discomfort fifteen minutes ago has escalated into a white-hot poker
snaking through his nasal passages. He gingerly pats the bandage his plastic surgeon placed over his efforts to re-shape the porridge of bone and cartilage into
what Hal hopes will be an reasonable replica of his former nose. He flashes
onto the moment of contact between it and Staci's Papi's fist. His brain replays
that moment over and over, and still it insists on going into rerun despite his
fervent wish to delete it forever.

He doesn't want to go to Tootsie and Max's, but he senses disaster if he
doesn't, so he will. But first, he needs a toke or two. Or maybe eight or ten.

Max is out of sight when Hal arrives. "He's in the bathroom," Tootsie informs him. "He may not come out." Her anger manifests itself in her offering
of food. Not brisket. Not chopped liver. Not bread pudding. "If you're hungry," she says, "get yourself something from the icebox. There's some sardines
left from lunch. He was too mad to eat, and I'm too upset to fix dinner."

Hal is in no mood to eat sardines, but he hasn't eaten all day. He could use
something that won't involve chewing. His nose hurts when he chews. Something soft. Like Jell-O. Tootsie always has a bowl of Jell-O in the fridge, its
traffic-light colors—stoplight red, caution-light orange, getaway green—an un-
expected note of cheer among the fridge's brown/grey leftovers—desiccated
brisket, wrinkled baked potatoes, salami gone bad. He reaches for the door's
handle and freezes.

There, stuck to the refrigerator like one of his kindergarten drawings from
fifty years ago, is the article from this morning's *Herald* about the Versailles fi-
asco. He had hoped that his parents would have somehow missed it, but no,
there it is, held front and center by a pizza-shaped magnet advertising Peesa
Pizza. Hal's Jell-O urge ebbs in a wave of disbelief. What will Tootsie do when
the big investigative piece comes out tomorrow—laminate it and hang it on the
wall?

He rips the article off the refrigerator, balls it up and stuffs it in his pocket. He wants to leave, but he can't. He's got to somehow defend his role in the impending demise of the Louis Quinze, or he'll never hear the end of it. He hasn't thought about what he's going to say, aside from claiming his innocence. After all, he hasn't really *done* anything to warrant such scrutiny. All he was trying to do was make a political comeback, and those behind-the-scenes shenanigans weren't his responsibility. That's just the nature of the game.

He opens the refrigerator and blinks into its sunny glare, scoping the crowded shelves stacked with the expected greige leftovers and anonymous lumpy packages wrapped in wrinkled foil. Several glass jars are packed with beige balls—gefilte fish? Matzo balls?—resembling the jars of preserved malformed fetuses he once saw in a Ripley's Believe It or Not museum as a kid. What little appetite he has quickly vanishes, but a neon orange glow from the bottom shelf catches his eye: Jell-O. He grabs the bowl, averting his eyes from the gefilte fetuses, and slams the door shut.

Ah. Jell-O. A virgin bowl, slightly mucous, almost set, its smooth mercurochrome-color translucence as yet unplowed. He tests its surface with a finger. It feels like soft skin. He grabs a soup spoon from the drawer and digs in, shattering the trembling viscosity into shivering orange facets. The cool fake-citrus sweetness slides down his throat in a syrupy swoosh, reminding him of childhood. For that moment, all is well.

"What are you *doing*?" Tootsie gasps as she bursts into the kitchen. "That's our *dessert.*" She grabs the Jell-O away from Hal and examines its fractured depths. "You're eating right out of the bowl! With a spoon!" She studies it some more, then thrusts it back at Hal. "You may as well eat the whole thing. You've already put your germs in it."

So Hal does. He runs the spoon through the Jell-O, now puddling back to its liquid origins, tips his head back carefully so as not to bonk his nose, and drinks it down. Tootsie emits a sigh of disgust. "I didn't ask you to come here so you could raid the refrigerator," she says. "Go see what's going on with your father. He *still* won't come out of the bathroom."

Hal wipes orange sticky stuff from his mouth with his hand and wipes it on his t-shirt, leaving an orange schmear. Who cares? What's a schmear on your shirt when you've got a marshmallow plastered in the middle of your face? Since the Versailles incident, his vanity has vanished with his pride. He has devolved from being an avid reader of GQ to thumbing morosely through the pages of the AARP magazine with its depressingly peppy articles about

Boomers Who Made It Big and Ninety-Year-Olds Who Joined the Peace Corps. He knows he'll be neither. Today a schmear of Jell-O on his t-shirt; tomorrow a blob of baby food on his nursing home bib. The future is looking bleaker by the minute with each forced step he takes in the direction of the locked bathroom door.

"Pop?" Hal raps on the door. He can hear the rattle of newspaper inside, underscored by low muttering. "Hey, Pop. Come on out." The only response is the gurgle of a flush followed by the inevitable rapid-fire clicking of the handle necessary to terminate said flush. "OK, Pop, you're done," Hal says. "Let's talk."

The flush decelerates to a pathetic whine. He hears the toilet lid slam down. Silence reigns once more on the other side of the door. Hal raps again. "I can open this with a coat hanger," he warns. "Don't make me get the coat hanger."

Several intermittent warnings later, he gets the coat hanger. "I'm opening the door," he announces, wiggling the unbent wire into the door lock. It opens with a little pop, then stops. Something is pushed up against the door, permitting it to open just enough for Hal to see the hamper, tipped on its side, wedged between the door and the tub. Through the crack, he sees Max sitting on the toilet lid, studying a particular purple fish on the shower curtain as if he had discovered a new species.

"Move the hamper," Hal says through the crack in the door. "We have to talk."

Max shifts his gaze to a orange fish higher up.

Hal really doesn't want to talk. He wants to go home and smoke a joint and order a pizza—a supersize pizza, a pizza with sausage and peppers and double cheese––and watch the Heat game on TV and forget that his life has turned to shit. But first he has to make things right with Max. How should he start?

Perhaps with Tootsie's words. "It's not what it looks like," he begins. "It's just politics. I hardly *know* these guys." He pauses. "I'm—I *was* – running for mayor. I'm not running any more."

Max rises, then disappears out of range. Hal's attempt to track his moves through the narrow crack is cut short when the door bangs shut again, almost taking his battered nose with it. This time, the coat hanger proves futile. He suspects that Max is holding the lock button in.

Hal hammers on the door, not expecting a response. At least he has a captive audience. "I had nothing to do with selling the hotel to build the condo," he pleads. "When I found out it was the Louis Quinze, don't you think I was upset? Don't you think I know what it means to you? Don't you think I'd do something about it if I could?" He waits for a Yes that doesn't come, so continues. "I didn't even know Milo had bought the property. He was just backing me, that's all. He's very supportive." He presses his ear to the door, hears nothing. "He thought I'd be a good mayor," he adds weakly.

He can sense Tootsie's presence behind him, knows that she's standing there, arms crossed, brow furrowed, lips pursed, Keds-clad feet planted solidly apart.

"He'll have a heart attack in there," she warns. "All this tumult, all this *tsuris*, who needs it? Get him out of there. I got enough to worry about what with the bleeding gums and the bunions and the running away in the rain, and now this. It's enough to give *me* a heart attack."

Hal isn't feeling so well himself. Not just his nose, but his Papi-punched gut is throbbing with waves of pain that wash over an intense craving for pizza. The combination is disorienting, dizzying, and he feels the need to grasp his belly and sit down on the floor, which he does suddenly enough for Tootsie's terror alert to escalate to red.

"Not you too?" she cries. "*Vey iz mir*! I'm calling 911!" Her Keds do a panicked little dance of indecision before they carry her in the direction of the phone.

"No!" Hal calls after her. "No 911! I'm fine! I'm fine!" He just doesn't feel like getting up right now. He leans his back against the door and takes deep breaths. Maybe he *is* having a heart attack. Is pizza craving a symptom? No. The pain is ebbing. His head is clearing. Tootsie is back.

"They're coming," she says.

Oh shit. He can't take any more of this. He scrambles to his feet and stumbles to the phone to cancel, to explain, to say that no, he's just fine, it was his mother. She's a little...you know. Wacky. And yes, he's sure he's fine. Positive. Thankyouverymuch. Sorry for the trouble.

"Jeez," he says to Tootsie, who is glaring at him when he hangs up.

"I'm a little wacky?" she asks. "I save your life and you call me wacky?"

"911? Who told you to call 911?"

"You scared me. You grab your heart, you plunk on the floor, what am I supposed to think?"

"What's going on?" Max yells from the other side of the door.

"Pop?" Hal says, energized by hope that maybe this will end now. "I'm fine, we're fine. Come on out."

But Max does not come out. His only response to Hal's request is an extended series of flushes which Hal presumes is intended to drown out his pleas as well as Tootsie's comments. Hal gives up. He's tired and hungry and frustrated with his own futility. "Call me when he comes out of hibernation," he says, and goes home.

They left the peppers off the pizza, the sausage is skimpy, and the double-cheese came single. Hal finishes off the last slice of pizza nevertheless, convinced that this is Domino's way of punishing him for his political and parental crimes and misdemeanors. To further his penance, the Heat is losing, their soggy performance as distressing a sight on his 60-inch screen as the news has been all day. Hal swigs the last warm drop of beer from the bottle, lights up yet another joint, and rearranges his battered body on the couch. Satiated with pizza, bloated with beer, buzzed from too much grass, he sinks into recrimination. Yes, he ate too much, drank too much, smoked too much, but, he blearily reasons, it's cheap therapy—the necessary evils he needs to blot out the memory of the silence behind the bathroom door.

He closes his eyes, shutting out the leaping forms on the screen, and dissolves into the past: He's six years old, high up on the terrace roof of the Louis Quinze beneath a white-hot sun. The air tastes like fresh popcorn. Above him, a shred of daytime moon floats above in the cloud-smeared sky like the remnant from a torn-off sticker. Below, a blue-ribboned sea spits foam on the milk chocolate shore. His sand-crusted sandals slap the tiles of the terrace as he walks, holding his Pop's hand.

They reach the edge and peer over the balcony. He sees the three pools, islands of blue in a concrete sea. Umbrellas sprout like blue-striped flowers, and red and brown people bake below like tiny chickens on chaises. He can hear faint music playing, *Good morning starshine,* very far below. Everything is very far below.

"Five hundred sixty-five rooms! Fifteen stories high!" Pop says. "The tallest building on Miami Beach. The most beautiful. The most famous. Always full." He reaches into the pocket of his cabana shirt, pulls out a Cuban cigar, and jams it between his teeth. He doesn't light it. Hal knows why. His mom doesn't like the smell of cigars, and she can tell when Pop has been smoking. Someday, Hal thinks, he'll smoke cigars. He wants to do what Pop wants to do.

"Do you know what I do?" Pop asks. The cold cigar moves with his words. "I am a builder. This is what I do. I've built lots of hotels, but never one like this one. People don't say 'Who's Max Wolfe?' They say '*The* Max Wolfe! Max Wolfe, the Hotel King! He built the most famous hotel in the world!'"

"In the whole world?"

"See those people?" Pop asks, waving his hand in a kingly gesture above the populace below. "They come from everywhere, all over the world, just to stay in my hotel. But they're not who I built it for. So, you're wondering. Who did I build it for?" He pauses dramatically. "I built it for *us*. For me. For Mom. And most of all," he says, placing one furry-fingered hand atop Hal's head as if in blessing, "I built it for you."

Hal nods, but doesn't understand. He doesn't need a whole hotel. Sure, it's great fun to swim in the pool, to play shuffleboard on the deck, to build castles on the beach. But he doesn't need his own hotel to do that. "Why for me?" he asks.

Pop takes the cigar from his teeth, examines it, then digs in the pocket of his cabana shirt for a match. He looks around, then, back to the wind, takes a long minute to light the cigar. "Not just for you," he says. "For you, and your son, and his son too. " He puffs vigorously on the cigar until its tip glows, then blows a ragged smoke ring. It disappears like a ghost in the air. "You know what a dynasty is?"

"I don't understand," Hal says.

"You will," Pop says. "Some day you will." He blows another ring into the wind.

Hal leans over the balcony. The hotel's curved façade cradles them like a giant angel's wing. He is gripped by a sudden urge to fly. A gust of wind parachutes his shirt, terrorizing him into a vision of soaring high above the toytown scene below. He throws himself backward and lands on the terrace with a thud.

He doesn't want to fly. He doesn't want to fly.

Hal wakes up on the couch with a start and the taste of yesterday's sausage in his mouth. His head aches, his stomach is queasy, and his nose feels like it's got teeth. It's morning. The sun is up. The birds are singing.

The *Herald* awaits outside his door.

CHAPTER XII

ZOE

Zoe's got bills to pay. She needs work, another steady client because Max isn't going anywhere. He refuses to leave the condo. He crawled under his quilt and only comes out to eat and pee, ever since the *Herald* article came out accusing Hal of being bought by the developers behind the soon-to-be demolished Louis Quinze and the soon-after-that construction of Fantabulissimo. Hal has explained to Zoe that it's all overblown, a lie, really, and he's not even running for mayor any more, for God's sake.

"That's not good enough," she tells him. "You've got to make it up to him somehow."

"How? How?" Hal seems genuinely flummoxed. "How can I undo everything?" She wants to believe him because he seems so sincere, but she did see that whole messy thing on TV.

For the first time, Tootsie has confided in Zoe. "Help me," she had begged. "You got to get Max out of this apartment. Take him someplace. Any place. He's not speaking to Hal. I can't even say Hal's name. 'Hal,' I say, and before I even get the '...needs to talk to you,' out, Max goes *meshuggeneh*. You gotta get him outta here."

Nothing has worked. Zoe went to the condo at Tootsie's invitation, tried to talk to Max, but he refused to come out from under the covers. Several more fruitless trips to the condo at Tootsie's insistence have made Zoe cringe whenever her cell rings. It's time to move on, get her career back on track now that she's ready to roll again. She's reunited with her beloved Zippity, all fresh and pink and perky, and she's got to make a living. Without Max as a guaranteed source of income, she needs to expand her horizons if she's going to get anywhere in this business.

The idea came to her after a day spent at the Swap Shop in Ft. Lauderdale. She makes the trip now and then to buy cheap t-shirts, two for $10. That day, she had selected a pink Garfield, a yellow Honey Badger and a real find, a tie-dyed Grateful Dead Dancing Bear.

"Far out!" she heard someone drawl as she held the t-shirt up to check its size. She turned to face a grinning shaggy-bearded gnome wearing an Aerosmith t-shirt. "I'da gotten that if you hadn't beaten me to it. Could always use another one. Five bucks! I paid twenty for mine. Back then. In the day. Concert. San Francisco. '89."

"Well, it's mine now," Zoe said.

"I'm just wandering around," said the gnome. "Friend dropped me off here, told me not to miss this." He jerked a thumb in the direction of the indoor-outdoor flea market jumble of booths and stalls being pawed through by sweaty throngs of people. "Never saw so much crap in my life. I love it." He nodded his head approvingly at the knockoff purses, cheap perfumes, auto accessories, stacks of dented canned goods, plastic jewelry, fake-tiger rugs, belts lined up like neatly-pressed snakes. "Wanna give me a tour?"

"Not really. I have to get back to work."

"What's that?" he asked.

"I drive a cab."

"Cool! I'll hire you. Show me around. Then you can drive me back to my hotel. South Beach. Save my friend the trip back here, give him more time with his girlfriend."

Zoe gave the gnome a head-to-toe appraisal, taking in his scruffy beard, his Aerosmith t-shirt, his frayed shorts, his flip-flops that exposed toes as furry as a hobbit's. His Rolex watch. Fake, she was sure. "That's a long trip," she said. "Expensive."

"No problem," he said. "How much?"

Make it high so he'll leave me alone, she thought. "$300. Up front." This'll be the deal-breaker, she figured. She had no intention of spending another minute with the gnome.

But he reached deep into the pocket of his shorts, pulled out a very fat roll of bills, and peeled off six fifties. "Here," he said. "And a great tip if you show me something outrageous to buy that I can show my friend."

So. The Rolex was real. "It's a deal," she said, and happily led the way. First stop: Wig Wonderland, shelf after shelf of wigs on plaster heads resembling decapitated women whose last day was a bad hair day.

"Cool," said the gnome. "But wigs? I see those all the time." On to the next: Bright yellow Porsche with a sign proclaiming that it was once in a "Miami Vice" episode. Not for Sale. "That's okay," said the gnome. "Got one. Don't need two."

Zoe had saved her favorite for last: the booth of the bejeweled Jesus. There, displayed within a glass counter was a zirconian display of interdenominational dazzle, including two varieties of Jesus––one sparkling on the Cross, the other a simple head shot with a Crown of Thorns resembling a rhinestone tiara; a mammoth rhinestone-encrusted cross; an equally dazzling Star of David, and a very large and sparkly Chai that Zoe thought was a poodle at first. Impressive as these bijoux were, they paled in comparison to the *pièce de resistance* that claimed a velvet-lined alcove of its own: a gold-plated medallion the size of a dessert plate depicting the Last Supper in "genuine cubic zirconium diamonds," as breathlessly proclaimed by the proprietor, a balding, mustachio'ed bundle of enthusiasm who, overjoyed by the gnome's disbelieving stare, clearly thought he knew a sucker when he saw one.

"How much?" asked the gnome.

"$2500."

"WHAT? Twenty-five *hundred?*" Zoe rolled her eyes.

"It includes the gold chain," the proprieter explained.

Zoe walked away. "You can take a picture of it for $10," he called after her.

But the gnome was fixated. He gazed at the glittering medallion with loving eyes. "Unbelievable," he pronounced. "Fuckin' unbelievable."

Zoe wheeled around. "So take a picture and show it to your friend. That's outrageous enough."

"Don't sweat it. I'm not spending $2500 on this." But the gnome was clearly enthralled.

"Special today." The proprietor revived, sensing possibility. He gripped the countertop with zirconium-ringed fingers. His nose blossomed with tiny drops of sweat. "Only $2000."

"$1000." The gnome's eyes narrowed in combat.

"$1500." The proprietor's lips twitched beneath his mustache. "It's one-of-a-kind."

The gnome considered this. "Fuckin' unbelievable," he repeated, shaking his head, then shrugged. "$1250. Take it or leave it."

The proprietor took it.

"$1250 for *that?*" Zoe couldn't believe it. "Are you crazy?"

"What can I do. It's the bling to end all bling." The gnome reached for the roll of bills, peeled off a pile of green, and grinned happily at an astonished Zoe. "What the hell. It's only money."

The proprietor couldn't do enough for the gnome. So ecstatic was he at this unlikely sale—cash!--that he quivered with happiness, his mustache perking up in a fuzzy replica of his grin. "Shall I wrap it for you?" he gushed, "or would you prefer to wear it?"

"I'll wear it." The proprietor placed the medallion around his neck with the reverence deserving of an Olympic gold medalist. The gnome paused to admire its blinding glitter in the mirror perched on the counter, pronounced a final "fuckin' unbelievable," then bid the fawning proprietor a fond farewell.

"Is that Monopoly money you've got there?" Zoe asked as they headed for the parking lot, where Zippity awaited. "Or did you just rob a bank?"

"Nope. It's as real as this medallion is fake. Don'tcha love it?" He lifted it to his lips and gave it a big smack. "My friend is going to freak out. This tops anything he's got. He's gonna want it. Maybe I'll sell it to him."

"Who's your friend, and when was he released from the asylum?"

"He's Lil Teddy Bare, the rapper, and his release is an album, not an asylum."

"Never heard of him," she said with a shrug. She searched the packed lot for Zippity's pinkness, spotted it several rows over, and led the way through the shimmering asphalt heat.

He paused in obvious delight as Zoe opened Zippity's door for him. "*This* is your cab? Far out. I love it." He slid into the back seat and ran his hands over the zebra slipcovers. "You wanna sell it?"

Zoe was stunned. Sell Zippity? After all she had been through? "You can't buy love," she said as she edged Zippity out of the lot and onto the highway. "Besides, this is how I make my living."

"Well, with this kinda cab, you could make a lot more money taking people on offbeat trips, not just carting them around. People will pay for offbeat. *I* did, didn't I?" His words were almost lost in the hot blast of air roaring through Zippity's rolled-down windows as they picked up speed, but they registered with Zoe. This guy had big bucks—he told her he was in the record business. The Beach was loaded with big bucks people, just like him. By the time they pulled up to his hotel, the Delano, he had planted the seed of an idea: Zippity Trips.

Zoe's at Kinko's, printing up flyers——pink with turquoise lettering: *Ask me about Zippity Trips!*—when her cell rings. Oh no. Tootsie again. Zoe's not answering it. She's had it with them. She's got a business to run. Not only her regular taxi service, but its budding offshoot: Zippity Trips! She's got a bunch of offbeat places in mind to suggest to potential clients who want something more than the usual tourist traps. She grabs the box of flyers and tosses it into Zippity's back seat. Now all she needs are customers.

Zoe's practiced eye catches the limp waves of a couple in matching Hawaiian shirts who signal her from the curb in front of the News Cafe. She makes a lateral move across Ocean Drive traffic and stops dead in front of the couple. They crawl, sun-dazzled, into Zippity's capacious back seat, where they encounter the freshly-minted box of Zippity Trips flyers.

The woman peels one off the top. "Ask me about 'Zippity Trips,'" she reads. "'See Miami like a Native. Offbeat excursions to wild and crazy places. Explore our hidden gems, experience offbeat adventures, eat local food without a reservation. There's more to Miami than sun, sand, and shopping!'"

She fans herself with the flyer. "Okay, where can you take us that's really cool?" She's as lean and tough as a strip of beef jerky. Her shirt, a green and yellow palm-patterned twin to her husband's, is half the size and twice as dry as his. Sweat foams over his casaba-shaped head, cascades from his grey-frizzled scalp onto cheeks as red and peeled as stewed tomatoes.

"Cool," he echoes. "Anywhere but the beach. I got fried."

Her first Zippity Trip! This twin-shirted couple is just begging for a nice, long ride, and she's the cabbie to take them.

"I got the perfect place," Zoe says. It's been a while since she's been there, but it's cool, it's fun, it's a good hour's fare down the road to Homestead, halfway to the Keys: The Sno-Pop orange juice processing plant, the last remaining OJ plant in South Florida. She makes a whiplash turn that evokes a screaming duet from the back seat, then speeds the cab west across the causeway, a palm-spiked streak of asphalt that spans the shimmery blue of the bay.

"Turn on the air-conditioning," says the wife.

"Don't need it," Zoe says merrily. "Feel that breeze!"

"Where we going?" The husband's face in the rear-view mirror is a red mask of terror.

"Homestead."

"Home? We're going home?"

"Home*stead*. Where the farmers live."

"If I wanted to see farmers I'd stay in Dubuque."

"This is an adventure," Zoe says. "You'll see."

The wife stares out of her rolled-down window. "I could use an adventure," she says. The wind snaps her pixie-cut bangs into a crown of little points. The landscape of strip malls, car dealerships, gas stations and apartment clusters holds her attention as they crawl through stop-and-go traffic on US-1.

The husband cranes his head out the window as Zoe turns the cab sharply off the highway onto a long and dusty road, leaving the urban scenery behind. They whiz past geometric fields, stark pine trees, lush lime and avocado groves, and the creeping suburbia of lookalike houses crowded together on what was once farmland. "Where are we?" he asks.

"Adventureland!" says Zoe. They veer into an empty parking lot in front of some odd-shaped buildings. *Sno-Pop Citrus Processing Plant,* reads the sign. *Visitors check in at the door.*

The husband blinks in the glare. "Are we still in Miami Beach?"

"You want cool? You got it." Zoe waves them inside. "Welcome to the only frozen juice processing plant in South Florida."

No one is there. The front office, a small room of lime-green-painted cinderblock, is furnished with a folding table and chairs lined up around the perimeter. On the wall are Sno-Pop posters of orange and grapefruit people with big toothy smiles and clothes made of leaves. The lady oranges wear high heels and lipstick. The gentlemen grapefruits sport fedoras.

On the table is a lined yellow tablet labeled "Visitors." The only signature is that of a Miss Vonda Wongle, teacher of a third-grade class from Banyan Elementary. The husband eyes the dust-laden fan that spins and shudders dangerously above them. "It's not even air-conditioned."

"Hey," Zoe calls. "Anybody home?"

"Hold your horses," a tinny voice replies. "I'll be out inna second." A distant flush and a couple of minutes later, a tall lanky man with a marionette's walk appears in the doorway. His long face compresses into a grin. "Welcome to Sno-Pop," he says. "Just call me Tyrone."

"Got time for a tour, Tyrone?" asks Zoe.

"Well, sure." Tyrone reaches out a hand the size and color of a raw beef joint. "Pleezta meetcha, Mr...uh."

"Goolsby," says the husband, staring at Tyrone's nose which looks rather frostbitten, white on the end with a tinge of blue. "We're the Goolsbys."

"Well, Goolsbys, you're in for a treat." Tyrone leads them through the door into a cool, dark hallway. There, as if something clicks inside his head, his loosy goosy demeanor changes to something tighter, measured, as automated as his voice has become: "The Florida story is a story of citrus," he begins.

The Goolsbys exchange a puzzled glance. "Cool," Zoe promises. "Very cool." They are outside again. It is not cool. The sun has found them, a hard and merciless midday sun that beats down as they parade over dirt to a windowless bunker.

Zoe's cell phone rings. Tootsie again, third time today. Shit. She's not answering it, especially not now. She's on her first Zippity Trip, and she's a long way from home.

"Great strides have been made in the production of processed citrus products," Tyrone intones. They enter the building. It smells like an orange the size of the moon. The sweet acidity enters every pore and emerges with every breath. Juice, not blood, seems to flow through their veins until they pulse with essence of orange.

"Thus came the development of frozen concentrate," Tyrone continues, "which in a few short years jumped to the top of the frozen food industry." Pupils narrowed to pin dots, the Goolsbys blink in the sudden darkness, blind for a moment to the roaring hailstorm of oranges that surrounds them. Gradually the scene comes into view: great vats of oranges being washed, the solemn lineup of sorters in orange-stained coveralls who study a barrage of spheres that barrel down a chute. The threatening hiss of sterilizing steam.

"Where are we?" whimpers Mr. Goolsby.

"In orange juice hell," replies his wife.

Zoe's cell phone rings again. She turns it off.

They hear the metallic whump of heavy machinery as they enter the next building, a grinding, clanking, death-like citrus squish that echoes in the suddenly autumnal air. They pass into another room. The temperature plunges. The palm trees on the Goolsbys' shirts sway in a palsied dance as they shiver in the cold.

"I'm *freezing*." Mrs. Goolsby hugs herself frantically, but Tyrone is on a roll: "The finished product is slush frozen, filled into cans, sharp frozen, then stored in warehouses at ten degrees Fahrenheit." He falls into a respectful silence as a roller-coaster of six-ounce cans rumbles down a giant incline.

"Are we done?" asks Mr. Goolsby. The tip of his nose is turning white, tinged with a little blue. "Can we go now?" But there's still the warehouse.

It's ten degrees according to the giant thermometer in the warehouse. Dwarfed by towering crates of frozen juice, they look up in awe at the majesty of citrus, the power of ice, the Florida dream. Tyrone throws his head back and raises his bony arms as if blessing each and every can. "By law, nothing, no, *nothing*, can be added to frozen concentrated orange juice produced in Florida. It is the PURE JUICE of FULLY RIPE ORANGES with only a PORTION of its water content removed!"

The Goolsbys are already outside, warming their faces in the sun. They drink their little paper cups of complimentary Sno-Pop, climb into Zippity Cab and sleep the whole way back. When they arrive at their hotel, they tip Zoe generously, whether out of relief or appreciation, it doesn't matter. Her first Zippity Trip has been a success.

When Zoe turns on her cell again, she sees that Tootsie has called her five times but left no messages. Now she's worried. Did something happen to Max? She calls Tootsie back. There's no answer. She tries Hal. Gets his voice mail, leaves him a message: "Is Max OK?" She drives to the Wolfe's condo. A police car is in the driveway. Not a good thing.

This is confirmed by the sight of Max being escorted inside by a police-woman seemingly oblivious to Tootsie, whose mouth and arms are both in ac-tion as she follows them through the lobby doors. Zoe slams on her brakes and parks, contrary to the valet's objections until he sees she's heading for the trio of Tootsie, Max and the grim-faced policewoman.

"...like a criminal!" she hears Tootsie saying. "He was just borrowing it! Five minutes he's gone, big deal, you'd think he was Al Capone with the fingerprints and the mug shot. You people should be ashamed, arresting a *meshuggeneh* old man."

Zoe sees Max's back straighten at that. She can't hear what he's saying to Tootsie but whatever it is shuts her up and puts a quick smile on the face of the policewoman. Zoe reaches them just as the elevator opens, and to Tootsie and Max's surprise, she jumps in for the ride up to their apartment

"So now you show up," Tootsie admonishes her. "I called you and called you and did you answer? No!"

"What happened?" Zoe asks.

"First I call because Max wants to go for a ride. I can't get him out of the apartment all week and now he wants to go for a ride, so I think, Well, this is a good sign, he's coming out of this *mishegoss*, he's asking for Zoe, this is good.

But do you answer? No. So I try again. He's getting *schpilkes* now, all excited to get out like it's me who's been keeping him inside like a crazy hermit. But do you answer?"

"No," Zoe answers for her. "And did you leave a message on my voice mail so I'd know what was wrong maybe? So maybe I could have come and helped, maybe?" "I don't like to talk to a machine," Tootsie says. "It's not a real person."

"I'm a real person. I listen to my voice mail. I would have called you back if I knew something was wrong."

"Well, you didn't answer," Tootsie protests. "If you had answered, nothing would have been wrong and he wouldn't be a criminal."

Zoe exchanges glances with the policewoman who has the look of someone who has seen it all but is still capable of appreciating creative irrationality.

"Okay, so it's all my fault," Zoe says as the elevator doors open. "But I don't know what *it* is. What did he do?"

"Wait. I can't find my keys," Tootsie says, fumbling in her purse at the door. The policewoman stares blandly ahead at the wolf's-head doorknocker. Tootsie's fumbling becomes more frantic as she paws deeper into the depths of her tote bag, its frazzled bunch of straw daisies hanging by a thread. "I know I had them this morning," she says, and dumps the tote's contents onto the "Welcome to the Wolfes" mat outside their door. She examines each item: pink plastic wallet, flowered glasses case, grey-tangled hairbrush, corroded lipstick case, Avon powder compact, several used tissues and a crumpled bunch of receipts, shaking each object as if the keys might fall out.

"I took 'em," Max says, his first words since they began their journey to the apartment. He reaches into his pocket and pulls them out.

Tootsie looks at him with a mixture of anger and surprise. "How did you get my keys?"

"In the police station. When you asked me to hold your purse while you went to the bathroom."

"You stole my keys in the police station? Why would you do that?"

"I want *my* keys back. You took my keys away. If I had keys to the car, I wouldn'ta had to borrow that guy's."

Tootsie grabs the keys and opens the door.

"Okay," Zoe says, exasperated. "Will somebody tell me what happened?" She turns to the policewoman as they file inside. "You know what happened?"

"Oh no. Oh no," Tootsie objects. "*She's* not gonna tell you what really happened. *She's* gonna tell you he's a criminal."

The policewoman shrugs. "I'm just escorting him home to make sure he gets here okay." A smile flickers across her thin mouth. "Let the missus here tell the story. If everything's in order, I can go."

"So go," Tootsie says. "We're fine. Go back to the Gestapo."

The policewoman leaves. Max settles into his La-Z-Boy and points the remote at the TV, clicking through the channels until it lands on CNN. He glares at what seems to be a fashion show, then resumes his clicking, muttering, "That's supposedta be news?"

"What?" Tootsie asks. "Like your arrest should make the news? Like they're interested in an old fart who steals cars?"

"He stole a car?" Zoe asks.

"Borrowed," says Max.

"Stole!" Tootsie disagrees. "Like a criminal! He steals it, they chase him, he crashes it. It's the OJ Simpson thing all over again."

"What OJ thing?" Max says. "I didn't kill anybody."

"Hold it!" Zoe throws her hands up to stop them. "Just tell me what happened."

"I just wanted to take a drive..." Max begins.

"So I'm at the sink peeling potatoes so he can have his mashed potatoes and gravy like always with his meatloaf," Tootsie says, "and I ask does he want peas and there's no answer. I ask again and ask again, still no answer so I go look in the living room and he's not there so I think maybe he's in the bathroom, no, not there, maybe in the bedroom, no, not there, not in the other bedroom, not on the balcony, so now I'm getting worried, where is he?"

"Worry, schmurry," Max says.

"He never goes to the pool since he got the nose thing because it's too much sun so I figure he's not at the pool but maybe I should take a look, so I go downstairs and I hear all this commotion in the lobby, yelling and commotion, so I'm a curious person and I have this feeling, sometimes I think I'm psychic, that maybe Max has something to do with it and guess what, he does!" Tootsie folds her arms and glares at him.

"If I had keys, I woulda taken *our* car," Max says by way of explanation. He points the remote at the TV. Quick bits of programs flash by like snatches of dreams: weather map, Auntie Bee, Eiffel tower, frothing Hannity, weeping dark-haired *telenova* actress.

"So," Tootsie resumes, "I ask What's going on? and Ruben, he's one of the valets, nice man, Cuban, says Your husband stole a car, and I say What? What are you talking about? and he says He jumped in that guy's Lexus before I could park it and then took off, and he points to the man. I've seen this guy on the elevator, not a very talky person, not even a hello, but now he won't shut up, he's yelling at everybody and there's a policeman who comes up to me and tells me Max stole this guy's car, like it's my fault or something. So I get my purse, *with* the keys, and ride in the police car until we get a few blocks to where Max has crashed the guy's car into a barrier."

"All that damned construction," Max says. "Who told them to block off 41st Street? Besides," he adds, "I hardly dented the car. Just the fender. Big deal."

"Have you told Hal?" Zoe asks. Where was Hal, anyway, she wonders. How come she's here and he's not?

"Do *you* know where Hal is?" Tootsie asks, "Because I don't. I called him and called him, just like I called you, but does he answer? No! What's with the fancy cell phones that you don't answer them?"

"Don't call him!" Max orders. "I told you, I don't want him here."

"So," Tootsie continues, "we have to go to the police station with all the criminals and he's booked like he's in the Mafia, fingerprints, mug shots, all that FBI stuff..."

"They let me go. It was all a mistake."

"Mistake? You could have had a criminal record, Mr. Mafia Big Shot. You think fingerprints and mug shots disappear? Please God they shouldn't put you up in the Post Office with the other criminals."

"That's just if you're Wanted," Zoe says. "They won't arrest him when he goes to buy stamps."

"You're lucky the guy didn't press charges," Tootsie says, heading for the kitchen. "You have me to thank for that. I told him you were senile."

"Senile?" Max yells. "That's how I beat the rap?"

"Beat the rap?" Zoe asks. "You've been watching too much TV."

Max slumps down in the La-Z-Boy and clicks off the television. He and Zoe stare at the pale grey screen. Zoe breaks the silence. "You want to tell me why you did that?"

Max shrugs. "I just wanted to get out."

"Max, I've been trying to get you out all week. You didn't have to steal a car to get out."

"Borrowed."

"You didn't have to borrow a car. I would have taken you."

Max studies the remote in his hand. "I don't know why I can't take myself. I can drive. I'm not senile."

"I know that. But you can't drive if you can't see. You had all those fender-benders before, remember? You could hurt yourself. You could hurt somebody else." Zoe pats Max's hand, a gesture he neither rejects nor acknowledges. She feels the slow pulsation from the tributaries of veins that map his hand; its rhythm seems to match her own. "You want to go for a ride? I'll take you wher-ever you feel like going."

Max turns to her. His eyes seem bigger, more liquid behind his glasses. "You know where I was going today?"

"Did *you* know?"

"I wanted to see the Louis Quinze one more time."

Not a good idea. She feels the pulsation of his veins quicken, and reconsid-ers. After all, he *is* entitled to say goodbye, to have some kind of completion. "Well," she says. "We can drive by, if you like."

"I want to go inside."

"I don't think you can do that. It's closed." But at his crestfallen look, she concedes, "Okay. We can give it a try."

"Now?"

Zoe hesitates. "Tomorrow. It's been a long day for you. We'll go tomorrow."

* * *

Max is waiting outside when Zoe drives up. He's wearing what she assumes must be an ancient suit: a brown tweed number with wide lapels and even wider pants. It may have fit him thirty years ago, but now it's outgrown him. He seems lost in yards of fabric; even the knot in his tie is too big, a bright yel-low sun setting beneath his chin. He climbs into the back seat, smelling faintly of mothballs and aftershave which she recognizes: Canoe, a little rancid, proba-bly from age. It's what Albert used to wear on their dates.

"Don't you look spiffy," Zoe says to his reflection in the rear view mirror. "All dressed up and someplace to go."

"I don't get dressed up. Not any more." He runs his hand over his head, smoothing down remembered hair. "I wore this the last time I was in the Louis Quinze, to sign the final papers. Tootsie tried to give it to Goodwill, but I kept it as a souvenir."

Well, she kept Zippity as a souvenir of Albert, so she understands. Sometimes you need a memory you can touch.

Max nervously fumbles at the knot in his tie. "Probably no one there will remember me now."

"Sure they will, Mr. Wolfe," Zoe says, although she's pretty sure that the place is shut down and no one is there. But he has to see that for himself. "You're unforgettable. And besides," she adds as a bonus, "you *built* the place."

"I did," he agrees. "It was my baby."

"My baby." With those words, Zoe connects: Max's obsession with the Louis Quinze is not just as a symbol of his role in the city's history. It's his time-travel back to the birth of his dream. It's his baby.

They round the bend on Collins. "Look! There it is!" Zoe announces. She's seen it hundreds of times before, but now she sees it through Max's eyes: not the decrepit hulk that remains today, but a languorous, curvaceous matron, an undulation of dazzling concrete that rules Collins Avenue.

Max leans out the window, straining to see. "Here, here, turn here," he orders, pointing to where the grand entry driveway should be, but Zoe can't turn. The driveway is blocked by a chain link fence that encircles the entire building. A security guard sits on a folding chair next to a sign that reads "Liquidation Sale Inside" with an arrow that points to an undisclosed location. Zoe pulls the cab up to the locked gate and jumps out. The guard snaps to attention.

"Hey!" he says, shoving his Big Slurpee cup under the chair and heaving his bulk to a standing position. "No parking here. You gotta park inna lot down the block."

"What's going on?" Zoe asks.

"What's going on?" Max echoes, scurrying out of the back seat. "What's with the fence? What's with the gate?"

"You wanna go to the sale? You gotta go around to the other entrance. The sale's in the ballroom."

"What sale?" Max's pink scalp gleams with sweat; his cheeks are at red alert. "Liquidation," says the guard. "Before they tear the place down. People been going in and out all week carrying all kindsa stuff out—lamps, TVs, dishes, beds, hair dryers, you name it."

"Hair dryers?" Max asks.

"Ironing boards. Coffeemakers. Telephones. Guy bought a mirror. Tripped right there," the guard says, indicating the curb. "Broke inta a gazillion pieces. Wanted to sue."

"Ironing boards?" Max asks.

"Let's go," Zoe says. "This is depressing."

"I want to go inside."

"No. No you don't," Zoe says. "Let's remember it the way it was."

"I came to see it one more time. I have to do that," he insists, pulling his arm away from her consoling hand.

"OK, Mr. Wolfe," she says with a sigh. "But I've got to park way away from here. It's a long walk."

"I'll stay with him," the guard offers. "I got nothing else to do."

"I don't need a babysitter." Max walks to the chain link fence and clutches it with both hands, peering inside. In his too-big suit, he looks like a kid whose mother buys him clothes she thinks he'll grow into.

"Don't move," Zoe calls back to him as she drives off. "We don't need any more cops looking for you."

She runs the three blocks from the parking lot back to where she left Max. He's still there, still clutching the fence where she left him. "I tried to get him into the shade," the guard reports, "but he wouldn't move."

"You said, 'Don't move,'" Max says. "I didn't move."

"Come on," Zoe says, anxious to get him inside, out of the sun. She's dying in her T-shirt; he must be baking like a cookie inside that tweed jacket. She follows the arrows to the sale entrance. Max looks confused as they enter.

"Where are we?" he asks.

"The ballroom," she says, but she's confused as well. The high ceiling arches above them, studded with tiny blue lights. The perimeter is festooned with elaborate but unlit chandeliers that dangle overhead like immense Halloween spiders. Below this elegance is, not a bejeweled crowd dressed in tuxedos and gowns, but a desultory parade of bargain hunters who weave among purple-tableclothed tables piled high with stuff priced in hand-lettered signs: dinner plates $1.50; gravy bowls $6; blankets $6; mattress pads $3; clothes hangers 50 cents; shower heads $3; finger bowls $2. Two kids are having a pillow fight next to a table piled high with limp pillows ($1.50). Lurid pink-and-green-flowered bedspreads ($14) spill off a table onto the floor; a woman in curlers debates herself concerning their suitability for her décor ("Pink. I don't know about pink.")

Max, dazed, shuffles to a table where tangles of knives, forks and spoons (50 cents) fight for space in metal trays. He picks up a fork, squints at the logo he can't see. "What's this say?" he asks Zoe.

"LXV," Zoe says. "I guess that's fifteen. For Louis Quinze, right? Fifteen?"

Max nods. He pockets the fork. "It's mine," he says when Zoe protests. "I don't hafta pay for anything in my hotel."

They wander into what, judging from the long row of marble check-in counters and fluted columns that support the two-story ceiling, must have been the lobby. It now resembles a Goodwill showroom crowded with monochromatic blonde wood furniture: headboards, nightstands, armoires, dressers, coffee tables, sagging couches upholstered in nubbly beige fabric. Max runs his hand over the geometric contours of a bureau. "Hmf," he says. "Modern. We didn't do modern, that cheap stuff. We did elegant stuff, French Provincial, like in France. This musta been what that hotel chain put in after they bought the place. They redecorated. They didn't have no taste."

Tall gilded mirrors and framed prints of Paris lean against a wall. A crowd of squat little lamps with dunce-cap shades huddles in a corner. Max lowers himself onto the velvet cushion of one of the sofas that encircles several marble columns like crimson lifesavers. The columns soar above the scene, their gold-rimmed fluting shimmering in the dusky half-light that filters through the few unwashed windows that aren't boarded up. Max looks up, following the columns' gilded path two stories up to the ceiling. "Steel," he says.

Zoe assumes he's referring to the fork. "You can always put it back," she says. "It's not stealing if you put it back."

Max ignores her. "Solid steel," he says. "More steel reinforcement than the Empire State Building." He reaches behind and whacks the column with his fist. "Like this column. Indestructible," he says. "Not just marble. Solid steel core. Built to last."

"Like the pyramids," Zoe says.

"Better." Max's gaze lowers to the surrounding scene once more. A guy with a do-rag knotted on his head and a girl in jeans and bikini top pull a mattress off a pile and lie down on it. Zoe hopes they don't start anything she wouldn't want Max to see, but they are merely testing it out. They roll back and forth, bounce a little, curl up on their sides as if sleeping. Satisfied as to its durability, they drag it off to the cashier's table near the roped-off front doors. Zoe wonders how many people have slept, as well as other things, on that mattress before.

"We kept the air conditioning freezing in here," Max says, "so the women could wear their minks." His eyes mist with memory. "It was classy then, in the fifties, the sixties. Movie stars, TV stars, politicians. Sinatra. Jerry Lewis. Jackie Gleason. JFK. This was the place."

Max leans back and closes his eyes. It's time to go, Zoe thinks. He's worn himself out from the emotion and the heat. He had refused to take off his jacket; the heat was intensifying its mothball odor, making her eyes water. The AC isn't freezing now—it's turned off to save money. No minks in this lobby, that's for sure. "Hey, Mr. Wolfe," she says, tapping him on the arm. "Ready to go home?"

He springs to attention. "See that stairway?" He points across the lobby. "Lemme show you something." Zoe has to hustle to keep up with him now as he churns in its direction, dodging blonde furniture, television sets and several determined customers who shove him right back when he pushes them aside.

They arrive at the foot of the grand, gilded double staircase to find it roped off and guarded by a bored security guard who is dabbing away with a glue pen at an elaborately decorated inch-long fake fingernail. "Can't go up, honey," she says when he tries to unhook the velvet rope. "It's off limits."

"Whaddaya mean, off limits?" Max protests. "We just want to go up and take a look."

"No can do," she says, examining her nail work. "Can't allow anybody up the stairs. Insurance, you know."

"Insurance? It's a *stairway*." He turns to Zoe. "She ruined the surprise. It's famous. It's the Stairway to Nowhere. You go up, you look around, you go down again. The mink ladies liked to make a grand entrance that way." He grabs the velvet rope again. "Let me show you."

"Hey!" the guard says. "Don't touch that rope."

Max unhooks the rope; the guard grabs it. It's a velvet rope tug-of-war with Max on the losing end until...

"Shit!" The guard releases the rope and drops to her knees. "My nail!" she says, groping the carpet frantically. Max makes his move. He scrambles up the stairway, tripping dangerously over his baggy pants in his getaway. He reaches the top, Zoe close behind. Below them, the guard is sending for the troops on her two-way radio.

Max surveys the lobby from his altitude. Zoe imagines that he's seeing–– not the spring-sprung sofas; the $72 TVs; the upended coffee tables, legs in the air like dead cats—but elegant women in furs, beehive hairdos braided like *challas,* and deep-tanned, Dep-gelled men in white dinner jackets. She can almost see him as he was in the photo she's seen in the Wolfe's condo, taken at a table in the nightclub: a dapper, dark-haired dandy. Now, sixty years later, Max

Wolfe, the Hotel King, spreads his arms, Pope-like, and embraces the room of his memory.

Reinforcement has arrived. A burly backup security guard storms one side of the stairway; the nail-challenged guard storms the other. There is nowhere to hide on the Stairway to Nowhere. Zoe and Max are trapped.

"Do you know who I am?" Max says as they are led to the exit by the backup guard.

"Yes. A lunatic," the guard responds.

"I'm Max Wolfe," he declares. "I *built* this hotel."

"And I'm Elvis," says the guard. "This is Graceland."

"He really *did* build it," Zoe says in Max's defense. "Can't you just let him say goodbye this one last time?"

"Sure. Goodbye," says the guard, and they're outside the door.

"Come on," says Zoe. "Let's go home."

But what's this? On display outside the entrance to the ballroom is a glass-enclosed scale model of Fantabulissimo itself. How did they miss seeing it going in? Zoe tries to shield it from Max. But he sees it, too:

FANTABULISSIMO, AN EXCITING NEW CONCEPT IN CONDO LIVING

AN OCEANFRONT RESIDENCE FOR THE UPSCALE LIFESTYLE YOU'VE ALWAYS DREAMED OF LIVING!

COMING SOON ON THIS SITE!

Inside the glass enclosure is a miniature replica of three soaring towers set within a gardenscape of pools and fountains. Teeny people sit on a wide white beach next to a brilliant blue ocean; more tiny people gather on balconies, sun by several pools, have lunch beneath tiny umbrellas, stroll among the plastic trees and flowers.

Max presses his nose up against the enclosure. It may be a small world after all, but it's not Max's world. "For this they're tearing down my hotel?" he yells. Ignoring the sign which warns *Do not lean on glass,* Max leans on the glass.

"Max!" Zoe cries. "Stop!"

But Max doesn't stop. He leans some more. The glass leans with him. Zoe rushes to stop him and does, but she knows disaster is just moments away. The teetering glass has reached the point of no return, balancing by a thread, but it's not too late to run and so she does. She grabs Max by the hand and they run, run, run as fast as his little baggy-pants legs will carry him.

They hear the crash half a block away.

CHAPTER XIII

HAL

"I don't know why the *Herald* had to start the story with the Versailles thing," Hal complains to Mandelbaum, his lawyer. "The reporter, that smart-ass Gomez, made it sound funny. It wasn't funny." He peels the cellophane off a peppermint ball from the big jar on Mandelbaum's desk and pops the ball into his mouth, puffing his cheek out like a chipmunk. "I ought to sue the bastards."

"Look," Mandelbaum says, "you got off easy in the story. You were lucky, you were only mentioned in the lead and you'll probably be dropped for the rest of the series. Technically you didn't do anything wrong, no money changed hands, you were just——" and Mandelbaum emphasizes this—"the *victim* of seasoned scumbags like Milo Minkoff and Carlos Cruz. That's a point we'll use if this goes to court, which it shouldn't."

Court. Hal doesn't want to hear that word. "Don't say that word," he says, but finds himself obsessively writing it in block letters over and over again on the yellow pad in front of him, *court court court*, like some lovesick girl writing her boyfriend's name, only he's writing from fear, not infatuation. He crumples the yellow sheet and stuffs it into his pocket.

"They used you," Mandelbaum continues. "You were their patsy, their hoped-for key to the politics of this project. Consider yourself lucky that it ended like this before you really got yourself into deep shit because let me tell you, you were headed down that road. You were right on the edge, ready to dive into that cesspool of contractors, developers, labor unions. Maybe you think a payoff here, a kickback there is just part of the job, but sooner or later you would have gotten busted."

"Busted?" He writes it on the yellow pad. *Busted.*

"It happens. This little episode may cost you in other ways, but you're off the hook felony-wise. So let the Herald use you as comic relief; it's not going to land you in jail. But," Mandelbaum adds, "maybe you should consider another line of work."

What kind of work? Hal wonders as the glass-walled elevator descends from the hushed offices of Mandelbaum, Mandelbaum and Wu to the sunwashed atrium of the lobby. What could he do at this point in his life, if not politics? What are his options? His seat on the commission was apparently safe for now, although there were rumblings about ousting him.

He still has his fans who, when he showed up for a few minutes of face time at the rally in his support, cheered him. They remembered the good times: boogeying down with the old folks at Douglas Garden; rapping with Fifty Cent at the Hip Hop Weekend; riding with the cops during a rash of tourist robberies. He was not only available for every photo-op, he made each one an event. He knows his strengths. He's a Clinton-esque charmer with a gift for remembering names, not just politicos or board chairmen or cultural arts mavens, but waiters, secretaries, mechanics, teachers, FPL linemen and kids. What else can he do with these talents at this age? Sell insurance? Be a Wal-Mart greeter? No. Politics is what he does. He knows how to make people feel special. He knows what it takes to be loved.

Except by Max. Max won't talk to him. Max relayed his message (*You're not just a Judas, you're a nincompoop*) via Zoe, who delivered the message reluctantly, adding her own encouragement for Hal to keep on trying to make up with Max.

"He'll come around," she said.

"Come around? He's been a total unremitting pain in the ass. You call that coming around?"

"He's just figuring it out. I think it's a matter of time."

Hal wants to believe her. Zoe now seems more attuned to Max's thoughts than anyone. Hal is baffled by their connection; it's almost as if they have a secret between them. Tootsie feels left out, a feeling she expresses on the phone to Hal each time Max and Zoe disappear on undisclosed errands.

"So where are they off to now?" Tootsie asks. Like he'd know. He doesn't know anything. He's shunned by Max whenever he shows up at their apartment trying to explain, to make amends, to prove to Max that he was inadvertently sucked into a plan whose diabolical end was unknown to him.

He really doesn't know himself why he got involved with Milo. He's spent many a grass-stained hour smoking himself into a stupor, trying to figure out how life came to this, sorting through memories stuck in his brain like cloves in a ham.

He still thinks about Staci. She pops up in his dreams, but not the way she did when he first had the hots for her. In these dreams now, she's wearing clothes. This is disturbing to Hal. Is he losing his lifelong horniness? Has age permanently deflated his favorite organ, which has been out of commission now for longer than he cares to remember?

Maybe, he tells himself, Dream-Staci is clothed because she needs to be dressed in her new life that she described briefly to him in a combination thank-you note/sympathy card/kiss-off, mailed shortly after the *Herald* story appeared. In it, she expressed her appreciation for his introducing her to new possibilities that went beyond the limited aspirations she had (she refrained from mentioning *Maxim*.) She has decided to go back to school to become a professional interpreter, and she already had several job offers as a result of the events at Versailles that day (events good for her, bad for Hal.) She is patching things up with her father with the help of her mother, and she is on her way to true independence. She expressed regret at Hal's misfortunes as chronicled in the Herald, and wished him all the best in the future.

In any case, she was gone from his life, if not from his dreams. He just wished they would include more nudity.

He wakes up from his nap (he's napping a lot these days) to the sound of his cell phone. Tootsie again. Her first words seem, to his fogged-out brain, disjointed and wobbly. Gradually, they make some kind of sense.

"...an hour ago!" she's saying. "So where could they be? He doesn't need a haircut, he's done with the periodontist until the next disaster, he won't go back to the bunion doctor, what's going on? If I was the suspicious type, I'd say, Aha."

Hal can't even imagine his father doing an aha, not at this stage of the game. "How long's he been gone?"

"Two hours! They shoulda been back an hour ago."

"Did they say they'd be back an hour ago?"

"They never say! They always say they're taking a drive, but I say an hour's enough for a drive. Where can you go for two hours? Boca? What are they doing in Boca?"

"Who said they were going to Boca?"

"They never say. Maybe they went to Key West."

Hal puts his head between his knees and hopes the blood returns to his brain. "Look, Mom. You're getting yourself worked up over nothing. They'll be back. They always come back."

And then, inexplicably, Tootsie is crying.

Tootsie never cries. Tootsie sputters, fumes, rages, mutters, growls, hisses. But she doesn't cry. The last time Hal saw Tootsie cry was when her bird died. Somehow, the mangy little parakeet she had bought on sale when the pet store on 41st Street closed, escaped its cage (also on sale), flew into the toilet and drowned. That was five years ago. She put a memorial sticker on the site (green parakeet with gold glitter), which greeted Hal every time he lifted the toilet seat in their guest bathroom to pee.

But she's crying now. Between blubbers, Hal can make out a few words: *years, heart, alone, bagel.*

"Okay, Mom," Hal says, alarmed at this uncharacteristic display of emotion. "Don't freak out. I'm coming over."

When he arrives, he sees Tootsie has pulled out all the old photograph albums which had gathered dust on the bottom shelf of the bookcase for years. To Hal's knowledge, no one had looked at them since his divorce over ten years ago. Neither Arlene nor Hal had wanted the padded white album with the gold-tooled "Our Wedding" inscribed on the front, so Tootsie took it. When the divorce was final, she had insisted on going through it page by page in Hal's presence as she mourned the loss of Arlene, whom she never really liked until she was gone, and the estrangement of her grandson Wally, bar-mitzvah'ed five years before the divorce and who still hadn't written her a thank-you note for the Swatch watch.

"Such a nice girl," Tootsie had said, sighing with each turn of the plastic pages. "Not such a great cook, but is that so important?"

That wasn't the reason for the divorce, but Hal hadn't wanted to go into the real reason, which was his being caught in mid-schtup in his car the parking lot of his gym with the girlfriend of a gym buddy of his, resulting not only in the end of one of the few friendships he had at the gym, but his marriage. Arlene took Wally to Arizona, got herself a younger boyfriend and disappeared from Hal's thoughts except at alimony time.

Tootsie, now dry-eyed, is thumbing through one of the older albums, its photos attached with triangular tabs glued to crumbling black pages. She stops at a picture of herself and Max taken in New Jersey soon after they were married. Her hair is carefully arranged in tight curls beneath a hat with a fly-away

veil, and her face is round and sweet as she looks up at Max. Max, in a rakish fe-
dora, has his arm around her waist; a lopsided grin (which Hal inherited) lifts
his Errol Flynn mustache to a slant. "I loved his mustache," Tootsie says, studying the photo. "When he shaved it off, I couldn't look at him for a week. His lip
looked like it had been put on a stretcher."

If Hal hadn't known they were his parents, he might not have matched the
photo with who they are now. It wasn't just that Max's beaky little nose and
teardrop earlobes had elongated with age, or that Tootsie's soft cushioned
cheeks had dehydrated to the texture of Triscuits. What created a disconnection
was the absence now of the warmth evident between the two of them as they
were in the photograph. They looked like they were in love.

Tootsie stares at the picture of the two of them. "If he doesn't come home,
I'll kill him," she says. She looks as if she might cry again, so Hal tries to distract
her, pointing to a picture of himself as a baby, cross-eyed, porcupine-haired and
fat as a side of bacon.

"No wonder you didn't have any more kids," he says. "You were probably
afraid you'd produce another one like this."

Rather than lift Tootsie out of her melancholy, this seems to drop her into a
pit of despair. Hal is bewildered as she breaks into sobs. "What's wrong?" he
asks. "I didn't turn out *that* bad, did I?"

"I wanted more," she says between sobs. "I just couldn't have more."

Hal had never heard this. In some happy space in his mind, he had always
thought he had no brothers or sisters because just having him was wonderful
enough. Apparently, this wasn't the case.

"We quit trying after all the miscarriages," she says. *All the miscarriages?* Hal
never heard any of this. It was as if the M-word had been as forbidden to say as
the C-and A-words had been. What else didn't he know about his family, his
life?

He has no idea what to say to Tootsie. "I didn't know that," is the best he
can do, followed by a weak "I'm sorry." It seems to provide some consolation,
because Tootsie's tears dry up and she resumes looking through the album,
much to Hal's relief.

She stops at a picture of herself on a beach, what must have been the Miami
Beach of the early fifties. Her hair is ruffled wildly and she's wearing a dopey-
looking bathing suit with a skirt. She resembles an old-movie starlet, someone
who never made the big time but who always played the star's kookie best
friend. The black-and-white photo is hand-colored, and Hal gets a flash of

memory, an image of Max at the dining room table with his tubes of transparent paint.

"Did Dad color this?" he asks.

"A hobby," Tootsie says. "Every night, he took over the dining room table. Look," she says, turning the pages, "like a coloring book." Indeed, several pages of photos are painstakingly hand-colored, until it comes to a sudden stop.

"He got busy with the hotels," Tootsie says in explanation. "Once in a while, he'd go back to it, but mostly he didn't."

But Hal is still lost in the long-ago image of Max at the dining room table. He imagines Max carefully dab color onto a photo with a cotton-wrapped finger, painting the sky bright baby blue, rouging Tootsie's cheeks the startling pink of a fifties movie star, converting Hal's black-and-white baby self into Technicolor. Where did that Max go?

Tootsie studies several faded photos in the album, running a gnarled hand over them as if she could erase time. People in old photos look older than they were, Hal thinks. Maybe he's just transposing onto them the years that have passed since then. "They're all gone," she says. "Some of them, I can't even remember their names." But she does remember every name—Dora, Bessie, Frieda––in one photo of some girlfriends posing next to a '40s coupe. Tootsie herself flirts coyly over one puff-sleeved shoulder. Where did that Tootsie go?

He feels sucked into the past, telescoped in time, and an unfamiliar feeling envelops him: nostalgia. He wants to flip the calendar back, not just to his own beginning, but back to where Tootsie and Max began. Do it different this time, he wants to tell them. Don't stop loving each other, don't grow cranky and mean. If you're different this time around, then maybe I'll be different, too.

He's putting the last of the albums back on their shelf when Max and Zoe arrive. Tootsie buries her relief in a verbal barrage that buries Hal's nostalgia as well. "Where were you?" she cries. "I worry myself sick, thinking you maybe had a heart attack after that bagel you had this morning, you had to load it down with lox when one piece is enough? and hours and hours go by so what do I think, OK, this is it, I'm going to be alone after all these years and why? because you're off looking for a heart attack, riding around, eating lox, who knows what you two do when you're gone, do you tell me? NO!"

Zoe and Max exchange a glance. "We were just riding around and lost track of the time," Zoe says, "and we stopped for ice cream..."

"Cholesterol," Tootsie says.

"...and rode some more." Zoe shrugs. "It's a nice day for a ride."

"I wouldn't know from a nice day. I been inside all day. Worrying."

"Maybe you could call next time," Hal suggests to Zoe as she backs toward the door, "and just let her know you'll be late."

"Right," says Zoe, and she's gone, leaving Hal to Max and Tootsie.

"So!" Hal says to Max, attempting to keep things upbeat. "You had a nice long ride today?"

"I could use a nap." Max heads for the La-Z-Boy, ignoring Hal. He tilts it all the way back and closes his eyes.

"All that aggravation, and this is what he does?" Tootsie asks Hal. "I'm already thinking God forbid funeral and he waltzes in and takes a nap?"

Back to square one. "Be happy you worried for nothing," Hal says. "Good thing you didn't order the deli platters for the shiva."

Hal would like a nap himself. He's going home. He rushed over here because he thought Tootsie was having some kind of emotional meltdown and maybe she *was* having it, but she made a speedy recovery, so what was the rush? His epiphany of nostalgia and longing has vanished with the reality of the present. He can't deal with whatever's going on with Tootsie and Max. He's got enough problems of his own.

Hal wakes up in the middle of the night. The digital clock glows 3:37. Another dream? He can't remember. But his mind is racing with a thought: What if something did happen to Max? Or to Tootsie? And it will. That was the real thought: Not *if*, but *when*. And then...what?

The thought that one and eventually both of his parents will no longer be around is a thought he consciously avoids, but now and then it pops up and surprises him when he's doing something that seems to have no connection to life or death or parents or anything related to those topics. Like today, when he was doing his depressing weekly shopping and sees some old guy in a golf cap trying to read the label on a box of cereal and Hal thinks he's doing that because there's no one to do that for the old guy any more, the old guy's never had to worry about labels or cereal or shopping for anything except maybe beer and chips and now he has to worry about roughage and whether he's getting enough vegetables or too much cholesterol, wondering *what happened, what am I doing here, why isn't Ethel here to do this for me?*

But there is no Ethel for this old guy reading cereal, that's clear. And Hal got really down about that because there's been no wife to read cereal for Hal either, not since Arlene took off, and all those other women, nubile and needy though they may have been, didn't want to pick out cereal for Hal, or anything else for that matter. They were enthralled with him at first, doing what all of Hal's women seemed to want to do for him, take care of him, make dinners for him, pick out shirts for him, plan vacations with him, and then one day, for no reason at least to Hal, they told him to get his own dinner and were gone. He may have chased them off, it's true, because after a while women do get boring, or clingy, or want to get married or live together or do something so cozy and domestic that he can't deal with it, so he'll do something mean or dismissive and then they're gone until the next one comes along. One always does.

Until recently. He hasn't had a real girlfriend since...well, before he started the Staci thing, not that Staci was a girlfriend, but she was a *potential*. If he had just a little more time and things hadn't happened the way they did (accident, father, Versailles, he doesn't like to think of them individually, just as "shit happened") then he's certain that the relationship would have progressed as all his relationships had done in the past: pursue, conquer, dump. Unfortunately, Staci went directly from pursue to dump, and this time he was the dumpee.

So all this went through his head in a flash while he was waiting in the checkout line at Publix today. And now, tonight, he wakes in a cold sweat from a dream—was it something to do with the old guy at Publix?—that made what had been abstract become something very real: that someday, Max and Tootsie––one of them, both of them––will be gone. He feels drained from an avalanche of emotion: grief, guilt, dread, abandonment, not just for Max and Tootsie, but for himself someday. He grasps at the tendrils of what's left of the dream, but they elude him, leaving little wisps of inexplicable clues: a golf cap, a banana, a pair of boxer shorts.

One thing he does know: he will take care of whomever is left, but he could never live with either Tootsie or Max. He would kill himself first. Beyond that, he draws a blank as to any other arrangements. It's not a subject he's ever discussed with his parents. They've never talked about death, never even mentioned the D-word, as if to discuss the issue will bring it down upon them. He knows there's a cemetery plot at Mount Nebo, but it's a piece of real estate that Max has only mentioned once, and that was to complain about the cost.

Hal sure isn't about to bring up the topic himself. They want to bring it up, fine. But he knows they won't. They have other things to worry about: Better to rail against the morons in government, argue about fixing the doorbell, lament the salt in lox, fuss because the cable's out, fidget with a broken toilet chain, dwell on the delay of a thank-you note, resent the signs in Spanish, envy the friends whose kids call daily, disdain the crap in the movies today, wonder why the Steinbergs never invite them over any more. Better to worry about anything but the D-word.

Hal looks at the clock: 4:18. He's got to get some sleep. Three more hours and it's time to get up. Go to sleep. He fluffs his pillow, turns it to the cool side, shuts his eyes tight. Sleep. Sleep. Think of a meadow, the meadow he was told to visualize in the one yoga class he went to with the girlfriend who turned out to be too airy-fairy for him. Okay. He's lying in a meadow. The grass is very soft, very green. The sky is blue, very blue. A gentle breeze is blowing. A puffy cloud is overhead. A little bird is singing.

4:32. He should have gone to medical school. Been a surgeon. Plastic surgeon. Boy, they rake it in. Like Phil Berger. A nose job, a boob job, a facelift or two, and bam, he's bought another house somewhere: Tahoe. Breckenridge. Asheville. Bet Berger's not wondering what he's going to do for a living at the age of 55.

Mayor. He didn't want to be mayor anyway. He just fell into politics, it was natural, they loved him, he ran away with his first election and got the bug. Who knew politics meant getting into bed with sleazebags like Milo? It's not in Hal's nature. Max knows that. He knows Hal isn't to blame for the Louis Quinze thing. He's just being irrational, he's mad at the world anyway, he'll come around. Hal has practically done handsprings to show him how sorry he is, what else does Max want from him?

4:56. Okay. He's in a meadow. Lying on soft green grass, looking up at the blue blue sky. Birds singing, breeze blowing, clouds puffing. If he sees his name mentioned one more time in the paper, he is personally going down to the Herald and pulverizing that Gomez. Punch him out. No warning, just pow, right on the honker.

5:23. Pee. Get a drink of water. Punch pillow. Close eyes. Okay. We're in the fucking meadow. Lying on the fucking green grass, looking up at the fucking blue sky.

Fuck.

Hal turns on the TV. He winces from the brightness as it washes the bedroom in pale blue light. Click. Televangelist. Click. Bette Davis. Click. John Belushi. Click click. CNN. Fox. YouTube. He stops at a view of a surreal meadow: Teletubbies. So soothing. So beautiful. He watches. Green grass. Blue skies. Happybabyface sun. Mellow music. Benign and squeaky-voiced Teletubbies. He wants to be one. He is one. He's bouncing along in a meadow. Bouncy, bouncy, bouncy...

...AND THERE SEEMS TO BE AN EARLY MORNING TIE-UP AT THE BIG BEND OF THE PALMETTO EXPRESSWAY...

What? What?

The clock radio. 7:30. He reaches over and slaps it off. He can't open his eyes. Tired. So tired...

...The phone wakes him. He squints at the clock. 10:17. Ten? Seventeen? Damn!

"What?" he yells into the phone, scrambling to get out of bed. He's got an appointment with Mandelbaum at...shit. Ten-thirty. He's not going to make it.

It's Zoe. "I can't talk now," he says, hurrying into the bathroom. "I overslept."

"I need to talk to you about your father," she says.

"It's going to have to wait," he says, turning on the shower. Steam clouds the room. He pulls his t-shirt over his head while he talks, drops his Jockey shorts on the floor. "I gotta go."

"He's acting strange."

"I'm really late for an appointment. I'll call you later, okay?" Without waiting for an answer, he hangs up. The shower is hot. It feels good. He wonders what Zoe means by "strange." He wonders why Mandelbaum wanted to see him. He wishes he had gotten more sleep.

Mandelbaum's news is not good. Not bad, either, he reassures Hal, something that can be handled, but it seems that Milo's attorney is attempting to implicate Hal in order to soften the indictment for Milo—something about Hal approaching Milo in this deal, offering political favors in exchange for Milo's help in running for mayor.

Hal stares at Mandelbaum with bleary, sleep-deprived eyes. The desire for a one-way ticket to some faraway place with understanding women and no drug laws overwhelms him.

"I didn't make the offer. He did. I may be stupid," Hal admits, "but I'm not guilty."

"I know," Mandelbaum agrees, "but I just want to get all the facts straight before I speak to his attorney. Tell me again the sequence of events."

Why doesn't Mandelbaum just ask him to stick his finger in the pencil sharpener over there, the electric sharpener next to the tastefully framed photo of Mandelbaum and Mrs. Mandelbaum and the three little Mandelbinos who inherited their father's droopy-dog eyes and considerable girth. Sticking his finger in the sharpener would elicit less pain than having to recount once again his role in the sequence of events that have led him to this unhappy state of affairs. But Hal does, with some tweaks of the truth, beginning with Milo's offer to back him for a mayoral run in exchange for a change in the height requirement for Fantabulissimo, which he sort of (*sort of? asks Mandelbaum*) said No to because his father built the Louis Quinze.

And even though the party at Versailles was a kickoff campaign party with some important contributors there, nobody actually contributed anything, not a cent. They were all Milo's buddies, and Hal didn't do one thing for them. And then he quit the race.

Apparently, that satisfies Mandelbaum. Except for one question: "How does your father feel about all this?" he asks. "It being his hotel and all."

Bring on the pencil sharpener. "We haven't discussed it," Hal says. And that's pretty much the truth.

The meeting with Mandelbaum has left Hal shaken, not so much because of what happened, but because it gave him a Yogi Berra moment: It ain't over till it's over. He's still in limbo, and until he feels his feet on solid legal ground, he's keeping his distance from anything or anyone connected with his problems. He hasn't been to a city council meeting since the Versailles incident, and —no surprise––hasn't been invited to dinner at Tootsie and Max's.

He has his hard-core supporters and hangers-on, people he's charmed in the past who remember his smile, his concern, his ability to remember their names, and who just couldn't believe he'd do anything that wasn't on the up-and-up. When they leave messages of support for him and greet him on the street with words of encouragement, he acknowledges them with the practiced grace of the natural politician. He then goes home to himself––someone he's finding it harder and harder to impress.

He needs an Etch-a-Sketch, something to erase the past and leave a clean slate. On that, he'd write a list: 1. Stay out of politics. 2. Listen to your Pop. 3. Don't neglect Wally 4. Pick one woman and try not to cheat 5. Get a pet, something warm and furry like a cat or a dog or a gerbil 6. Stop smoking weed because it makes you make stupid lists.

He's popping popcorn in the microwave for dinner when the phone rings. He doesn't want to answer it. It's much better not to answer it, much better to stand in front of the humming microwave, hypnotized by the sound of the accelerating momentum of popping corn, the Zen of Orville Redenbacher: *Pop. Pop. Pop pop. Pop pop pop. Popopop. POPOPOPOP.* Mesmerized, he meditates on the popcorn bag as it lazily spins on the turntable, slowly ballooning from virgin to pregnant.

The phone keeps ringing. He ignores the flashing message light. The microwave's *ding* snaps him out of his reverie, and he grasps the bag gingerly with practiced hands that tear the bag diagonally, permitting a steamy, sensuous whiff to escape, teasing him with its movie-concession perfume before he rips it fully open and dives into the first, crisp puffs.

The damn phone again. All right, all right. He picks it up with a greasy hand, ready to slam it down. He's not in the mood to speak to anyone.

"Hal? It's Zoe. You got a minute?"

"I'm pretty busy right now," he says, licking his fingers. He doesn't want to hear any more bad news.

"It's your Dad. He seems better now. I thought you should know."

"Well, that's great." Maybe Max has forgiven him. "What's he doing?"

"He's getting out. He's talking." She hesitates. "He's got a new hobby."

"Hobby? What kind of hobby?" Hal gets a flash of Max at the dining room table, hand-coloring the family photos. "Is he painting?"

"No," Zoe says after a long pause. "He's driving."

CHAPTER XIV

ZOE

It started innocently. A few weeks ago, shortly after the disastrous trip to the Louis Quinze, Max had needed socks, or so he said. It was a nice day, so they took a drive up to Aventura mall, a long way to go for socks but that's where Max said he wanted to go, so they went. Zoe was happy to be back on the Wolfe payroll again, and happy, too, that Max wanted to get out, to resume life, to do things again. Even if the thing he wanted to do was buy socks.

So. They're in Aventura. They buy the socks, six pairs of Gold Toe at Macy's, all black, on sale even. To celebrate, they go to Johnny Rockets and order forbidden things: hot dog with chili and onions, fries and a chocolate shake for Max; hamburger (slight guilt––she's cheating on McDonald's) and root beer float for Zoe. Giddy with adventure, Max says he wants to do something else wild and crazy: he wants to drive the simulated race car video he sees in the game arcade.

How can that hurt? So Zoe agrees. Max shoos a kid away from the machine and climbs in the driver's seat. He grips the steering wheel. Zoe drops in the quarters. And he's off! Scenery–houses, trees, cheering crowd––zips by on the video screen as the car caroms off walls and leaves bright explosive splashes of color where he hit something. A flashing row of numbers indicates his escalating speed; the explosions splatter with increasing frequency. And then the ride abruptly ends.

"Again!" Max says like a little kid. "I want to do it again!"

He does it again—five times. Zoe is out of quarters, not to mention patience. There's a lineup of pissed-off kids waiting for the video game, and she's tired of fending them off. Besides, Max has to get home. Tootsie will no doubt be waiting at the door, arms braided at chest-level. Zoe, in an attempt to include her, had invited her to come along, too, but Tootsie had refused, perhaps due to Max's comment, "If she goes, I don't."

Max stalls when they get to the parking lot. "It's too hot," he says when Zoe opens the cab door. She opens all four of Zippity's doors to cool it down, and he still won't get in except on one condition: she lets him drive.

"No way!" Zoe says. "You're not driving my cab."

"Why not? I did good back there in the video car."

"Good? You set the record for smash-ups. Did you see the score?"

"Higher isn't better?"

"Listen, Mr. Wolfe. It's one thing to drive a video car. Driving a real car is another story: you don't have a license, you can't see, and it's *my* car you want to drive." She's got to get him home. She doesn't want to face Tootsie's wrath. But first she's got to get him into the car.

"If you don't get in, I'm going to call the cops to take you home," she says. "You want to ride home again in a police car?"

No. Max does not want to ride home again in a police car. He gets in and slumps down in the back seat. Zoe, relieved, wends her way out of the parking lot until she's stopped by a lineup of Bob's Barricades. Great. They have to go all the way around now. This section of the lot has been blocked off, apparently freshly re-painted with parking stripes.

"Damn," says Zoe. "No wonder it was so hard to get a space."

Max, however, is not dismayed. Actually, he's become quite animated. He rolls down his window and points excitedly at the empty lot. "No cars!" he says. "I can drive here!" At that, he opens the door, jumps out, and opens the driver's side door. "Move over," he demands. "I want to go for a little spin."

Zoe's first inclination is to drag him back inside the cab, but she doesn't have the heart. He's had so many downs lately. Right now he's up; she doesn't know when she's seen him so up. Why not keep him there just a little bit longer? What harm can he do in an empty parking lot?

She quickly shoves aside one of the barricades and edges Zippity through. "Just a *little* spin," she cautions him. "Take it slow, and stop when I tell you to stop."

He nods eagerly and gets behind the wheel. He's wearing the same intense expression he wore when he got behind the wheel of the simulated race car. He flexes his hands, bones prominent beneath translucent skin spattered with coffee-colored spots. His orthopedic shoe stretches toward the accelerator. He squints at the dashboard, fiddles with the gear shift, and says with a touch of disdain, "Hmf. Automatic shift." Zoe's having serious second thoughts, but it's too late. And he's off! Zoe hangs on tight, bracing herself against the glove compartment. The freshly painted parking lines zip by in a blur as he careens around the lot, jerking the wheel happily.

"Slow down!" Zoe yells. He brings it down a notch, turning the wheel all the way to the left, then the right, making a lopsided figure 8.

"How's that?" he asks. "Slow enough for you?"

"No," Zoe says, deeply regretting this entire detour. "I want you to stop."

Max gives it a little more gas. "Just another minute," he says, and picks up speed again.

"Stop," Zoe yells, waving her cell phone in his face, "or I'm calling the cops."

Max sullenly obeys, and at Zoe's insistence returns to the back seat. As they exit, Zoe realizes that the lot is a scribble of yellow tracks imprinted from Max's wild ride over the freshly-painted lines, and Zippity's matching yellow tires attest to their guilt. Outta here! Zoe guns it, hoping the security guard in his golf cart won't realize that the pink car speeding away is leaving the scene of a crime.

"That was fun," Max says. They edge into I-95 rush-hour traffic.

"Why do I trust you?" Zoe says. "I must be losing my mind."

Max is quiet a moment, then, "I'm not losing mine."

Zoe would beg to disagree, but doesn't. "I didn't say you were."

"I'm not senile," he says.

"I know that."

"I am a man of action."

"Well, you've seen enough action for one day." So has she. She's worn out. Who knew getting socks would be such an ordeal?

"I just got a little excited. Next time, I'll take it easy. I won't go so fast." He stares out the window. "Next time, I'll stop when you tell me."

"What next time? There'll be no next time." She has to change lanes. She's behind a longbed trailer stacked high with shiny new cars. She hates those; she always visualizes one of those cars coming unshackled—they never look that secure, like the person chaining them together was drunk or stoned or just careless––and imagines the bright blue Volvo on the end flying off the truck and landing smack on top of Zippity, right in the middle of I-95 rush hour. Trapped, seatbelt-strapped, she braces for her demise––flattened by a flying Volvo.

The image grips her, along with a major hot flash. The gleaming Volvo bobs and bounces on the truck ahead, its grille the demented grin of a member of

Blue Man Group. Her hands, slippery with sweat, slide around the steering wheel as she attempts to change lanes; the car occupying that space responds with an angry honk. She swerves back into her lane momentarily, then swings wildly around the longbed truck, its receding image imprinted with *objects are closer than they appear* in her sideview mirror.

"See what I mean?" She raises a fist in triumph at her success, ignoring Max's terrified yelp. "You want to drive? *This* is driving. Driving isn't toodling around some parking lot or steering a video-game car. Driving takes skill. It takes coordination. And basically, you gotta be able to *see.*"

"I can so see," Max protests. "I saw my racing-car score." Zoe can hear the pout in his voice.

"That's not going to win you a driver's license. And a license, you're not going to get."

"They took it away," he grouses.

"Which is why we get to do stuff together!" Zoe says more perkily than she feels what with the hot flash and the sweat and the sudden desire to pour the contents of her water bottle over her head. "We have fun, don't we?"

Max is silent a moment, then concedes. "The parking lot was fun."

"See?" She extracts a super-size Kleenex from the box on the passenger seat and wipes down her face and neck. "And Johnny Rockets. When's the last time you had a hot dog? With *chili*? And *onions*? Tell me that wasn't fun." She pulls the neck of her T-shirt away from her body and blows into the gap.

"Life is a cabaret."

"Yeah." *Whatever.* Zoe takes a swig from her water bottle before squirting a little down her chest. "You got to take your fun where you find it."

"I found it in the parking lot."

"Look. That was a special treat, and we almost got busted for it. Think of it as a fond memory."

"There are other parking lots to drive in. Or, how's about I drive on streets where there aren't any cars?"

"There are no streets without cars in Miami. It's against the law to have streets without cars. Anybody sees a street without a car, they call the street police, and they'll rush abandoned cars over to fill the space. That's why Miami has more cars per square foot than any other city in the US." She catches his magnified eyes in the rear view mirror. "It's a fact."

Stunned into silence, Max stares back at her.

"So," Zoe concludes, "there are no empty streets to drive on."

Max leans forward over the seat. "You think I'm senile, don't you?"

"Come on. I was just kidding. I don't think you're senile. It was a joke."

"I drove okay on the lot," he says. "I drove fast, I drove slow, I drove in circles, I even did like Sonja Henie, a figure 8. Senile people can't do a figure 8." Dispirited, he sinks back into the seat. "Who knew the paint was wet? I had fun. I did okay."

Zoe blasts the AC on high and tilts all the vents in her direction. *Ahhh. That's better.* But as the temperature falls, so does her resolve. Really, what harm did he do? So they left the parking lot in yellow scribbles, so what? It was the first time she had seen Max so elated. He was a different Max, a confident Max, a bold and happy Max. She had, for one brief crazy spin in the parking lot, glimpsed the Max who once was king.

"Listen," she says, despite a fluttering sensation in her gut that she may live to regret this, "I'll tell you what. Next time we go out, if I can find us an empty parking lot—I mean really empty, like deserted and unpainted—I'll let you drive. But you have to promise to follow the rules."

"What kind of rules?"

"First, you have to listen to me. When I say stop, you really gotta stop. When I say slow down, slow down. When I say It's time to go home, that's when you stop, turn the car off, get into the back seat, and let me drive home. You got that?"

Max gives it a moment's thought. "Can I drive a little bit fast?"

"No."

"*You* drive fast. Why can't I drive fast?"

The fluttering sensation in her gut becomes a big red flapping flag imprinted with YOU WILL LIVE TO REGRET THIS. Praying for a negative answer, she asks, "Do you want to do this or not?"

"Okay," Max says. "It's a deal."

Two days later, it's Max, not Tootsie, on the phone, telling Zoe he needs a ride; he's got an appointment. "What appointment?" Zoe is suspicious.

"A haircut."

"You just had a haircut. You need a haircut like I need a mustache."

"Well, it's been growing a lot lately. It grows a lot when it's hot."

"You just want an excuse to drive." Zoe can't do it now, can't deal with the crazy driving thing right now, all she wants is to pull into that McDonald's over there, the one she's been thinking about since she dropped the barefoot mother

with the three sand-crusted kids off at their hotel and realized she's got to vacuum out the beach they left in the back seat. But not before she satisfies her
sudden craving to grab a Big Mac for sustenance. "You don't need to go anywhere."

"Yes I do. I need to go anywhere." Max sounds desperate. "I need a haircut
very very badly." *Who is that?* Zoe hears Tootsie ask Max. *Who are you talking to?*

"I don't know where you can get a haircut," Zoe says, feeling for some reason that she, too, has to speak in code. "I haven't found a good place to get a
haircut yet." Not that she's looked for someplace he can drive. She was kind of
hoping he'd forget the whole thing. Apparently not.

I didn't hear the phone ring, Tootsie is saying. *Who is it?*

"I'll meet you in front in a half hour," Max says, and hangs up.

Zoe's got indigestion. The Big Mac isn't sitting right and it's all Max's fault.
She had planned to take the burger to a bench at the little park by the water and
watch the Jet-skis plow up the bay while she leisurely savored her snack in all its
bovine yummy-ness. No. Instead she had to grab the Mac on the run, eat it in
the car, drip it all down her favorite Hello Kitty T-shirt. She dabs at the
ketchup smear that stains Kitty's prim little W-shaped smile and slurps what's
left of her Diet Coke noisily through its straw as she drives.

She sees Max standing on the curb in the condo driveway. He's not alone.
Tootsie, arms folded in a furious lock, stands with him, unacknowledged by
Max who waves happily when he sees Zoe. This, Zoe recognizes, spells trouble.
She resists the urge to make a quick U and disappear, and pulls up to the curb.

Tootsie's words follow Max as he climbs into the back seat: "Haircut
schmaircut. You two are up to something, don't tell me you're not, you're always off somewhere, you know what I'm talking about but I don't even want
to think about it."

"So stop thinking about it." Max pulls the door closed.

Zoe thinks she knows what Tootsie is thinking, and the concept appalls her.
"It's not what you think, if that's what you're thinking." Tootsie responds with
a glare. "We're just going for a haircut. And a ride."

In the rear view mirror, she sees Tootsie fuming as they pull away from the
curb.

"I got a place for us," Max says eagerly.

"Are you crazy?" Zoe says. Her paranoia slips down a notch when she realizes what he means by "place."

"It was on the news at noon. They closed the garage at the Biscayan. The building's going to be renovated. Nobody's there. It's blocked off." She hears something she hasn't heard from Max in a long time––maybe never: a chuckle. "It's all ours." He chuckles again. "It's perfect. I know that garage by heart, every twist and turn. I built it! I could drive it blindfolded."

"No way!" Zoe says. A spiraling parking garage is the last place she wants to drive with him. Just the thought is terrifying. She has a problem taking those curves, and she can *see*. It's out of the question.

Max is chortling now. "Nobody's there," he says. "It's all ours."

"All ours? It's not ours. It's not anybody's. It's blocked off."

"Big deal. There are ways." Max settles back in his seat. "Let's go."

Okay, Zoe figures. It's pointless to argue with him. They'll get there, he'll see for himself that they can't get in, and that'll be that. Once the garage is ruled out, she'll find some place, maybe an after-hours school parking lot if she can find one that's not roped off.

The garage is blocked. Its yawning entrance is gated off with barricades, reinforced by a big CLOSED sign. Max only sees it as temporary. "Move it," he says.

"What do you mean, move it?" Zoe is relieved at the sight of the barricade. "That's illegal." And that, she thinks, should settle it. Only it doesn't.

"If you don't move it, I will." With that said, Max is out the door.

"Hey, hey!" Zoe rushes after him. "Get back in the car!"

"Okay, then. You do it." He heads back. Zoe reaches the barricade. It really *is* barricaded. She was going to feign an attempt, but she doesn't have to pretend. The barricades are chained together––solid, locked, there's no simple way to...

She looks up and jumps aside. Zippity is headed straight for the barricade, Max behind the wheel. The barricade goes down in a splintering crash, and he's off! Zoe is too stunned to yell as Zippity zips by her and begins a rumbling climb up the parking ramp. She finds her voice as she runs after it: "Are you out of your fucking mind?" Somehow, Zippity has rounded the first curve unaccompanied by the crashing sound she expected to hear. She runs, panting, up the second ramp. Zippity is out of sight, but she can hear its engine Doppler-echoing its way upward. How can Max, half-blind Max, do that? Even she, expert that she is, finds spiral ramps make her dizzy and fearful that some part of the car will come into serious contact with the unforgiving concrete curves. Is he traveling by sound, like a whale?

Winded, she leans against the wall at Level 3, listening for disaster. The engine sound fades into a distant hum, then stops. Zoe holds her breath. What happened? The hum picks up, grows louder and louder until she can hear the familiar rattle––Zippity's heartbeat that she takes as much for granted as her own––grow louder and closer. When she sees her cab make the final descent of the exit ramp, she remembers to breathe.

Max brings Zippity to a stop at the exit barricade. Zippity's front bumper is battered but unbowed. Zoe runs over, discovers the barricade is locked by a bolt that's easily undone, and pushes it aside. Max grins triumphantly from behind the wheel, exposing teeth she's never seen before. Never has she seen him so happy, not even after his wild ride through the mall parking lot. He's bouncing in the seat like a kid. "That was fun!" he says.

Zoe flings open the driver's-side door and unhooks Max's grip on the steering wheel. "Get in the back seat, pronto." She practically carries him to that destination. "We are so outta here. You want the cops after us again?"

They roar away from the crime scene. Max turns for one last, lingering look. Not until they are safely back on the causeway does Zoe calm down enough to share her thoughts with Max: "Looney tunes! Fucking looney tunes! You are a certifiable nut case."

Max's euphoria, in decline but still undimmed, allows him to overlook that comment. "Did you see how I took those turns? Smooth as glass."

"Lucky! You were damned lucky! You could have killed yourself! And what about my bumper? What about that?"

"It was like I was flying," he reminisces. "Automatic pilot. I could feel it, knew all I had to do was keep turning the wheel to the left, turning turning turning all the way up, keep turning to the right, turning turning turning all the way down. I coulda done it with my eyes closed."

"You might as well have. Why do you think they didn't renew your license?"

"The test guy didn't like me." Max's mood downshifts at the memory. "He said I didn't stop at the stop sign, and I *did.*"

The first time Zoe heard that excuse, she halfway believed him, but now her sympathies were completely with the test guy. She's convinced that Max not only went right through the stop sign, he probably didn't even see it. "I'm not arguing with you." She turns sharply into the condo driveway. "But I will tell you this: I am never, repeat never, letting you drive again."

Max doesn't get out when the valet opens his door. "What about my haircut?" he asks.

"What about it?" *I'm driving away, far far away, and I'm never ever coming back.*

"I didn't get my haircut." And then he reaches over the front seat and touches her on the shoulder, a move so unlike him that she jumps back, startled. "Maybe tomorrow?" Before she can say, "Maybe never," his face breaks into the happy smile she's only seen twice the entire time that she's known him: once after completing his mall parking lot escapade, and today at the triumphant end of his ramp ride. His eyes swim behind his glasses—*are those tears?*—and he says, "Thank you. I forgot what it was like to be happy."

She watches through the lobby doors as he waits at the elevator, hands clasped behind his back, watching the numbers change. He looks somehow taller, more upright, a little smile flashing across his face, sunlight between clouds. When the elevator swallows him up, Zoe imagines what awaits him when Tootsie opens the door, and knows what she must do.

He said Thank you. She leans forward and presses her forehead to the steering wheel. *Oh shit. He said Thank you. He's never thanked me before, never smiled. I made him happy. How can I leave him now?*

So when Max calls to ask when can they drive again, she offers him a deal. Twice a week, she'll pick him up. Empty parking lots only, no ramps. Speed: under 20. He'll stop when Zoe says Stop, slow down when Zoe says Slow down. When she says it's time to go home, he'll stop with no argument, turn the car off, get into the back seat, and let her drive home. They'll always be back in an hour, on the dot. These are the rules, and Max readily agrees.

But how can they explain this to Tootsie? They can't. The only reason they can give her is they're just taking a drive. Well—that's not a lie, is it? Tootsie doesn't have to know who is doing the driving. When Zoe picks Max up for their outings, Tootsie remains in the kitchen, furiously stirring whatever she's stirring, not responding when Zoe calls out, "We'll be back in an hour."

Which they always were, until yesterday, when they got careless. They had stopped for ice cream.

After several days of sampling various parking lots—one had too much gravel, another was fine until they were chased off—Zoe had discovered a lot in a dingy strip mall that was perfect for Max's driving needs. Deserted, off on a side street, its only occupants were a couple of cars that appeared to be abandoned. The stores in the mall looked closed with the exception of a vacuum cleaner repair shop and an ice cream parlor which appeared defunct at first sight. Although Cone Head was clearly in the final stages of retail life, Max suspected otherwise. The neon ice cream cone in its dusty window was dim but still flickered brightly enough to catch Max's eye.

"Let's get ice cream," he said, not moving from his seat behind the wheel after a rousing tour of the parking lot.

"Time to go home," Zoe said. "Time to move to the back seat."

"I wonder if they have chocolate chip. I could use a scoop of chocolate chip."

"It looks closed. Let's get going." She slid out of the passenger seat and opened Max's door. "Come on, Max. A deal is a deal. Stop stalling."

Max got out and scurried toward the beckoning light of Cone Head. "It's open," he announced. Before Zoe could catch up with him, he was inside.

Cone Head was indeed open, but just barely. The clerk, a lava-complexioned kid who apparently had eaten more than his share of ice cream, looked up, startled, from the comic book he was reading.

"You got chocolate chip?" Max peered into the scratched glass panel that needlessly protected a row of empty stainless-steel containers.

"All's we got are some Good Humors over there in the case. Not much left. We're fixin to close soon."

"How about strawberry?"

Zoe attempted to steer Max out the door, but he wouldn't budge. "Let's go, Max. They're out of everything."

"No strawberry either? What kinda ice cream place is this?"

"We got Good Humors," the kid said, miffed. "That's ice cream."

"I'll take a Good Humor, then." Max jerked away from Zoe, fished an ice cream bar out of the cooler, unwrapped and bit it before Zoe could stop him.

"Seventy-nine cents," said the kid. "Plus tax." Max jerked his thumb toward Zoe. "Ask her. I didn't bring my wallet."

Resigned, Zoe paid the kid for two and snagged a Good Humor for herself. Max was already at the car. "Oh, no you don't," Zoe yelled. "No dripping ice cream in my cab." She spotted a rickety wooden picnic table on the sidewalk outside Cone Head, and waved him over. "Let's eat here. And hurry up."

They seated themselves gingerly on the splintered seat. "Nobody here," Max observed between bites. "Another dead strip mall." The chocolate shell of his Good Humor slipped dangerously, revealing the ice cream's pale nudity. Big vanilla blobs dripped on the table, resisting Zoe's attempt to mop them up with the tiny napkins she had found inside. "Strip malls: small potatoes. That's what

Hal does. When he's not pretending to be a lawyer or doing politics." Max slurped up an errant drop before it ran down his hand. "He coulda done better."

"How do you mean?" Zoe figured Hal was no dummy being ivy league and all, but she had to agree with Max. Somehow Hal had managed to screw himself up royally. "What could he have done?"

Max looked off into the bare asphalt of the parking lot. "He coulda taken the business I handed to him and made it grow. That was my dream, that we'd work together, father and son. He was a good boy, my little pal, but then he went to college and that was that. He didn't want any part of it." He bit morosely into the Good Humor. "All he hadda do was keep it going, isn't that what they teach you at Yale? I did the hard part already, took over the company when I was just a kid, and made it what it was. I was the King of Miami Beach!" he said with a flourish that threw a big chunk of chocolate coating onto his shirt. He looked down, plucked it off and stuck it into his mouth.

"Take it easy, Mr. Wolfe." Zoe reached over with her napkin and tried to wipe off the remnants, but a dark fudgy smear remained. "Don't get yourself all worked up."

"He never listened to me. I said black, he said white. I said Develop, he said Politics. I told him, 'Wally's got the smarts in your family, and he didn't get 'em from you."

"Wally?" Then she remembered what Hal had mentioned once in passing, something about Wally the Thankless Little Shit who sells time shares in Tucson. "Hal's son?"

"Yeah. My grandson." Max examined the carbuncle of ice cream left on the stick of his Good Humor before disposing of it in sad little licks. "I haven't seen him much since Hal and Arlene got divorced. I think Wally's in real estate in Arizona. Development, I bet. He got it from me. Smart boy."

"Hal's smart. He just made some mistakes." She took Max's ensuing silence as encouragement to butt in deeper. "He *knows* he made mistakes. And he'd really like to let you know how he feels." More silence. "He feels really sorry. Really really sorry."

Max's eyes narrowed behind his glasses. "Are you his girlfriend?"

Huh? "No! I'm just trying to help."

"What do you care? We're not your family."

That stopped her. She didn't know why she cared, only that somehow, in her loneliness, she had adopted this wackadoo family and made them her own.

That, she realized, made her as nutty as they were. "You're right," she conceded. "It's none of my business."

"Right. You gotta butt into somebody's business, butt into your own family's, not mine."

She picked a slab of chocolate off her Good Humor and bit into it. "I don't have any family. My parents are gone, and so's my husband."

"Gone? Where did they go?"

"They died."

"Your husband died?" Max frowned at that. "I thought you were divorced."

"No. He went and died on me. It's been six years now." She took a moment to lick the fast-dissolving ice cream that threatened to drop off the stick.

"Well. I'm sorry to hear that." Max's face puckered in sympathy. To her surprise, he patted her on her shoulder. "Divorced is one thing. Dead is another."

"I still dream about him." She did. Just the other night, she dreamed that she and Albert were bowling in their bedroom. They were naked except for the cowboy hats, and were eating Spaghetti-O's from the can. She had woken up from the dream sad and hungry.

Max rolled his napkin into a little ball and stuffed it into a crack in the table. "I still dream about Sandra Dee." A shy smile unpuckered his face momentarily, and Zoe got a flash of the young Max she had seen in the old photo. "She used to come to the Louis Quinze with Bobby when he'd perform there. I looked pretty spiffy in those days. We made goo-goo eyes at each other, but we never *did* anything, if you know what I mean. I think Bobby was jealous—you know, Bobby Darin, you remember him?"

"Sure. I used to have a crush on him."

"Sandra Dee. She was the cutest little shiksa I ever saw. Blonde. Big flirty eyes. Cute little button nose." He paused. "She probably looked like you when she got old."

Zoe didn't know whether or not to take that as a compliment, but it didn't matter. What mattered, she realized when she checked her watch, was that they were going to be late. "Tootsie is going to go ballistic. We've got to get going."

But Max was still back in Gidget-land. "I usta flirt with the ladies, but it never came to anything. Ava, Marilyn, Rita, they all were crazy about me. Tootsie, she'd get upset but I wasn't a runaround and she knew it deep down." He stuffed the napkin ball so far into the crack that it disappeared. "Tootsie was the only girl I ever loved."

Zoe was so startled to hear the word *love* come out of Max's mouth that she didn't relate it immediately to Tootsie. His confession didn't mesh at all with the image she had of the two of them. Maybe she heard him wrong. "Tootsie?" she asked.

"Who else?" He gave her a reproving look. "You think maybe it was an arranged marriage or I knocked her up and we had to get married?" He paused. "Not that it couldn'ta happened. She was a hot little number back then. We were always going at it."

Zoe couldn't imagine.

"You wanna know what we called it?"

"Not really."

"Hokey-pokey. That was our secret word. 'Wanna do the hokey-pokey?' one of us would ask and next thing you know, we'd be in bed. It was a popular dance back then. At parties, they'd do the hokey-pokey and it would get us so riled up that we'd have to leave."

So, Zoe was tempted to ask, what happened? When did that stop? Instead, she agreed. "You married for love, then."

"Whaddaya think?" Max was indignant. "You think maybe I married her and didn't love her?"

There. He said it again. "No, no. I just thought...well, you two are always arguing, mad about something or other, but..."

"You ever lived with somebody for 65 years? Living with her is no trip to Disney World, I'll tell you that. But," he added, "I can't think of anybody else I'da wanted to spend sixty-five years with. Or," he conceded, "who woulda wanted to spend it with me."

"You're a good match," Zoe said.

"Yeah," Max agreed. "It wouldn'ta lasted this long if there wasn't some glue to hold it together. We got that glue."

Somehow, the image of the two of them stuck together didn't move Zoe, but his profession of love, for whatever reason—the passage of time, the fear of being alone, the tenacity of glue—did. In their own way, Tootsie and Max really loved each other, and this came as an odd relief to Zoe, as if she were a kid who found out her parents weren't divorcing after all. She linked her arm through his and helped him disengage from the picnic table. "Come on. We're really late. Better get that glue ready because Tootsie's probably coming apart by now."

Max climbed reluctantly into the back seat, and aside from a brief burst of lyrics, *you do the hokey-pokey and you turn yourself around,* he spoke only once on the ride home: "Sandra Dee. She was one cute little shiksa."

By the time they arrived at the condo, Max's mood had dropped to his pre-drive level, but something had changed that day. Zoe had gotten a glimpse of the Inner Max, the soft sweet center inside that hard shell. Behind that stubborn façade was someone who, just like anyone, needed love and wanted happiness. When he was behind the wheel, he was happy. She could relate to that. If letting him drive could perform such a miracle, then perhaps that simple, if illegal, act of kindness could provoke another miracle: Maybe he would soften enough to reconcile with Hal.

It was time to reveal their secret.

CHAPTER XV

HAL

"He's *driving?*" Hal chokes on a kernel of popcorn, has to put the phone down until he hacks it up. "What do you mean, he's driving?" He places the kernel's soggy remains on the granite countertop.

"Just with me. Under controlled conditions..." Zoe says.

"He can't see! He doesn't have a *license!*" Hal pushes a glass into the refrigerator's water dispenser; it ejects an errant spray onto the floor before it hits the glass. He takes a gulp and wishes it were vodka. "Are you out of your mind?"

"No. And neither is he, by the way." She pauses. "He's happy. I think that counts for something."

Hal can't argue with that. He truly wants his father to be happy. Hal wishes he could be happy himself, but this news isn't doing it for him. "He could kill somebody. He could kill himself. He could kill *you.*" Not a bad idea, Hal thinks. "How happy would that make him?"

"He's not going to kill anybody driving in an empty parking lot at 20 miles an hour," Zoe says. "That's it. That's what we do. I let him drive around for an hour, and he goes home happy."

"He drives in circles? In a parking lot?" *He's paying her for this?* Hal takes another swig of water and reconsiders. "Has he hit anything?"

"There's nothing to hit. Actually, he's not a bad driver. One time he even..." she pauses. "Well, trust me, he's not bad."

"One time he even what?"

"Nothing. I just wanted to let you know that his mood seems to be better and maybe it would be a good time to, you know, make things right between you."

"Has he said that?"

"No, but he's mellower now. He actually smiles sometimes. That's a good sign, right? Smiling sometimes?"

Hal can't remember the last time he saw Max smile, unless smirks count. Smirks at something seen or heard on the news, usually accompanied by a comment that included a variation of the word "Idiot." (*see: schmuck, putz, moron, nitwit, nincompoop, pinhead, bonehead, knucklehead.*) That had been the extent of Max's expression of joy for the past six months, which, Hal realizes with a start, is about the time his license was revoked.

Max's mood had darkened steadily since then, plunging into total eclipse when he discovered the Louis Quinze/Hal connection. But with this sudden automotive-inspired brightening of his outlook, maybe, just maybe, Hal could emerge from the shadow of Max's gloom and resume his position as #1 (and only) (if disappointing) Son.

"Smiling is good," Hal agrees. "But what makes you think he'll smile at me?"

"I don't know if he will," Zoe concedes, "but I figure if he's ever going to be in the mood to listen to your apologies, this might be it."

"What do you know about his moods?" Hal's own mood isn't lifting with this busybody telling him what to do. A twinge of jealousy—how come Zoe likes Max more than him?—prompts Hal to blurt, "What do you two talk about, anyway? Driving around, getting him in trouble. Maybe you should mind your own business."

"Maybe you should mind *your* own business," Zoe snaps. "It's your business that's gotten your father all pissed off. Think about it. You've done some really really dumb things and you don't know why he's upset? Grow up. Get a real job. Ditch the pony tail and lose the earring. The sixties are over."

"What does that have to do with my father's moods?"

"Maybe he'll see you differently if you change your image and get out of politics."

"I *am* out. Don't you read the papers?"

"Also, it wouldn't kill you to show him you're sorry."

"You think I didn't try? I almost killed myself trying. What am I supposed to do—throw myself at his feet and beg for mercy?"

"Might work."

Hal considers this for an insane moment. It's not like life has been such an awards ceremony lately. He'd do almost anything to cross this dismal turn of events off his list of Things That Keep Him Up At Night. "Any other bright ideas?"

He can almost hear Zoe think in the silence that follows. "Are you really serious about changing things between you two?" she finally asks.

"Well, what do you think? But what else can I do? I can't turn back the clock." He flashes back to the moment after graduation when he rejected the future Max had planned for him. "You got a magic wand handy?"

"Seriously. 'Sorry' doesn't work. You could tattoo 'sorry' across your sorry ass, for all your dad would care. But if you want to make a dent in his stubbornness, then," she pauses, "be a man of action. *Do* something. It's not good enough just to talk about it. "

"Do what?"

"I don't know. Get off your butt. Figure it out. Get a plan," she says. "Give your dad a reason to believe in you. He really *wants* to believe in you."

"What makes you think he'll listen to me?"

"I can tell. He's just too proud to admit it." Zoe thinks for a moment. "Will Tootsie ask you to dinner? If you're sitting under his nose, he'll have to listen."

Tootsie hasn't asked him to dinner since Max stopped speaking to him. Tootsie phones him every day to give him a Max report, but as for ingesting any of Tootsie's cooking, he has been spared that. Oddly enough, he finds himself missing the familiarity of it, like an abused child might miss the parent he's been separated from by the courts. He's even missed the parched stringiness of Tootsie's brisket, the rigor mortis of her string beans, the ceramic stiffness of her mashed potatoes. He's like a pregnant woman who craves an ice-cream-and-pickle-relish sundae; he knows it's repulsive, but he wants it.

"She's not asking me to dinner," he says. "I don't even know if she's cooking any more. The last time I was there, I ate Jell-O."

"So invite them out to dinner. If Max will go, you're home free."

Max agreed to go out to dinner, if––Tootsie relayed to Hal when he called to invite them––Hal didn't take them to one of those fancy-schmancy places with the *faygeleh* waiters.

So, once again, it's dinner at Humperdink's.

When Hal arrives to pick Tootsie and Max up at their condo, Tootsie has news. "We got another raise in our condo maintenance, this on top of the assessment we just paid for, what? a new gym? we need a new gym? I never use it anyway, not since that time I tried to walk on the treadmill like Dr. Weinberg said to do if I didn't want to, God forbid, break a hip like Elsie Rosenbaum, you know she never got over that, and Weinberg said Pop should use the treadmill too but does he, NO, so I go on the thing and nearly kill myself, it doesn't *stop*, it just keeps going and going and I couldn't get it to stop and I nearly fell off, so how healthy is *that*?"

"I'm not ordering brisket," Max says. "I want the chicken in the pot."

"Anything you want, Pop," Hal says. "It's on me."

"They got shrimp? I want a shrimp cocktail first."

"Harriet," Tootsie continues, "you know Harriet Fishbein in 1710, she bought the Katz's corner apartment? she says she's not paying the assessment, her son-in-law's a lawyer in Kendall and he said if we all sign up we may have a case to sue..."

"Everybody wantsta sue," Max says. "It's a lawsuit world."

"...so what do you think, do you think we should sign up or just pay up, I don't know, who knew? who knew when we bought this place thinking okay, that's that, but NO, every year it's something else, more maintenance, another assessment and for what? the pool leaks? the balconies are falling off? it's always something...Stop!" she cries, spotting the looming neon letters of the Humperdink's sign two blocks away. "There it is!"

Hal resists his usual urge to respond with a smart-ass answer, so pleased is he that nothing seems to have changed. It's almost comforting to hear them resume what is normal conversation for them, as if the Incident had never occurred and Max had never shut him out of his life. Here they are, a family once again, and he has been forgiven.

Max sinks into the vinyl seat of the booth; the table reaches him at mid-chest. He looks so little, so frail. An image of Max sitting in a booster seat crosses Hal's mind, and a wave of sadness washes over him.

The waitress has purple hair and a tableau of tattoos snaking down both arms. Max doesn't notice, and peers closely at the oversized menu she has handed him, his nose almost touching the shiny plastic page. "How you folks doin' today?" the waitress asks, shifting what little there is of her weight from one silver-sneakered foot to the other.

"Isn't this whatsername's table, the waitress with the braids on top of her head?" Tootsie asks, eyeing the waitress with suspicion. "She sick or something?"

"Braids?" The waitress taps her pen against a front tooth, bringing Hal's attention to the ring in her nostril. "You mean Ilse? I think she retired."

"Retired? She's not coming back?" Tootsie looks stricken, as if her best friend had moved to Albuquerque. "Why would she do that?"

The waitress shrugs. "I'll be right back with your rolls," she says, and before Tootsie can further lament the departure of Ilse, their present waitress has van-ished into the kitchen, leaving a violet afterimage shimmering on Hal's retina.

"How does she blow her nose?" Tootsie asks. "What's with that?"

"They have shrimp cocktail, right?" Max asks. "I know it's here somewhere but I can't find it."

"Right here, Pop." Hal points to it on Max's menu. "Anything you want, just name it."

"Jumbo shrimp," Max says. "I want the really big ones. The jumbo ones."

"Jumbo shrimp it is!" Hal can barely suppress his relief. Max is talking to him. Zoe was right. He's happy. That was easy. If circling a parking lot is all it takes to guarantee happiness, Zoe may have hit on the therapeutic tool of the century.

"What's on the Early Bird?" Tootsie asks. "I might try the stuffed cabbage. I haven't made that for a long time."

"Forget the Early Bird." Hal beams with his own generosity. "It's my treat. Go to town!"

"I could go for a lobster," Max says.

"No lobster on the menu, Pop. I thought you wanted chicken in the pot."

"It's a whole chicken. Who eats a whole chicken?" Tootsie objects. "Here, you want chicken?" She rattles the menu at him. "They got chicken fingers."

"I don't want just the chicken's fingers. I want the whole chicken." Max pauses. "And some pickled herring."

Tootsie throws her head back and rolls her eyes. "Oy. I told myself I wasn't going to say anything about salt and I'm not saying a word, just go ahead and bloat, take your blood pressure over the top, all I ask is that when Dr. Weinberg says 'I *told* you not to eat salt!' that you tell him it was your idea, not mine. I give up. I'm not saying a word."

Max reaches over to the condiment bowl and stabs a pickled tomato. Fum-bling, he manages to slice it into quarters, one of which he pops into his mouth, his lips pleating around its sourness. "Mmm, mmm. Nothing better than a good pickled tomato."

Hal finds himself stiffening with the old feeling of irritation and snaps him-self out of it. He's happy, isn't he, that things are slipping back into their old pattern, that Max seems to have forgotten his anger at him, that everything is what once passed for normal? "I'm going to have the brisket," Hal announces. "Just for old times' sake, to remind me of our Friday night dinners." There.

That should nail it. He's part of their family again. The shrimp cocktail arrives: six monster shrimp clutching the edge of a metal bowl. Max grasps a shrimp by its celluloid tail, plunges its head (if it had a head) into the tiny pot of cocktail sauce and pops it whole into his mouth. Hal watches, fascinated and repelled, as it disappears between Max's pursed lips, plumping out his hollow cheeks like he's trying to swallow a mouse. Max's look of bliss as he chomps the crustacean to oblivion is a signal to Hal: This would be a good time to share his thoughts.

"So!" Hal butters a pumpernickel roll with great intensity. "I wanted to tell you what's on my mind." He butters his hand accidentally, but goes on. "I've really, really regretted what happened. I know how much it's hurt you, Pop."

Max dips another shrimp into the cocktail sauce pot and examines it closely before allowing it to join its fast-disappearing sibling. He chews contentedly, seemingly unaware of Hal's attempt at conversation, and delicately places the tail on his plate alongside the nether remains of shrimp #1.

"Nothing I say will make up for that, I know." Hal clears his throat. "But I'm going to do what I can to stop this thing in its tracks."

Max glances at him and makes what Hal hopes is an approving gesture: a slight nod, accompanied by pursed lips, which immediately open to admit shrimp #3, dripping with the last glob of sauce Max has wiped from the pot.

"Here's the plan. I'm going to tell the planning board everything I know, about Milo, about the payoffs, the loopholes, about everything. I'll take the blame for what I did. It's political suicide, but I don't care. I'm through with politics."

"I need more cocktail sauce," Max says around the shrimp. "How they expect you to eat six shrimp with a shot glass wortha sauce?" He looks around and waves his arms in the air as if he's being attacked by a bat. "Where's that waitress? Get her to get me some sauce."

"If you didn't drown the shrimp, you wouldn't need more sauce," Tootsie says. "You're supposed to *dip* them, not drown them, how can you even taste shrimp that's been sloshed around like that, you could be eating shoelaces for all you know so why don't you just order a bucket of cocktail sauce?"

Hal shuts his eyes, takes a deep breath. Ommmm. Ommmm. All is well in the universe. Good thoughts. Good thoughts. "How's the stuffed cabbage, Mom?" he asks in an attempt to derail Tootsie's runaway train. "Bet it's not as good as yours," which he remembers as mushballs of overcooked rice and meat surrounded by limp cabbage leaves stapled together with a hidden toothpick which invariably stabbed him in the gums.

"Hours it took me to make that stuffed cabbage," Tootsie says. "*Hours.* Not like this, it's probably thrown together with tomato soup and frozen this-and-thats, you know how it is with restaurants, they don't take the time to make something homemade, but believe you me, I took the time, I made the effort, and even though it may not have been appreciated, you knew it was good. I was known for my stuffed cabbage." She pauses. "You know what a *balabusta* is?"

Hal reaches for the Yiddish grown stale in the folds of his brain and comes up with, "Good cook?"

"That, too!" Tootsie agrees. "A *balabusta* is a good housewife, a good cook, a good at everything!"

"A *balabusta*," Max says, still waving for the waitress, "you ain't."

Tootsie's buoyancy deflates. Her shoulders beneath her pilled pink cardigan sink like punctured water wings. Hal tenses, awaiting the usual Tootsie re-bound—indignation, an insult, a purse-mouthed glare. Instead, Tootsie falls silent and pokes listlessly at the pale membrane of cabbage cloaking the meatball. The fork seems too heavy for her sparrow-boned hand, flopping impotently as she attempts to penetrate the cabbage's tough hide. Hal fights an urge to reach over and cut her food for her, like a child, and is overwhelmed by an image of himself as the parent of these two infantile people. *Behave yourselves,* his image says. *Sit up straight. Stop playing with your food.*

The idea frightens him, that his parents are dissolving into ancient children, dependent children, children he'll have to feed and bathe and comfort. "You *are* a *balabusta*," he says in a panicked attempt to revive the familiar combat between them that he once abhorred but now desperately desires. "Pop's just kidding you. Hey, Pop. Just kidding, right?"

"Nope."

"Sure you are," Hal insists, trying to keep it light, doesn't want to piss him off, not now, not just when Max has signified his forgiveness by that little nod of acknowledgment when Hal announced he's through with politics. "Mom's a *great* cook. A great..." he gropes for the word, "*everything.*"

Tootsie raises her head slightly from her cabbage-leaf puncturing, sparse eyebrows lifted in the hope of seeing agreement from Max, who is now flagging the waitress with a red-splotched napkin. The waitress's limpid gaze sweeps over him, pauses briefly, then moves on.

"You see that?" Max fumes. "It's like I'm invisible. Whadda I hafta do to get noticed around here? Stand on the chair?"

"*No.*" Hal grabs his arm as Max makes his move. "I'll get you some cocktail sauce. Just sit down, for God's sake."

Max complies reluctantly. Hal wends his way through the restaurant, grabs two tiny sauce pots from the counter and scurries back, fearful of what awaits him at their table. Thankfully, Max and Tootsie have not budged nor, it appears, exchanged a word. "Good," Max says with the arrival of the sauce, then swings into action, nabbing the first of the three remaining shrimp that grip the edge of the bowl in what Hal imagines is sheer terror.

"You're welcome," Hal says. The sarcasm is lost on Max, who is busy sucking the meat out of a shrimp tail. Hal looks over at Tootsie. Her attempts at penetrating the cabbage wall have remained unsuccessful. Hal can't take the tedium of watching her poke about. He grabs his own knife and fork and performs surgery on the spot. The cabbage opens easily, exposing a meatball so traumatized by Tootsie's probing fork that it disintegrates without its protective covering and collapses into the surrounding tomato sauce.

Hal has lost what appetite he walked in with; he just wants to go home. He can't watch his parents eat. It makes him inexplicably sad. He toys with his brisket, takes a bite. Hmm. Not bad—certainly more tender and flavorful than Tootsie's flat, dry version. He stabs another piece, sops it up with rich gravy, takes another bite. This is how brisket should taste, he thinks, and stuffs in yet another mouthful.

But something is missing. What could it be? Not the taste of burned onions he's come to expect, not the carrots cooked to a paste, not the hard chunks of turnip Tootsie thinks gives it flavor.

It's the careful, loving tending of a *balabusta*.

And that, he realizes as Tootsie attempts to guide a soupy meatball morsel onto her fork, is all that she ever wanted to be.

"You're not just a *balabusta*," he says in a burst of truth-stretching acknowledgment. "You're the Martha Stewart of *balabustas!* The best cook, the best housewife, the best at everything."

Tootsie and Max look up, startled, at Hal's announcement.

"I am?" Tootsie asks.

"You are," Hal says, immediately regretting the possibility that he may have taken sides.

"See?" Tootsie says to Max. "And he should know. After all, I raised him."

"Know what you raised?" Max waggles the last shrimp by its tail, spattering-painting the table with sauce. "A back-stabber. A sellout to that...whatsis name, Milo. You raised a *politician*."

"I am *not* a politician." Hal speaks with such force that the couple at the next table swivels their heads in mid-mouthful to stare. "Haven't you been listening to me? I quit!"

"Okay," Max says. "If you're not a politician, then what are you?"

Tootsie breaks the silence. "He's a good son," she says. "That's what he is. A very good son."

* * *

Hal doesn't remember driving his parents back home; he only knows that he did because they're not in the car any more. He drives without purpose as if he's trailered to the car ahead of him, just another bead in the necklace of red brake lights strung out as far as he can see up Collins. He doesn't want to go home. He doesn't know what he wants.

He's not a good son. Not to Max, he's not. He's willing to publicly flay himself, set himself up for who knows what kind of vilification and revenge, what other proof does Max need to forgive him? Doesn't Max know that Hal *needs* his forgiveness? He wants to be the good son.

Lost in regret, Hal becomes vaguely aware of driving west over the causeway towards Miami, finds himself entangled in some kind of detour, and winds up on a dead-end street in a barren neighborhood of nailed-shut windows and doors. He pulls over and parks there, punishing himself with the creepiness of this setting, to think.

Max is right. If he's not a politician, what is he? He'll never be what Max wanted him to be: his successor in the Wolfian empire, the continuation of Max's legacy. He's even failed at his alternate career: he's nothing more than a so-what attorney who could have been great, who could have risen through the ranks to full partner. He could have had his name on the door instead of buried in tiny font on the firm's letterhead below larger-font attorneys who couldn't match him in smarts but exceeded him in drive and ambition: two qualities he mistakenly thought he possessed for politics, but not for the practice of law.

Now it's too late. Too late to start over and climb his way to the top of the legal ladder, to the name on the door, to the recognition he deserved and could have won if only his goal had been law. What was he thinking when he made the decision so long ago that politics was his calling, that he could make it in that world, that he was *special*. He's got to get a life. Get a life get a life. But what can he do that *matters*?

He'll go to New Orleans, that's what, build houses for Habitat for Humanity. Hammer. Paint. Work with his hands. Yeah. He's never been to New Orleans—why is that? Or... he'll volunteer to save the icebergs. Global warming. The earth is melting. He met Al Gore once, shook his hand *Welcome to South Beach, Senator!* when Gore was...what? Running for President? He forgets. Or...the Peace Corps. Is he too old for the Peace Corps? That's what he could do. And go...where? Where do they send you? Mongolia? Somalia? Too scary. He should have done Scary when he was young and stupid. That would have pumped up his resume, now pretty limp at this stage of the game. Why didn't he do those things when there was still time?

He's parked in his garage—he doesn't remember doing that—and is riding the elevator to his apartment. Now he's putting his key in his lock. Now he's inside. Now he's lighting a joint, standing on his wraparound balcony looking at the older condo across the way, its residents still cursing his condo that obliterated their once-great view of the ocean. Hal sees their condo as showtime, shadow puppets behind Pottery Barn sheers, people living their lives: lovers quarreling, children fighting bathtime, liver broiled in Formica kitchens, agitated cellphone conversations on balconies, TVs glimmering bluely.

He moves around the corner of his balcony to watch the causeway, a gilded snake of cars inching across the bay toward the lights of the city. A dew drop of light marks the path of a sailboat as it glides across the dark bay waters. He wonders who's inside––lovers in the V-berth? Or a retired couple living on their boat, frying in stale Crisco the fish they caught, serving it up with a couple of beers, radio playing softly in the background—maybe one of the stations he accidentally comes across while he's punching buttons on the car radio, the station with the female DJ who serves up fifties songs along with advice in her soft sexy voice to listeners who call in the night with their most intimate problems, problems they would never tell anyone except her and the hundreds of listeners out there who understand, people listening to those old songs that remind them of high school or a lover who never called back after they left all those messages on the voice mail, *why couldn't he just call back, just pick up the phone and say, well, it's not working, that's all, it's just not working and we should see other people,* and then she'll play "When I Fall in Love" and "My Funny Valentine" and the listeners sigh and remember.

Night lights are a magnet for Hal, stoned and alone on his balcony. Pin-point lights from ships and freighters delineate the horizon, a diamond chain on a sheet of black satin. In daylight the horizon is clear, cruise ships sailing like great paper hats to the Bahamas or the Caribbean, tourists on board dressed in their nautical best, ready to party, to scarf the lobster at the giant buffet, to eat their way to Cayman and St. Maarten and Cozumel, a little seasick if the ocean gets rough but having a damn good time while they're at it, a damn good time because they paid good money to have a damn good time and by God, they're going to have it.

When's the last time he had a good time? He can't remember. He can't even remember how he got home.

Something's got to change. *He's* got to change. He needs a new image. What was it Zoe said? Grow up. Ditch the earring. Lose the pony tail.

Maybe she's right.

Hal presses the earring into the cotton of the Zale's jewelry box from whence it came. It wasn't his first earring, nor his second. Nor is it a real diamond. After losing two real diamond earrings (one in the bed of his then-girlfriend Lauren, who refused to return it when he said he couldn't marry her because, well, he *was* married, actually, at the time; the other he thinks he ate in a slice of sausage pizza at a Heat game), he bought a zircon replica which passed for the real thing. He stares at his bare ear in the mirror, rubs the lobe. He already misses the earring. He feels naked without the speck of sparkle, now nesting in its cotton bed.

Maybe he should let his hairdresser take the next step: the pruning of the pony tail. But if he waits for an appointment with Fernando, he may chicken out. He rummages through the kitchen drawer and finds a pair of shears whose last duty was to clip a coupon for Rogaine. In the bathroom, he examines the back of his head in the mirror and is momentarily shocked at the regression of his hairline since his last inspection, a cranial low tide revealing flesh he had hoped would never see daylight. And yet, here it is: a peninsula of pale, tender skin, glowing in the halogen brightness.

He reconsiders. Maybe cutting off the pony tail is a bad idea. It's the only real proof that he can grow hair and grow it well. What's there is pulled back in a grey-streaked sweep, captured in a tight black band at the nape of his neck, dangling to his shoulders in a lazy coil. But if he is to move on, the deed must be done. If nothing else, this should prove to Max that he's serious. Hal takes several deep breaths to gird himself. It's not just a haircut, he tells himself; it's a hair *bris*. It's a symbol. Scissors in one hand, pony tail gripped in the other, he begins.

The scissors gnaw away at the coil, hair by stubborn hair. It's harder than Hal imagined. Each bite of the scissors brings from his throat, unbidden, a grunt of regret––too late now—until, still gripped by the band, the pony tail is free. His head feels strangely light, as if it might float off like an errant Macy's parade balloon. The hair that's left springs free in a frizzled curtain around his ears. He resembles a geriatric Clarabelle. He should have gone to Fernando.

Hal gently lays the pony tail on the kitchen counter. It seems to gasp for breath, then goes limp. Hal is filled with an immense sadness as he strokes the length of the coil and says goodbye to his youth. Goodbye to dreams, to ambition, to his secret fantasy of becoming a rock star. The pony tail and earring were a statement: he was a child of the eighties. He thought it would last forever.

He bags the pony tail in a sandwich size ZipLock, then makes room for it and the earring in the Muriel cigar box he's had since he was a kid, where they join the other icons of his life: his lucky aggie marble; the collar from his first and only dog, Wilbur; his Beach High ring; his first driver's license; a champagne cork from his wedding. Hal shuts the Muriel box, leaving the dark-eyed, red-mantilla'd beauty on the lid to watch over the treasures within. Once she was his fantasy of an older woman; now, decades later, she's half his age.

His phone is ringing. Now what? He checks caller ID, sees it's Zoe, doesn't pick up. She's persistent. It rings and rings and rings, hardly resting between rounds. She's not leaving a message. He can't stand it any more.

"What?" he barks into the receiver.

"How'd it go?" She sounds obscenely chipper.

"I cut off my hair. Does that tell you anything?"

"You got a real job?"

Hal winces. "This isn't about a job. It's about my father."

"You cut it for *him*?"

"He stonewalled me when I tried to talk to him. Like I wasn't even there."

"Talking isn't enough," Zoe says. "Actions speak louder..."

"I *have* action in mind. He wouldn't listen."

"What kind of action?"

"I can go public with my role in the political shenanigans of Milo's developments, describe the payoff offer to add twenty stories to Fantabulissimo. I'll go to the planning board, the MDPL, the Urban Arts Committee, do what I can to reverse the preservation loophole his lawyers jumped through so Milo can demolish the Louis Quinze. Public humiliation, forty lashes, whatever it takes. I'll be a whistle-blower. Maybe this could stop the demolition. I tried to tell Pop this, but he just ignored me," Hal says. "He thinks I'm ...*nothing*."

"He said that?"

"He called me a politician. To him it's the same thing."

"So you..."

"Cut off my pony tail. Maybe if I have a new image he'll take me seriously. Maybe he'll listen now." Hal catches his reflection in the dark kitchen window. What's left of his hair has risen perpendicular to his ears. He has to do something. Shave it, maybe. "I've made myself into a freak."

"It's a good thing," Zoe says. "Really. It's a good thing."

"Maybe I'll shave it. Shaved heads are in." He hears a loud slurping noise, the sound of a straw sucking air at the bottom of a cup. What's she doing—eating her McDinner while he's going through this crisis? "Why did you call, anyway? Why all of a sudden is my business your business?"

"I like to keep my clients happy."

"Since when am I your client?"

"Not you. Your father. You know it's just his pride that makes him behave that way with you, and maybe if you really act on your plan, he'll be different. This might be a good time for that––I see him coming out of that black pit he's been in. He's in a better mood now than since I've known him, and I want to keep him that way. Mellow." She pauses for a final slurp around the cup. "I hope whatever went on between you two tonight doesn't set him back. I don't know why you two can't just get along." He hears the rattle of what he imagines is the McDonald's bag.

"Are you finished?" he asks.

"Nope. I got an apple pie here, still hot."

"I mean, are you finished with your Dr. Phil number? Because I have to go. There's a razor waiting for me."

"Don't do it! You have everything to live for!"

"I'm shaving my head, not cutting my wrists. How's that for a new image?"

"Fine, if you're looking for a job as a Mr. Clean lookalike."

Not what he's looking for, even if he'd been serious about shaving his head.

"Look," she says. ""Don't just *talk* about doing something," she pleads. "*Do* something."

Hal hears the crackle of cellophane, then a munching sound. "Hey, I don't want to interfere with your dining experience. I'll handle this my own way. Just butt out, OK?" Before she can answer, he hangs up.

He refuses to pick up when she calls back, but listens to her message later:

"Your dad talks about being a man of action. So be a man of action. Make a difference, and you'll make him proud. He's more than just a cranky old man. I think he'll surprise us all."

CHAPTER XVI

MAX

They're making a party out of it? A party? They're blowing up my hotel in three days and celebrating? Why is this on TV?

The news guy thinks it's funny. He's making a joke about it. What's so funny? Big deal channel 7 news guy, if this is what you think is going to get you on CNN, well guess what, you're always going to be local because you've got no brain, you're just a little local pitskeleh who thinks it's funny to say Big doings on Miami Beach this Saturday, the Louis Quinze is going down!

Why am I listening to this crap? I'm turning it off. Just bad news on top of bad news. I don't need to hear about all the mishegoss going on in the world. Where's the remote? Tootsie, where did you hide the remote? *She always hides the remote..* No, I'm not sitting on it. Wouldn't I know if I was sitting on it? *Oy. Here it is. I'm sitting on it.*

I smell cabbage. She knows it gives me gas. Why doesn't she just serve a bowl of Maalox on the side? Yeah, yeah, I'll be there in a minute. Start without me.

What's this? Now it's on CNN? What's it their business the Louis Quinze is getting blown up, like it's national news? There's going to be A VIP party? Catered in a tent? With a band? It's a funeral, for God's sake, not a wedding. VIP? What's that? Very Important Putzes? Somebody's got to stop it. It's all Hal's fault, he didn't have to help them. But no, he turned into one of them.

Why don't they take care of what's there instead of tearing things down? There'll never be another Louis Quinze. They're building crap now, you see it everywhere, falling-down gone-with-the-wind cardboard crap, not solid like we built. Coulda kept building like that, too. Hal and I shoulda been partners, shoulda carried on that kinda quality I was known for. When he was just a little pisher I'd promise him, this'll be yours some day, the hotels, the whole business. We'll call it Wolfe and Son. He was a smart kid, we were buddies, I was so proud of him. Good-looking, too—looked like me, people said. Who knew he'd go to fancy-schmancy Yale and come out a two-bit politician?

Politicians. They're all over the TV, like vermin, like cockaroaches. Maybe you get a good guy now and then like that mayor, whatsisname, in the fifties, I did a coupla favors for him, he did a coupla favors for me. The Louis Quinze wouldn'ta been built without his help. But times were different then. We didn't have to tear down stuff to develop Miami Beach. There was nothing there to tear down. A coupla big houses, a lotta sand, some coconuts, nothing special––and look what went up. An architectural wonder, that's what they called it in Life Magazine. Yeah, Life Magazine: big spread with photos of movie stars around the pool, bathing beauties on the beach, Sinatra in the club, and me, standing on the diving board, all dressed up in a suit and tie. Great shot. I was famous.

Those were the days. Tootsie looked good then. Maybe not as good as Ava or Marilyn or Bette. I looked good to them, too––that's between me and them, I'm not a big talker—but Tootsie was cute in her way, with a mouth on her that was funny then. Now she won't shut up. What happens to women when they get old, they can't put a lid on it?

The world is turning to shit. I don't know why I even turn on the TV but it's like passing an accident, you don't wanta look but you gotta. What happened to good news, like V-J Day or the walking on the moon thing? Bad enough I gotta listen to pundits, those nutcase news guys spouting their opinions, but there's all this famous-people crap they call news, movie stars showing their bazooms.

We never saw bare bazooms in the movies; we just saw the tops of them. Like Jane Russell. She had nice tops. We didn't need to see nipples, we knew they were there. That's the trouble with movies today. No imagination. And look what they call music these days. It all sounds alike. Tony Bennett is music. Frank Sinatra. Rosemary Clooney. Real names. What kind of name is Snoop Dogg? You know his mother didn't name him that.

Tootsie named Hal. Harold Arnold Wolfe. It sounded dopey to me but Tootsie liked the way it rhymed so who was I to argue, like she said, two days of labor entitled her to the last word on the subject. If I'da known he'd be our only kid, I woulda put up more of an argument, but I figured I'd get to name the next one. Hal hated the Arnold part and changed it to "A." Harold A. Wolfe. Sounds like a politician.

I've forgotten a lot. But sometimes I remember things I haven't thought about for years. They pop up for no good reason, just bing, *and it's like I'm right there again. Little bites of time.* Bing. *I'm leaning against the fridge in our first apart-*

ment, drinking grapefruit juice from a jar while Hal sings a song from kinder-garten about a teapot. Bing. *Tootsie is getting dressed for some fancy charity some-thing. She's straightening the seam of her stocking. The window is open. The bedroom smells like summer rain.* Bing. *I'm making my way to the dining car on the Orange Blossom Special from New York. Between cars, a whoosh of hot steel air, an eardrum-splitting clackety clackety, tracks flying under our feet then* wham *the door slams shut. We sit at a table covered in a starched white cloth and order tomato soup and club sandwiches stuck together with frilly toothpicks and tea served in little pots. The silverware and glasses rattle and shake. Out the win-dow, the sun sets behind an orange grove. The whole world looks orange.*

* * *

Ding.

Max slams the carriage of the old Underwood to the margin. It's surprising that the typewriter's ribbon hasn't dried up altogether, but the type is still legi-ble, if faint, when he presses his forefinger hard against the licorice keys one at a time. He never learned how to type, but hunt-and-peck works just fine.

Dear Miami Herald,

Some kind of telephone system you've got, press one for this, press two for that, never a real person. You wait and wait and then you get disconnected, is that any way to treat someone who's been a subscriber for fifty years? So I'm writing you, even though you never published one, not ONE, of my Letters to the Editor.

This isn't a letter. This is a warning.

Tell those developers, don't tear down the Louis Quinze!!! Here's a headline for you: SAVE THE LOUIS QUINZE, THE MOST FAMOUS HOTEL ON MIAMI BEACH! It's built strong, to last centuries! I know this because I built it! Look it up! It's in the history books! Did they tear down the Eiffel Tower because it's old? Even the Leaning Tower of Pisa, look at that! It's leaning! But do they tear it down? No!!! And it's really old!

STOP THIS DEMOLITION OR I WILL. I am a man of action! If I don't hear from you, I'll know it's up to me, so call me at 305-555-2920. If my wife an-swers, hang up and call again. Sometimes I can't hear the phone.

Best wishes,

Max Wolfe, Developer

Where did Tootsie put the stamps? She's been paying the bills since his vi-sion went downhill, so now he doesn't know where anything is. Here's a bunch of them, a little stuck together but okay. How much is postage? What's this with the space shuttle on it? Twenty-two cents. Or is it 27? Probably enough, but just to be safe, stick on another stamp, how about this one? Some kinda flower, looks like 10 cents, that should be more than enough. He carefully licks their backs and sticks them onto the envelope he's hand-addressed in big block letters to the *Herald*. He has to hurry downstairs to the mailbox before Tootsie gets back from shopping.

As he drops the letter into the slot, it occurs to him: What if the *Herald* doesn't call him? What will he do? He's only got three days to come up with something.

CHAPTER XVII

ZOE

Max hasn't mentioned it and Zoe hasn't brought it up, even though it's been national news all day that the Louis Quinze will be imploded in three days, reduced to a pile of rubble in one explosive, made-for-media moment. Not one word on the subject as they drive to the mall for new orthopedic shoes; not one word on any subject, actually, on the way back. Maybe Max hasn't read the paper or turned on TV today. Well, good luck, because if he has, there's probably some kind of implosion of its own going on beneath that little pink scalp that Zoe would rather not deal with.

Hal called today when the news of the impending demolition went public. "You said, *be a man of action*," he said. "So, I figured, what have I got to lose? I'm already a loser. So, I went into action."

He did the hard part first. He appeared before the Miami Beach Commission and repented for his sins, which he spoke in a loud voice to cover up his nervousness. First: His exploitation of the loophole that enabled Milo's past buildings to attain heights surpassing legal limits. Second: His taking the bait of Milo's promise of the mayor's seat if Hal repeated his height sleight-of-hand for Fantabulissimo. Third: His failure to counteract Milo's posse of lawyers whose questionable legalities overrode the historic designation of the Louis Quinze, enabling its imminent demolition. In short, he was guilty of succumbing to outside influence to the detriment of the city of Miami Beach (but not punishably guilty, Mandelbaum had assured him). Certain members of the commission sank slowly in their seats as he spoke, themselves participants in such sneaky shenanigans, as Hal well knew.

That done, he then met with the chairman of the Miami Design Preservation League, who, given Hal's recent Versailles adventure and resultant public humiliation, had initially refused his phone call. But Hal had turned on his charm, this time with heartfelt intent, and convinced the chairman of his sincerity. Also, as he pointed out, being as he was in the last throes of his political influence, Hal might be the MDPL's last hope to prevent the death of the Louis Quinze.

Although the members of the MDPL were highly suspicious of Hal's request, they were desperate. Their fruitless struggle, legal and extra-legal, to save the Louis Quinze had escalated to the point where, in the spirit of their founding mother, Barbara Capitman, certain members had taken to chaining themselves to the surrounding fence. Others had set up a candlelight vigil which resulted in their arrest when, in their zeal, they briefly set the hair of a curious bystander on fire. Their antics had garnered them some faint publicity which was, unfortunately, bad timing, lost in the avalanche of media attention at the height of Art Basel and its of-the-moment celebrities, undercover parties and overrated art. The impending demise of the Louis Quinze paled in kitschy comparison.

In a last-ditch effort to prevent the demolition, Hal joined with the MDPL chairman and requested an emergency meeting today of the Planning and Zoning Board to rescind the demolition permit. Overwhelmed with pending studies on whether the tennis courts should be clay or hard, or how many trees should be allotted for Alton Road, or if Burrito Benny's window menu display could exceed the three-square-foot maximum to allow for their 200-plus selection of burritos of all nations, the planning board agreed to take up the question of demolition permitting tomorrow, if they had time.

"Three days," Hal had groaned when he relayed this information to Zoe. "How will we stop this in three days?"

"Two days, actually," she had corrected. "Today's almost over."

* * *

Well, so much for optimism. Hal calls Zoe the next morning to wake her with the bad news he just received from the MDPL: After all his efforts, the demolition has been scheduled as planned. This news dilutes what would have been his good news: Prompted by Max's witnessing on TV Hal's appearance before the commission and his plea for a repeal of the demolition edict, Max wanted to talk.

"At first he was his cranky self, not willing to do more than admit that he knew I was sorry," Hal says. "But then he said the most surprising thing. He said he was sorry, too."

"Sorry for what?" Zoe asks, although she could compile a long list of things Max could be sorry for, if he truly regretted his ways.

"That he hadn't trusted me. He hadn't believed I would do what I said I would. But somehow, watching me really try to make my case to the commission, seeing me expose myself like I did, well, I guess that did something that made him see me differently. I think he was more surprised at his reaction than I was. And I *was* surprised. The most I expected was some kind of grudging forgiveness. But he went further.

"He said that when – not if – but *when* the Louis Quinze is saved from demolition, he wanted to buy it from Milo, and then renovate it. With me as his partner."

"It's hard to renovate a demolished building." Zoe climbs out of bed and takes the phone with her to pee.

"He doesn't know that yet, and I can't bring myself to tell him. He'll find out soon enough."

"You'd better tell him before he watches TV this morning."

"I know. I know." Hal is silent a moment. "I tried to tell him it might be too late to stop it from happening, but he wasn't listening." He pauses. "Are you peeing?"

Zoe confirms that with a flush. "At least you tried, you really did. And he knows that."

"I hope. I hope he doesn't think I just screwed up again. I screwed up, all those years ago, not going in with Pop like he wanted. Too late now. Shoulda done it then."

"Coulda shoulda woulda," she says around her toothbrush.

"Wise words. But unless there's some kind of miracle, the demolition's on schedule, and we've got to come up with some way to keep Pop away from there, at least till it's over."

"*We?* You, not me," Zoe says. "That's your department."

"He might do something crazy. You're better at handling him than I am."

"What can he do that's crazy?" As if Max didn't already have a crazy person's rap sheet. She amends the question. "What could he do about it anyway? *I'm* sure not taking him there."

"He's a sly old fox. You gotta watch him."

"Me watch him? *You* watch him. I'm just his driver."

But she knows she's more than that. She's Max's caretaker, his confidant, his watchdog as well. How did that happen? At first it was just a job and a guaranteed income, but now she really cares about Max even though he drives her wacko, and look where that's gotten her. She's had to put Zippity Trips on hold for too long already. This nutty family is stalling her career.

"All I'm saying is keep him busy the day the implosion happens," Hal insists. "They're televising it live in the morning, and they'll be showing it on the news all day. Take him someplace where there's no TV."

"There's no such place. Why don't you just unplug it? That'll solve the problem."

"Are you out of your mind? He's perfectly capable of plugging in a TV. Besides, they've got three sets. Just get him through the day. Once it's over, he'll be okay. But before, who knows? He's done some wacko things."

"I know what he's done. I was there."

"You were," Hal says with what she wants to think is regret. "And I appreciate it. You've had to deal with a lot. He's a handful."

"I've been the clean-up crew."

"I know."

"You say you know, and then you make another mess I've got to clean up. Think about it. None of this would have happened if you had a shred of conscience."

"That's not fair. What do you think I've been doing all week, trying to make up for everything?" Hal sighs. "He's had this little window of happiness. It's going to be a disaster when it closes."

"Okay, I do give you credit for that. But disappearing your dad for a day isn't part of my job description."

"I'm pleading with you. Just keep him occupied tomorrow. I don't want any more trouble."

"Then you gotta help me out here," Zoe told him. "I can't levitate him out of the house. Talk to your mother. Think of an excuse. Get him into my cab and I'll do the rest."

The cable is out. At least, that's what Max thought when he turned on the news and all he got was snow and static. "So there'll be no TV at the Wolfe abode tomorrow," Hal says when he calls Zoe to tell her what he's done. "I paid one of the maintenance guys in their building to disconnect the box in their hallway."

"How's Max reacting to no TV?"

"Nuts. Totally nuts. He tried to call the cable company to complain but was put on hold," Hal says. "He almost broke the phone banging it on the kitchen counter. He said he needed to know what was happening with the demolition. So I guess he already heard the news." Zoe hears Hal's sudden intake of breath, then silence.

"Hello?"

"I'm here," he says on what she knows by now to be a smoky exhale. "I was afraid I'd have a problem with Mom, but I told her what was up, how Pop would go into meltdown if he watched it happen. She said he was already melted down, she couldn't take any more melting. So she said okay but made me promise it'd get turned on again before "The Young and the Restless" on Monday."

"No TV tomorrow, right? So I can take the day off?" *Good,* Zoe thinks, *I'll cool off in a movie, go to Macy's sale, I could use some new shorts...*

"Not so fast. You need to take him somewhere, get his mind off what's happening. If he and my mother have to spend the day together, one of them might not survive."

I really need some shorts. All my shorts have shrunk up. It's weird they all shrank at the same time. "Tootsie won't go for that," she says. "She'll think we're going to shack up somewhere romantic, like the Publix parking lot."

"She was surprisingly okay with it. He's been driving her bonkers ever since he heard the news. She said she wanted some time to herself anyway because she needed a break, that having him around now was like living with Nixon on his worst day."

"So how do I get him out of the condo and out on the road?" Zoe resigns herself to tight shorts for a while, at least until the next sale.

"I'm working on some reverse psychology. I told Mom to tell Pop, 'Now don't you go calling that Zoe to take you out tomorrow,' so Pop will probably call you."

Zoe's phone rings right after she hangs up from Hal. It's Max. He wants to take a ride tomorrow.

"Great," she says. "We'll go someplace special."

"I got a place in mind," he says. "Pick me up at nine." And with a click, he's gone.

Zoe stares at the phone. She knows where he wants to go, and she's not taking him there.

Max is waiting out front when she pulls up. He's wearing the brown suit. She knows why.

"We're not going there." She'll pre-empt him before he even asks to go to the demolition site.

"I have to watch," he says. "I saw the Louis Quinze being born. Now I have to watch it die."

"I'm not going to let you torture yourself. I have an awesome day planned."

"I don't need an awesome day. I need to be there." He opens the door on the passenger side and settles into the front seat. Zoe gives him a sideways glance. He never rides shotgun. Another bad sign.

"Seatbelt," she says. He obeys. Zippity pulls away from the curb with a subdued chug, a cab on a mission. Zoe takes a turn off Collins and heads west.

"Hey!" Max lunges at the wheel. "It's straight ahead. Where are you going?"

Zoe jams on the brakes. Zippity shudders and screeches to a halt at the curb. "Get in the back," Zoe orders. "What are you doing, grabbing the steering wheel like that? I'm driving! Move your skinny ass! I said I had an awesome day planned, dammit, and I meant it."

Max sits immobile for several seconds. To her relief, he picks himself up and gets into the back seat. Scrunched down in his too-big suit, he seems to glower at her from the depths of a brown paper bag.

"Okay, that's better." Zoe pulls away from the curb and flicks on the radio. NPR. Old Click and Clack replays are on. The day has taken a sunnier turn. They're bantering about fuel pumps and brake fluid with a giggly girl from Omaha, and all is right with Zoe's world again.

"Here's the plan," she says, peering at the egg-shell top of Max's head visible in the rear view mirror. "We're going someplace special so you can drive. No, not just drive. Drive *fast*. Wanna guess where?" Max's reply is grim silence, but she forges ahead, laying out the plan she had lain awake plotting until two in the morning: They'd travel far, far away, far enough away to bring them back after the demolition was over, doing something distracting enough to take his mind off of it, with enough forbidden food to satisfy his lust for danger.

"Homestead Speedway," she announces. "The racetrack! How'd you like to drive as fast as you want on the speedway?" She hadn't figured yet the logistics of doing that, but somehow she'll make it work. Receiving no response, she continues happily. "Didn't I tell you it would be an awesome day? So, first stop: Dilly Deli, to pick up a picnic lunch. Herring? Lox? Anything you want. Pickles? Pastrami? You name it, you got it. We'll snack and speed, snack and speed. Can you imagine a more awesome day than that?"

Max has straightened up enough so she can see his magnified eyes in the mirror. "Hmf," he says. She takes it for agreement.

Goody. A parking place right in front of Dilly Deli; oh shit, it's a loading zone. "Let's go," she says, opening Max's door. "We've gotta make this quick. This isn't a real parking place."

"I'll wait in the car," Max says. "Leave the keys in case I gotta move it."

"Get real. You're not moving it anywhere." Zoe has a flashback of their last excursion to Dilly Deli. "You're coming with me." He doesn't budge. "Okay, I'm taking you home. You and Tootsie can stare each other down all day."

That works. With Max grudgingly by her side, she unloads her purse into the kiddie seat of the shopping cart and pushes it to the deli section. There's a line. She takes a number: 86. "Seventy-nine," calls the deli guy into the mike. "Eighty." The lineup of customers at the counter checks their tickets as if they are Bingo cards. "Eighty-one." *Yeah, eighty-one here. I'd like a pounda chopped liver, oh bout a half pounda egg salad, and gimme summa that green stuff there, yeah, that stuff.*

"Eighty-two." *That's me, eighty-two. Turkey, sliced thin? I mean really thin, like shave it, you know? So you can almost see through it? Quarter pound. It's low-fat, right?*

Max is peering into the deli case. "I want salami," he says to Zoe. "And creamed herring. And lox."

"Eighty-three. Eighty-three." A guy with a greasy comb-over and high-waisted Dockers waves his ticket. After careful deliberation, he orders the shrimp with pasta salad. He changes his mind in favor of the bean and corn salad, then questions the source of the poultry that gave their lives for the chicken salad. When he debates regular tuna salad versus the low-fat version and asks for a taste of each, Zoe can't take it any more.

"Just pick something, doofus," she mutters.

"What?" Comb-over halts in mid-taste, tiny plastic spoon clenched between tuna-clogged teeth. "You got a problem, lady?"

"You're the one with the problem," she says. "Make up your mind. You're not picking out a ring at Tiffany's. It's *food*."

"Don't rush me. I'm not going to be rushed. You're in a hurry, go to Burger King." He drops the used spoon into the little bucket on the counter and turns to the deli guy. "I think I'd like to taste the lobster salad."

Before Comb-over can get the spoon to his lips, Zoe grabs it and shoves it into her mouth. "It's yummy," she pronounces. "Now get a pound of it and move your sorry butt out of here."

"Did you see that?" Comb-over yells at the waiting crowd. "She *ate my taste.*"

The crowd shuffles uneasily, studying their number stubs with renewed interest.

"Sir," says the deli guy, an experienced hand at counter-induced altercations, "please place your order so we can move on."

Comb-over glares at Zoe, turns to the deli meister and in a cold and level voice says, "Give me a taste of lobster salad."

"Okay, that's it," Zoe says, wheeling around. "Come on, Max, we're outta here."

But Max is gone. And so is her purse.

"Max? Max!" Zoe shoves aside the customers eager to take her place and takes off on a run. She barrels out the front door of Dilly Deli.

The loading zone is empty. Zippity Cab is gone.

CHAPTER XVIII

MAX

Max grips the steering wheel with both hands, ignoring the blare of horns he's leaving in his wake. It's hard enough to see over the steering wheel; how do they expect him to concentrate with all that racket? He has to slump down even further to reach the brake and accelerator with his toe. *Shoulda moved the seat, how does she do that?* He gropes around under the seat, tries to force the lever forward, gives up. Well, it's not that far to the Louis Quinze. He can make it if these jerks would just get out of his way. He leans on the horn *A-ooo-ga* and swerves up on the curb momentarily to pass a station wagon from Ohio on the right.

He feels alive, tingling as if he'd been struck by some magical lightning bolt. His mission has begun. If there had been some plan to this mission, his escape from Dilly Deli would have figured into it, but who knew? He just got lucky. When he woke up this morning he only knew that he had to do something, anything. And somehow he knew that going somewhere, anywhere, with Zoe would make it happen. *My brain still works. If I wasn't all there, how would I have known the perfect moment to grab Zoe's purse with the keys and get the hell outta Dilly Deli? How would I have remembered how to start the car and drive in traffic? The brain cells are all there, and they work just fine.*

None of this woulda been necessary if those jerks at the Herald had bothered to answer my letter. I bet they think I'm some old fart they don't have to pay attention to. Well, here's a headline for them: Old Fart Stops Louis Quinze Demolition.

Max brings Zippity to a head-snapping halt as traffic comes to a standstill. A barricade up ahead is preventing access to the Louis Quinze and traffic has been detoured. *Okay brain cells. Get to work. Get me out of this mess.* Caught up in the ooze of bumper-to-bumper traffic that lumbers like an articulated beast around the detour, he bullies his way across lanes without acknowledging the honks, screams and curses coming from cars he barely misses. Just before the barrier, he sees what he thinks is a sign with an arrow. *What's that?* He leans forward, squinting. *Parking? Is that for parking?* He makes a sharp left and finds himself in a long line entering a car-filled expanse of grass and dirt that stretches off into the distance, ending in a chain-link fence surrounding the Louis Quinze. The entry to the dirt-lot is blocked by a scowling parking attendant.

"Five bucks," barks the attendant.

"I gotta pay to park? What, are you kidding?"

"Five bucks," the attendant repeats. "Nothin's for free, buddy."

Max grudgingly hands the attendant five dollars he scavenges from Zoe's purse, then weaves Zippity through rows of parked cars, past families toting coolers, couples holding hands, kids on cellphones, bleary-eyed partiers still up after a night on the town. They're all carrying phones, cameras or binoculars, and they're all excited.

What's so exciting? They're blowing up my hotel. Doesn't anybody care? As Max edges Zippity closer, he sees the snowy peaks of a mammoth tent. A large banner with the message *VIP Event: Invitation Only* bars the tent to common-ers who, attracted by the rhythm of a salsa band and the charcoal fragrance of grilling meat, peer in curiously as they walk by. An army of Friendly John porta-potties stands sentinel. Max stops the car and glares at the VIPs, plastic wine glasses in hand, who mill about white-tableclothed picnic tables laden with platters of food. It's all ghoulishly festive, like those old photographs of people celebrating at a lynching in the South.

A voice crackles over a loudspeaker: *Two minutes. Two minutes to count-down.* A warning siren goes off. The crowd cheers and surges toward the fence. Cameras and cellphones are held high over heads in anticipation. A gutted al-abaster monument, the Louis Quinze waits with Marie Antoinette stoicism, its blank and shattered windows revealing nothing. The crown of Max's kingdom is now a desolate shell doomed to imminent death. Max must ride to the rescue.

Somehow, he knew this moment would happen all along, as if beneath his cloak of despair had been hidden a brilliant plan, a plan just revealed to him in a flashback of CNN memory: the image of a solitary Chinese man holding back a tank in Tiananmen Square.

Max is that solitary man. Max will hold back the tank. Max is a man of action.

CHAPTER XIX

ZOE

Now what? Zippity cab is gone, her purse is gone, and Hal isn't answering his cell. Zoe pockets her phone again and ponders her next step. Call Tootsie? God no. Call (*oh, the humiliation*) a cab and catch up with Max? She knows where he's headed, but how will she find him? The Dixie Chicks ringtone sings from her pocket, startling her out of her immobility. It's Tootsie.

"Bring him home *right now*," Tootsie says without a Hello. "He's up to something and that something is trouble and you got to bring him home."

"What are you..."

"I got it here in black and white, right here, a letter to the *Miami Herald*, it came back postage due today, the dumbkopf, he didn't put the right postage on it, what does he know from postage, I pay the bills, when's the last time he stuck a stamp on an envelope, so it comes back and I open it to see what this is, and what is it he's writing them about? The Louis Quinze! *This is a warning,* he tells the Herald, *stop this demolition or I will* but what do they know, they didn't get the letter, how are they supposed to know he wants them to stop anything, and would they care anyway? so before he does something crazy I want you to bring him home *now.*"

Zoe feels she's been transported to another dimension. Time slows to a sludgy pace. Traffic floats serenely down Alton Road. The green-haired girl coming out of Dilly Deli gazes at her lovingly with egg-yolk yellow eyes, and that homeless guy is Jim Morrison, alive and well and singing to her, *Baby won't you light my fire*. Once she took acid and felt like this. Maybe she'll stay this way forever.

Tootsie's voice snaps her back. "Zoe? Zoe? I'm calling the police."

Traffic resumes its feverish pace. The green-haired girl still has green hair, but her loving egg-yolk gaze has become a slit-eyed glare. And Jim Morrison is blowing his nose in the street.

"No! Don't call the police," Zoe says, suddenly alert. "I'll find him."

"He's lost?"

Shit. "He took my cab." Pause. "I think he went to the Louis Quinze."

"The Louis *Quinze*?" Tootsie's voice reaches a decibel Zoe would have thought was even beyond Tootsie's range. "They're blowing it *up*. Isn't that why you took him away for the day? To get him *away* from the blowing up. And what do you do, you lose him!" Tootsie stops. Zoe waits. She braces herself for Tootsie's inevitable realization of the true situation, which comes in an octave known only to dogs and small insects: "He's *driving*?"

"That wasn't part of the plan." Although, Zoe has to admit, that was part of the plan, the bait that would lure him far, far away. But, like a fish that snags the bait and then escapes, Max had stolen, not just the bait, but the whole boat. And now he was driving—*driving*—it to the one destination she had busted her ass to avoid. And she had no way to catch up with him. Unless...

"Can you drive over here quick and pick me up?" Zoe braces herself for the big No, but what else can she do? She could try and get a cab, but (thanks to Max's purse-snatching) having no money would entail a confrontation with a pissed-off cabbie who wouldn't get her there on time anyway unless he let her drive and good luck with that happening.

"Pick you up?" Tootsie is saying. "I'm not picking you up. I'm calling Hal. He'll find him."

"First you've got to find Hal." Zoe feels like she's in one of those Escher drawings she's seen where people are climbing stairs that seem to go up but then they're going down and where they're really going is nowhere. She's going nowhere, and Max is going somewhere, and where he's going isn't good. "Hal's not answering his cell. I left messages."

"Why isn't he answering his cell?"

"I don't know! How should I know? Why does it matter? You want to find Max? Pick me up! And *hurry.*"

"I'll get there as soon as I can," Tootsie says, mollified. "Wait out front so I don't have to park, I'm not a very good parker."

Also, not a very good—or speedy—driver, Zoe remembers. By the time Tootsie picks her up it could be tomorrow and what's about to happen could be yesterday's news. "Never mind," Zoe amends, gritting her teeth with the realization of what she'll be forced to do. "I'll get a cab. Stay put. I'll call you later."

"Wait, wait..." are Tootsie's last words before Zoe hangs up and races to the street to flag down the cab she spotted, a cab now stopped at the light, a cab with passengers in the back seat and a red-faced cabbie who yells "Whaddayadoin?" at Zoe when she opens the door and orders the passengers out.

"It's an emergency," Zoe cries. She tugs at the arm of a spike-haired kid whose preoccupation with the video game between his hands is barely broken until his phone goes flying out the door, thanks to Zoe's frenetic action. The kid follows the phone, the mother follows the kid. Zoe slams the door behind them and mashes down the lock. "The Louis Quinze," she commands the stunned cabbie. His response is negative.

"Gedouttamycab or imcallindacops. I got passengers, you crazy nut, gedouttahere!" The mother pulls on the door handle, pounds on the window, points to her kid's tear-stained face and his hand clutching the mangled phone. Horns blare as the light changes to green. The cabbie gives the cars behind him the finger, an apparently damaged finger, bandaged with a Donald Duck Bandaid. "Fuck off," he yells at the clot of cars, a deja-vu moment for Zoe which summons the painful memory of the day this adventure began.

"Just go, go, *go*." She leans over the seat and points ahead. "It's life or death."

"For *you*, if you don't get outta my cab."

"A hundred bucks. A hundred bucks if you get me there in ten minutes. Two hundred if you get me there in five."

"The Louis Quinze?" He accelerates quickly, blending into the traffic flow with a goodbye wave to his former passengers. "Idn't that getting blown up today?"

"That's why it's an emergency—somebody might get blown up with it."

He deftly executes a U-turn at an intersection without hitting any of the pedestrians scurrying out of his way. Zoe, reluctantly impressed by his ability, still has to control the urge to take the wheel herself, especially when the cab slows and then stops dead. Traffic has frozen at the intersection of Alton and 41st where a parade of Lubavitch families trundles babies, baby buggies, strollers and an assortment of kids of all ages to the nearby Chabad house, defying the walk/don't walk light as its little green man changes to the big red hand, then back again. The last straggler finally climbs the curb, oblivious to the cacophony of honking horns and shouts from drivers. Traffic inches forward once again, picks up a little as they turn onto Collins.

"We're not gonna make it," Zoe says. "Drive on the median."

"What?"

"I'm a cabbie. I've done it. You can do it. It's an emergency. Drive on the median."

"You're a cabbie?"

"Yeah."

"Where's your cab?"

"It's at the Louis Quinze. Drive on the median."

"What's your cab doing at the Louis Quinze?"

"Getting blown up if you don't drive on the median."

"Okay, Babe, but you'll pay for the ticket." The cab thumps heavily onto the median strip, its back wheels whirring before they make the climb, and they're off, skirting signage poles, thumping off, then onto the median again between turn lanes, passing drivers whose expressions vary between astonishment and anger.

Zoe hears the whine of warning sirens from the direction of the Louis Quinze. "It's happening," she yells. "Hurry! It's happening! It's going to blow!"

The cabbie skirts the barrier set up across Collins, and, urged onward by Zoe's shouts of encouragement, barrels through the parking lot, scatters the onlookers, and bores through the chain link fence surrounding the hotel. She sees a flash of pink in the distance. It's Zippity! "There he is!" she cries. "Follow that cab!" Max has paved their path for them, a wide stretch of dirt marked by tread marks and people shouting and pointing in the direction of the hotel.

The countdown is on, echoing over the loudspeakers: *Seven. Six. Five.* She suddenly realizes Max's true mission as the pink flash aims at what was once the grand entrance of the Louis Quinze.

"Hey!" the cabbie yells when she flings open his cab door and takes off on a run. "Where's my two hunnert bucks?"

But Zoe hears only the shatter of breaking glass and a gut-grinding crunch, a sound nearly drowned out by the raucous salsa beat coming from the VIP tent as the countdown continues.

FOUR!

Stop stop stop there's a car in there

THREE!

with a person inside, a real person

TWO!

Stop!

ONE!

Max!

Chapter XX

MAX

This is it.

Max braces himself for the final run, the moment it seems he's been preparing for his whole life. His hands, speckled as a grouper, grip the steering wheel with the power of a sixteen-year-old on his first solo drive. His toe on the accelerator presses daintily yet strong, Baryshnikov on wheels. He peers over the steering wheel, makes out the swirled gold LXV emblem embossed on each glass door of the entrance to the Louis Quinze, and aims dead center. He knows what he must do: Brake before he reaches the doors, get out and stop the tank.

Save the Louis Quinze, he'll say to the astonished crowd. *This is your history.*

And time will stop. And history will go on. And he will have saved the day.

The Louis Quinze looms closer and closer. He can hear the warning sirens. He has to reach it before the countdown.

But what is that he hears? *Seven. Six. Five.* It's happening?

His heart pumps madly. He accelerates. The golden LXV scroll grows closer and closer. *Brake! Brake! On the left! Or is it right?* His toe shifts in a two-step dance, left, right, left, which is it? *Stop! Which one is Stop?*

With a mighty crash, the door with its golden scroll is gone, splintered into diamond facets, dazzling him with cosmic light that seems to go on forever while he spins and spins and spins. He comes to a crunching halt against a column in the lobby, the lobby where he once reigned, where ladies wore spangled dresses and men wore tuxes, where on opening night he climbed the Stairway to Nowhere with Tootsie on his arm and they descended like Bogie and Bacall, like Frank and Ava, like Lucy and Desi. Like gods. And here he was again in the lobby, columns stretching high above to a blue-sky ceiling sprinkled with stars that once twinkled. He has to make his speech. He has to tell them, no, no, this can't be over, this can't end, this must go on forever.

In the sudden quiet he hears a word, the last word Max hears before he hears nothing at all:

One.

CHAPTER XXI

ZOE

The sound is the sound of the sky splitting open, a crack beyond thunder, an eardrum-shattering, bone-rattling percussion unmatched since Zoe sat next to the speaker at a Creedence Clearwater Revival concert when she was in high school. A staccato series of booms follows like aural dominoes while concussive bursts of light explode from each floor. An avian tornado of pelicans, ibises and shrieking birds big and black as Van Gogh's crows whirls into the sky. Then a pause, as if the building is taking a last breath. In slow motion, a floor at a time, it accordions in on itself.

The crowd applauds as the building disappears into a massive plume. Their cheers are punctuated by barking dogs, wailing kids and howls: *Woohoo, Wow, Oh my God, Unbe-leeevable!* Zoe is stunned into silence, then finds her voice, a hoarse croak of "Max!" choked through an inhalation of thick dust from the khaki-colored cloud that billows from the implosion site, then rolls towards them as the wind shifts in their direction. The crowd's cheering turns to coughing with its advent, and they backpedal in hasty retreat.

The stampede of hacking people pulls t-shirts and jackets over their heads or snatches napkins from their coolers to cover their noses and mouths. Zoe muscles her way through the panicked crowd to get to Max, who must be somewhere behind the dust cloud and beneath the rubble that just moments ago was the Louis Quinze. She stumbles over a blanket-covered stroller steered by a wild-eyed mother wielding a cellphone, scrambles to her feet only to be pummeled by a Hefty bag stuffed with a very large man whose darting eyes are the only thing she can see through the hole he has poked in the bag. And then she can see nothing but a blizzard of beige as the cloud descends and obscures everything in sight, even the fingers she spreads out in front of her face.

She hears music still playing from the VIP tent. A frayed thread of wonder weaves through her racing mind: *Gloria Estefan?* The cloud tastes gritty; she can feel it in her teeth, in her lungs. Where is she? She stops dead, afraid to move, afraid she'll bump into, fall off, or trip over something. Which way is Max?

The cloud begins to thin like a stretched-out cotton ball, and she can make out forms once again. Everything and everyone seems to have been dipped in flour, a baby-powder of fine dust that coats hair, clothing, cars, palm trees, picnic coolers, radios and cameras. The VIP tents and tablecloths are snarled or gone with the wind, but a few hearty partyers still wander the area carrying drinks and plates of albino food like ghosts at a mashed-potato buffet. Everyone else is hellbent on deserting the scene. The parking lot is a long line of schmutz-covered cars snaking their way to Collins. The sun, once completely obscured, glows through the haze like a light bulb through gauze, and a cool breeze sweeps away the cobwebs of cloud. Fire hoses spray water in great arcs to settle the dust. The air begins to clear, revealing helicopters hovering overhead. Palms and pines sway softly in the sudden silence as if nothing had happened at all. Some people are taking photos of each other against the background of the wreckage. Amazingly, there is no sign of destruction outside of the fence; inside, it looks like Hiroshima.

Zoe reaches the crumpled chain link fence Max barreled through and crawls inside. An orange-vested contingent of guys in hardhats and dust masks is racing her way, shouting orders to stop where she is, but she won't. She won't stop until she reaches Max, but she can't tell where he might be. The Louis Quinze has been condensed into what looks like a toppled wedding cake. Geometric piles of wreckage––torqued squares that were once windows, twisted triangles of steel, shattered blocks of concrete––are stacked into what could pass for a mammoth Louise Nevelson sculpture. Arcs of water from fire hoses juxtapose rainbows across the grey landscape in a Wizard of Oz effect.

Already there are signs of life in the distance. Bulldozers and extractors lumber to the scene and begin to crank through the debris. Like a dinosaur scavenging for dinner, an extractor slowly lowers its clunky head over a pile and noses it curiously. A bulldozer is more aggressive, its claw scraping voraciously through metal and glass. Zoe jumps up and down, waves her arms, screams, "Stop! There's somebody under this!" But the machines forage blindly as robots, unmoved by Zoe's antics. She hears a siren in the distance. The guys in hardhats are bearing down on her.

"Help!" she yells. "There's a car here. With a person in it!"

"There she is!" The guys spot her. Their big boots stumble through the rubble, aimed in her direction. They're not looking very helpful. Don't they know what happened? Didn't they hear? Those people who witnessed Zippity's dash through the doors—where did they disappear to? These guys don't look in any mood to listen. She scrambles through the wreckage, searching for some nook or cranny within the pileup in which to hide. She knows Max is here somewhere, and she's not leaving without him.

She ducks into a gap between chunks of debris. She can hear the hardhat guys call to one another, hunting her down. "Over here, no, over there." Footsteps crunch over concrete next to her. She holds her breath. The footsteps pass.

The Dixie Chicks warble from her cellphone. She smothers the sound and quick answers it. It's Hal. "I left you *four messages,*" she whispers hoarsely.

"What the hell's going on?" he asks. "Where are you?"

"I'm in what's left of the Louis Quinze. Where are *you?* Your dad's somewhere in this mess, and you've got to get help."

"What? What are you talking about?"

"He drove here. Before they blew it up. And now I can't find him." She hears the footsteps again. "Just get here," she rasps into the phone. "I can't do this by myself."

"You can't *find* him? What do you mean you can't find him? You were supposed to watch him." He pauses. "You're not telling me he was *inside* the Louis Quinze."

"I'm telling you that."

"Fuck. Oh God. Fuck fuck. Oh God."

"Maybe he's OK." She listens for some affirmation of her desperate hope, but is greeted only with silence. "Miracles hap..."

"Shut up. Just shut up. I'm on my way."

Zoe crouches in her hiding place. Should she throw herself on the mercy of the hardhats, or wait for Hal, who may not find her if she keeps crouching here? Surrender is the only option, she realizes, if she's going to get help for Max. She scurries out with her hands held high. "I can explain..." she begins as two men rush towards her.

"Just get out of here," says one. "We can only deal with one nutcase at a time. Right now we've got to find the lunatic who drove inside."

"You know about him?" she asks, relieved that she isn't the real object of their search, and that they'll help her find Max.

"Yeah, all those people pointing and screaming was a tipoff, but it was too late," says the other. "It happened too fast. Now we gotta find him. I don't know what your excuse is for being here, so just beat it before you're arrested for trespassing."

"I'm not leaving." Zoe plunks herself down on a chunk of concrete and grips its edge. "I know him. He's Max Wolfe. He built the hotel and he's in my cab!"

"Well, don't expect to drive it outta here," he says. "We probably won't find it and your friend for days."

"No! You've got to get him out of here *now*. I saw where he went in. I know just where to look."

"Wherezat?"

"He went through the front doors. He's in a pink cab..."

"Pink?"

"...probably in the lobby. We can start there."

"There's no lobby left. And there's no 'we' here," he says. "It's me and him," he points to his buddy who is kicking at some loose chunks with a steel-tipped boot, "and those guys." He motions to several other hardhats who are roaming the site, kicking up little puffs of dust. "You gotta leave."

Zoe leaps off the concrete slab and takes off, surprising herself with her nimbleness as she scampers over jutting steel bars and melted puddles of plastic. She's not sure where the front doors would be; the site is an apocalyptic landscape of mangled girders and blasted concrete, a dust-coated monochrome that stretches on and on, ending at a placid beach fenced off from the neighboring hotels. The ocean takes over from there, bright sun flinting off deep blue waves. Several motorboats plow through the water in circles, drawn to the scene and its aftermath.

She runs, expecting to hear the thunder of steel-tipped boots behind her. She turns to look. The hardhats are standing where she left them. They're talking to someone whose arms windmill at high speed...is that Hal? Yes, it looks like Hal, something about his stance, the way he points an accusatory finger in her direction. She can't tell what he's saying, but from the angle of his head—thrust forward, shoulders hunched—she imagines he's not sending compliments her way.

And then she hears it. Faint bleats from an indeterminate direction: *A-ooo-ga a-ooo-ga*. Although weak and distant, it's a sound she would know anywhere: the voice of Zippity Cab. She gallops toward it. But then it seems to change location. Here? Here? She can't tell. Zippity's horn grows louder, then seems to come from everywhere at once, *A-ooo-ga a-ooo-ga* echoing around her with the ubiquity of a car alarm in a parking garage. Here! Max is here!

She jumps up and down with the energy of a cheerleader on Red Bull, frantic to be noticed by the hardhats and Hal. They run toward her, then, catching the sound of the horn themselves, break into a dust-churning dash.

"Here! They're somewhere under here!" Zoe cries as a herd of hardhats descends on her, followed by a panting, sweating Hal.

"They? There's more than one?" the hardhat asks, and rasps that information into his two-way radio. "Two down, two down."

"Uh, one down," Zoe corrects. "The other one's my cab."

The area quickly swarms with hardhats, fire rescue, and various tools and machines of extraction. Zoe and Hal are shunted aside, left alone to deal with each other as the crews burrow beneath the wreckage. Zippity's horn becomes weaker and more feeble (a-ooo-ga a-ooo-ga) as Hal's diatribe escalates, accusing her of neglect, lamenting his poor judgment to trust a dingbat like her with his father.

Zoe's anguish dissolves into anger. "And where were you?" she accuses. "You disappear whenever there's something going on with your parents. You didn't even answer your phone when I called to tell you your father took off with my cab. I needed help! I left four messages! What were you doing—screwing some bimbo? Getting punched out on live TV? Playing golf?"

"I don't play golf."

"I don't care what you were doing. You are *useless* when it comes to your parents."

Hal crosses his arms and stares over at the crew bustling over the site. "I was trying to stop the demolition. That's why I didn't return your calls. I was in the middle of negotiating."

"Negotiating? Who with? The devil?"

"Yeah, you might say." He presses his lips together and frowns. "Milo. The developer. It was a last-ditch effort to convince him to call off the implosion."

"Well, that worked nicely."

"I was desperate. I *knew* he wouldn't listen after I exposed what he did to the commission—on TV, yet—but I had to try. I'm surprised he didn't strangle me when I tried to talk him into renovating the place instead of tearing it down." He bites at a hangnail. "Here's how desperate I was: I tried to pay Milo off. He laughed at me. Called me an asshole for believing him, that he had con-nections way more important than I'll ever be, and that there's no way to stop Fantabulissimo. And there's not a damn thing I can do about it."

Zoe shades her eyes with her hand and squints into the sun to watch the men at work. "Well, at least you tried," she concedes. "And you made up with your dad. That's the important thing. That counts for a lot."

Hal's face crumples and Zoe is afraid he'll cry. "We weren't *finished,*" he says, his voice watery. "We had just started. He trusted me. He wanted me to be his partner. There was lots more we had to say and we didn't get to say it." He wipes his nose with the back of his hand, then uses that hand to gesture in the direction of the digging. "Now I'll never get to say it. I *failed* him."

"You didn't fail him. He knows that. And he'll tell you that when they find him," she says in a burst of sunny optimism that's as much for her own benefit as Hal's. "It's not too late to say what you want to say."

"It's too late for everything," he wails, now in a full-blown crying jag that Zoe doesn't know how to handle. "It was too late from day one, the day I met with Milo."

His cell rings. Hal composes himself and answers it, but Zoe can tell by the look on his face that it's Tootsie. He takes a deep breath. "I'm here...Yeah, it's gone, the hotel's gone... Well, we're looking for him... Um. Not sure. Don't worry, he'll be fine...No, don't come. Just stay put, Mom...No, there's nothing you can do, please don't come. Mom, don't ...no, no, don't...*please* don't come ...Mom? Mom?" He stares at the disconnected phone. "Shit. She's coming."

That threat fades in significance at shouts from the crew. Zoe and Hal break into a run. She leaves him behind and elbows the men aside who are gathered around a crevice. She peers into the blackness, sees nothing. And then the sun catches hold of the darkness and snags on a flash of pink.

"It's Zippity!" she cries. "It's Max! We found them! They're here!"

Hal arrives, panting dangerously, and she pulls him toward the crevice. "Look! Here they are!" she cries, delirious with joy that instantly dissipates when she hears the comment "It's probably flat as a pancake" from a hardhat.

Zoe and Hal are unceremoniously shoved aside, and the men and machines take over. They watch with trepidation from the sidelines, shaking. And then Zoe realizes Hal is holding her hand. She doesn't know when that happened, only that her hand is gripped tight in his sweaty fist and her fingers are losing circulation. But this is no time to make an issue of digital numbness, so she focuses on what's happening now.

The workers move swiftly, removing metal and great chunks of concrete from an ever-widening gap. Fire Rescue stands ready, apparently expecting the worst. A crane arrives to lift the largest slab away. At an angle beneath the slab lies a crumbled marble column, its steel core intact. Beneath that, sheltered by the column, is Zippity Cab.

Once the column is lifted away, Zippity is visible, up to its fenders in crumbled concrete. Its windows are opaque spiderwebs of cracks and its hood is a concave crumple. But Zippity's roof, though battered, is unbowed, protected by the half-toppled column.

"Max!" "Pop!" Zoe and Hal shout, pushing forward. They're held back as a rescuer clambers into the opening. Hal struggles against a beefy hardhat who finally relents and lets him go. Zoe and Hal rush to the edge of the crevice, fearful of what they might see.

"Is he okay?" Zoe cries. Hal says nothing, and Zoe realizes he's holding his breath. Great chunks of crazed windshield are carefully peeled away, revealing Max slumped over the wheel, leaning on the now-mute horn. His glasses are pretzeled on the dashboard, their lenses gone. Zoe and Hal stand back as rescue extracts Max from the cab, lifts him to the surface, and places him on a stretcher. Floured in dust, he looks like an anorexic chicken rejected by KFC.

"Pop?" Hal says. "Can you hear me?" Max's face is all but concealed by the oxygen mask; his eyelids, thin as onionskin, flicker briefly before he is deposited into the belly of the fire rescue truck. Hal climbs in after Max. "I'm riding with him. Meet me at Mount Sinai." He throws his keys to Zoe. "My car's over there on the grass, the black Mercedes. Wait for my mother. Don't let her drive." The siren sounds, and they're off, wa-waaaing down Collins to Mount Sinai's emergency room.

Zoe has no idea when Tootsie will show up, or even where, until she sees off in the distance a commotion of sorts, pinpointed by a mini-dust cloud stirred by a tiny figure being chased by some hardhats. Of course. It's Tootsie. Zoe runs to intercede, and immediately regrets it when Tootsie transfers her frenzy from the workers to Zoe.

"Where is he? Is he okay? You said you were taking him *away* from the blowing up, not *to* it, and now look..."

Zoe grabs Tootsie's arm and steers her toward Hal's car, parked askew on the grass. "He's fine," she says, not knowing exactly how fine Max is, but at least he looked somewhat alive. "They took him to the hospital. Hal is with him. We're meeting them there."

"My car..." Tootsie begins, but Zoe doesn't care. Why should she care about Tootsie's car when Zoe's own car, her brave, beloved Zippity Cab, is squashed like a pumpkin down below, a battered martyr to lunacy. She pictures Zippity, the stalwart heroine of this debacle now wounded and alone––even, possibly... she stifles a sob. No, no. She can't allow herself to think the worst, not just about Zippity, but especially Max. Zoe's heart is torn, but duty calls. "Don't touch my cab," she yells to the crew of workers who look baffled at the order. "I'll be back later. I want to be here when you take her out."

The workers scatter over the piles of wreckage, intent on their real job: disposing of acres of rubble so another building can rise from the ruins. The extractor cranks up; the bulldozer claws the ground, impatient for the future. Like the Phoenix, Fantabulissimo will rise from the ashes.

Once Max is in the hospital and acknowledged to be alive, if not conscious, Zoe hustles a cab and heads to the demolition site, taking the keys to Tootsie's abandoned Lincoln for the return trip. She arrives to find that the excavated spot where Zippity and Max were found has been bulldozed, its location marked only by the shattered marble column, now being hoisted by crane onto a dump truck. But where is Zippity?

Zoe flags down the crane operator, who pauses long enough to tell her: "You wanna claim it for insurance, they gonna charge you for the tow, but it's prolly at Hunk-a-Junk, that salvage place on 27th Avenue where they take mashed cars and such. You better get on down there before they scrap it."

Scrap? She runs to where Tootsie left the Lincoln, hops in and floors it. Unaccustomed to speed, the Lincoln responds reluctantly and chugs to the maze of warehouses and junkyards on 27th Avenue. There it is: Hunk-a-Junk.

She spies a mash of pink inside the chain link fence, screeches the Lincoln to a halt and bangs on the fence gate until a bouncy little man in a wide-brimmed hat scuttles up to ask what she wants.

"My car," she says, pointing. "The pink one. I want it back."

"Why you wan it back? Is no good. Just good for parts, scrap. Is crap."

"Is *not* crap," Zoe protests. "Is *family*."

"Worth more as crap," he says, pointing to a teetering tower of colorful metal layers occupying the back of the lot. Each layer, Zoe realizes, is a flattened car.

"No!" Zoe rattles the gate furiously. "No! You can't have her!"

"I already got her."

"Well, I want her back. She's mine."

"Not yours any more. Is abandoned. I tow. You take it, you owe."

"How much?"

His face disappears in the shadow of his hat as he counts on his fingers, coming up with a figure she knows is outrageous, but she's not arguing, for how can you put a price on a life? Surely Zippity can be saved, even restored to her former glory. Boyd has done it before. Boyd can do it again.

"No can do." Boyd places a paint-glossed hand over his heart. "This time she's a goner." Zippity's carcass, unceremoniously deposited by the tow truck at Boyd's, is almost unrecognizable by now, having endured not only the implosion, but two towings, the last of which completed the pancaking of her front end as she was dragged down I-95 at rush hour. "I don't even know if there's much in the way of parts to save," he says. "I wish I had good news, but I'm afraid it's time. She's reached the end of the road."

Zoe is numb. This can't be the end. After all they had been through together, and all they had been to each other, how can she say goodbye? She leans against Zippity's mangled body, collecting herself. "I need some time alone with her," she says, and pulls on the door handle. It comes off in her hand. "Oh, God. She's fading fast. Please, can you could get her to open? I want to sit with her a moment."

Boyd manages to pry open a door. "There's glass all over," he reports. "Don't go in until I vac it out." He power-slurps out the shards, then leaves discreetly. Inside, Zoe discovers a dust-powdered furry dice on the floor and a long-forgotten MacDonald's bag: remnants of happier days. She closes her eyes and remembers.

Boyd is tapping on the cracked rear window. "Are you okay? You've been in there a long time."

Zoe's tear-streaked face appears in the glass. "We were together a long time. It's hard to say goodbye."

"I thought of something. Maybe there doesn't have to be a goodbye."

"You can fix her?" Zoe's soaring moment of joy is waved down by Boyd.

"No. She's not fixable. But...remember when I told you about the Cadillac Ranch?"

"You mean, that graveyard for Cadillacs in Texas? Where they stick them in the ground with their butts in the air?"

"Think of it as a memorial. A memorial for Zippity." He pauses. "We could bury her nose first in front of my shop with those sassy tailfins way up high. It would be a real attraction, a sculpture, kinda. That way, she'll always be there, and you could visit her whenever you want."

Zoe nods. She could visit. Yes. That would be good.

Tentacles of tubes and wires attach Max to bottles and monitors. A syncopation of beeps, boops and Max's faint snore beneath the oxygen mask provide a meditative New Age soundtrack punctuated by Tootsie's bedside laments aimed at Max, who is about as attentive to her exhortations now as he ever was when conscious. "What, you had to go be a big hero, who do you think you are, Superman? and for what? you coulda been dead for all you know." Receiving no response, she changes tactics. "Max, Max, just open your eyes, is that too much to ask? Just open them so I'll know you're in there."

Hal, slouched in a chair, sighs. "He can't hear you, Mom. The implosion may have damaged his eardrums. Give it some time."

Tootsie's face crumples into a tight little ball and her eyes spill over with tears. "I don't want to go home without him." She pokes at Zoe's arm with an accusatory finger. "You were supposed to take care of him. How could you let him steal your car?"

"*Let* him?" Zoe asks, backing off.

"Lay off, Mom," Hal says.

"Well, then you tell me," Tootsie wails. "Why did he have to go and do this?"

That's a question Zoe has asked herself over and over. She thinks she knows the answer. "Because he's a man of action."

"What?" Hal looks up from the hangnail he's picking at.

"Don't you understand what he was trying to do?"

"Kill himself maybe?"

"I don't think that was the plan. He was trying to...I don't know...take a stand." Zoe isn't exactly sure what she means, but something is starting to come together, something she realizes had been building within Max, something she saw but misinterpreted. Beneath the guise of a cantankerous old man hid a young man who still dreamed of glory, whose future wasn't in his past. If what he built could last forever, then maybe he would, too. "This was his last chance to make a difference. You've got to give him credit for trying."

"Some difference," Tootsie says. "Nothing's changed. The Louis Quinze is bombed to kibble, and up goes Fancypants."

"Fantabulissimo," Hal corrects her glumly.

"Well," Tootsie says, "you should know, shouldn't you, with all the cart-wheels you did to get the thing built, and you can say you're sorry all you want..."

"I *am* sorry," Hal says in despair. "I did everything I could to stop the damned demolition. Pop knows that. We were just starting to understand each other, and then...*this*. Don't you think I'd do anything to take it all back?"

"Would you two just cut it out?" Zoe interrupts. "What's the matter with you people? Here he is, out like a rock, breathing from a tube, peeing in a bag, but he's *here,* and you're fighting like he's not. You're so busy blaming me and each other that you're missing the whole point of what he did."

"There's a point?" Tootsie asks.

Zoe can't take much more of this. "I'm watching TV," she announces. She grabs the remote and thumbs it, stopping abruptly at what looks like the Louis Quinze in mid-collapse.

The news is on. The implosion is the featured entertainment. As a video re-play of the event fills the screen, Channel 7's Renaldo Cohen explains in mournful tones: "The Louis Quinze, jewel of Miami Beach during its heyday in the 1950s and '60s, became just another pile of dust on Miami Beach's archi-tectural landscape today. This latest victim of progress was imploded, ending its reign as celebrity central, host of such stars as Sinatra, Elvis, the Beatles and Tammy Faye. Rising in its place will be Fantabulissimo, a sixty-story, three-tower condominium."

"Turn it off," Hal says. "I don't need to go through this again."

But there's more: Renaldo and his news partner, the ever-chipper Renee O'Reilly, are apparently knocked out by what happened next:

Renaldo: *But, in a shocking turn of events, apparently someone was inside when it went down!*

Renee: *Yes, Renaldo, you won't believe this, but someone DROVE THROUGH THE BARRIER JUST BEFORE THE IMPLOSION. Here's ac-tual video footage shot by an actual viewer who was actually on the scene!*

The footage, taken from a distance, is shaky and out of focus, but there is no mistaking the blur of pink that zips past the barrier and crashes inside before disappearing in an eruption of concrete, steel and dust. The voices of the videographer and his friend can be heard over the background boom: "What was that, a car?" "You think?" "Maybe it's some kinda sensor or something." "Yeah, or an explosive thing, like, to set it off." "Cool."

Renaldo and Renee reappear on-camera, brows stiffened into Botox-frozen attempts at expressions of serious concern. Renaldo: *Renee, we have word, as yet unconfirmed, that the driver of the vehicle was Max Wolfe, the original developer of the Louis Quinze. Apparently, he plowed into his hotel just as it went down.* Renee: *Unbelievably amazing, Renaldo! This is a story we will be following, so stay tuned for more news at eleven.*

"That's him?" A nurse they haven't seen before stands open-mouthed in the doorway holding a brown plastic tray filled with white plastic food. "Mr. Wolfe here, that's who they're talking about on the TV?"

"What's that you've got there?" Hal wants to know. "Is that food? He's got tubes up the wazoo and you're bringing him dinner?"

"He's on the schedule." She plunks the tray down on the swivel bedside table. "Did he really ram into the Louis Quinze? Is that why that reporter is asking us questions? Because of Mr. Wolfe here?"

"Who's asking questions?"

"Well, they found this guy Gomez from the *Herald* in the hallway, nobody knows how he got there, he just snuck himself up and there he was, asking all kinds of questions nobody would answer. The supervisor hadda get a security guard to get him outta here." She deftly sidesteps Hal to peer closely at Max. "Izzy famous?"

CHAPTER XXII

MAX

Izzy famous? *The question seeps through the murky depths of Max's comatose brain, and something stirs.* Yes he iz, *responds the something, not in a voice, but as a thought.*

But where iz he? Buried somewhere deep and dark, Max can neither see nor move. Izzy dead? No, he can't be dead. If he were dead, he wouldn't be able to hear, and he had heard the question: Izzy famous?

He sinks back into his murk, for how long he can't tell, but something rouses him again. A sound. A voice.

Remember that first time? the voice says. You followed me home from the streetcar after I smiled at you, next thing I know you're knocking on my door and Mama asks, so who is this? not happy because she already decided I was going to marry Schmuel, the kosher butcher down the street with the yellow teeth, but I liked your chutzpah, following me home like that but there was something about you, that funny little mustache you had, never mind you went and shaved it later but I'll tell you, that's what got me, the little mustache that tickled when we kissed on the rooftop, do you remember? and after nights of that and more, lots more, I said, yes, I'd go anywhere with you and next thing I know we're married and I'm leaving the Bronx with Mama wringing her hands saying *vey iz mir, vey iz mir,* and we're on the train to Miami Beach where you said the streets were paved with gold but when we got there the Miami streets weren't paved with gold, they were covered with schmutz, trees and trash from a hurricane and I wanted to go back to the Bronx but you said no, no, just wait, you'll see, this will all be good.

He knows that voice.

And Max, I never told you this or maybe I did, I hated the place for a long time, it was a hot sticky buggy *Yenneveldt* and I missed my Mama but because I loved you, I learned to like this place okay, so I want you to hear this CAN YOU HEAR THIS? I'm not sorry I spent all these years with you even if I said I wished I never married you those times when I'd get really fed up because you can be a real schmuck, you know, yelling at the TV, acting like I'm not there and...well, never mind, what you got to know is I was never really sorry I married you because even if you're a schmuck you're also a mensch, like when you paid the doctor bills for the doorman's sick kid, and even if I didn't like the fancy schmancy people you used to hang around with during the hotel days, I was always proud of you even if you're a real pain in the tuchus.

He tries to answer but he can't, he's stuck in the muck deep in the dark and all he can do is think the words he wants to say: Tootsie? Is that you? Then he sinks again, and the dark closes in for how long he doesn't know.

And then he hears the voice again, the voice he thinks is Tootsie's, scrambled with another one that's saying Go home, get some sleep, he's not going anywhere.

I don't need to go home to sleep, says the Tootsie voice. I can sleep perfectly fine in this chair here. I went home last week and I couldn't sleep, so it's better I stay here where I can watch him since I'm not sleeping anyway.

Well, eat something then. The cafeteria's open. They have chicken noodle soup and the meatloaf's not bad.

What are you talking about, chicken noodle soup? They don't know from chicken noodle soup, it's canned, it's Campbell's, how you expect me to eat that canned stuff? And don't even talk to me about meatloaf.

Well, you've got to eat something.

I ate his Jell-O.

You can't live on Jell-O.

What do I have to live for, if he *and the voice breaks into a sob* if he, you know, does the D word?

He's not going to die. You heard the doctor. The steel column and Zoe's cab saved him. It's the coma we have to worry about.

Waaaah! The Coma!

I'm in a coma? Get me outta here, Max tries to yell, but he can't. All he can do is listen.

Look, Mom.

Mom? That voice, it's Hal.

I haven't had any time alone with Pop. Go get something to eat. Take a walk. Take a nap. I want to talk to him alone.

Hal's a good boy. A very good boy.

Don't upset him. The doctor said he might be able to hear everything you say so don't say anything that'll get him *fatootzed*, you know what I'm talking about.

Take a walk, Mom. Eat something before the cafeteria closes.

Fifteen minutes. I'll be back in fifteen minutes. Don't upset him.

Max hears the squeak of sneaker-clad feet, and then silence except for beepboop and wshhht sounds from tubes and machines and the echo of hallway voices. Very close to his ear, he hears:

Pop, if you're in there, listen to me. I'm sorry you're a captive audience, but now I'm going to say what I wanted to say for so long.

Beepboop. Wshhht.

Okay. First of all, I'm saying I'm sorry. I know I said it already, but I need for you to really understand. I'm sorry for so many things, the things you and I talked about before your...your accident. I tried to make up for the stupid, stupid stuff I did by telling it all before the commission, tried to get Planning and Zoning to stop the demolition, tried to stop it myself. I tried to bribe Milo, but he laughed at me. That's what I get for getting mixed up with a scumbag like Milo and all his scumbag friends. I am a scumbag.

Boopbeep. Beepboop.

I know what you're thinking: Why get mixed up with all those creeps in the first place? I don't know. It's complicated. I thought it was my last chance to *be* somebody, to pull my life together because it wasn't going anywhere. I wanted to do something to make you proud of me, even if it was a political thing. So when Milo promised that I could be mayor, I fell for it. Stupid. I didn't really want to be mayor. I know you hate politics, but it's all I'm good at. People liked me. They voted for me. Go figure.

Beepboop. Wssht.

Oh hell. It's all just excuses. I don't have any excuse. I know you're disappointed in me. I know you wanted me to be you. But I'm not and I never was. Trouble is, I don't know what "me" is. And now it's too late to find out.

Boop.

You're a hard act to follow, Pop. I mean, how many people got their picture in *Life Magazine*? You're part of the Miami Beach story, you put it on the map. And you started from, what, being a carpenter in the Bronx, to building the Louis Quinze, and now it's gone. You made something out of nothing. I know you think I made nothing out of something.

Beep.

You have to know this, Pop. It wasn't me who blew up the Louis Quinze. It wasn't even Milo, or any of the other creeps that were involved. It was Time. And I know you think that's just bullshit, but time is money on Miami Beach, and I don't mean in the usual way. Time sells—the olden times, the pretend past, the way it looked, not the way it really was. It's fantasy history. People want what they imagine life was like then, and they always imagine it was better.

It hurts for me to say this because I know it hurts you, but the Louis Quinze was old, at least in Miami Beach years. People don't want that kind of Old. Those art deco buildings on South Beach, they never looked as good when they were new as they do now, all fixed up and trendy. Lots of them were pretty shabby, even on their best days. You can save a building, but you can't save the past. It's gone, like all those celebrities you thought would be here forever. Two weeks later, nobody remembers who they were. Like Vanilla Ice. Pee Wee Herman. *I don't know from those people.* And Dr. Ruth. *Her I know. She's cute.*

Wsssht.

It's sad but true, Pop. The Louis Quinze was old news. Sure, it should have been renovated and given a new life, but so should everyone. That's called reincarnation, and I wish I believed in it.

I hope you meant it when you said you forgave me. Not just for this Louis Quinze thing, but for not being you. I could never be as good a You as you were, so I thought maybe I could be a good Me. Well, so much for that plan.

All this has made me think about Wally. Your grandson. He's been a disappointment, but maybe I'm just disappointed that he's not the Me that could have been.

Sit me up, Max tries to say. I got to talk to you.

He hears the sound of a door opening, the squeak of sneakers.

Mom, what are you doing back so soon? Did you eat something?

The soup looked watery, and the meatloaf looked pork-y, so I got something from the machine. Peanut butter crackers. Want one?

Would you mind waiting outside? I'm talking to Pop. I'd like some privacy.

What are you saying you don't want me to hear?

Go outside! Hal's talking to me!

Look, look, he's making a face, says Tootsie, that's good isn't it, if he's making a face? It means he's waking up.

It doesn't mean that, Mom, you heard what the doctor said. It's just reflexive.

Reflexive, reshmexive, I know what I know. He's waking up. Look, his mouth is all pooched up, like he's trying to say something. What is it, Max, what's that you want to say?

He's not saying anything. He just does it, that's all, you can't read anything into it that's not there. He did it when I talked to him too.

What's happening? says another voice. *I know that voice.* Is something wrong?

Oy vey, it's Zoe. Who invited you?

Zoe? Who is Zoe?

I brought a book to read to Max, says the Zoe voice. I thought maybe he'd like to hear something besides you two fighting. *Max feels a hand cover his.* Max, it's me, Zoe. I brought you an Isaac Singer book from the library. I liked the title: *Enemies, a Love Story.* Remember? You told me he was a great writer. You told me they named a street after him.

Zoe. I remember Zoe.

I'll read it to you when everybody leaves.

Who's leaving? I'm not leaving. I'm going to sleep right there in the chair where I been all week, and what does he need from such a book about enemies, he doesn't need more bad news, he gets enough of that from the television.

Okay, fine, I'll just move this chair over here *Max hears a low scraping noise* and you can sit in that chair and listen, too. Zoe clears her throat and reads. " 'Chapter one. Herman Broder turned over and opened one eye. In his dreamy state, he wondered whether he was in America, in Tzivkev, or in a German camp.' "

German camp? What is this *mishegoss*, you have to read to him about Nazis? If you got to read, read something happy. He always liked Art Buchwald. Read him some Art Buchwald.

Let her read, Mom. Zoe knows what she's doing. She probably knows Pop better than we do.

Boop. Beep.

Zoe continues. "'He even imagined himself hiding in the hayloft in Lipsk. Occasionally all these places fused in his mind. He knew he was in Brooklyn, but he heard Nazis shouting."

He likes Art Buchwald. But what do I know? I'm only his wife.

" 'Full awakening required an act of volition,' " Zoe reads. " 'Enough! he told himself, and sat up. It was mid-morning.' "

Zoe reads, for how long he can't tell. Hours? Days? The story ends. Herman Broder's three women--Yadwiga the balabusta, Tamara the sexpot, Masha the motherly—weave together in Max's brain, becoming one: Tootsie. He hears her speak:

Look, look, he's making a face, don't tell me it's reflux, I can see his eyes moving like they're trying to open, look, look, did you see that?

Mom. Don't get yourself all...

No, I see it, too! Your mother isn't making it up, look, his eyelids are fluttering. He's trying to talk. Something's happening! Buzz for the nurse, hurry!

Max rises to the surface of the murk, sinks, rises again like the "yes" "no" "ask again" answers in the inky sea of a magic eight ball. Yes. No. And then it's yes. Yes. Yes. Fuzzy shapes are moving about him. He hears voices, excited. The feel of hands. His name called in all its variations, questioning. Pop? Max? Mr. Wolfe? Yes, he tries to answer, and then does. Yes yes yes.

* * *

Max squints through his new glasses at the TV set on its perch over the beribboned basket of bright shiny fruit and a forest of chrysanthemums sent by he doesn't know who, maybe those people he's watching live on the 6:00 news, televised as they chant and wave signs beneath his window.

Max! Max! Max! they chant. Renaldo Cohen is interviewing two of the sign-waving multitude: a loose-limbed guy with a pouf of pink hair and a freckled pixie of a girl wearing a t-shirt that reads "S.O.B." Renaldo questions its meaning.

"Save Our Beaches!" she pipes in a squeaky-toy voice. "Max is The Man!" The chant of *Max Max Max* swells in response, and signs reading "Mighty Max" and "S.O.B." wave wildly above the crowd. "Max, we love you!" squeaks Pixie Girl. Pink Hair pumps his fist in the air to punctuate that thought.

Renaldo has to shout his next question. "But he almost got killed for nothing. He couldn't save the Louis Quinze. Was it worth it?"

"What matters is that he tried," Pink Hair yells above the crowd. "Before, nobody cared. Now, *we* care. It's our city, too!"

"Back to you, Renee," Renaldo says as the crowd roars approval. Renee O'Reilly appears onscreen, eyebrows knitted into an appropriately somber expression.

"According to his family, Max Wolfe is recovering nicely," she says, "and will not be charged with breaking and entering, as earlier reported. His adventure, along with the efforts of his son, former commissioner Hal Wolfe, has prompted an unprecedented public response which some in the S.O.B. movement hope will create change in the way developers operate on Miami Beach. When asked for a statement, developer Milo Minkoff replied, 'Does an eighteen-wheeler stop when a chicken crosses the road?'"

"What an idiot," Zoe says. Max had forgotten she was there. She reaches up and turns off the TV. He can hear the muffled chanting from the crowd beneath his window. *Max Max Max.* "You're the Man of the Hour," she says.

"I am a man of action," he agrees. He presses the button that raises the head of his bed and tries to see out the window. He wishes he could thank the people below. He wishes he could stand at the window and wave to the crowd, like the Pope.

"You ready to go home?" Zoe asks. "The doc says tomorrow's the big day."

"I'm ready today. The food here stinks."

"Tootsie says she's fixing her special brisket for you." Zoe adjusts the thin beige blanket that covers him. His knees tent the blanket in two little bumps. He's lost weight, he can tell. Lucky he didn't break any bones, or he'd be fricassee, just a pile of toothpicks in what little juice he has left. "She says she's going to fatten you up like a goose."

Brisket. That sounds good. It sounds like home. "Tell her I want some chopped liver, too. Salami and pickles and herring." He's getting hungry just hearing himself say the words. "And lox. Lotsa lox."

"I think whatever you want, Tootsie will get for you." Zoe checks her watch. "I've got to go or I'll miss my bus."

"Who's taking me home tomorrow?" Max doesn't want to mention Zippity, doesn't want to bring up Zoe's cab since he was responsible for its demise, although, according to the clamoring crowd below, it was all for a good cause. Still, he feels guilty.

"We'll figure it out," Zoe says. "Maybe Hal. Maybe Tootsie." She gives him a wave from the doorway. "Maybe even me. It'll be a surprise."

By the time he's dressed in the new sweatsuit and sneakers Hal brought him after Zoe left last night, Max is raring to go. He refused the breakfast tray (*Cream of Wheat! More white food.*) in anticipation of the bagels and lox he's been thinking about since he woke up, but it's another hour before he can check out. He sits on the bed, channel-surfing with the remote in search of news starring himself. Disappointed that the only remnant on TV of his heroism is a two-second shot of last night's crowd beneath his window and a mention that he's going home today, he perks up when the nurse who comes in to take his temperature and blood pressure asks for his autograph. He signs his name with a flourish on the napkin that came with the breakfast he didn't eat, and settles back to watch Dr. Phil and his parade of dysfunctionals do their thing.

It's okay with Max that his exploits have disappeared from today's news, for he knows that his fame will be lasting. Hal had called this morning to tell him that it was official: the name "Max Wolfe" will be long remembered. In cooperation with the Miami Design Preservation League, Hal has established a foundation that will focus on the legal and architectural strategies for preserving historical sites, designed to ensure that nothing like the destruction of the Louis Quinze will ever happen again.

The Max Wolfe Foundation for Historical Preservation. Max likes the sound of it. He rolls the name around his mouth, savoring it as if it were a kalamata olive: *The Max Wolfe Foundation for Historical Preservation.*

Happily musing on the possibility of eternal esteem, Max is startled to see Hal at the door of his hospital room—with Zoe. Ah, they're *both* taking him home; that must be the surprise. Max is too excited at the prospect of going home to give their togetherness much thought, but he does notice that they seem to be chummier than he remembered, whispering together as they wheel him down the hall and into the hospital elevator. Hal waits with him as Zoe gets the car. That was odd, too.

And then he understands why.

"Surprise!" Zoe calls as she pulls up. She's driving Zippity Cab, in all its glorious pinkness. He didn't kill Zippity after all! Max, to his own surprise, bursts into tears––tears of happiness, of joy, of relief that Zippity is still around. A survivor, just like him.

But... there's something different about Zippity. Max peers through his new glasses, not sure what he's seeing: something's changed, but what? It's like the time Tootsie dyed her hair red. Max knew something looked different but he couldn't put his finger on what it was. And now...

"Meet Zippity Three," Zoe says. "My new Prius."

"New-ish," Hal corrects. "Four years old. A real deal."

Max's relief dissolves into grief. So he killed Zippity after all. He was the executioner, and his punishment is having to ride in this...this *imposter*. "They couldn't fix Zippity?"

Zoe shakes her head sadly. "No. Totally totaled. But we gave Zippity a decent burial—a memorial. You'll like it—it's Zippity forever. When you're better, we can visit her."

"I want the old Zippity. This one's not the same."

"Listen," Zoe says, "the hardest thing I had to do was say goodbye to her. But I had to come to terms with it. The fact is, Zippity is dead. Dead dead dead."

"The D word." Max shudders with the finality of it.

"And that's the way it is," Hal says, and opens the door for Max.

He won't get in. "It's not the same," he protests.

"Nothing stays the same. You think it will, but it won't," Zoe says. "You have to move on."

Zoe runs her hand over Zippity Three's shiny new surface. "Look at her. She's really kinda cool, don't you think?"

Max takes a closer look at the latest version of Zippity Cab. "Does it have the same crazy zebra seats?"

"You bet. And brand-new furry dice. And it's the same color pink. Didn't Boyd do a great job?"

Max studies Zippity's new incarnation, then concedes with a shrug. "Not bad."

Hal helps him out of the wheelchair and attempts to steer him into Zippity's open rear door. Max freezes in place. "What's wrong now?"

Max waves him off. Nothing's wrong. He's fine. Very fine, in fact. So fine he has a question:

"Can I drive?"

EPILOGUE

Zoe turns on her rooftop light and settles behind the wheel of Zippity Cab. She loves her cab, loves its flamingo pink color, its zebra seat covers, its furry dice dangling from the rear view mirror. She loves it almost as much as she did Zippity One, which she visits regularly to reminisce about the old days. Zippity's memorial has become a point of interest, even featured in a *Herald* story with a photo of Zoe in her saucy pink cap embroidered with "Zippity Cab," hugging Zippity's newly vertical tailfin. As much as she loves Zippity Three (she prefers to forget there was ever a Two), it will never replace Zippity One in her heart. First love is never forgotten.

But thanks to Max and his TV moment of glory, Zippity Three is instantly recognizable, its pink hybrid presence garnering cheers wherever they go. Hal subsidized a website for Zippity Trips, and now there's a waiting list for her business. She's amazed at how many people—tourists as well as native South Floridians––want her to chauffeur them to the offbeat places she listed: the SnoPop Orange Juice plant, the Swap Shop, Alabama Jack's. Zoe had always known that Miami is more than just a Star-of-the-Moment showcase; Miami is an Adventure.

Hal had lent her the money to buy Zippity Three, but his interest hasn't stopped there. He's invested in Zippity Four—another used Prius, this one for Keisha. In her excitement about Zoe's new venture, Keisha had suggested even more destinations: the Lyric Theater, Dorsey House, Purvis Young, the Senegambian African Hair Village. "We'd need another Zippity to cover all that," Zoe said. And so Keisha, now retired from Home Depot, became a Zippity Trips guide.

Hal is already thinking of a Zippity Five, and has sold his share in the strip malls he owns to finance what he sees as an exciting new venture. "We can incorporate," he says. "Hire more drivers. Train them to be like you."

"Me?"

"Yeah, you. You create an experience. You know the city inside out. You've got personality, character, smarts." He pauses. "You're terrific."

Zoe is momentarily stunned. "Ya think?"

"Why else would I invest in you?" Zoe sees a look in his eyes she never noticed before, and is swept with a desire to do something crazy: kiss him.

Hal doesn't taste like a recently-ingested Big Mac, like most of her previous encounters, nor does he smell of paint primer, like Boyd. Hal tastes like mint and smells like pine. The last person who had kissed her with his heart and soul had been Albert. For the others, kissing was the price of admission to an action movie.

She had kissed a lot of frogs. It's crazy, but maybe she's finally found her prince.

* * *

A molten sun throws a lick of flame onto the charcoal ocean, melting the night away. Its light spreads over the horizon until the sea glows cerulean blue. Sandpipers tiptoe over the beach leaving trails of tiny forkprints; a pelican dives into the surf. Crisp and clean as fresh laundry, a breeze swirls through Zippity's open windows as Zoe pulls into a parking space.

Ocean Drive is empty at this hour except for a homeless guy sleeping under a palm whose fronds swish above him like fans. The wrapper of Zoe's Egg McMuffin rattles as she bares it for a bite. This is a time of quiet celebration, a celebration she wants to begin at dawn, her favorite time of day, and to share with her new and faithful companion, Zippity Three.

Today is Zoe's birthday. Today she is fifty.

Boyd's gift to Zoe is a custom-made car cover for Zippity One that he pulls over her in inclement weather. Turquoise vinyl, flannel-lined, with "Zippity Cab" written in pink. "It'll keep her rust-free for another 50 years," he said, and then wished Zoe the same for herself.

Later today, she will celebrate with the Wolfes, who have become the family she always wanted. She still drives Max wherever he needs to go. Sometimes Tootsie goes along. She and Max sit in the back seat and bicker, but something has changed. Somewhere during the ride, Zoe will hear one murmur to the other, "Wanna do the hokey-pokey?" And then they want to go home.

Tootsie has promised not to make a birthday brisket. Max has promised to turn off CNN during dinner. Hal has promised to be there. He said he has a surprise.

Life itself has been a surprise. When she lost Albert, she thought she had lost herself. All she had left were good memories with no hope of making more. Sometimes she thinks Zippity inherited Albert's spirit, and he somehow guided her here.

Still, who knew that by fifty she would have all she ever wanted? Friendship (Keisha), children (Keisha's kids), a family (the Wacky Wolfes), a thriving business (thanks, Zippity), and the possibility of love.

This must be what happiness is.

Zoe slurps the last of her Diet Coke and licks the remnants of Egg McMuffin off her fingers. The morning sun climbs a cloudless sky. Ocean Drive is waking up. Two toasted tourists toting folding lounges wave to Zoe as they pass her on their way to the beach. A car pulls into the space behind Zippity, then another, and another.

And so a new day begins.

THE END

Acknowledgements

I am deeply grateful to friends and fellow writers who read my novel in its many incarnations, including my writers group in Miami and the Flatiron Writers in Asheville, NC. I want to give special thanks to Madeleine Blais and Jackie Miller, whose extensive comments and enthusiastic support encouraged me throughout. Thanks also to the city of Miami Beach: endless source of all things wacko, provider of characters you just can't make up, and the inspiration for this story.

Made in the USA
Columbia, SC
13 June 2021

39330891R00143